Totally Bound Publishing books by Amy Craig

Single Books
Lost in LA

LOST IN LA

AMY CRAIG

Lost in LA
ISBN # 978-1-83943-939-1
©Copyright Amy Craig 2021
Cover Art by Erin Dameron-Hill ©Copyright January 2021
Interior text design by Claire Siemaszkiewicz
Totally Bound Publishing

LOST IN LA

Dedication

For Nana, who found time to bake.

Chapter One

Wylie stood in the shadowed hallway of the two-bedroom apartment, her fist clenched as she brainstormed ways to fight an eviction notice.

Dottie, her roommate, was texting her from the security of the bathroom.

Couldn't she face me? After four months of cohabitation, Wylie knew very little about the woman. She mostly found it funny when the overpaid nanny confiscated candy from her sugar-restricted charges, retreated to the bathroom and savored the contraband where no one could see her. Today, Wylie struggled to find humor in the situation. Breathing through her frustration, she released her fist and sank to the floor. "The wrappers in the trashcan give you away," she whispered. "We both know what you're doing in there."

She looked down the hallway and focused on the living room couch where Dottie's orange-and-white cat luxuriated on the corduroy fabric, as smug as its owner. White mini-blinds cast stripes of sunlight on the room's beige carpet, valance drapes and dusty brass fixtures. As a native of Santa Monica, Wylie understood that the furnished apartment on Montana Avenue and Fifth Street relied on its location to attract tenants. The nineteen-hundred dollars a month sublease let her walk to the beach where she taught yoga, but the cat paid nothing for his sunlit pleasure. *Maybe I'll take you with me. I could hold you for ransom until Dottie adds me to the lease.*

The cat yawned.

You're right. You're not worth the trouble.

Steam seeped beneath the bathroom door, as nebulous as her counterarguments and self-doubts. Ignoring the tacky feel of the semi-gloss paint, she leaned against the bathroom door and pulled her fingers through her long blonde hair. *This is what I get for being too trusting and naïve. I should have put my name on the lease. I should have known better than to get myself into this mess. I could find Dottie a boyfriend. A girlfriend. Whatever. Threaten to reveal her undocumented cat. Light her bed on fire.* She laughed and released her hair to cover her mouth. *Shit, that wasn't appropriate.*

She rapped on the bathroom door. "Dottie! Let's talk about this situation like grown women. I'm this close to finishing two-hundred hours of professional certification and landing a full-time job with benefits. What am I supposed to do now? Live on the streets?"

Her ostensible roommate remained silent.

"There has to be another alternative."

The faucet ran as Dottie added hot water to her tub, ignoring their shared utility costs and the environmental impacts of her two-hour bath. "What's done is done. Cousin's in and you're out."

Wylie exhaled, finding it impossible to reason with a woman who lacked the courage to face her. "This isn't right. Don't you have to give me some notice or something? Don't you even feel bad about what you're doing?"

"Not really."

She hung her head. *It doesn't matter if she stays in that bathtub until the floor caves in. Her name's on the lease and she calls the shots.*

"I know I promised you a year —"

Wylie's hope soared.

"But we all thought my cousin would fail her semester at UC and have to repeat it. Maybe, like, twice. Now that she's graduated, she's decided to come to Los Angeles to pursue her acting career." The plastic snap of a toiletry bottle echoed in the tiled room. "My aunt called and told me this morning. What am I supposed to do?"

"Tell your mom you already have a roommate? One who's never been late paying rent?" She considered kicking down the door and upending the bubble bath all over Dottie's head. "A roommate who changes the litter box for the cat you're not even supposed to have in the apartment!"

"Leave Snickerdoodle alone."

Wylie eyed the cat. "I love animals."

The cat stood, repositioned himself and presented his ass to Wylie.

Wylie stared at the bathroom door. "This is bad karma!"

"Sorry, kid."

"Your cousin will never make it to her auditions on time." Her words sped up and she stood, hoping her hard-won native logic could override the aspirations of a wannabe actress. "Your cousin needs to live in one of the San Fernando Valley neighborhoods. The Central and Eastside neighborhoods would be even better if she's looking for a deal."

"She's a trust-fund kid."

"She might decide this apartment isn't a good fit. I don't want you to end up with zero roommates. Maybe she could sleep on the couch for a while." Water sloshed on the other side of the door and Wylie crossed her fingers, hoping her magnanimous offer cloaked her desperation.

"That's the thing. My cousin wants the second bedroom. My aunt already wired me six months of rent."

Of course she did. Wylie bit her lip and decided to play her final card. "I guess I could take the couch."

The bathwater stilled.

Wylie clung to a moment of hope.

"You'd still have to pay me the same rent."

The counteroffer hit Wylie like a rogue wave. Her eyes widened and she slapped the door in disbelief. "You can't charge me the same amount you're charging for a bedroom."

"Why not? My name's on the lease. We're not friends, Wylie. Take it or leave it."

She opened her mouth to accept a month on Dottie's fur-strewn couch.

The other woman pulled the plug on the bathwater. "You know what? Scratch that. I don't want to put up with three women sharing one tiny bathroom. It's not like we're desperate."

Tears streamed down Wylie's cheeks as she hung her head and let her hair shield her face. The draining water sucked away the last bit of her hope. *Right now, I'm the definition of desperate.* She cleared her throat, determined to retain her pride. "How long do I have until your cousin shows up? Like, a week?"

"She'll be here in the morning."

Wylie stared at the bathroom door. "Are you serious?"

"Honestly, I thought you'd be gone by now."

She wiped away her tears. "Funny. I'm still here."

"You should probably leave tonight and make a clean break."

Laughter bubbled up in Wylie's throat, displacing her desperation. "This is not helping me out. This is, like, the definition of not helping me out."

"I guess you can stay the night. I'll use your deposit to pay for a cleaning service."

"You're funny, Dottie. Fucking hilarious."

The woman remained silent for a minute. "Sorry, kid."

Wylie retreated to a bedroom full of mismatched furniture and cursed her stupidity. She shoved her clothes into her duffel bag, folded a set of sheets and crammed them on top of her clothes. *People have done more with less.*

Dottie emerged from the bathroom wearing a towel and a hair turban straight from the archives of the home shopping channel. She tossed an envelope of cash on the bare mattress. "Here's your deposit. I hope everything works out."

Wylie stared at the clumsy script bearing her name, Wylie Winidad. The sight of the familiar envelope brought tears to her eyes and she shook her head, realizing Dottie had never felt the need to deposit her hard-earned cash. "Thanks, I guess."

The woman nodded and retreated without saying another word.

Wylie picked up the envelope of money and shoved it into her purse while she considered her predicament. *Why do bad things happen to good people? I've done everything right since my parents left town. How am I going to scrape together the money I need for a deposit on my own place? I need to figure out a way to take care of myself, but there's no way I'm calling my parents. Most of the people I know have moved away and like…grown up.*

She thought of her mom and dad ensconced in an Oregon complex full of California refugees. *'They'll be the hardest years of your life,'* her mother had said, boxing up a lifetime of dishes and serving pieces. *'You're only twenty-six years old. Instead of fending for yourself, why don't you tag along with us?'*

'Because I belong here.'

'Oh, honey, you'll always belong with us.'

Wylie blinked away the sting of tears. *'Thanks, Mom.'*

The next day, her parents had driven up the coast in a rental truck full of furniture and left her in Santa Monica with a wardrobe of frayed designer jeans, a jumble of high-priced loungewear and the athletic gear she needed to host her beachside classes.

She'd gotten drunk with Natalia to celebrate her independence. Clinking glasses, they'd toasted having everything they needed. Most of their sporadic interactions involved yoga classes and cocktails, but Wylie knew her best friend would let her crash for a few days if she happened to be in town. Unfortunately, the spunky yoga enthusiast worked as a studio scout and her social media feed showed her scouting battle sites on the Horn of Africa. *Who would let me in? Nobody. I have nobody left in this town.*

She wheezed as the reality of her situation set in. The muscles in her airways tightened and stress impeded her breathing. *Now is not the time for an asthma attack.* She focused on calming her rapid inhalations, but the muscles in her neck and chest tightened as panic set in. The pain of the clenching muscles echoed through her body. Doubling over, she scrambled for the rescue inhaler in her purse and dumped out the contents of the bag. The metallic inhaler caught her eyes. She pumped the cartridge, slumped to the floor and waited for the rush of the short-acting bronchodilator to relieve her systems. *What would I do without my medicine?*

Twenty minutes later, her breathing slowed and she wondered when the misery of this day would end. Trusting her heart rate to remain stable, she struggled to her feet and hefted her duffel bag, testing her strength against an upset stomach and shaky limbs. *I can do this.*

Dottie sat on the couch in a pair of pajamas, her turban in place while she watched a cooking show with the cat.

I'm surprised she's not hiding in her room.

The cooking show went to commercials.

Dottie looked up. "Do you need any help with your stuff?"

Oh, so now you're helpful? Wylie shook her head, dropped the first duffel bag by the front door and returned to the bedroom to grab the second one. She straightened her spine as she walked between her former roommate and a television chef demonstrating how to make pasta. "Adios, Snickerdoodle. It's been swell."

The cat's eyes remained closed.

Dottie petted the animal and kept her gaze locked on the television, determined to learn the secrets of boiling water.

Whatever. Wylie opened the front door to a small concrete balcony leading to the flight of stairs. The midday breeze caressed her face and she looked toward the water, knowing that change came with the tide. She hefted the first bag, balanced the two weights and looked over her shoulder at the pair sitting in the dusty, beige living room. "I guess that's goodbye. I hope you, your cousin and your cat all get cavities."

Dottie looked up. "What?"

"Nothing," Wylie said. She pulled the front door closed with her foot, kicked it for good measure and muttered a string of expletives. *That was petty, but I deserve a medal for not slapping the woman and throwing a lamp at her precious television set. Violence never solves anything, but damn, it would have felt good.*

After trudging down the stairs, she found her SUV in the parking lot, loaded her bags and climbed into the driver's seat. The sun-warmed interior smelled like a mix of beeswax and the sweet almond oil she used to condition her skin. *I can figure out how to solve this problem. I'll just have to work harder to get ahead.*

She picked strands of cat fur off her black yoga pants and cataloged her wealthy clients who lived in the hills over Palisades Park. She felt comfortable collecting twenty-five-dollar class fees when everyone wore coordinated sets, but she doubted her practitioners wanted to empathize with her situation and host her in their lush guest houses. *They've never invited me to grab a bite to eat, stroll around the farmers' market or stop by for a drink. At the end of the day, they admire my yoga form, but their patronage will probably disappear if they discover I'm desperate. Nobody wants to feel obligated to the needy. They're afraid they'll recognize something familiar about the person they're trying to help.*

Pulling out her phone, she searched for extended-stay apartments and temporary solutions to get her out of a crisis state. The action felt reassuring and positive, but the social media listings looked like scams and the preludes to money wire requests. She found a cluster of weekly rentals on the other side of the valley that met her budget, but she shook her head, knowing the cost of the commute would eat up her funds. Dejected, she closed the browser application and wondered whether Oregon might be a better solution in the long run. *At least when I'm there, someone else will be pumping my gas —* she rolled her eyes *— if I can afford it.*

Her stomach rumbled and she thought about the days when her parents had footed the bills for her favorite fast-casual restaurant serving barbecue and grilled foods. Garlic rolls, a Caesar salad with salt and pepper chicken and a can of natural-essence sparkling water sounded delicious, but she knew independence came with concessions and sacrifices. *I want to find a way to make this life work on my terms. Given my situation, splurging on a twenty-dollar meal would be as irresponsible as skipping the water bill to pay for false eyelashes. That's one of the problems with living in LA. You're surrounded by luxury and hot people, but you don't know who's legit and who's hoping you won't see through their façade. What's the difference between necessity and prep work?*

She found a ballpoint and ran the numbers on the back of the deposit envelope. The five-hundred-dollar refund and the April rent sitting in her bank account fell short of the amount she knew she needed for a place of her own. Desperate for solutions, she thought of the yoga instructor overseeing her certification and wondered if Cynthia would play mother hen to a yoga chick in need. *If that doesn't work out, I'll just live in my spacious SUV until I scrape together enough cash to put down a deposit and find a roommate of my own.* She put the vehicle in gear and navigated toward Cynthia's big-name yoga studio that catered to the Silicon Beach set in Playa Vista. *Two weeks, max. Even I can do that.*

She pulled into the faultless parking lot of Cynthia's studio and wondered how many hours of sweat equity separated a beachside practice from the bricks-and-mortar achievement of a studio. Beyond offering three types of yoga, Cynthia taught the two-hundred-hour certification class Wylie needed to land a job with health insurance.

The woman spends more time taking selfies than improving her practice, but I've already completed forty online hours and finished the first half of the studio work required for my accreditation. If this morning proved anything, it proved I need a way to manage my asthma. If Cynthia won't house me, maybe she'll fast-track my accreditation or serve as an employment reference. I mean, I could teach her class blindfolded — she turned off the ignition. *Who am I kidding? I'm just trying to get by right now.*

The class ended at one o'clock and Cynthia clapped her hands for attention. "I'm going to grab lunch at the Modesto food truck. Feel free to stick around if you have any unanswered questions."

Wylie peered through the studio's windows and saw a food truck with horizontal wood panels. Positioned near the street corner, the truck's multicolored prayer flags and painted bistro sets created a park-let and a final destination for a long line of customers waiting to place their orders. *It must be pretty good.* Her stomach growled.

Realizing she had left all her food in Dottie's apartment, she hurried to catch up to Cynthia. The woman had the toned arms of a lifelong yoga practitioner and the honed polish of an athlete. Her white teeth sparkled with the uniform shine of veneers and her dyed bob remained as black as her yoga pants.

They stood in line and surveyed the menu.

Wylie shifted her balance, searching for common ground before she encroached on their professional relationship with a litany of personal requests. "So what do you like to eat here?"

"The veggie wraps are amazing. I don't know what they put in the sauce, but it makes you forget to count calories and just believe in happily ever after."

Wylie raised her eyebrows and scanned Modesto's menu with more interest. The food truck's offerings focused on seasonal produce, lean protein and hot grains, but she wondered why the proprietor had named it after a town in the central valley. "I guess they're not selling hamburgers today?"

Cynthia rolled her eyes. "*Ew*. Who would eat a hamburger these days?"

Wylie inhaled, figuring her chances of crashing on the woman's floor had fallen a notch. She took a deep breath. "Do you have any other accreditation classes I could attend in the next few weeks? I'm super interested in wrapping up the coursework and finding a permanent position. Like, let's get this done as soon as possible."

"Are you going to keep your beachside practice?"

So you do pay attention. Wylie decided to hedge her response and shield her desperation. "Yeah, I just realized that I need to get benefits or earn more money to survive in this town."

Cynthia nodded. "My accreditation program is a good starting place, and you've got good form."

"But?"

"You can't rush these things. Develop a little patience. It will improve your practice and your daily life."

Wylie thought of the long, dark hours awaiting her if she could not find an alternative to sleeping in her SUV. "I'm not sure patience is the only thing I need."

Cynthia looked at her. "What's wrong?"

"Um, my roommate kicked me out."

The instructor raised her eyebrows. "What'd you do?"

Nothing! Wylie wanted to scream, but she exhaled. "What can I do? She's letting her cousin move in, like, today."

"That's a bummer," Cynthia said like someone who wanted a paleo cookie from the pool's snack bar. "There's only so much you can control."

She waited for the woman to caveat her statement with a note of empathy. *That's a bummer, but you can stay with me for a few weeks. That's a bummer, but I know a few women who could put you up for a spell. That's a bummer, but... It's not my problem.*

"I'd like to control her into a dose of common sense."

Instead of coming to her rescue, Cynthia laughed and scanned the food truck's menu. "Take it from me, Wylie. There are only so many factors you can control."

A vendor in his early thirties leaned out of the window and asked for their orders.

Cynthia moved forward until she stood directly beneath him. "I'll have the veggie wrap and a side of sweet potato fries."

The man smiled. "Big calorie splurge, Cindy?"

Cynthia looked at Wylie and smiled. "Isn't it cute how he calls me Cindy?" Without waiting for a response, she turned back to the vendor. "It's in honor of my friend, Wylie. She's reminding me what it's like to be young, ambitious and impulsive." The woman winked. "I just hope my metabolism is on board with this plan."

Wylie swallowed as the vendor glanced at her with bright green eyes, but he dismissed her and focused on the customer at the front of his line. "Oh, I think you could take her down."

Cynthia laughed and handed the man a credit card to pay for her meal. "That's why people keep coming back to you, Nolan. Your food's good, but your sense of humor is even better."

"It must not be a high bar," Wylie said. She kicked a piece of gravel near the curb and thought about how she would spend the remainder of her day.

The vendor laughed.

She looked up, meeting his bright green gaze. *Shit, that snide comment came out louder than I thought.* Embarrassed by her retort, she blushed, intending to apologize for being rude. *Common courtesy — your mother taught you to be polite to strangers.* The words stalled in her throat.

His charming grin and lively gaze hummed with amusement.

The longer she stared at the man, the more she feared they would remain strangers.

Raising his eyebrow, he broke the connection and scanned her body.

She stood proud, knowing she looked good in her athletic gear. His appraisal would take in the swell of her breasts and the neat indentation of her waist. Remembering to raise her chin, she let her smile grow. *Yoga pays off, doesn't it? Have you decided I'm more than another customer? Do you see something here you want?*

The vendor met her gaze and bit his lip.

Smiling, she tried to ignore the warmth spreading through her chest. The man's unique eyes caught her attention, but his style choices and elevated physique gave her a reason to linger. His neat fade suggested a standing appointment with a barber and mimicked the hip street aesthetic of the food truck, but a small line of skin separated his beard from his sideburns. *Did you flinch at your last appointment or did your barber have a problem making the ends meet?*

"Like what you see?" Nolan asked.

She stopped admiring the strong lines of his jaw and grinned. "It's an interesting menu."

He laughed and stood up straight, spreading his arms to encompass the food truck and healthy menu. "We aim to please."

"Looks like you've got a line today," Cynthia said, clearing her throat and vying for the vendor's attention.

"Good thing," Nolan said. "Humor won't keep us out of the red."

The instructor dropped a five-dollar bill in the tip jar. "Maybe you just need another gig." She raised her eyebrows.

Wylie coughed and bit her lip at the innuendo, trying not to laugh at the thought of the yoga instructor propositioning the younger man like a typecast cougar. A trickle of laughter slipped passed her defenses and she clapped her hand tight against her lips, pretending to clear an errant cough from her throat. *What happened to the mascot from the tiki lounge?*

They both turned to stare at her, his eyebrows raised and her eyebrows frozen from one too many injections.

She widened her eyes and tried to look innocent. "What? We all have our strengths."

Cynthia's brow twitched.

"You said Modesto makes good food, so let's do it."

Nolan's finger hovered over a mobile dashboard and a credit card reader meant to obviate daily trips to the bank. "So, what will you have?"

She stared at the menu and pondered which combination of dishes would keep her stomach full the longest. Moisture pooled in her mouth and she swallowed her spit, wondering how people managed the pain of chronic hunger when the country had so much food it spoiled and grocers threw it out. "How about a deal?" she said, focusing on Nolan. "I'll promote your truck on social media in exchange for a free lunch of your choice."

"What?" Cynthia mumbled about the right way to do business and shook her head. "He has my card. Just order a wrap." She waved at the men in their Friday shirts.

Wylie watched her leave and focused on Nolan, who was responding to an issue within the food truck. *We might be interested adults, but until I put my life back together, the only booty call that I'm making is a midday visit to a public restroom.*

"Sorry about that," he said, "but no-go on the promotion deal. I could retire if I had a dollar for every social media influencer who wanted a free meal. Let me guess… You have, like, thousands of followers?"

"Something like that." She smiled. "I teach a beachfront yoga class at Palisades Park and my clientele would love your menu." *Blink. Blink.*

"Great. Tell them about Modesto the next time you want to do a good deed for a budding entrepreneur."

"What?"

"You don't look like you need free food."

She blinked and looked at the waiting line of customers clutching credit cards. She winced, realizing her offer pitted a slim upside against the nourishing reality of free food. For a moment, she considered twirling her hair and wondered if Cynthia's brand of flirtatious humor would have gotten her further with the man. *Stick to your principles.* She took a deep breath. "So no free lunch?"

He crossed his arms and looked down at her. "This is like the story of my life. People see what I have and they want a piece of it."

She glanced at the menu. "Well, you're selling food."

The obvious comment elicited a laugh and defused his defensive posture. "I'm just stating the facts. My menu's good enough to cultivate a loyal social media following without your added exposure. I'd run out of food if I gave my goods away to everyone who asked for a handout."

"Well, at least you'd have friends."

"Hardly. I'd have dependents."

Isn't that my greatest fear? Hanging out in my parents' basement, unable to support myself while the rest of the world gets ahead? She blew out her breath. "Fine. Your loss. Just remember, reviews can go both ways."

He raised his eyebrows. "Are you threatening me?"

She smiled. "No. I was offering to take a chance on you. My reputation for your food. The least you could do is to return the favor."

The man leaned on the stainless-steel shelf holding his mobile dashboard. "You want to be partners? How about this? You pay for your meal and I'll give you a promo code. If your followers track down my truck and place an order within the next week, you can have ten percent of the profits."

"What do they get for mentioning the code?"

"Ten percent off their order. You and I are splitting the proceeds."

Wylie considered the potential payout of their deal. The reality of living without showers and laundry facilities had begun to sink in, but this man did not need to know that fact. She wondered if he could see the desperation beneath her athletic gear and clean blonde hair. *How long before this patina wears off?* Visibility made her feel vulnerable.

A woman coughed behind her.

She shook off her insecurities and decided she had nothing to lose. "What's the code?"

Nolan cocked his head and looked at her like a rare ingredient, then he smiled and winked. "Mini Mako."

"Excuse me?" she asked, knowing their conversation straddled a fine line between flirtation and schoolyard banter.

"Oh, you know the song. *Bay-bee…*"

She shut her eyes and frowned as a K-pop children's song wormed its way into her subconsciousness. Before the song had taken over every preschool in the nation, it had endured as a simple camp song with a gruesome ending. She thought about the years she had spent on dusty SoCal campuses where summer childcare masqueraded as noble summer camp.

I'm nothing like a mako shark. They're large, fast and decisive. I'm…peaceable and intentional? She scanned the impromptu nickname for a shred of truth, but the song's lyrics drowned out her objections and she involuntarily tapped her foot, indulging in the simple melody before adult reality roared through her consciousness like a sneaker wave. She opened her eyes and stared at the man, shaking her head to clear the annoying rhythm. "You did that on purpose."

His smile widened. "It's memorable, just like you."

I'm going to see this man again. The realization heightened her awareness of how she stood and she straightened her shoulders. *Why him?*

Nolan matched her posture and straightened to his full height. If he felt the same awareness she did, he hid it behind the casual friendliness that seasoned his food. A prep cook called out a question and he answered it without breaking her gaze. Ten people stood in line behind her, but Wylie leaned forward, wondering what might be on the chef's menu.

He swallowed, his throat working like he had encountered an unexpected morsel. "Mini Mako? It's an easy promo code to remember and I want you to come back."

She shook off her awareness of their mutual attraction and reminded herself that she no longer had the luxury of flirting with handsome men. "I'm not an idiot. Why don't you go with something more uplifting? Like 'FreshToFit'?"

"Mini Mako."

"My name is Wylie."

He repeated her name and seemed to taste the sounds. Then he eyed the line of people waiting to place their orders. "Take it or leave it."

"Fine." She sighed, wondering if 'Mini Mako' would elicit anything more than a few laughs on social media. *Haven't they ever seen* Jaws?

"So what will you have?"

She scanned the prices on the menu. "Lentil soup."

He nodded at the cheap selection, but she couldn't tell if he approved of her choice or recognized the budget decision.

"Small or large?"

"Large." She let the frustration of the day seep into her voice.

His finger hovered over the mobile dashboard. "Anything else, Wylie Coyote?"

"Just Wylie."

He smiled and typed her name. "That'll be six dollars."

She handed the man her credit card, thankful that the delayed billing cycle would buy her time to balance her finances. She knew the money would have gone further in a supermarket, but the splurge had been worth it to get more face time with Cynthia.

Nolan looked up. "I'll throw in some sweet potato fries to sweeten the deal."

"Aren't you generous?"

He smiled and winked at her. "The orange color will brighten up your post."

Twenty minutes later, Wylie sat in the shade of a sycamore tree and finished her lentil soup. She savored the quiet satisfaction of a full stomach before she arranged the empty soup container on a bed of large green leaves. *My followers won't know it's empty. Can I make a haphazard stack of sweet potato fries look like art?*

Her phone's camera brought the truck's logo into focus and let the vehicle's horizontal wood panels and painted bistro sets fade into the background. She considered a series of captions before she began to type.

Delicious find in Playa Vista. Seasonal produce, lean protein and hot grains. No upcharge for a handsome proprietor and somewhere to rest your ass. Mention 'Mini Mako' this week for ten percent off your order.

She tagged the Modesto food truck and calculated her followers would have to spend sixty dollars to offset the price of her lentil soup. She looked at the remaining sweet potato fries in her composition and thought, *Good thing the fries were free.*

She popped one into her mouth and watched another food truck employee begin to pack up the bistro tables. The diminishing crowd on the sidewalk went back to their daily pursuits and left her in the shade of the tree, alone and unobserved. *I'll need more than luck and good looks to get myself out of this situation.*

Chapter Two

Walkers, bikers and people-watchers thronged the lush twenty-acre park overlooking the Pacific Ocean, but Wylie chose a spot away from the area where she normally hosted her yoga classes. Palisades Park might connect with the broad beach from *Baywatch*, but she gambled that the television series' iconic episodes had never profiled the expansive asphalt of this particular parking lot.

She ignored the scrubby hills on the other side of the Pacific Coast Highway and walked past children playing on a rope playground. Their guardians tapped their smartphones and looked at her with mild interest. Wylie did not smile back. Instead of their village aspirations, she had come here to drown her thoughts with the anonymity of a parking lot, acres of open beach and the sounds of crashing waves. She dropped a towel on the sand and pulled on a baseball cap to shield her eyes. *Is this what people do all day when they don't have a job or a place to go? They find places to get lost?*

Tower eight looked empty in the mid-afternoon light. Wylie wondered if lifeguard stands north of the pier remained unstaffed until Memorial Day. She thought of climbing the tower's steps and claiming the structure. *Maybe I can sleep there for a while?* She turned and looked at the public restroom facilities and rinse-off showers near the parking lot.

An LAPD cruiser pulled in.

She faced the water. *Maybe not.*

The sound of the waves overrode her uncertainty until a woman's off-key singing became too loud to ignore.

As the performer came closer, *Free Bird* lyrics dissolved into a vocalized guitar riff. The woman settled on the bare sand, too close for comfort and too loud to ignore.

She covered her ears. "Do you mind?"

The woman shrugged. "This is my spot but feel free. You can sing along."

"What do you mean, this is your spot?"

The woman stopped singing and looked at Wylie. Age spots covered her tanned skin, but her blue eyes and mainstream sun-streaked brown hair could have easily blended with the crowds inside a neighborhood coffee shop.

Then Wylie looked closer and saw the woman's unpainted toenails, faded jeans and ragged hoodie. She wondered if the freestyle beach performer had enough change to cover a cup of coffee. She pulled her knees up and rested her chin on the thick material of her workout gear. "Don't worry about it," she said. "Sing as much as you want. It's a free world."

The frayed woman stood and dropped down to the sand beside her. "I'm Penny Lane."

"Wylie," she answered, wondering if Penny Lane's performance had been a tribute or a clue to the woman's underlying mental condition.

Penny Lane leaned back and yawned. "It's such a pretty day. Why are you sitting out here all by yourself?"

Wylie kept her eyes on the ocean. "I just needed a break."

"Sure, but I mean, don't you have people?"

"No," Wylie said. She watched a gull cruise over the wide Pacific and thought about the long car ride separating her from the family she could claim. "I don't have people."

Penny Lane laughed. "I have too many people — people who want things from me, people who want to steal my stuff. I come out here to get rid of too many people and just think about the important ones."

Wylie hoped silence would get her out of the conversation, but her new friend kept talking.

"I used to live on the bluffs overlooking the ocean or camp out at Will Rogers State Beach. It sounds ideal, but I had million-dollar views and nothing but the clothes on my back." She cleared her throat. "Well, I had a tent, but when most people think of homelessness in Los Angeles, they think of faceless forms sleeping on the concrete in Skid Row, Venice and Santa Monica. That wasn't my MO."

Wylie glanced at the woman then looked up at the dense brush climbing the hillside on the other side of the freeway. She realized that without her SUV or a clear solution to her problem, the steep landscape could easily become her only option for a home.

She realized that her family and account balance gave her choices, but pride and ambition were forcing her to play the long game. The possibilities of roughing it had seemed vaguely romantic until she'd met Penny

Lane and thought of the dangers hiding on the steep slope. *I'll swallow my pride and take the bus to Oregon before I let myself feel that exposed.*

Money and the state of their family finances felt like a thread woven throughout the tapestry of her childhood. She knew her parents worked hard to pay the bills, but she wished she had been older before she had seen the seams and learned to balance a checkbook. She wished she had experienced Disneyland without wondering about the cost of the ticket. As graduation approached, her parents had pushed her toward college degrees with six-figure incomes, but Wylie had balked and planted her feet on the beach. Her parents had retired and moved to Oregon, giving her a final choice to follow them. Instead, she had moved out, more determined than ever to stay in the basin and prove she could earn a living as a freelance yoga instructor. *What would I have done without a marketable skillset?* She turned her back on the coyotes, snakes and human predators camouflaged by the steep slope and focused on being a sympathetic listener.

"It's not so bad," Penny Lane said. "A few years ago, we had a pretty big community out there. I liked it, you know? It made me think of my family back in New Jersey. My mom and I lived in a borough called Palisades Park. I think she would have gotten a kick out of this beach if she had lived long enough to see it."

Wylie stopped looking at the ocean and laid her head on her knees as she asked Penny Lane, "What happened to her?"

"Old age. Poverty. She got sick and waited too long to ask for help."

Wylie nodded, but she realized that the gulf between them had widened. Her mother relied on an established relationship with a primary care physician.

Penny Lane smiled. "So after she passed, I came out here and found a new home. Except, instead of just facing poverty, I had to spend my time wondering what people wanted from me. Most of my new friends had a touch of mental illness. People usually have a reason they find themselves sleeping rough."

Wylie closed her eyes for a moment. "I'm sorry I don't have any spare money to give you."

Penny Lane laughed. "A couple of years ago, local residents formed the Pacific Palisades Task Force on Homelessness. They put in the hours and cleared the bluff through a combination of outreach, treatment and housing. They had plenty of money. It didn't work."

Wylie looked at the woman. "Why not?"

Penny Lane took a deep breath. "People came back."

"Why?"

"It's got to be the whole package," she said. "I'm one of the lucky ones. I ended up making friends with an older guy named Larry and lived with him for a few years. He was my best friend, but he had Parkinson's disease and it just got worse and worse." She took a deep breath. "He committed suicide about three weeks ago. He died."

Wylie nodded to show she understood.

"But I took care of him and stuck with him until the end. He was on Supplemental Security Income, so he paid all the bills and everything. One day, he sent me to the grocery store, and when I came back, he was gone."

"That's so sad."

"I don't know why he wanted to die alone."

They sat in the cocoon of the ocean waves.

"Maybe he wanted to protect you," Wylie said.

The woman nodded. "Maybe."

Hoping Penny Lane's anxiety responded to the rhythm of tasks, Wylie sketched circles in the sand. "Sometimes I find it helpful to write down my to-do lists. Even if I don't stick to the lists, they dampen my uncertainties and reassure me that I have a plan and proof of what I've accomplished."

"Never been much of a planner," Penny Lane said.

"Start with a small decision."

"I want to donate his clothes to the homeless shelter. I know people could use them."

Wylie nodded. "That's a good task! Start small."

The woman started singing *Free Bird* again.

At least she's looking forward. Wylie wondered if she could break down her needs into similar increments. It seemed so much easier to make choices for other people than to make choices for herself. "My roommate kicked me out too," she said. "She didn't give me any warning and everything I own fits in two duffel bags."

Penny Lane stopped singing. "That's a light load. You're more flexible when you're young." A minute passed and she finished the next verse. "I figured something bad had happened to you. You're too young and pretty to be sitting out here by yourself. You don't look like you're even enjoying the beach."

Wylie toyed with the sand and thought of Penny Lane's story. "I don't have a lot of room to complain about my choices. I just need to find a new place to live until I get my life sorted out."

Penny Lane looked up at the hillside. "Yeah, we're always one step away from success. My stuff's probably still up there under a bush. I bet one or two of the people from the old camp never even left their spots — the ones who didn't want four walls and a roof to cage them in."

"You shouldn't go back there," Wylie said. She stood, brushed the sand from her yoga mat, shook out her towel and folded it over her arm. "It's just going to seem normal again. You'll forget Larry and the security of what you had when you two were together."

Penny Lane stood and stretched, her sweatshirt riding up to expose the smooth white skin of her stomach. "No. I came out here on the seven-twenty to remember him. You can spend hours with your head propped against the glass, watching the blocks pass and worrying about what you're going to do next. We used to take the bus out here and enjoy the view. It's a cheap way to reflect."

"Reflect on what?" Wylie asked, ignoring the twenty-five-dollar fees she charged her students to capitalize on the sounds of the ocean. An hour of solitude improved their bodies, but it also gave them an opportunity to pinpoint their negative tendencies and bad habits.

The woman fingered a small vial hanging from her necklace. "Reflect on what would have happened if our lives had turned out differently."

"And if they hadn't? What if this reality is your only option?"

Penny Lane laughed. "You're so young. Don't you see how many options you have left?"

Wylie glanced at the hills. *Don't you see how much you've lost?* She kept her mouth shut, determined to respect a woman who had befriended her without asking for anything in return.

The haggard woman smiled. "Larry and me, we were just grateful for where we were and what we had left. Fate and circumstance might have narrowed our choices, but we still got to make the final decisions."

Wylie nodded, looked at the scrub-covered hillside and doubled down on her resolve to stay in Los Angeles and find a way to earn a living in the star-studded town. "Thanks for sitting with me."

"Don't you have anybody you can call? Friends? An ex-boyfriend you could call?"

"Not really." She looked at the kids running around the playground. "They're all living paycheck to paycheck like I am. Nobody I know has the means to settle down."

Penny Lane hummed the chorus of her song. "Some of us never do."

* * * *

The threat of rush-hour traffic and meaningless gas consumption pushed Wylie toward the allure of a solid building. Tired of using her phone to search for housing solutions, she took shelter at a one-story library. From the outside, suburban homes and towering eucalyptus trees created a scenic diversion, but Wylie paused the moment she stepped inside. Screaming kids filled the children's section and more than one sleeping person occupied a bench in the lobby.

She walked past the nameless men and women, determined to avoid their fate and limit her empathy to Penny Lane. Then she took a deep breath and applied for a library card to use the computers. Two hours later, the lackluster results of her search left her feeling exhausted and frustrated.

She thought of Penny Lane's question. *'Don't you have anybody you can call?'* She sought out a quiet corner of the library and sighed. *I didn't want to go there.*

"Wylie!" her ex-boyfriend shouted into the phone.

House music filled the background and she sighed, relieved he had taken the call. "Rusty," she said, "it's good to hear your voice."

"Are you coming to the opening tonight?"

She plugged her other ear to block out the competing noise of the library. "What opening?"

"I have a new club. The Social Club. I put you on the list."

Wylie looked at her yoga gear and wondered how bad she smelled after an entire day of elemental exposure. "No, I don't think I'm going to make it to the opening. I need a favor, though. Could I sleep on your couch for a few nights? My roommate kicked me out."

"I told you Dottie was a bad choice."

Wylie exhaled. *You also told me we were exclusive and threw plates at the wall when I called you out on it.* She ignored the sinking feeling in her stomach and focused on getting what she needed out of the conversation. "Turns out you were right."

"No can do on the couch. I have a new girl and she's not the sharing type."

"Sure," Wylie said. She closed her eyes. "Of course."

"You should come to the club."

She looked at a bedraggled woman staring at a bulletin board. "Maybe when things settle down."

"Yoga on the rooftop," Rusty said like he had invented the idea. "We could do a happy hour special. Don't get drunk and fall off!"

"Hilarious." Wylie prepared to end the call, but the reality of her situation merged with the hunger clawing at her empty stomach. Desperation made her hide her memories of life with Rusty and focus on the bright spots in their relationship, like the time he had bought her flowers. The only time. She steeled her resolve and swallowed her pride. "Rusty, wait! Before you go.

Maybe I could pick up a few shifts at this club? Like, don't you need waitresses or something?"

"I don't know if Candy would like that."

"Candy? Seriously?"

Rusty defended his new girlfriend. "She's Southern."

Wylie amended the man's statement. *She's a Southern stripper.* "I need to pull in some extra cash if I want to get my own place. My mom will probably co-sign a lease, but I have to cover deposit and rent. Right now I just don't have enough."

"All my money's tied up in the club."

"Rusty, I'm not asking you for money."

He stayed quiet and she bided her time listening to the pulsing house music. She imagined him scratching his hair and finding purpose in the tangle of his reddish-brown locks. *Or did he find a tick? Why did I ever fall for him? We yelled as much as we made up.* Then she remembered the man's pathetic first attempt at beachside yoga. *Even in Downward Dog, he seemed more like a stray than I did. Now who's the lost cause?*

"Sure. I mean, what's the worst that can happen?"

Wylie took a deep breath. "You mean that?"

"I'll text you the address. Just come by at five and wear all black."

"Won't that make it hard for patrons to see me?"

Rusty declined to answer the question.

She checked their connection and heard him respond to a question from someone in the bar. Tired of dangling at the end of the line, she thought of ways to grab his attention. "Rusty? Remember that time we went to Vegas?"

"Vegas?" The background music transitioned to a new track. "Yeah. Five gallons."

"Five gallons?" she asked.

"Sorry. We're setting up the bar. Look, Wylie... I have somewhere I have to be right now."

She looked at the shelves of books and the neon sculptures above the library doors. "Lucky you." She hung up the phone, returned to the beach and saw Penny Lane sitting beneath a streetlight at the edge of the playground.

The woman made eye contact and her face brightened in recognition.

"Get in," she said. "I'll buy you a sandwich for dinner, as long as it's cheap."

"You'll have to leave the village."

She laughed. "We can buy a week's worth of peanut butter and jelly sandwiches for the price of something from the village."

Penny Lane toyed with the radio. "Some people never figure out that fact."

Wylie drove the two of them to a small grocery.

"I took your suggestion," the older woman said when they arrived in the parking lot. "I donated all his clothes."

"And?"

"And it felt good."

Wylie grinned and climbed from the SUV. She selected a bag of bread, nonperishable spreads and a couple of liters of water. When she returned to the car, she found Penny Lane seated on the tailback, her legs swinging as she used a stack of yoga equipment for a backrest.

Ten minutes later, the woman bit into her peanut butter and jelly sandwich and smiled. "I told you to get the chocolate. You need to take advantage of life's small pleasures."

Wylie chewed the gummy mess in her hands, mortified to recall the days she'd spent counting calories or completely avoiding them. "I'm saving my money."

"For what."

"Rent. Life. Whatever happens to me next."

Penny Lane sipped from a dented water bottle. "Don't spend too long worrying about what happens next. I'm proof of what happens when you stall out."

Wylie took a deep breath. "I took your advice and called an old boyfriend."

"Wait. Did I give you that advice?"

She smiled. "More or less."

"That sounds like terrible advice. He must be a dick if you're still out here with me."

"He offered me a job at his new club."

The woman nodded. "But nowhere to sleep. Typical man."

"He has a new girlfriend."

Penny Lane counted the cars in the parking lot. "Larry never knew what was good for him either. He should have kicked me out and found someone who could do more than take care of him. He should have found someone to *love* him."

Maybe he loved you, even if you didn't love him back. She remembered the days she had spent trying to mold Rusty into the man she'd thought she wanted, someone full of energy to pass the time. Rusty had always barged into his apartment with a loud declaration. '*Honey, I'm home.*' Half the time, Wylie had jumped up to greet him, but the other half of the time, she had felt annoyed when he'd interrupted her meditations and Savasana pose. *I need a man with quiet intentions, but right now I need to eat this sandwich.* "What are you going to do next?"

"Either find a job or find a way back home. That man's benefits spoiled me. I've been thinking of life back at the camps, wondering if I could do it again. He kept me out of that environment."

"It wasn't so great?"

Penny Lane polished off her sandwich and pulled her hood over her hair. "It had its perks. I got attached to the beach, but I don't want to see any more friends drink themselves to death. I don't want to spend my days collecting cans and bottles for recycling or relying on donations." She gestured to the groceries and the small plastic utensils they had used. "Not that I'm not grateful."

Wylie smiled and imagined Penny Lane in Rusty's beat-fueled club. The woman would probably sit at the bar with canned beer and get a kick out of the pretentious customer base. "What kind of job could you do?"

"I'm more of a caregiver without the right credentials."

"Tell me about it." Wylie wiped the crumbs from her athletic wear. "I don't know why we need licenses to be good human beings."

"Lawyers."

Wylie laughed. "Well, you can sleep in the SUV with me tonight. There won't be any cause for litigation. I'll even let you tune the radio."

Penny Lane looked at her for a moment but shook her head. "It's a generous offer, but I figured I'd just take the seven-twenty back to downtown."

"And do what? Do you still have Larry's apartment?"

Her gaze focused on the horizon. "I have friends."

Wylie started to pack up the groceries. "Lucky you."

"You could come with me," Penny Lane said.

She looked toward the ocean. "I'd rather take my chances on the beach."

"Just stay up at the state park where there's more darkness and cover. The police sweep the beach, so you've got to stay in your car or hide in bushes. Watch out for the bugs and ground squirrels...or just keep moving. I can't tell you how many times I heard about people waking up in their vehicles to find a police officer rapping on the window or shining a flashlight in their faces. 'Just keep moving' can only get you so far."

"Just keep moving," Wylie repeated, wondering how much sleep she could get if she had to move her vehicle every two hours.

Penny Lane closed her eyes and took a deep breath like she was summoning a buried memory. "You need to find one of those 'safe parking' programs. I think they cater to veterans, but some of the sites even have showers and bathrooms and support staff."

"I don't need support staff," Wylie said.

Penny Lane raised her eyebrows.

"Come with me?"

The older woman shook her head. "I've been out here for a long time. Whatever you do, just don't leave your vehicle parked on the street for more than seventy-two hours. They'll tow it and you'll be shit out of luck."

Wylie laughed, hoping she wouldn't find herself stuck on the streets for that long. "This is just temporary," she said.

"So what are you going to do?"

"Hide in plain sight." She looked toward the ocean. "Keep my head above water until I figure out how to get a room or an apartment."

Penny Lane nodded. "You're young and pretty. You might be able to do it."

"And if I don't?"

The woman gestured toward the crumbs from their meal. "Well, you've already got one friend on the streets."

* * * *

Wylie woke with the sun, thankful that she had been able to grab a few moments of sleep between her dark stretches of paranoia. Within the confines of her SUV, the sounds of the Los Angeles night had fueled her fears. Every human voice had seemed ominous, jerking her awake and pushing her to check the locks on the vehicle's doors.

As she stretched the cramps from her muscles, she began to respect the cautious wariness in Penny Lane's eyes and wondered how the woman had survived so many years of sleeping rough. *I made it through one night because I lucked out in plain sight and nobody bothered me. What happens on nights two and three? Night twenty-three? I told myself I could last two weeks, but she's living in a whole different reality.*

A bench with metal strips disguised as armrests caught Wylie's eye, and the anti-homeless design and hostile architecture of the surrounding neighborhood no longer looked benign or intended to thwart skateboarders.

As she stretched and began her yoga flow, she began to see the green space south of the Santa Monica Pier with a whole new perspective. The park where Ocean Park Boulevard met the ocean had given her refuge for the night, but she realized that the leaning palm trees and open lawn near lifeguard tower twenty-six would not open their arms for everyone.

I have the morning to myself. She stood, craving the warmth of the sun and the open freedom of the beach.

Raising her arms above her head, she realized that she needed a shower as much as she needed food and freedom. *Okay, if my class meets every other day, I'm going to have to make sure my 'on' days start with a shower.*

She eyed the wide Pacific and wondered how cold the water would feel if she risked a swim and pretended her body odor took second place to washing her clothes. February had passed in a blur of hearts and decreased class attendance, but Wylie's childhood swims had taught her the temperature of the seawater peaked in September. *There's a reason the surfers wear wetsuits.*

A woman wearing wedge sandals stopped walking and struggled to sip her coffee while her Chihuahua pulled at a narrow lead. Wylie smiled. *That's not my life right now. I have sandwich materials and it's easy enough to find a shower to rinse off, but I need to wash my clothes as well.*

She scanned the park and thought of Dottie, ensconced in a dated apartment with every creature comfort she needed. *I hope she and her cousin are bonding over botulism, but I need to find a laundromat.*

Chapter Three

The complications of life without a fixed dwelling filled Wylie's day with boredom and frustration, but at five o'clock sharp, she arrived in front of Rusty's new club to start her first shift. The old brick PG&E power station by the railroad tracks filled a city block, but strings of patio lights and a private security team promised curious Westside gawkers that the Social Club had opened for business.

Wylie parked her vehicle behind the building and considered its location in Chesterfield Square. Twenty miles from the coast, the obscure Los Angeles neighborhood had a reputation for high crime and a heavy minority presence. She knew residents worried about gang violence, but palm trees surrounded the litter-free park and she wondered if heart disease and cancer were the bigger threats. *What's Rusty doing out here?* she wondered as she checked her makeup in the rearview mirror. *Whatever it is, this commute had better be worth the tips.*

She walked toward a back door where the smells of a kitchen combined with the fumes of fresh paint. "I'm looking for Rusty," she said to the kid smoking a cigarette. "Today's my first shift."

The man took a drag and examined her black pants and V-neck shirt. "You're overdressed for the floor."

She looked at the man's spotless white apron and gel-slicked black hair. "I doubt you're in charge of the front of the house."

His eyes narrowed, but he shook his head and moved aside. "Good luck, *mamacita.*"

The industrial kitchen gave way to a huge space with exposed ductwork and smaller nooks furnished with leather finishes and gleaming chrome. Workers ignored the blaring house music as they polished the bar and swept the floor, waiting for the sun to go down.

Wylie scanned their faces, looking for her ex-boyfriend's reddish-brown hair amid the clusters of black-clad servers struggling to talk over the amplified feed of a local radio station. She eyed the waitresses milling near the bar and realized the busboy's assessment of her clothing had been correct.

The women's skirts barely covered their assets and most of their tops could have passed as bras. Wylie felt like a rookie auditioning to join the cheer squad amid a sea of midriffs and exposed cleavage. She looked at the DJ assembling his gear and laughed when he stood up and revealed an oiled chest and leather armbands. *They'll take me as I am.*

Rusty waved from the front door and beckoned her over. "You made it."

"I did." She looked around the room and locked eyes with a private security officer. The man's dispassionate expression made him look like a musician whose advertisements peppered downtown billboards. The images of a square-faced, jacked-up musician from Columbia promised to fuse traditional music with catchy, guitar-driven pop-rock, but Wylie doubted the bouncer knew how to carry a tune. She focused on Rusty. "How did the soft opening go last night?"

Her ex-boyfriend paled. "We had some trouble."

She exchanged looks with the bouncer, but he remained mute and waited on a bar stool, one foot resting on the stool's chrome supports while he cradled a tablet device.

"Not quite the clientele we were hoping to attract," Rusty said.

She thought of the neighborhood surrounding the railroad tracks and wondered what outcome her ex-boyfriend had expected when he had invested in a glittering spotlight near Chesterfield Square. *Shouldn't you build to meet the community's needs? How would you even know the community's needs unless you asked them or lived there?*

Rusty smiled at his hired help and slapped the man on the back. "Don't worry about it, though. We've posted a dress code on social media and taped a copy to all the public doors. It's covered. It's cool."

"Is it?"

The bouncer raised his eyebrows and handed Wylie the tablet.

She scanned a recent post on the bar's landing page.

Out of respect for all our guests, the Social Club has expanded its common-sense dress policy to require that all guests maintain traditional grooming standards, wear appropriate attire – e.g. collared shirts are preferred for male guests – and avoid sagging or culturally incendiary clothing.

Patrons wearing overly casual and overly revealing clothing will not be admitted.

Wylie glanced at the gaggle of waitresses waiting to make cash from exposing their assets. "This dress code leaves a lot of room for interpretation."

Rusty laughed and jerked his head toward the bouncer. "I'm counting on Jed to enforce the code as he sees fit."

She met the bouncer's gaze.

He rolled his eyes.

"I'm curious to see who he lets in." She exhaled and balanced her feelings toward Rusty against her new appreciation for life without paid utilities. She needed this job, but she also knew that most proprietors stopped at 'no shirt, no shoes, no service'. "Are you sure this is a good idea?"

Rusty nodded and jerked his thumb toward the waitresses. "C'mon. Come meet the girls. They'll show you where you can get changed."

"I didn't bring any other clothes."

Rusty considered her outfit and shrugged. He waved off her objection and pulled her toward a bleach-bottle blonde whose black skin shone beneath the overhead lights. "I'm sure the other girls can find you something to wear."

Wylie took a deep breath and wondered if she would fare better asking for donations along the beach path.

When Rusty assigned Wylie to Dede, the other waitress took a good look at her understudy, nodded and led her to a locker in the employee changing room. "How you know Rusty?"

"We dated for a while."

The waitress stopped and crossed her arms, barring the door. "And?"

"And I called him and told him I needed a little extra cash."

Dede raised her eyebrows at the honesty behind Wylie's answer. "It happens to the best of us." She led Wylie inside the spare room lined with lockers and vanities with 1980s round lightbulbs.

Another woman sat on a stool, her lips pursed as she took selfies beneath the flattering lights.

Dede shouldered a metal locker and spun the dial until the mechanism released. "Kolinda didn't like the haul last night, so I doubt she'll be coming back for a second shift. You can borrow some of her stuff."

Wylie stared at the open locker. "How'd you open that?"

The woman looked at Wylie and glanced at the woman applying makeup. "Were you ever this green?"

The second woman laughed but declined to answer.

"Okay. So, thanks for the clothes," Wylie said.

"You might want to add some more makeup too. The customers pay for flash. Do you have body glitter?"

Wylie thought of the organic cotton cosmetics bag stashed in the SUV. She shook her head and Dede pointed toward a woman applying black liquid eyeliner. "Jeanie will loan you some."

When Jeanie failed to blink at the request, Wylie decided the communal makeup had a better chance of transferring pink eye than luring Wylie's customers into bigger tips. "I'm good. I'll pick some up tomorrow if this works out."

"Nothing in Chesterfield Square works out," Jeanie said. She put down the eyeliner wand and toyed with her red highlights. "You have to make shit happen in this part of town." She turned to face Wylie and evaluated her blonde hair and stretchy black pants. "What do you know about this neighborhood?"

"Not much," Wylie admitted. "I just followed the directions on my phone."

Jeanie raised an eyebrow that carried more liner than natural curve. "Nothing rang a bell when you punched in the address?"

Wylie scanned the two women. "I had to take the freeway to get here?"

"The 54th Street Massacre? The riots?"

She felt the limits of her age and confined experiences. "I guess I wasn't old enough to pay attention when all that happened."

"Shit," Jeanie said. "All that's been defining my life since I was a kid." She met Dede's gaze and took a deep breath. "Not that it was your fault."

"What happened?" Wylie asked, hoping the story had a happy ending.

"Gang violence erupted between men who should have known better than to be in the same place at the same time. The tension killed a bunch of fourteen-year-olds in 1984, but the painful part is, it happened again and again. We're going on thirty-five years of being 'that part of town'. If people mention something else about this neighborhood, it's the Grim Sleeper, and that ain't good either." She rolled her eyes and turned back to the mirror. "So we've got a reputation for gangs and serial killers. That's all anybody ever talks about when they mention our home."

Wylie struggled for an appropriate response.

Jeanie met her gaze in the mirror. "Except for Rusty. He said he's going to try to build something new. Boy doesn't understand what he's getting into, but Dede and I ain't going to blame him for trying." She raised her eyebrows. "Ain't going to blame you until you screw up, either."

Wylie glanced at the door to the main floor and nodded, hoping the woman's view of Rusty as a shrewd businessman was a better casting choice than the lead she would have picked. *He's always been a temperamental, romantic fool.* Her new coworkers' allegiance to the man said something about the circumstances of the club that Wylie must have missed. Like a family, the waitresses were suspending their personal interests and working together to get something done. *This isn't the Tragedy of the Commons, but what kind of something is it?*

She held up Dede's black top and wondered how the web of straps and ties would support her breasts.

Jeanie and Dede swapped neighborhood gossip, oblivious to her concerns.

She got the distinct impression that the women had known each other from another venue. *A venue with poles*, she added before the judgmental thought made her blush with embarrassment. *We're all here trying to make a buck.* She faced the metal lockers, pulled off her V-neck and considered what to do with her bra.

"Take it off, girl. You're young enough to handle it."

Wylie shook her head and unclasped the garment. She pulled the black top into place and realized the bulk of the fabric belonged to a hood. The two triangles in front crossed over her cleavage and ended in ties that would anchor the top behind her neck and at the small of her back.

These had better be very good tips. She anchored the strappy top on her shoulder and wondered how many shifts it would take to pad her account balance and secure an apartment lease with her name on it.

"Did you guys know Candy before you started working at the Social Club?"

Jeanie and Dede looked at each other and laughed. "Girl, everybody knows Candy Cane."

Wylie blew out her breath and wondered how much her ex-boyfriend knew about his new business partner. Then she considered her situation and shrugged. *Who am I to care?*

Jed opened the doors at seven o'clock and a slow trickle of suited office workers and off-duty drivers pooled around the bar for happy hour prices. Wylie and the other waitresses lingered on the periphery of the room, waiting for darkness and the South Los Angeles neighborhood to turn toward the allure of nightlife.

Dede fixed her hair. "It's going to be slow until nine o'clock."

Jeanie laughed and nodded. "We won't close down until three or four."

Wylie swallowed and wondered how painful it would be to survive this night and host her beachside yoga class in the morning. *Maybe I can time these shifts so I have a day to recover.* She watched Dede reapply her lip gloss and took a deep breath. *Maybe I should just buy heavier concealer.*

Rusty started yelling at someone outside the main entrance and Dede and Jeanie rolled their eyes. "Here we go again. Let's grab a drink while he's not looking."

Instead of following the women, Wylie moved toward the front door, confident that Jed and Rusty had enough muscle power to keep her safe from harm.

"'Overly casual' and 'overly revealing' leaves room for misinterpretation and inconsistency," said a honeyed voice with the rhythm of a poetry slam champion. "At a minimum, your phrasing could be perceived as targeting and social profiling."

Rusty countered the man's argument. "I'm just trying to maintain standards and run a quality establishment."

A couple of people laughed and Wylie wondered at the size of the crowd outside the building.

"Man, you realize the dress code you published is straight-out racist?"

"No," Rusty said. "I would never call myself a racist. I care about this community."

"You guys pushed out an immigrant community, gentrified a historic building and posted blatantly racist dress codes, but now you care about the community? I'm not buying that."

"Me neither," a woman said. "Do you want my money or not?" Rusty hemmed and the sound of the crowd swelled. "It's as good as yours. You gonna take it or leave it, white boy?"

Wylie craned her neck to see the crowd, but before she could maneuver around Jed, the big man took a look at the crowd and lifted a presumptuous velvet rope. "Come on in."

The first person in line, a woman in a neon green bikini, sauntered into the room with the confidence of a Brazilian samba dancer. As she strode toward the bar, her glowing skin and lean thighs captured the attention of every person in the room. Wylie smiled. *It might be overly revealing, but she knows she looks good.*

The men following the dancer wore an assortment of scarves and bandanas more appropriate for Burning Man. As their number swelled, Wylie wondered if the Social Club had morphed into the newest headquarters of the Pride parade or an outlet of the community theater's costume department.

The waitresses flocked to the colorful crowd and escorted them to booths and private tables. Within ten minutes, Jed and his staff had admitted enough patrons to fill the bar's empty spaces and push the DJ to abandon his formal setup. He plugged in his phone and selected a playlist, filling the room with a pulsing beat that obviated conversation and made the crowd's default activities transition to drinks and side glances.

Dede grabbed Wylie's hand and pulled her toward the crowd.

"I'm coming," she said, but she turned toward the front door, confused by Rusty's absence and the warm voice of the lead protester. *I swear he sounds familiar.*

Jed stood by, arms crossed and ready to intercede as Rusty traded barbs with a man in a new baseball cap, a torn hoodie and sagging jeans. Wylie thought the protester looked like a stand-in for an old music video.

He continued talking to Rusty about social movements with a teasing humor designed to deescalate the confrontation.

She gasped, recognizing the food truck vendor. "Nolan."

Both men turned to look at her.

She remained focused on the newcomer. "What are you doing here?"

The man's green eyes softened and he pulled off his baseball cap to run his hands along his smooth fade. Wylie watched his movements and his idealistic presence captured her attention more soundly than the bouncer's muscles and heavy intimidation. She realized Nolan had taken the time to scrape away his five o'clock shadow and she smiled at him. *At least he cares enough about his cause to go all in.*

He looked at her and smiled, his disarming indifference to her appraisal giving her reason to blink.

51

"Just engaging in a little social advocacy, Mini Mako," he said.

She shook her head at the presumptive nickname. "Just Wylie."

Rusty cleared his throat and gestured toward the man. "You know this jackass? He's trying to tell me how to run my business. I need his help like I need an immigration raid."

Wylie moved closer to Nolan, knowing how quickly her ex-boyfriend's frustration could turn into broken plates and swinging fists. Hoping to insulate the food truck vendor from the consequences of playing Robin Hood, she put her arm through his and faced down her ex-boyfriend. "We've, uh, been friends for a while. He runs a great food truck."

Rusty crossed his arms like a Napoleonic version of his bouncer. "Aren't food trucks passé?"

She barely heard his words. Every one of her senses yearned to focus on Nolan and explore his presence and what it might mean in her life. The sensation hit her like a jolt of electricity and her mind struggled to process the spark. Nervousness and self-awareness battled for her attention as she took a deep breath and attempted to calm her reaction.

"It's pretty good, Rusty. Lots of local produce. Maybe you should listen to what he has to say about the dress code. He probably sees more of Los Angeles in a day than either one of us can see in a week. His perspective could help your business."

Her ex-boyfriend shook his head. "This isn't 2008. People want quality experiences and I don't see the king of Korean BBQ leading the charge for vegan wraps. Quite frankly, your boy doesn't know what he's talking about."

Nolan took a step forward. His action changed the momentum of the conversation and all eyes focused on him. "You don't get it, dude. Quality comes in many forms. The people in your bar care about their outfits as much as your desired patrons do."

Wylie blinked. *So the man cares more about equality than profit margins and sweet potato fries.*

"LA isn't all glitz and old Hollywood." Nolan gestured to the curious neighbors responding to the noise of his costume protest.

The men and women stood in line to present their licenses to Rusty's bouncer and join the newest party in their neighborhood. Muscle shirts revealed bodies honed on manual labor and a woman with false eyelashes wore a white Coach jacket proclaiming, 'He's Never Gonna Treat You Like He Should'.

"Twenty million people can't be hotshots in this town," Nolan said.

Wylie felt the crowd's curiosity shift toward impatience as they began to vent their restless energy. "Man, what's the holdup?"

Nolan glanced over his shoulder and met the protestor's stare. Both men took deep breaths and nodded before Nolan focused on Rusty's pretentious discrimination. "I'm telling you... The sooner you figure out who controls the power and influence in this neighborhood, the better it's going to be for your business."

Rusty snorted. "Like the freaks you brought to my club?"

"Yeah. Every one of them lives within a quarter-mile of this club."

Rusty closed the distance to Nolan but stopped short of making contact. He looked up, glaring at the man. "I grew up in this town! Don't pretend you know it better than me, just because you're channeling some lame-ass hipster vibe!"

The men at the front of the entrance line traded glances while echoes of Rusty's shout rippled through the crowd.

Wylie coughed, knowing Rusty's origin story involved more than a few interstate migrations. "Yelling isn't going to solve anything," she said.

Rusty shifted his stance like a nervous boxer.

Someone in the crowd cracked a joke. The punchline died before it reached them, but the crowd's unexplained laugher ignited the situation.

Rusty shoved Nolan's chest. "Go sell your veggie plates in Burbank and Century City. I'll call the police if I ever see you near my club again."

She felt Nolan's muscles tense.

He ignored Rusty's assault and narrowed his gaze.

The club owner pushed him.

"Do it again," Nolan dared the man.

Rusty lifted his chin, ready for the physical altercation. He jumped in place while his bouncer stood by, paid to assure he would win.

Considering the possible outcomes of their impending fight, she took a deep breath, dropped Nolan's arm and glared at her ex. "Let it go, Rusty. They're all going to pay your cover and buy your drinks."

When the two men continued to glare at each other and ignore her, she tugged on Nolan's arm to create space, but the man refused to back down from Rusty's self-righteousness. *Fine, let the social justice warrior and the prick go at it. I don't need to be the victim of their idealistic testosterone match. They'll recover, but I won't be part of it.*

"I'm selling an experience," Rusty said.

Nolan rolled his shoulders and narrowed his gaze. "Aren't those Burbank office workers the same people who are going to buy your overpriced beer? What do you have? Three VIP booths? Dude, Bernie Madoff's off the rotation. You try to sell as many bottles as you want, but real business owners know profits come from the masses." He pointed a finger at the club owner. "You're alienating the masses."

Wylie caught Jed's eye and mouthed a command. "Candy."

The bouncer nodded and disappeared into the club as the abandoned crowd began to object and complain.

Wylie eyed the assembly and realized their socially charged argument held center stage and served as the main attraction in lieu of entrance to the club. She had no doubt the two men could handle themselves, but the threat of a fight and two ruined businesses gave her the courage to slide her shoulders under Nolan's arm. She beamed her biggest smile toward Rusty and tried to play peacemaker. "It's not too late to tweak the dress code."

Nolan looked at her. If he found himself surprised by her presence, he accepted it and left his arm in place.

The weight encouraged her to keep going, confident that the man could handle himself if her tactics failed to end the argument.

Rusty frowned at their display of solidarity. "Tweak it to say what?"

She scrambled to reword Nolan's objections without sacrificing her ex-boyfriend's pride. "Why don't you focus on safety? No flip-flops etc. Make it about customer experience. You can still encourage people to dress up without alienating your neighbors in the process."

"Safety?" Rusty narrowed his eyes, his wrinkled forehead a visible objection to her argument.

"Maybe your insurance agent can get you a policy discount?"

Candy came bouncing out of the club, her heels clicking on the asphalt as she pulled at the hem of her red dress. She waved at the crowd and hooked her arm with Rusty's. Yellow exterior lights caught the flash of her garish earrings. "Baby, the club is almost full."

He peered into the interior. "Yeah?"

Rusty's focus shifted and relief swept through Wylie. She sagged against Nolan's side and registered the heat where his arm rested along her shoulders.

Then the man opened his mouth and starting talking to Rusty again. "One night of success doesn't guarantee another one. Build up your base before you get uppity enough for a velvet rope."

"Uppity?" Rusty planted his foot and shook off Candy.

Oh my God. Can't the two of you let it go? She turned to Nolan and cupped his face, hoping her expression said as much as her words. "You made your point."

The man looked at her, his eyes widening.

Unable to ignore the heat building between their bodies, she took a deep breath. *Is this why we met? Are you the one who needs to be saved?*

He opened his mouth.

Rusty spat on the ground.

The sound of the discharge might as well have been a gunshot.

Gauntlet thrown, Nolan looked at Rusty without a pretense of civility.

She lost it, grabbing the vendor's sweatshirt until he had no choice but to turn and face her.

Surprise flashed in his green eyes.

Claiming his lips with a kiss, she erased all other options and felt his mouth open in surprise. She slipped her tongue between his lips, lost in his rich and exotic taste. *How can he taste like citrus, mint and spice all at the same time?*

Pulling her close, he grasped the straps knotted at the small of her back.

She pressed her hips against his, and leaned into his touch, trusting his strength to hold her.

The crowd started to cheer.

She broke the kiss and blinked, her senses lingering on the taste and feel of Nolan, but the threat of impending violence pulled her attention to Rusty.

"I have this," Candy said. She pulled Rusty toward the front door of the club.

Wylie wondered how her sky-high heels gave her any traction.

Her ex-boyfriend looked over his shoulder and shook his head in disgust. "Get a room," he said. "If you can afford it."

Nolan moved to set her aside and go after the man.

She pulled him back and locked her arm around his neck, anchoring him to the spot. Her attraction to him surprised her, the interest as deep and primal as gnawing hunger. Could she afford an indulgence like lust? She pulled back, comingling their breaths in the foggy evening air.

He raised his eyebrows.

She captured his lips again, eager to check out her body's reaction and the taste of his kiss again. *This kiss is just for me.* Angling her head, she tested his resistance to see where the pleasure might end. It didn't. When his taste threatened to steal her awareness, she pulled away and scanned the volatile surroundings.

Nolan captured her hips, reclaiming her undivided attention. He pulled back. "I'm thinking about that room."

She blinked and sorted through her emotions. *Which need can wait? The job or the kiss?*

He raised his eyebrows and kneaded the muscles of her lower back, his touch both a reminder and an invitation. "I'm all for taking this somewhere else," he said. "Somewhere where we won't have an audience."

Her brain registered catcalls and whistles from the crowd. She shook her head and took a deep breath, breaking the connection she craved. "You were ten seconds from feeling Rusty's fist instead of my lips."

Nolan eyed the club's front door and let go of her. "I think I got the better deal."

But did I lose it? She shook off the tingling sensation of his lips and headed toward the pulsing beat of the club. His cardamom taste lingered on her lips and she smiled, hoping for a third encounter.

"Wylie, wait. Where are you going?" He reached for her hand and stalled her retreat.

The simple gesture felt more intimate than his lips, but she took another step toward the packed house. "I'm going inside to do my job. Earn some tips. Pay the rent."

He dropped her hand and looked at the strappy top she wore. "What happened to the carefree blonde yogi?"

I don't know. Self-consciousness let her turn the question back to him. "What happened to your hip street aesthetic?"

He looked at his shoes and frowned. "This isn't hip?"

She looked at him, a self-proclaimed champion of the underclass, standing alone in a parking lot while his supporters chose partying over indulging his righteous cause. *Did he pay them? I bet he gave them more than sweet potato fries.* Shaking her head, she decided to soften her insult with a smile. "You look more ridiculous than the crowd you brought with you."

He scanned her from head to toe.

She ignored the memory of their kiss and the unexpected heat lingering on her lips.

"This isn't you," he said.

Laughing at his unprecedented conclusion, she shook her head and thought of Penny Lane and the waitresses who had taken her under their wing to improve her outfit. *What can you know of me after twenty-four hours?* She replayed the tension of the agreement between Rusty and Nolan, her empathy stretching to cover Candy Cane. *What would it be like to live so far from home? We're all just trying to survive, aren't we?*

Nolan knew so little about her circumstances. She shook her head and looked at the man's ragged hoodie and sagging pants. "I'm not the one wearing a costume."

Chapter Four

Wylie woke up at nine, checked the charge on her cell phone and gave thanks that the phone's USB connection had not drained her car's battery. She smiled through the exhaustion of her late-night shift as the vehicle's engine rumbled to life. *It's a small victory, but I'll take it.*

Her muscles ached as she climbed out of the vehicle and took a deep breath of the crisp morning air wafting through Hotchkiss Park. Signs surrounding the neighborhood park had advertised a requirement for residential parking permits, but Wylie had seen several spots as she cruised the early morning streets to avoid a paid lot.

By the light of day, dogs played on the park's lawn as their owners ignored the leash laws and kept an eye out for the park ranger. *So, we can all bend the rules.* She considered the million-dollar houses surrounding the tree-lined lawn.

She headed toward the park's green restroom building and slowed to consider an avant-garde statue that looked like a papier-mâché depiction of family life. A weathered plaque attributed the public art to Eino Romppanen and listed the work's title as 'Oneness'.

A musician spread his tattered blanket on the lawn near the statue. "You like it?"

Did the local kids use it for spitball practice? She shrugged her indifference, choosing politeness over honesty.

The man laughed and opened his guitar case. "The groundkeeper told me this park used to be the site of the Mooney Mansion. Strange things happened to the people who lived in that old house. Rat poison took out an old widow. Another man's pocket pistol went off and shot a hole in his back. That's plenty enough to haunt this place, but a murder in the 1880s sealed the building's fate."

Wylie looked for the remnants of an old structure and imagined a grand house built to take in the ocean views. She thought of Chesterfield Square and the legacy of violence marking the site. *Would its legacy be the same if it had ocean views?* She turned to the musician. "What happened to the old house?"

He grinned at her. "It burned to the ground in 1904."

"That's not so strange." She shifted her weight and eyed the restroom building. "Whatever happened, it seems like a perfectly lovely park. I'm glad people like you and I get to enjoy it."

The musician jerked his head toward the weathered white statue. "You ought to know what you're enjoying. I figure that statue's a ward against evil spirits. If you spend enough time in this park, you'll realize that when the wind drops, the hairs on your arms are still standing on end."

Wylie rubbed her arms.

"The only 'Oneness' these folks believe in is their property values. If I were you, I'd move your car out of the residential zone."

Wylie kept her arms crossed over the athletic gear she had donned under the cover of darkness. The Social Club's borrowed black top sat on the back seat of her car and she wondered how she would return it. The musician strummed his guitar and she lingered for a moment to listen to the haunting music. Then she found herself staring at the bright line where his T-shirt dipped and revealed pale white skin. *How much time does he spend in this park?*

The man ended his song and looked up.

"How do you know I'm not a local?" she asked.

He shaded his eyes. "I recognize the locals," he said as his smile widened. "You ought to stick around and get to know us."

Biting her lip, she wondered if the invitation hovered between flirtatiousness and hospitality. *Like I would know the difference.* She focused on the things she could understand, like the pressure of Nolan's lips against hers. His taste lingered in her memories like a sweet worth unwrapping when she found time to savor it. "Thanks, but I have somewhere to go."

The man nodded and looked at the strings of his guitar, tuning the frets to summon the chord he wanted to hear. "Lucky you," he said without looking at her.

Wylie left the park and her strides lengthened as she passed an outpost of a ubiquitous café and rental business anchoring the county's public beaches. Instead of being annoyed with the chain's red-and-white awnings, she normally appreciated their presence and used them as a signpost to guide patrons to her class location.

This morning, the rich, buttery smells emanating from the café teased her senses with memories of hot coffee and morning croissants. *Those savory breakfasts cost me ten bucks.* To ground her senses, she focused on the ocean and ignored the peanut butter and jelly sandwich sitting in her stomach like a lump of modeling clay. *Screw the croissants.*

She put down her mat, dumped an armload of foam blocks on the sand and stacked a pile of extra beach towels near the lifeguard stand. The extra gear lived in the back of her trunk and allowed her to advertise drop-in classes with an open motto, "Come as you are!"

Then she eyed her regular short-term parking lot on Barnard Way and wondered how long it would be until she could afford little luxuries like hot food and paid parking. *It doesn't matter*, she told herself as she began to stretch. *The walk did me good. This is just a minor setback.*

She moved into a second pose and the sand beneath her toes felt refreshingly cool. As an approved commercial fitness trainer, she had the right to conduct classes on the sand near Palisades Park, but it was up to her to recruit the customers. In exchange for the privilege, she paid tribute to the city of Santa Monica and stuck to a fixed schedule so anyone with an itch for yoga could find her.

The men and women came to her through social media posts and friendly referrals, but she treated them all the same. For twenty-five dollars a class, they could stretch, strengthen their muscles and follow her lead as they breathed in the fresh salt air.

Today, twelve people showed up at class time and unfurled their beach towels or coordinated yoga mats. They waved their phones in the air to acknowledge a transfer of funds and greeted each other like old friends. Wylie made a point of greeting each of them by name, bowing her head as the wind captured her greeting. "Namaste."

For the next hour and a half, the group of twelve navigated their beach towels and worked up a sweat as they followed her through a series of poses. She tried not to grin when one of her favorite patrons fell over. Price Ross grinned as he brushed the sand from the side of his face and scrambled to his feet.

"Don't worry." She went up to the man and offered him her hand. "You can rinse off the sand at the showers or take a dip in the ocean."

He laughed, shook his head and grasped her hand. "I should have known better than to come out here after hitting the town."

Tell me about it. The stress and exhaustion of the last two days made it difficult for her not to smile at Price's self-conscious reparations.

He jerked his head toward a man standing beyond the group. "I think you have another admirer."

She followed his gesture, prepared to redirect a 'shadow' participant who thought they could mimic her class from a distance and evade her fees. Instead of a freeloader, she locked eyes with Nolan, shirtless and barefoot as he stood in the sand in a pair of black running shorts.

Her mind jumped to the previous night and the look of surprise that had flashed in his green eyes as she had claimed his lips. The taste of citrus and spice had faded from her memory as the evening progressed, but she had found herself scanning the crowded bar, somehow hoping the food truck vendor had braved Rusty's wrath and dared to come back.

"He's just a friend." She hastily looked away and focused on correcting Price's sand-strewn posture. "Maybe we got our times mixed up for a breakfast date. Don't worry about him."

The man nodded and lowered himself back into the high lunge of the Salutation pose. He smiled as he used his arms to maintain his balance. "Your date looks delicious."

Wylie blushed and told the man to focus on his practice.

He winked at her.

I don't have the luxury of admiring Nolan's abs. She ignored Price's wink and focused on the rest of her class, extolling the virtues of their beachside practice. "Choosing to do your poses near water can be incredibly soothing. Let your bodies connect with the lulling sounds of nature, the rhythm of the waves. As we transition into our next pose, shelve your to-do list and gaze at the ocean. Consider where your practice can take you."

Price laughed. "I hope yours is taking you to crepes and hot coffee."

Wylie smiled but ignored Nolan's presence as she led the remainder of the class. *Nolan's just a friend — a friend who tastes like cardamom, a friend who found me on the beach and doesn't know how to move on without making this awkward.*

Five minutes later, she risked a glance and found him standing with his back to the sun. She could not see the expression on his face, but she had no problem sneaking a peek at his shirtless body. *He must spend a lot of time loading supplies and wrestling with the hardware. Who am I kidding? I could definitely eat him for breakfast.*

When the class ended, she chatted with the twelve participants as they folded up their towels and promised to return in two days. She watched the last one leave and reminded herself to view them as people instead of dollar signs.

Nolan came to stand beside her on the sand. "Looks like a good crew. How much did you make?"

"About three hundred bucks," she said as she looked up at him and attempted to keep her eyes off his ripped abdominal muscles. The memory of his chest pressed against hers suddenly seemed more interesting than the taste of his lips. *The only thing better than the feel of his kiss would be the feel of him naked.* She cleared her throat. "Not that's any of your business."

"What happened to our partnership? I shared my truck's profit margins with you. That's deep."

She snorted and slipped on a lightweight jacket. "I'm lucky you didn't scare off my customers. What are you doing out here? Stalk much?"

Nolan laughed and braced his hands on his hips. She tried not to follow the line of his biceps and wondered what kind of heavy lifting came from working at a food truck. *Loading supplies? Troubleshooting the truck's diesel generator?* The shirtlessness still distracted her sleep-deprived mind until he interrupted her thoughts.

"I looked you up and figured I'd go for a run and check out your class," he said.

The morning sun picked out the beads of sweat running down his pecs. Wylie looked away and focused on the apartments, bungalows and houses climbing the hills to claim the highest ground. The high rent of her former apartment had felt like a business expense, but she knew Nolan's food truck moved all over the city. She recalled the lentils and sweet potato fries that had been her last taste of flavor. *I can't subsist on room temperature groceries for two weeks. How long before I cave and blow twenty dollars for a hot food fix?* Hoping to distract her stomach, she focused on the barefoot man standing in front of her. "You live nearby?"

He nodded and offered to hold the stack of extra towels none of her participants had needed. "I share a house with a couple of friends. Plus, I wanted to know how much traffic your little business gets. That ten percent coupon could hit my bottom line."

"I doubt it." She glanced at his chest and wondered if skin-to-skin contact would do more to take her mind off other cravings. The thought of taking Nolan back to her SUV for a quickie made her laugh and she shook her head as she turned toward Ocean Avenue and starting walking.

He fell into step beside her and matched her stride. "So, do you want to get lunch? I have a few things to talk about—like, mainly that kiss."

"I was just trying to keep your mouth shut before you said something stupid and gave Rusty a reason to deck you."

"Mission accomplished," he admitted. "But what about the second one? Let's get food and do it again."

"Or not." She kept walking and hid her smile. *Doesn't he need shoes?*

"You don't like hanging out with me?"

She stopped and turned to face him, scanning his chest and the shadows of dried sweat on his suntanned shoulders. "It's not that." She swallowed and decided not to string him along. "Things are just complicated right now."

He considered her for a moment and shifted the weight of the towels in his arms. "I'm good at solving problems."

She shook her head and reached for the load he had offered to carry. "This is my problem to solve. Come back in a few weeks. By then, I'll either have gotten it together or splurged for a one-way ticket to see my parents in Oregon."

He surrendered the towels and braced his hands on his hips. "So you're telling me that there's a chance you'll just be gone?" When Wylie nodded, he shook his head like she might have spent too much time in the sun. "I'm not looking for a hookup. I'm asking you out on a date."

"I get it," she assured him, "but it's not a good time for me right now. Between the beach sessions and Rusty's bar, I'm emotionally maxed out."

Nolan shook his head. "That guy's a tool."

"Yeah, well, he's a tool who's offering me a paying job."

He scanned her branded athletic gear and raised his eyebrow.

Looks can be deceiving. She held her tongue, grateful he withheld his opinion of her financial priorities. *Would he have given up so easily if I still wore the stripper's top?*

"At least let me help you carry this stuff back to your car. You can barely see where you're going with all that stuff in your arms," he said.

She held on to the burden. "It's not that bad."

"Please? It'll keep people from staring at my chest."

She laughed and handed over the towels. "Fine. I won't keep turning down the help if it'll get you out of my hair. I'm just parked up near the park."

They fell in step and she thought about the last protestors who had left the Social Club, arm in arm as they traded good-natured jibes with their new neighborhood friends. "Did you think that crew would make Rusty change his dress code?"

Nolan nodded. "Money has a way of talking. I bet his take was higher than opening night."

"I wouldn't know."

"He's gambling on that old PG&E building. The lease is dirt-cheap for the first year, but he'll have to make a profit if he wants to recover his sunk costs."

Wylie glanced at him and wondered why he didn't have a T-shirt tucked in the back of his running shorts like everybody else who jogged on the beach and required backup layers to buffer their exposure. The intimacy of their walk grew as they got farther and farther from the rhythmic allure of the water. She adjusted the bag on her shoulder and looked at the anonymity of the milling crowds. *I should have just given him my number and ignored him until I got my act together. He's going to figure out what's going on and judge me.*

Eager to deflect the conversation from Rusty's business acumen, she glanced at Nolan and raised her eyebrows. "You seem to know a lot about commercial property development for a guy who mans a food truck."

He made a noncommittal noise and shrugged. "It interests me."

"I bet." She turned the corner and looked for her vehicle in the shadows of Hotchkiss Park. She thought she had left it on Hollister, but turned toward Strand in case the stress of the last twenty-four hours had left her mistaken. The green-roofed houses and apartment building stood where she had left it, but she admitted reality. The SUV was gone.

"Seventy-two hours," she said, thinking of her conversation with Penny Lane. "She told me I could leave my car on the street for seventy-tour hours."

Nolan gestured to a blue and white sign for Tommy Tee's Tow Service. "Some of these agencies can be aggressive about enforcing their contracts."

Wylie focused on the dingy sign and read the metal proclamation. Red text swirled with warnings about unauthorized vehicles and the penalties associated with blocking access. "But I wasn't blocking access. They can't just tow me for no good reason, can they?"

Nolan brushed a hand through the longer hair on top of his head. "How close did you park to the opening of that driveway? Residents get territorial about their access if they have boats, RVs or stuff they need to get out. Trust me. The food truck has skated through more than one sloped driveway."

The thought of owning a boat or RV made Wylie choke on her laughter. She dropped her bag of yoga props and braced her hands on her knees. "This is surreal. What am I going to do now? That little SUV was everything to me."

"I'll give you a ride to the tow yard," Nolan said. "My house isn't that far away. Just hang out here while I go get my car."

"No, I'm not a damsel in distress. It's bad enough I let you carry my stuff. Just leave it there. I'll figure it out." She avoided Nolan's gaze and looked at the guitar player passed out beneath a large shade tree. *He tried to warn me. How long does it take to look at the world with a new perspective? How long does it take to identify new dangers?*

"Wylie?"

She shook head and scrambled to recalculate her finances. Retrieving her vehicle from the tow yard would probably cost her upward of three hundred bucks. *There go the proceeds from this morning's class.* She cursed her stupidity. "I should have just slept in this morning."

Nolan cupped her elbow and captured her attention. "Hiding from life never solves anything. Let's just go spring your car. You can thank me by agreeing to lunch."

The warmth of his touch heated her skin and made her aware of goosebumps raised by the ocean wind. She shook her head and pulled her arm free. "You don't have to do that. I should have known better."

"Are you this hard on your clients?"

Wylie looked at him.

"Do you expect them to get everything right the first time?"

She shook her head. "No, but I'm not paying you for life advice."

Nolan laughed and swung an arm over her shoulder. The casual gesture surprised Wylie, but she relaxed into his warmth and stopped inventing new ways to curse Tommy Tee and his tow service.

"C'mon. I'll even bring you to your house first so you can drop this stuff off."

She froze and slipped away from his warmth. "Nolan, I have it."

His gaze narrowed and he stared at her.

Raising her chin, she hoped her wind-tousled hair and athletic gear disguised two days of sleeping in her SUV.

"Where do you live?"

Wylie swallowed and considered lying to the man, but pride and perjury seemed like two very different outcomes. A few weeks of stress might make her stronger, but 'domestically challenged' and 'urban camper' sounded like cute euphemisms for her homeless state. They discredited Penny Lane and the musician who had done his best to help her. She replayed kissing Nolan at the bar and casting herself as the savior, but the reality of her predicament made her feel weak. She raised her chin. "I'm between apartments at the moment," she said, hoping to acknowledge her reality without accepting it as her fate.

Nolan nodded as the pieces fell into place. "What happened?"

"Why did something have to happen?"

He shifted his weight. "Are you into drugs or something illicit?"

She reached for the stack of towels and pulled them tight to her chest. The smell of salt and sand anchored her senses and buried her tears of frustration. "No, it's not like that. My roommate kicked me out, and I've been living in my vehicle for a few days to save money. Anyone would do it."

"Most people have friends with couches."

"Well, my friends are out of town." She tucked a piece of hair behind her ear and tried not to feel like the confession reflected on her self-worth.

"All of them?"

She took a deep breath. "I don't seem to have friends as much as I have business relationships. A few weeks in my car isn't going to kill me, but losing my yoga clientele would be borderline tragic."

He shook his head and scanned the tree-lined street. "You don't know what you're up against, Mini Mako."

He reached for the towels and pulled them from her arms. "Let's go get your car."

"Nolan, I told you, it's not" — she watched him turn and walk back toward the water — "your problem."

"Hey, Rikard, can you grab the Bronco and meet me at the rental spot where Ocean Park meets the beach?" He nodded and gave the man directions to find his keys. "I appreciate it," he said before he hung up.

"Is this an old Bronco or a new Bronco?" Wylie asked, making light of the situation.

Nolan looked at her and his posture stiffened, no longer as carefree and confident as the man who strode through town without shirt or shoes. "Does it matter?"

"Sure. An old one would be pretty cool. Authentic, as long as it's in good shape."

"And a new one?"

"Well, I'd be a little worried about your life choices and the outlook for your food truck. Maybe you're not very good with your money."

He laughed and lengthened his stride. "If it's an old one, you're in for a bumpy ride. They steer like tanks and the death wobble is enough to make you second-guess the quality of American engineering. Don't even get me started on the braking systems."

"So it's a new one."

Nolan smiled. "Not exactly." He scanned the busy sidewalk and the groups of tourists evading men on bicycles and women with untrained dogs. "Let's save that analysis for another day. I have another proposition for you, partner."

Wylie tensed, wondering if she had misread the entire situation. Rusty's bar might have been a coincidental meeting, but Nolan's appearance on the beach began to lean toward suspect behavior. She stopped short and scanned the street for support. *What impression did I give him? I knew I shouldn't have worn that top.*

Nolan held up his hand like he could read the tension in her shoulders. "Come pick up some shifts at the food truck. I talked one of my roommates into covering for a prep chef, but I know he'd rather spend his days on his own start-up."

She turned her face toward the ocean. "You don't have to take care of me. I'm a grown-ass adult."

"I'm not trying to take care of you," he said. "I'm trying to meet a need."

The tension and vulnerability of the last two days flooded her eyes with tears, but she blinked to disguise them. "That's not necessary. Rusty's job pays well enough. I'm going to get by on tips. I'm going to get an apartment where I control the lease and have a say about who comes and who goes. I'd never treat someone like Dottie did."

Nolan reached for her arm but dropped his hand before he made contact. "Dottie?"

"My old roommate. We never connected and she threw me out as soon as she got a better offer. Shouldn't we have formed some type of mutual respect after four months of living together?" A tear rolled down her cheek. "What's wrong with me?"

"Are you crying?"

"No, of course not."

He cupped her elbow. "I don't think anything's wrong with you, Wylie. Maybe the problem lies with Dottie." He tapped his head. "Maybe there's nothing there."

Trying not to laugh, she took a deep breath and wiped her eyes. His touch sent awareness spiraling up her arm, but the upheaval in her life made the complications of a relationship seem monumental. She stepped to the side and rubbed her arms, forcing him to release his hold. "I'm usually not this needy and vulnerable. It's like I had momentum in my life and someone pulled the rug out from under me. You don't have to pick up the pieces and help me put my life back together. I'm more than capable of doing it myself."

"Never mind what Dottie did. You're learning to trust your instincts, and you'll pick a better partner next time. On the other hand, my instincts say Rusty's club is one step away from an implosion. The people working there don't have any loyalty to him. They're just in it for the money and that's a bad combination in a bad part of town."

"That's not true," she said, thinking of the two former strippers who'd taken her under their wings. "They're hoping the club becomes a big draw."

"Does that mean they're going to stick it out and support the community when tips get thin? Put in extra hours to do maintenance work? Let Rusty know when someone's stealing from the till?"

"No, probably not." She wiped away a rogue tear and pulled out her inhaler to relieve the tightness in her chest.

"It's okay to cry when you're frustrated."

She shook her head. "It's the spring tree pollen." *Or the stress of watching my life collapse around me and feeling powerless to stop it.* "I barely notice my symptoms this time of year. It's nothing like ragweed and asthma peak week in September."

Nolan nodded. "I'm just saying, let Rusty get his feet wet before you pick up any more shifts out there. The man's sitting on a tinderbox and he's too blind to see it."

"Who turned you into the wise man on the mountain? It's just a pretentious bar."

He stared at her. "Yeah, and you're just one person in a crowded building with poorly lit exits. Who's going to save your ass when shit goes down?"

She thought of the women who'd loaned her the clothes and makeup she needed to attract attention and tips. *Nolan's right. Their matronly instincts probably rank below their need for self-preservation. Aren't we all looking out for ourselves?* She thought of Penny Lane's quiet generosity. *What happens when you remove money from the equation of friendship?*

"In the meantime, come work with me. Better yet, come live with me. We've got an open room in the shared house where I live."

Wylie bit her lip as the offer came too close to what she needed. Her instincts told her to give him the Downward-Facing Dog and flee to protect her self-interest, but she remembered the way he'd smiled as his stream of friends had paraded into the club. *He's not demanding change as a condition of his interest. He's trying to solve problems. He's offering me options.* "You don't have to do that."

"I don't have to do anything."

She laughed at the proud boast. *Wouldn't that be a luxury?* "Then what gives?"

He ran a hand through his hair. "You're the first social media influencer to take me up on my offer of a partnership. Most people just want something for free without putting in the effort."

"I don't think the promotion is going to amount to much."

"Yeah, but you're willing to try it. And I have a feeling you'll keep trying things until you find a way to win. I admire that attitude. So many people spend their life complaining instead of taking action. It's something I've been guilty of in the past."

"But now you're reformed?"

He laughed. "Well, it's a work in progress. Please don't worry about the housing situation. It's not the intersection of a reality-show compound and a juiced-up dating show. My roommates and I choose to live together so we have more time to run our businesses." He looked at the empty street and shrugged his shoulders. "What other option do you have?"

"I have options," she said, but her voice wavered. "I can move in with my parents."

He raised his eyebrows. "What are you, sixteen?"

She crossed her arms and wondered how a man could stand on the street, bare-chested and open to a world of possibilities, while her tiny world felt like it might be on the verge of caving in. "I've spent a lot of time on Craigslist in the last few days. Converted garages, tool sheds and outdoor tents are starting to look very appealing to me."

He shook his head. "That's hardly glamping."

"You don't get it," she said. "I told you I want to control the lease."

"Why?"

"Because I didn't like feeling inferior to my last roommate. She held all the power."

"Power's only a bad thing if you don't trust the person who wields it."

Wylie shook her head. "I barely know you and I've never met your roommates."

"You know where I work and what my lips taste like."

She raised her eyebrows.

"That last bit of knowledge came at your own volition," he said.

"So you'll use that against me?"

He laughed. "No, but Cynthia will vouch for me."

"Oh? Did you negotiate with her for further tips?"

Nolan shook his head. "Not my style, but I'm saying you know more about me than you would know about a stranger who walked off the street to answer a sublease advertisement."

"The promise of control is, like, the one thing that's been keeping me sane at night," she admitted. "What does it say about me if I give it up?"

"It says you recognize a better deal when you see it."

She blew her bangs from her eyes. *Just a shower, a washing machine and a solid lock on the door that keeps me from jerking awake every time something goes bump in the night.* She took a deep breath and considered how much she could afford to spend on the luxury of a good night's sleep. She had left Dottie's apartment determined to control the high ground, but Nolan's invitation felt like a luxury she wanted to afford. "I don't need much. How much is the rent?"

Nolan smiled. "Seventeen hundred dollars."

It's a dump. She practiced her poker face. *He's beautiful and it's a dump with corrugated tin walls.* "And the deposit?"

He scanned her yoga ensemble. "Three hundred."

She shook her head, sensing a trap. "That's below market."

He shrugged. "Take it up with the landlord. You can't get into too much trouble sharing a space with five other people. They've all got too much on the line to step out of bounds."

What if I want you to step out of bounds? She considered her options and recent experiences with Dottie. *I wanted a place of my own.* The woman's loyalties stung, but her eviction notice had pushed Wylie to scrutinize the insecurities of her new living situation. "Who is the landlord?"

Nolan started walking toward Ocean Avenue.

She fell into step to avoid losing the possibility of his offer.

"We've never had any problems with management and repairs. You've just got to pass the review board."

She rolled her eyes, knowing her freelance finances would never pass corporate screening metrics. *I knew this was too good to be true.* She stopped walking and shook her head to put an end to this conversation. "The review board's probably super strict."

He looked back over his shoulder and smiled as he also came to a stop. "Review board might be an exaggeration. It's a southern California house full of millennials trying to incubate new businesses. We vote on everything from toilet paper ply to the size of our grocery budget. Just convince the other roommates you have something to add to their community. I'll show you around the house and you can meet the people working from home. If you don't like it, split."

The allure of trading automotive upholstery for a bedroom door gave her the courage to bury her insecurities. "I'd be willing to consider it." She smiled, shielding the truth of how much she needed his offer to work out before she lost her courage and started pricing bus tickets to Oregon. "Yoga never goes out of style. If there's a lawn or something, I can teach classes on my off days."

Nolan nodded and started walking again.

She cleared her throat and hurried to catch up. "I mean, I'm willing to give it a shot if they're willing to consider me. It's got to be a mutual fit."

"Good call, Mini Mako."

Wylie frowned and struggled to connect the pieces of their conversation. "You said it's a business incubator. What's next for you after the food truck?"

"I want to expand the truck into an established restaurant," he said.

"Of course you do."

"What does that mean?"

She rolled her eyes and looked at his haircut, wondering if her move would level the ground between them or set the pendulum in motion. She thought of Cynthia's established yoga studio and Rusty's ambitions for the club. *Is everyone further along with their plans?* Nolan's self-awareness and generosity felt too good to be true. She decided to test his reserves and try knocking him back. "You have to sell a lot of sweet potato fries to maintain that haircut."

Instead of taking offense, he laughed. "People have done a lot more with less."

She almost missed her step.

Chapter Five

She watched Nolan wave to a suntanned blond man wearing a button-down shirt. The man stood near a polished 1970s Bronco with all-terrain tires and milky green paint. The vehicle reflected the sunlight like a piece of polished jade. The truck's stainless-steel hardware gleamed and the headlights shone behind clear glass.

Someone took a lot of time to restore the old body and outfit it with modern gear. She imagined Nolan covered in grease with a wrench in his hand. His muscles supported her fantasy, but she doubted his passion for food trucks extended to restoring classic cars. *So where did he get the truck?* She watched him shake hands with his roommate — one of them a poster boy for corporate stewardship and the other still shirtless from his mid-morning run.

"Rikard, this is Wylie, my new friend."

Friend? What else would he say? Homeless charity case? She shook off the questions and looked at Rikard, knowing she had to impress the blond if his approval stood between sleepless nights and a real room and board. "Wylie Winidad," she said as she offered her hand.

The man shook it, but his look lacked the warmth of Nolan's first and second looks. If anything, Rikard reminded her of the kind of man who relocated to Los Angeles but still checked the smog levels every morning. She ignored his critical assessment and hoped her wind-blown hair and hard-earned muscles marked her as a local with something to offer instead of a naïve transplant who still needed explanations of the Santa Ana winds. "Thanks for coming to my rescue."

"What exactly are we rescuing you from?"

"My car got towed."

"She's interested in the empty bedroom," Nolan said at the same time.

Rikard raised his eyebrows and focused on his roommate. "And you decided to screen her application wearing only a pair of running shorts?"

Nolan laughed, but the sound of his amusement died in the wind as the men looked at each other and Rikard waited for a response. Wylie expected Nolan to defend his invitation, but Rikard's stance shifted and he shook his head before he opened the Bronco's passenger side door and claimed the back seat. "Whatever."

She looked at the powder-coated Bronco and realized she would be riding shotgun if she climbed inside the vehicle. Trying to lighten the mood, she looked at Nolan and called him out on the extravagant ride. "It's worse than a new Bronco. It's a custom-build."

He smiled and crossed his arms, seemingly ready to defend himself. "So what does that say about me?"

"Did you do it yourself?"

"No."

"Then your daddy has money."

"Not exactly." He widened the gap of the passenger door and raised his eyebrows.

Wylie considered her options and climbed into the vehicle, admitting that pride kept her from phoning her parents, but two nights of sleeping in the SUV had enhanced her willingness to embrace life's gifts where she found them. *So Nolan's got some money and maybe a good heart. I don't mind being his cause of the week if it gets me out of this mess. It's not his fault that I have none.*

Nolan claimed the driver's seat and she winced as he pressed his sweat-caked skin against the vehicle's pristine interior. *It's his truck.* She typed the address of the tow yard into her phone. *Let him worry about staining the leather.* After giving him directions, she shifted to find a comfortable position. "We should be there in twenty minutes."

She glanced over her shoulder at the man who kept his face turned to the wind. She could imagine him sitting in the driver's seat of a Frankenstein truck, his sleeves rolled up as he locked eyes with a parallel driver and revved his engine. *Hey, man, my Bronco is worth more than your Porsche.* The second the light changed, they would careen through the supercharged nightlife of an urban drag race, but who would win? *I have no taste for men who risk their lives at a hundred miles an hour.* She resolved to be polite. "So, Rikard, where are you from?"

"Everywhere."

She looked to Nolan for backup, but he kept his gaze on the road and let her fend for herself in the open-topped truck. Turning in the seat until the seatbelt curtailed her movement, she focused on Rikard. "How many everywheres?"

The blond turned away from the scenery and looked at her. "I grew up in a Denver suburb, went to college in Ithaca and followed a finance job to New York City. Does that make it three?"

"But you're here now. I'm counting four."

He nodded and mimicked Nolan's focus on the traffic.

The wind pushed his hair away from his face and he looked younger for a moment, maybe less than forty. *'I'm not trying to take advantage of him,'* Wylie wanted to say, but she held her tongue against the unspoken accusation.

Rikard took a deep breath. "I knew all my neighbors in Denver, but the residents of the New York apartment building turned out to be geriatric holdouts who refused the collegial comfort of independent living facilities." A smile teased the corner of his mouth. "I wouldn't consider myself a nomadic millennial, but apparently I have lousy taste in leasing agents."

"Were they sweet geriatrics?" She smiled. "Like, did they bake cookies and ask you to change lightbulbs?"

"No," he said, "they barely acknowledged me. One day I came home from work and realized I didn't know any of their names — not even the name of the doorman. The residents complained so often that management tended to fire the contractors before they could settle into the job. Not like it would have mattered, though. I was working so much that when I got time off, I would kind of just sit at home or scroll my phonebook, wondering what had happened to my college friends."

"You're leaving out the girl." Nolan switched lanes. "There's always a girl."

Rikard snorted. "She hasn't qualified as a girl since puberty hit and she decided to use what her mother gave her." His silence said more than a character assassination ever could. "Lisa was gorgeous and she knew it."

Unsure of how to respond, Wylie looked back and forth between the men.

Their gazes connected in the rearview mirror and Rikard took a deep breath.

"I fell hard for Lisa and followed her west," he said. "You could say she found me at a vulnerable moment, but I admit I was looking for an excuse to bail on the east coast. Our relationship didn't last long once we landed in the midst of Hollywood glamour, but she introduced me to Nolan and the co-living commune."

"That's a mature way to look at it."

"That year was a dumpster fire," Rikard said.

She swallowed.

"Either way, Lisa made herself scarce, but I realized I still had a community."

Wylie nodded and thought about her parents. They'd done everything they could to raise her in Los Angeles, but their achievements had fallen short of the wealth needed to shield her from the realities of bills and a mortgage. Was that awareness a blessing or a curse? Either way, she sympathized with Rikard's loneliness, but his desperation felt too close for comfort. She wondered how far she would take her attraction to Nolan under normal circumstances. Candy's distraction had given her a reason to bail on the Social Club kiss, but she had been on the verge of leaving with the man. Shaking her head, she looked at Rikard's aloof, sun-bleached profile. "But you didn't go back to Denver?"

He nodded. "My family comes from Croatia. Croats are Slavic people, but it turns out I also hate the cold."

She laughed and turned back in her seat, wondering if Nolan would tell her his origin story. But instead of giving her a chance to fill in the missing pieces, he turned the tables on her instead. "What about you?"

"Born and bred here," she said, fighting to hide the vulnerability of her situation. *Isn't that what they all want? A carefree California blonde with a comical situation?* She thought of Penny Lane and wondered what Nolan would have done if her skin bore the effects of the sun and crow's feet framed her eyes. *Well, for one thing, he probably wouldn't have been as amused when I kissed him.*

"Family?" he asked, prompting her to respond.

She blushed and hoped the open top would disguise the color on her cheeks. "Oregon."

Nolan glanced at her yoga gear. "Like, new-age mysticism Oregon?"

His frown made her wonder if he had decided to reevaluate his interest in helping her.

"No, just mainstream retired urbanite." She smiled to reassure the man, but she made herself laugh, imagining what she would have done if she'd followed her parents to the Pacific Northwest and found herself at a rally for a twenty-first-century cult leader. *Hell, I would have turned around and come home. Los Angeles has no problem doling out new gender identities, but religious quirks might be the last frontier of social diversity.*

She thought about stringing Nolan and Rikard along, but she felt too vulnerable. "They just wanted a lower cost of living."

Both men nodded like the concept resonated.

Does it? She ran her hand over the fine-grained leather of the passenger seat. *I shouldn't try to mix with the finance and entrepreneurial crowd, but I'm not going to look a gift horse in the mouth...unless it's creepy. Please, don't let this turn creepy.*

Her phone chirped with directions and Nolan changed lanes, following the navigation system into a maze of one-story industrial buildings. A sign for Tommy Tee's Tow Service marked a parking lot near a weathered cinderblock building and a chain-link fence guarding a tow yard.

Exposed steel beams presided over an overhang near a loading dock, and rust stains dripped down the building's exterior. Knowing she would have to start in the office, Wylie focused on the front door, where concrete breeze blocks sectioned off a walkway and overgrown begonias filled two terracotta pots. Someone had paid good money to erect the mid-century feature, but she eyed the yellowed polycarbonate panels serving as a roof and figured that person had probably moved on. "I guess this is it," she said.

Nolan put the Bronco in park and reached into the back seat to grab a shirt from a small pile of belongings stashed in the footwell. "I'll go in with you."

"That's not necessary."

He pulled the shirt over his head. "You'll get bored without me."

"You're not even wearing shoes," she said, watching his lean muscles flex. *I think I hate his shirt.*

He grinned and retrieved a pair of surf-inspired flip flops from the center console. "Happy now?"

"Getting there." she said. She did not bother to suppress her grin.

"How long have you two known each other?" Rikard asked.

Nolan opened the driver's-side door. "She kissed me last night at a bar."

Wylie met Rikard's gaze and saw dismissal in the way he shook his head, like she had never learned to hold her liquor. "It wasn't like that," she said.

"Whatever."

Whatever? She opened the passenger door and hurried to catch up with Nolan. *Maybe it was like that? One kiss from a good-looking man and I'm reevaluating my priorities when I've never been more desperate?* The admission slowed her steps and she looked back at Rikard for a moment. Nolan might have left his friend sitting in the back seat of the truck like a faithful hound, but it was not her job to wait patiently at Nolan's side until he issued a command or asked her to follow a scent.

She jogged toward Nolan to overtake him, but he ignored her approach and strode toward the entrance of the building. She reached for the door's metal bar and seized it first. "It's my car."

"After you." He gestured toward the shadowed interior and fell back.

Squaring her shoulders, she faced the painted cinderblock structure and considered its weathered façade. More than a decade had passed since the building's architect eschewed the privilege of windows and placed his faith in the palm tree struggling in a thin bed of gravel. "They're probably going to be ruthless."

Nolan met her gaze and nodded.

She focused on a series of printouts taped to the door. The yellowed papers listed the company's hours and identification policies. "Standard stuff." She continued reading and bristled when she realized she would have to add ATM fees and processing charges to her impound fees. "Why can't they just make it seem fair?"

"It is fair. They've combed the rules books for decades to squeeze every last dime out of their business."

"Maybe I'll send them a potted plant with my thanks."

Nolan put a hand on the small of her back, but she shook off the calming influence, raised her head and marched into the office. An ancient black vending machine offered a bag of Doritos and a package of Hostess cupcakes. The wood wall paneling marked Tommy Tee's Tow Service as a member of the American Trucking Association and a proud sponsor of a local golf classic. She attempted to reorient her perception of the place as a bastion of the community before she noticed a certificate of appreciation from law enforcement. *Why do I get the feeling they've been working together longer than I've been alive?*

"May I help you?" a receptionist asked. The woman's tight, bleached curls paled against her tan and lined skin. Wylie glanced at the bottle of lotion sitting on her desk. Its sweet floral fragrance failed to hide the scents of stale cigarettes and grease originating from behind the desk.

"Yes," Wylie said. "Your company towed my vehicle this morning."

The woman nodded and reached for a stack of tickets. "Name?"

"Wylie Winidad," she said.

The receptionist flipped through her stack of paperwork, licking her finger between each sheet. The black and white clock on the wall ticked as the older woman made her way through a stack of tow yard receipts.

Nolan shifted on his feet.

She wanted to touch him and anchor his restlessness, but she kept her hand pinned to her side. *How many vehicles could they have possibly towed before noon?*

"Yep. Your vehicle was parked illegally. Property owners have the right to remove cars from their driveway after the car has been parked there for more than one hour."

"Can you prove that it was parked illegally? I think I was clear of any driveways."

"Did you take a picture?"

"Who takes pictures of their cars when they park?"

The woman raised her eyebrows and turned the paperwork to reveal an inkjet image of the SUV's shadow blocking a tapered driveway. "We do."

Wylie took a deep breath. "What do I need to do to get my car back?"

"Documents and cash," the receptionist said. She put more lotion on her hands.

Wylie gritted her teeth. "How much?"

The woman pulled out a handheld calculator and began adding up the fees. "Are you paying with cash or credit?"

"Credit," Wylie said while she struggled not to grind her teeth.

The woman nodded and looked at a list of processing fees. The total bill went up by two and a half percent before she put down the calculator. "Towing and storage charges related to the impoundment come to three hundred seventy-two dollars and forty-eight cents."

"What?" Her gaze widened at the total. "The SUV was there for less than three hours."

"Oh, we only operate in twenty-four-hour increments." She unleashed a saccharine smile and pointed toward the yellowed printout behind a drugstore frame. "A minute past midnight is as good as another day in my book."

"Are you even open at midnight?"

The woman pointed toward a sign. "Twenty-four hours."

Wylie had the urge to jump over the counter and rip the aged paper from the wall. The thought of leaving the office in handcuffs kept her sane and she pulled her wallet from her purse. "Just give me back my car."

"Sign here," the receptionist said.

Nolan cleared his throat. "She changed her mind and she's going to pay cash. Take the convenience fee off the bill. I also want to see a signed copy of the property owner's towing authorization."

The receptionist glanced over her shoulder. "That paperwork's in the back."

He smiled and leaned across the desk. "So go find it," he said, his voice as measured as his presence in a room reeking of lemon wax and abandoned cigarettes.

Wylie responded to the glimpse of the steel beneath Nolan's good humor and stepped closer to him. What had Cynthia said? *'Your food's good, but your charming sense of humor is better?'* Had the studio instructor known about the strength behind Nolan's smile before she propositioned him? "You don't have to do this," she whispered, afraid of sounding vulnerable within earshot of the candy-scented plywood vulture.

"It's just business," he said. "I don't like seeing people take advantage of their customers. Bandit tow trucks aren't allowed to actively look for cars to tow. Even if a scout spotted the violation, someone had to authorize the tow on behalf of the property owner."

The receptionist returned and shuffled the papers on her desk. "Charlie's out on another call and said he forgot to turn in the signature page."

Nolan cocked his head, but Wylie cupped his arm and smiled at the receptionist. Nolan had given her a lead and she felt more than capable of taking it. "I'll give you a hundred dollars to release my car," she said to the woman.

"But the fee's more than three hundred."

"This feels a lot like a towing scam. How much does it cost to respond to a police report?"

The woman shook her hair-sprayed head. "I could tell you two would be trouble the moment you walked into the office."

Wylie smiled. "Given the state of the office, we'll take that as a compliment."

Nolan pulled a hundred-dollar bill out of his wallet and placed it on the counter. The receptionist looked at the pair of them and shook her head before she tested the bill for forgery, ripped up the paperwork and radioed for Wylie's vehicle. "Charlie will bring it out front?"

Wylie turned to Nolan and raised her eyebrows. "I thought Charlie was out on a call."

He laughed, but the receptionist frowned. She opened her mouth to respond, but the phone rang and she inclined her head toward the door. "Have a nice day."

When neither of them moved, she looked over her shoulder and beckoned a second woman to come to her aid. The receiver rang again, its digital shrill too loud amid the soft whir of the air conditioning and outdated computers. The receptionist cleared her voice for the new customer. "Tommy Tee's Tow Service. How can I help you?"

The second woman came to the counter. "Is there a problem?"

Nolan shook his head and turned his back on the woman.

Left to choose from his wake or the frowning administrator, Wylie fell in behind him, too dazed by the encounter to consider other alternatives.

"You shouldn't have given them anything," he said.

She eyed the chips waiting behind the grimy glass of the vending machine and decided against rounding up her bill with the addition of an impulse purchase. "You're probably right, but I'm ready to get this mess over with." She considered his easy confidence amid the wood paneling and craft store frames. "You already saved me a few hundred bucks. I'll pay you back as soon as I get to a bank branch."

He glanced at the ATM shoved in the corner, its buttons worn smooth and ringed by black grease. "What? You don't want to use these fine facilities?"

She grinned and opened the door for him, hoping road noise would disguise the growl of her stomach. "I promise you I'm good for it, eventually."

Nolan looked at her lips.

She took a deep breath. For a moment, she considered giving him the casual kiss of a girlfriend, something as soft a meaningful as a thank you. *I can't afford that risk right now. I have nothing to back up the gesture and no right to push the limits of our friendship.* She pulled back and the pleasure of extracting her car faded against the reality of the day. She shielded her eyes and added up the debts behind her promises. "I'm going to pay you back, Nolan, and we're going to forget about those kisses. If you're serious about letting me join this commune thing, I need to know where I stand. I need to know that we're even."

"Even?" he asked.

She nodded.

"How can two people ever be even?" He walked toward the Bronco and slowed, matching his stride to hers. "Are you keeping score?"

"I saved your ass last night when Rusty would have taken a swing at you. You got me out of this mess, so we're all good."

"Sure, we're good." He glanced at her, smiled, and waved to Rikard lounging in the back seat. "Let's go."

The man's amusement undercut the sincerity of his comment and gave her reason to doubt her actions outside Rusty's club. "I'm going to pay you back." She reached for his arm to affirm her intent.

"I heard you."

"Why can't I say thank you?" She felt her skin warm against his arm.

He shrugged. "It's not a big deal. Anybody would have done it."

Anybody. Letting go of his arm, she exhaled and approached the truck. The Bronco's polished hood reflected their image and she defended her line in the sand. *I'm going to see this man again. Every morning if this commune thing works out. I'm not just anybody. Anything that happens between us has to start from common ground.*

She shook her head as a tow operator in a jumpsuit returned her vehicle to the freedom of the street. He flipped her the keys and saluted their ingenuity as he headed into the main office. Wylie held her freedom in her hand, but she looked at Nolan standing near the driver's side door and admitted her attraction to him. His eyes were as green as the hood of the Bronco and she wanted to remember the taste of cardamom on her lips. Knowing she had her limits, she acknowledged her attraction and redefined her terms. *Consensual and based on common ground.* He raised his eyebrows and she asked him, "What's the address of the house?"

Nolan nodded and gave her an address on Monument Street in the hills of Pacific Palisades. He opened his mouth to say more, but stopped and turned to Rikard. "All good?"

The blond leaned back, his hands supporting his head. "I mean, a few people offered to buy the Bronco, but I told them you wouldn't part with it."

Nolan climbed into the driver's seat and put the key in the ignition. "Why not? Everything has a price."

Rikard glanced at Wylie as she approached the customized truck. "Trust me," he said. "They weren't offering enough."

* * * *

Wylie rolled down her windows, turned up the radio and picked up a live concert from KXSC. The independent, student-run radio station from the University of Southern California reminded her that other twenty-six-year-olds were still figuring out their lives. "It's called getting an advanced degree," she muttered as she turned up the volume.

The wind and the music filled her senses. She climbed the hills of Pacific Palisades and turned onto Monument Street, expecting to find a rambling structure from the 1970s — something mismanaged and made of stucco that had escaped modernization and vexed the neighbors for years.

As the street rose, she scanned a stately eucalyptus tree. It presided over homes that pushed the boundaries of local building codes and tight lot lines. *So it's an economically diverse neighborhood.* She followed house numbers and watched pavers and ornamental shrubs flash at the edge of her vision. When the scale of the white shingled façades and terraced rooflines only grew with the views, she shook her head and wondered if she had misheard the commune's address.

Then she passed a late-model Mercedes parked on the downhill side of the street, its wheels turned toward the curb. "No way," she said to herself. "This is way out of my league." Yet her phone chimed to indicate she had arrived at the correct address.

Wylie looked at the right side of the street and exhaled. The address Nolan had given her had brought her to a newly constructed contemporary home guaranteed to have views of the Pacific. She counted three levels and eyed the spacious rooftop deck, wondering how many neighbors had been pissed off about that feature.

Unsure about where to park or how to turn around without driving to the top of the hill, she put the SUV in park and took a deep breath. *There's no way a room in this house is seventeen hundred dollars. What is it? The maid's closet?*

Nolan and Rikard pulled up behind her in the green Bronco and she used the rearview mirror to watch Nolan reach for a garage door opener. She turned to face the house and confirmed her suspicions when the door rose and revealed an empty parking space next to a sleek Corvette.

She leaned out of the window to say she'd changed her mind, but Nolan gestured for her to claim the open spot. Wylie hesitated, wondering if she would be able to reverse her commitment, but she heard Nolan's yell through the open window. "Don't worry. You'll fit."

Wylie eyed the commune once again. "I doubt it," she said, but she closed her eyes for a moment and pulled into the garage as Nolan parked his custom job on the steep and exposed street.

Chapter Six

"The basement level includes a large media and game room, laundry facilities and Antonia's bedroom. She's been the only woman roommate in the house for the last year or so. We attempt to give her some privacy, for what it's worth."

Wylie followed Nolan's gestures, but her comprehension failed to advance past the amenities of the media and game room—a drop-down projection screen and a semicircle of eclectic seating that filled the majority of the space. On either side of the impromptu theater arrangement, a ping-pong table graced one wall and a bar setup worthy of a magazine spread anchored the other wall. She saw her bedraggled reflection in a mirror behind the shelves of liquor bottles. *I'm in way over my head.*

"Are you coming?" Nolan asked, one hand on the stair railing leading to the next floor.

She swallowed and looked at the collection of recliners like a streetwise Goldilocks. *Could I be at home here?* Boxy, overstuffed chairs looked straight out of nineties sitcoms, but she could see herself sitting in them, her bare feet tucked in the corners as she mindlessly ate popcorn.

At the edge of the grouping, a masterpiece of molded plywood and red leather looked like a relic of the 1950s. She shook her head, knowing she would never be comfortable in it. For a moment, she wondered if the owner had a white cat or a pretentious rosewood tray to rest on the matching ottoman. "I don't own any furniture," she admitted. Nolan and Rikard looked at each other and she felt the need to clarify. "My last place came furnished."

Rikard's face remained expressionless, but Nolan shrugged and put a hand on an autumnal-colored loveseat with velour fabric and scrolling dark wood trim. The piece looked like a relic from grandma's 1970s basement and she wondered if it smelled of old smoke and subtle mold. "You can have the seat of honor until you pick out one of your own."

She looked at the brown-tone floral fabric. "Thanks, I think."

"The main level has an open floor plan with a European kitchen, dining room, living room and large sliding-glass doors." Nolan climbed the concrete steps. "We do a lot of seamless indoor-outdoor living and entertaining on this floor. When the weather's nice, we tend to leave the doors open and use the pool decking as an extension of the room."

"Pool?" She scrambled to follow his lead as he disappeared around a corner at the top of the stairs. She raced to the top step, eager to keep track of him in the unfamiliar house, then stopped in the formal reception space on the main floor. An infinity pool filled the small backyard and disappeared over the horizon, leaving her with breathless views of the hills and the distant ocean.

Rikard climbed the stairs and bumped into her.

She finally closed her mouth. "Sorry." She looked at the expanse of the living area and found three people sitting at a large table with ballpoint pens and blank white forms.

"It's a nice house," she muttered, looking for refuge on the main level.

The seated committee members eyed her with unsuppressed interest. A woman with short brown hair smiled, but the expressions on the two men ranged from critical evaluation to dazed disinterest.

Wylie raised her hand and waved, forcing a smile to her face. "Hi," she said, "It's nice to meet you guys."

She looked over her shoulder and located Nolan, his lips pursed as he waited for Rikard to join the congregation on the landing. "Busy texting while we were at the tow yard?"

Rikard smiled and claimed a fourth chair near the roommates. "We agreed to evaluate every potential roommate on the same criteria." He gestured to the open edge of the table. "Wylie, have a seat."

The room's occupants looked alert as she swallowed and realized Rikard's approval had not been the only thing standing between her and a good night's sleep. She turned to look at Nolan.

He took a step forward then hesitated.

The tic in his jaw suggested a simmering frustration and she realized his roommate's decision to summon the group and stage the coup had surprised him. She watched him rub the dried sweat from his trimmed beard and glare at Rikard. *The line between his beard and sideburns might be a sign of control, the precision cut a warning instead of an omission. He's more than capable of making the two ends meet.* She waited for him to react to Rikard's challenge.

She replayed images of Nolan presiding over his food truck and leading the group of protestors to Rusty's bar. His lips might have melted beneath hers, but she realized he carried an intent behind everything he did. *Why did he find me this morning? Why did he take up my cause?*

The man shifted his weight.

She turned to face the three roommates who were waiting to judge and evaluate her. *Isn't this the reason I decided to skip out on corporate America?* Taking a deep breath, she chose a seat at the table and took matters into her own hands, offering a smile to each of the roommates. "I'm Wylie Winidad."

The woman with short brown hair raised her hand and waved it from side to side like an excited child. "Antonia."

"Jack," the intense man said with a brief nod. Bold glasses hid warm brown eyes and Wylie wondered what circumstances had brought him into the group.

The man who had greeted her arrival with dazed disinterest blinked like he had trouble focusing without artificial light. "Neil."

"Hi, Neil, it's nice to meet you."

Rikard cleared his throat. "So, let's get down to business."

Nolan approached the table and pulled out a chair. Its wooden legs skimmed the polished floor, summarizing the tension from Rikard's ambush.

Rikard rolled down his sleeves and waited until everyone refocused on him. "Upstairs we've got a fabulous master suite, three large guest rooms and seventy square feet of living space masquerading as a sixth bedroom." He looked at Nolan for a second then turned his attention back to her. "Don't worry. It's also got a lock on the door, a window and a wardrobe."

Wylie smiled as the banal description sent relief flooding through her system. Then she wondered whether Rikard's humanist concessions might be a trap. She envisioned a space built for a nanny or a home office, but reasoned the room at the top of the stairs would be infinitely more comfortable than the front seat of her automotive haven. "That explains why it's so cheap."

"Pretty much," Antonia said. "The last person who rented it got a loft bed from one of those big-box stores that designs and sells ready-to-assemble furniture. They set up their computer desk below the bed."

"I don't have a computer. I just use my phone."

Jack and Rikard looked at each other but held their comments.

Antonia made a note and looked up from her rubric. "What do you do for income?"

Wylie smiled, more comfortable on familiar ground. "I teach yoga on the beach every other morning. I'm working on my official certification."

"That's awesome," Neil said, his droll tone conveying the enthusiasm adults maintained for artwork students carried home from elementary school.

She nodded, pleased to get a response from the man. "It is pretty cool. I love watching my clients progress and improve their physical and mental wellbeing. As soon as I complete my training with the national organization, I'll be able to get a full-time job with health benefits."

"Are you still going to keep your beach class?"

Wylie spread her hands on the table. "I'm going to try. Full-time doesn't have to mean nine-to-five, but I don't want either endeavor to suffer."

"Good call."

"So, Nolan described this as a commune?"

The question hung in the air without any takers.

"What does that mean, exactly?"

Antonia smiled. "It means we work together and try hard to be there for each other through thick and thin. It means we don't pass judgment and bail on each other based on whims."

Oh, Dottie, you wouldn't last a minute in this house.

"We try to dine together and gather on Thursday nights for something we call 'the Games'. It's a no-holds-barred opportunity to call out each other's moral and business failures, but also to offer support. Nobody in this house has the right to be passive-aggressive, selfish or avoidant with other roommates."

"That sounds intense."

The woman laughed. "It's not like you're facing down men the size of linebackers screaming 'Fuck you! Fuck you! Fuck you!'"

"I would pee in my pants."

"Smart woman," Neil said.

"The Games have their benefits," Rikard admitted, "but they can feel contrived if nobody's honest about their motivations."

Wylie frowned and worried the man's questions about Oregon cults had preceded some other household obligations the occupants had yet to explain to her. Then she remembered Nolan's advice to add something to the community as a way to gain their acceptance. "I could lead house yoga sessions. It's always helpful to work through poses with friends and share notes on modifications that you find helpful." She thought of Nolan showing up shirtless and turned away from the table to hide her blush. *I could definitely get behind group sessions, jack up the heat in the open-concept living room and lead a few sessions of hot yoga. I wouldn't mind seeing them all these men in their running shorts.*

She turned back to the table and found Antonia staring at her. She swallowed, wondering if the other woman would be foe or friend. *Wait? Who says I'm even doing this?*

Jack cleared his throat. "Structured exercise could benefit everyone, but we're not living together because we want to spend our days chasing peace, love and harmony. Just so you're clear... This isn't a household that's used to extensive recreational drug use and hooking up with multiple partners."

Wylie focused on the man and tried not to look at Nolan. "I understand you're all trying to incubate new businesses." The warning about good behavior felt too close to home, given her thoughts on household eye candy. *Look, but don't touch*, she told herself. *Especially Nolan. I'm the one who told him to keep it professional.*

"But you're not. Do you think you can empathize with a bunch of stressed-out entrepreneurs?"

She scanned the group and met every person's gaze. "I respect what you're trying to do. It's hard to run a small business — or a large one. I know how important it is to manage your brand and make sure you deliver a consistent and high-quality product."

Rikard nodded and his small smile reminded her of the relaxed man who had turned his face into the wind. "Don't be fooled by Jack's pragmatism. The freezer's full of tempeh burgers, Neil hung a bunch of macramé plant holders by the pool and Antonia's got a wax pool from the drip candles she's been nursing for three years."

Neil cleared his throat. "I mean, Rikard's right. It's not a hacker house. StartupHouse in San Francisco might have gained national attention, but people have been living this way for a long time. The Glint closed, but I think the Rainbow Mansion and Blackbox Mansion are still going strong. Who knows? I'd have to check the blogs."

Wylie nodded like she understood any of Neil's references. She looked to Nolan for clarification and he steered the conversation back to the logistics of running this household. "I told you we vote on everything from toilet paper ply to the size of our grocery budget. Each roommate also has a sphere of influence to help the household run seamlessly. It's a method of governance that cuts down on duplicate expenses and builds a sense of community dependence."

Clapping her hands in excitements, Antonia bobbed in her chair. "I have the socials. I organize theme parties and invite speakers who might appeal to everyone in the house. We use a messaging app to keep up with daily chatter. You can just connect your calendar if you download an extension from the app directory."

Wylie thought of her phone's calendar and the sparse series of appointments it helped her maintain. *Yoga instruction, yoga certification and birthday reminders for people I hardly ever see. The occasional job interviews and doctor appointments. Who would be interested in that level of detail?* She smiled at Antonia and hoped the warm expression covered the sense of isolation that had begun to creep into her consciousness. "Works for me."

Jack jerked his head toward Antonia. "She does a good job with soft skills. Laundry falls under her purview as well, but that just means she counts the bags before the laundry service picks them up. I manage the cleaning crew, but that doesn't mean I do it."

He looked at Wylie with raised eyebrows and she smiled as she envisioned him hauling a mop and bucket between the three levels. "No, of course not."

"You ought to try planning dinner for thirty, Jack. It's not all soft skills." Antonia leaned back in her chair. "Nothing's worse than feeling alone in a room full of people."

The man shrugged but declined to take her bait.

"I'm on groceries," Neil chimed in. "Put your name on anything you buy that you want to keep to yourself. The rest is up for grabs. Let me know if you have any dietary restrictions."

Wylie nodded and turned to Rikard.

He looked at her and took a deep breath, his head cocked in consideration.

Stuck on your misgivings from our first impression?

The man exhaled. "Accounts payable. We have a house credit card, but all the bills and reimbursements go through me. I also collect rent."

Nolan broke the ensuing silence and saved Wylie from defending her ability to pay on time. "I handle maintenance issues. So each resident's sphere of influence makes the household run more smoothly. We've all tried living on our own and found ourselves bogged down with logistics when we wanted to focus organizational energy on managing our businesses."

His deep voice surprised Wylie and she smiled, hoping the benign gesture would hide her response. She had been working so hard to give roommates equal attention that she had overcompensated and almost forgotten him. "What does that leave me?"

They exchanged looks.

"Neighborhood relations," Antonia said.

She considered the clarification. "I don't get it."

"You're used to working with the public, right? We need someone to go to the community meetings and stay abreast of any council changes or code amendments."

"Is that what the last roommate did?"

Antonia nodded. "He probably took it a little too far. He's living at the top of the hill with a cougar named Beth."

Wylie bit her lip and tried not to laugh, but Neil cracked first and all six of them began to smile.

"So, you think you can do this?" Nolan asked. "It's not a big room, but it comes with a lot of perks."

"And responsibilities," Rikard added.

"Yeah," Wylie said, "I think I can do this. I think it would be a lot of fun." She took a deep breath and added her conditions. "But I want a year's lease. I want something in writing. And I kind of want to see the room."

"Of course," Jack said. "We won't hang you out to dry."

Uneasiness twisted her stomach. *I don't have anything but their word and my intuition about Nolan.* She thought of Dottie's passive-aggressive eviction and wondered if it had been the best thing that could have possibly happened to her this year. "Okay. And maybe a thirty-day clause to change my mind? Call it a probation period in case this whole dream-house-thing is a façade and you're all a bunch of freaks and geeks."

Nolan laughed, but the other four roommates looked at her like she had personally insulted their mothers. "I'm sure it will be great," she added to cover the faux pas. "Assuming you guys are good to go, I'm in."

"We'll vote on it while you go upstairs and see the room."

She rose from the table and followed Nolan up the stairs to the third floor, conscious of the four sets of eyes following their movements. "Which one of you has been here the longest?"

"I have," he said without stopping.

Just keep your hand on the railing and your eyes off his butt. She followed him to the landing, where he ignored a window-filled hallway and a glass-paneled door leading to a rooftop deck. The other side of the hall led to the smallest bedroom she had ever seen. White particle-board furniture filled the space, but the loft bed and freestanding wardrobe looked perfectly at home. She stepped inside the room and imagined unrolling her yoga mat in the remaining space. Then she looked up and gauged the sturdiness of the overhead beams. *It doesn't matter whether the beams are strong enough. I doubt an aerial swing would fit.*

"What do you think?" Nolan asked from the hallway.

She turned to face him and stopped mentally organizing two duffel bags full of clothes. "I mean, my old room was bigger, but this house has got way better amenities."

He nodded but stayed in the public foyer. "I'm glad you like it. Do you want to see the deck or some of the other rooms?"

"The deck would be fun, but I'm not interested in seeing what I can't have."

"I can empathize," Nolan said. He turned to the glass panel door and opened it to reveal a flat section of roof topped with deck flooring, a small couch and a low coffee table that would not compete with the view of the surrounding hills and the glittering Pacific. A break in the railing led to an outdoor staircase that connected the deck to the patio surrounding the pool on the main level.

Nolan lowered himself to the couch. "So, do you want to get lunch?"

Her stomach rumbled and she leaned against the side of the house. "You already asked me that question. Do all the residents try to eat together?"

"If it happens, it happens." He spread his arms along the back of the couch. "I guess if you're going to be living here, we should establish some ground rules."

Wylie smiled. "Do I need to open a messaging account for this?"

"I just want to clarify that kiss. You're not obligated to like me back."

She walked toward the couch and sat with her back against the armrest, careful not to touch him. "I like you plenty. I like the way you taste and the way you pulled me against you when we kissed."

"But?"

She exhaled and looked at him, knowing a man who would strike a deal for a bowl of lentils would also respect a locked door if she locked it. "I figured I could do this homeless thing for two weeks, save up money for a real deposit, finish a class I'm working on and get on with my life." She took a deep breath and looked at the rows of multi-million-dollar houses lining the hillsides. For a few days, she had been one of the thousands of faces loitering beneath the green southern California canopies, but she wondered how many people had seen her. "Then I tried to do it. Honestly? I barely slept the last two nights. I don't know how people survive that lifestyle without losing their minds."

He nodded. "The country spends a lot of time and money trying to get people off the streets. Some of the programs work. Some of them don't."

"I know most homeless people feel like they don't have a choice, but the reasons aren't that cut and dry. I met a woman named Penny Lane who seemed like a real sweetheart, someone who should be manning the front desk of an elementary school. She looked so much older than she should."

"The elements can be harsh," he said, but he maintained the distance between them.

"And I always had a choice. I always had the money to bail on my California dream or hide in a hotel room until I felt safe enough to try again."

Nolan pulled his arm from the back of the couch and pivoted to face her. "But you didn't bail. You tried to stick it out. I told you, Wylie, not many people would face those kinds of risks."

"Doesn't it matter that I was scared?"

He reached for her then seemed to change his mind, pulling back his arm until it rested in his lap. "No, it just makes you human."

She looked at his hand and wished she dared to reach for it. *Which armchair is his? The comfortable cushions or the expensive stylish leather? Only one of them could be right for me and I'm too scared to confirm whether I'm right or wrong.*

She turned her face to take in the sweeping view. "I like hanging out with you. I like all this and I appreciate it, but—"

"You're feeling vulnerable," he said.

Wylie let the word fill the space between them. "That's one way to put it."

"I get that, Wylie, but don't confuse my patience for disinterest."

She swallowed, wondering how long it would take her to let down her guard and seek him out. *Keep it together, girl. There is more than one way to screw this up.*

Rikard opened the paneled door and crossed his arms as he stood in the midday sunlight. "All right, Wylie, we all voted. You're in."

She grinned and jumped up.

A look passed between the two men.

She steadied her reaction and understood the vote fell short of unanimous. *Wait! Who voted against me? What was the margin?*

Nolan stood and walked past Rikard, leaving the two of them standing on the deck.

She started to move past the blond, but stopped and bit her lip, searching for the words to soothe their rocky start. "I want us to get along," she said. "I want to fit in."

Rikard raised his eyebrows. "We get along just fine."

"But you don't like me."

He cocked his head and considered her. "I don't like unexplained actions."

"That's what I am?"

"No. To me, you're a threat. Most of the parties and social events happen on the rooftop deck." He gestured to the staircase leading to the wider space above them.

"Nobody except Nolan ever comes out here, yet I find the two of you out here, as comfy as lovebirds."

Wylie looked at the intimate haven where they'd stood and wondered if she had trespassed on an unwritten rule. She told herself that her first day in the house should be about making friends and settling into the rhythm of a shared space. "Why doesn't anyone else use the deck?"

"We all have our havens," Rikard said, "and this one has always belonged to Nolan. I would think twice about interrupting him when he's sitting out here alone." The warning lingered as he strode toward the door and left her standing on the exposed decking.

She wondered what Rikard found lacking in her presence.

He paused at the door to the house and turned to face her. "The code for the exterior doors is nine-six-nine-six. Don't get yourself locked out."

Wylie looked at the keypad and nodded, accepting that bad beginnings could lead to bad outcomes. *I could make a point of getting to know him, but do we all have to be friends to live here?* Memories of sitting in the carpeted hallway of Dottie's apartment overwhelmed her system. *I don't want to be powerless and afraid of my footing.* Deep breathing exercises calmed her flight response until she felt confident enough to follow Rikard inside the building. She found Antonia standing in the hallway with a bottle of champagne.

The woman with the short brown hair grinned and popped the cork. "Welcome home!"

Chapter Seven

After they'd helped finish the first bottle of champagne, the men realized the dynamic in the house had shifted and abandoned them. Wylie spent the rest of the afternoon sitting on the couch with Antonia and her laptop.

"Co-working, co-living, co-creating," Antonia said, "we do it all together." She toyed with her short brown hair and winked. "Sometimes we're even co-sleeping."

Wylie choked on her champagne and wondered if the alcohol had affected her hearing. Which roommate? She could not imagine the high-spirited woman crawling into bed with Jack or Neil. *Maybe it had been Rikard.* She swallowed. *Please don't let her say Nolan.*

"I used to live in a tech house in San Francisco. They hosted hackathons and salons in the living room and invited Silicon Valley's best and brightest to participate. You can't imagine how exciting it is to see all those men and women hunched over their laptops, muttering to themselves and shouting code across the room. They're all focused on the bottom line, but I could just tell they hadn't given up their desire to change the world."

"Please tell me you didn't just pick one and ambush them in the hallway?"

Antonia laughed. "Not quite, but every session got me going, and after the lust faded, it got me thinking as well. I think it's time for society to understand co-living can be more than a millennial trend. Those programmers came together because they desired a lifestyle without property ownership, but co-living has so many solutions for the global population. Multi-generational houses aren't new, so why shouldn't we accept multi-relationship houses as well? Better energy efficiency, better urban density and better social networks make people happier."

This champagne makes me happy. She finished her glass and realized she had not eaten lunch. "So what's your techie contribution? Matchmaking?"

"Not quite," the woman said as a Cheshire Cat smile spread across her lips, "but you're close. Think event management for entrepreneurs. I know how they think, even if they can't articulate their tactical needs without digressing into big picture issues and social injustices. Most of my events are pitched as talks or trade shows that draw hundreds of people at a time. During cocktail hour, participants workshop pitches and ideas while they're networking. You'd be amazed at what they come up with after they leave their comfort zones."

"You're leveraging their lusts and passions," Wylie said. She imagined a room of determined entrepreneurs rehearsing their elevator speeches as they scanned a crowded ballroom for potential connections. It would only take one handshake before the threat of losing leads pushed them to interact and sent a wave of connections rippling through the room like falling dominoes. "But how do you make money?"

"Ticket sales or hosting fees. I'll admit I've gotten more than one wedding invitation with a handwritten note that they met at one of my events."

Wylie imagined wandering through a restaurant and knowing every mind in the room worked differently from hers. *It's one thing to leverage technology to host yoga classes, but it's another thing to build it.* She put her glass on a long, polished coffee table that housed books and kept clutter from interfering with work surfaces. "How did you get from lust to running your own business? I mean, I teach yoga, and it's such a predictable path—self-promotion or studio work. I can't even imagine what type of innovation would come next."

Antonia nodded. "You've got to lose your security to innovate."

"Check," Wylie said, but she kept her mouth shut when Antonia raised her eyebrows.

"I was living in Chelsea for a few years, since I moved to New York City, but the publishing house where I worked folded without notice. I realized that I had fifteen days to find a new position or pack up five years of my life and move on."

At least you had fifteen days. She focused on Antonia's backstory instead of reliving her plight.

"Moving in New York City takes work. You need to have a lot of money saved up and trying to find a decent apartment is like *The Hunger Games* with fewer costumes. When I got down to five days without any leads, I started expanding my search to different living situations. Maybe a room would work for a few months? I had a blog on the side and I recalled going to a PR workshop hosted at a co-living facility. When I researched it, the Common came up, but so did a host of co-living locations scattered across the country.

"San Francisco sounded sexy, but" — she drained her glass—"it's so freaking cold up there! Not dry cold…wet cold. It's the fog. It just seeps into your clothes and messes with your hair. I bought the best neoprene jacket I could afford, but I still remember the feeling of raindrops seeping down my neck!"

Wylie thought of the dense, patchy fog that could blanket the hills when the conditions were right. "Remind me not to invite you for a run when it's drizzling."

"No way," Antonia said. "These days, I'm strictly a warm-weather type of woman. The rest of the county watches the hills when the Santa Ana winds start to blow, but I'm the person who's outside, face to the wind, soaking in the heat. It's like a five-year-old opening the door to a furnace. You can feel the radiation and close your eyes, believing you'll always be warm."

"Maybe you and Rikard should partner on a business venture. He confessed his family comes from Croatia but he also hates the cold."

Antonia rolled her eyes. "It's kind of sexy to listen when he gets going in Croatian on the phone, but he and I have never hit it off. Sometimes I doubt if he even likes women."

"I think he followed a woman out here."

"Figures," Antonia said. She stood and stretched, like a cat rousing herself from a sun-soaked nap. "It only takes one bad apple to ruin a good man for the rest of us. Let's get food before I say anything I'm going to regret."

Like what? Wylie wondered as she followed the woman's lead. *Like you've been living in your SUV for a few days and this is all too good to be true?*

"How did you and Nolan meet?" Antonia asked.

"We've met around town once or twice and my car got towed. He helped me get it out of the lot and realized I was looking for a new room to rent."

Antonia nodded as she began pulling large aluminum takeout containers from the refrigerator and arranging them on the center island. "Let's see… We've got quinoa enchilada casserole, vegetable lo mein and that cranberry and pecan cabbage slaw that never fills you up."

"I vote for the casserole," Wylie said. "I can't believe all this food comes with the rent."

The other woman smiled and peeled back the cover on the casserole. The roommates had eaten half the contents, leaving an expanse of saucy aluminum and a glimpse of chicken and quinoa spilling from the inner layers.

Wylie's hunger returned with a vengeance and her stomach rumbled. She looked at Antonia, hoping the house's climate system prevented the other woman from hearing her body's response to the thought of hot food. "But I'm fine with whatever you want to heat up."

Nodding, Antonia gathered the necessary utensils. "First lesson of co-living"—she stopped speaking until Wylie looked up and met her gaze—"you've got to speak up for what you want, but learn to choose your battles. Some things are non-negotiable. Put on a sweater if seventy-two degrees feels too cold, but don't waste time battling the men for control over the thermostat."

Wylie laughed. Dressing in layers felt like one of the ten commandments.

"That doesn't mean they're always right. Don't let the rest of the roommates steamroll you into watching action movies and living off man-food."

"Man-food?"

"Wings. Grilled meat. Sriracha sauce. There's a reason Thais call it 'rooster sauce'."

Laughing, Wylie opened a cabinet door and searched for ceramic plates. "I won't give up the fight," she promised. "Besides, it seems like Neil does a good job ordering the groceries and managing the variety and food."

The other woman laughed and pointed Wylie toward the right cabinet. "That doesn't mean he's unbiased. He'd feed us nothing but lentils, sourdough and probiotics if we let him."

The unmistakable sound of Wylie's hunger filled the room. She grinned and realized there were some aspects of her new living situation she would just have to accept. "I like sourdough."

"Not when Neil makes it," Antonia said. "The bread's delicious, but it fills the whole house with a warm yeasty smell that you can't escape." She dished out her portion of casserole and pointed Wylie toward a microwave. "Beware the container in the back of the fridge marked 'starter'. You'll be sorry if you open it, but you won't make the same mistake again."

Wylie nodded, but her brain barely registered the words. The feminine, celebratory indulgence of champagne with Antonia faded as she watched her meal rotate in a stainless-steel microwave. *How did I ever believe I would make it two weeks on my own?*

When lunch ended, Wylie left Antonia at the kitchen table and trudged up the stairs, aware she owed Rikard a rent check and Nolan a reimbursement. As she crested the landing, her feet began to move as slowly as her brain. She realized the combination of quinoa, chicken and champagne had hijacked her blood supply, but the hillside house and the feeling of possibilities gave her an excuse to shut down her defenses. *I just want to rest for a minute.* She turned toward the seventy square feet of living space she could claim.

The white loft bed and freestanding wardrobe persisted, but someone had taken the trouble to bring her duffel bags up from the car and set them near the door. A laundry bag, a stack of sheets and a soft waffle-weave blanket sat beside them with a note. She leaned down to get the note and inhaled the soft remnants of citrus and spice that had escaped a round of laundry detergent.

Wylie dropped to her knees and read the note.

Hope you're getting settled in. We'll get you a parking permit so Rikard can have his spot back. First in, first out. I hope you're going to last longer than one of your yoga classes. Your first shift is at five o'clock. Don't wear the stripper top.
Nolan.

She looked at the slant of the letters and recognized the energy behind Nolan's legitimate welcome. Then she closed her eyes in recognition of the space she had requested. *He could have left this note for anybody.* Tears welled beneath her lids. *I could be any one of the people living on the street.* Worried that one of her new roommates would see her moment of weakness, she closed the bedroom door and told herself she was crying from a stress letdown. The tears streaming down her cheeks had nothing to do with Nolan's distance or the fear she had felt in the middle of the night.

* * * *

The next day, Wylie slept until nine and dressed for her certification class with a refreshed outlook. She thought of her certification instructor as she followed her phone's instructions to the studio. *I won't have to suck up to Cynthia for a place to stay, but what will mother hen think when she realizes one of her yoga chicks has taken up residence with the fox? She'll probably be jealous.* The thought of letting a comment slip kept Wylie entertained throughout the accreditation class.

"Now that we've covered teaching methodology, anatomy and physiology, our next classes will incorporate yoga philosophy, ethics and lifestyle. Remember that most of our customers expect to leave in a certain state of mind."

Wylie eyed the rest of the training attendees in the Playa Vista yoga studio. *What kind of mindset does the Silicon Beach set expect when they walk through the doors of this studio?* She thought of Cynthia's propensity for taking selfies and wondered if the woman had a calendar or a self-help book to fill in the lifestyle words. *It doesn't matter what Cynthia wants.* She rose to her feet. *I'm going to finish this series and become a legitimate instructor, eligible for a stable job with benefits.*

The class ended at one o'clock and Cynthia clapped her hands for attention. "I'm going to grab lunch at one of the food trucks. Feel free to stick around if you have any unanswered questions."

Wylie glanced out of the studio windows and wondered if the Modesto food truck was waiting. Relief and disappointment washed through her system when she stepped outside and realized Nolan's truck was not among the old bread trucks and renovated airstream trailers idling in the parking lot.

"Did you find a place to rent?" Cynthia asked. She stopped alongside Wylie. "I thought of a friend I could ask for you."

"I did find something," Wylie said, determined to be polite and avoid generating any animosity in the woman she had paid to qualify her as a yoga instructor. "I think it's going to work out."

"One of the other class members said she saw you working at a bar called the Social Club." She scanned Wylie's color-coordinated ensemble and raised her eyebrows, as though the class pet had revealed exactly what Wylie had worn for her shift at the bar. "I didn't realize you were that hard up."

Take it in stride, Wylie told herself as she smiled. "Just helping out a friend. My ex-boyfriend owns the bar."

The woman's eyes widened, straining the limits of the maintenance injections keeping her face preternaturally young and Zen. "What's he doing out in the Westside? That's very" — she waved her hand — "avant-garde."

Wylie ignored the woman's disbelief and smiled with the innocence of a lamb. Cynthia's predilection for post-collegiate vendors and salt-and-pepper stunners kept her firmly anchored near the laidback lifestyle of the coast. "Do you want me to get you on the list?"

The woman blinked. "That's not my kind of place."

"Then why did you ask me about it?"

She was speechless for a moment but recovered with time-honed skills. "I just wanted to make sure you weren't rifling through the lost-and-found bin. I know what it's like to feel a bit desperate."

Were you too distracted to empathize the first time I told you I needed a place to live? Wylie smiled and thought of the stocked refrigerator and hillside views that had replaced the cramped conditions of her SUV. *I'm not on the street anymore, but I'm not that far from feeling desperate. I'm not lost, but nowhere near found.* The reality of the admissions softened her response. "Thanks for looking out for me, Cynthia. I appreciate it."

The woman fluffed her hair and waved at a group of men striding out of a two-story office building. "No problem," she said, but her gaze remained fixed on the swarm of office workers wearing chinos and business casual. The door opened once again and a smaller group exited the building. Cynthia smiled and zeroed in on a salt-and-pepper stunner wearing a vibrant Hawaiian shirt. She grasped his arms and kissed both his cheeks while the remainder of his group shifted and frowned, mouths open as they tabled their conversations until she released her prey.

I doubt she met him in the yoga studio. He probably owns the building.

She felt uncharitable and considered her options for the remainder of the afternoon. She had a beachside class to teach the next morning, but the benefits of her new hillside home eliminated the litany of errands that would have filled her afternoon. She brought a copy of her lease to the parking office, applied for a residential permit and sat in the parking lot to fill out the Post Office's online change-of-address form.

Once she'd submitted it, she looked up and scanned the southern California street. *Maybe I should go back to the library and check out a book.* She thought of the people sleeping on the library's benches and wondered what Penny Lane had chosen to do with her day. *Would Nolan have offered her the room?*

She called her parents on the way back to the house and omitted the part of the story where Dottie had unceremoniously kicked her out of the apartment. "So this new house has a ton of features and six bedrooms. You'd love the view," she said.

Her mother let the comment hang between them. "But it's so far from the beach and your job."

Wylie listened as her mother knocked a wooden spoon against a ceramic bowl, the beat as steady and predictable as the rhythm of a metronome. She remembered the foggy tradition of muffin mix on Saturday mornings, her mom cradling a bowl of dough while she reviewed her list of errands and Wylie's scheduled activity. *What time did she get up each morning to beat my alarm clock? It shouldn't matter if I thought the dehydrated blueberries tasted like bits of sand and sweet jelly. I should just be happy she made the muffins in the first place.* The distance between their present locations overrode her feelings about her have-it-all childhood. *She probably uses fresh blueberries in Oregon.*

"Are you sure it was a good move? What about the commute?"

"Minimal," Wylie said. "I'm just higher up."

"Well, that's one way to get ahead."

A moment of silence stretched between them and their conversation veered toward family gossip and the intricacies of life in Oregon. "We're thinking about buying a house. The lack of sales tax has been nice for our daily living expenses, but your father's running the numbers to see if we can swing property taxes. Wouldn't it be nice to have somewhere permanent?"

"What kind of house?" Wylie asked. Her mother gave her the address and she pulled up the listing for a contemporary home they never could have afforded in California. *They've earned peace of mind and shaded luxury. What was the point of all those sixty-hour workweeks if they weren't going to pay off?*

"A cute little cottage with a spare bedroom for you," her mother added. "We hope you'll come visit when your yoga empire allows you the freedom to take a vacation."

Wylie smiled at the open invitation and parallel parked on the street, remembering to turn her wheels toward the curb in case the vehicle's brakes failed. "'Empire' might be an exaggeration."

Her unspoken words stopped the rhythmic sound of her mother's wooden spoon.

"I'm sure you'll find something nice for the two of you," she added to fill the silence.

"You can always come home."

Wylie glanced over her shoulder and focused on the allure of the wide Pacific. Antonia's preference for warm weather resonated and she had a hard time imagining the whales migrating between Alaska and the Baja peninsula. "I appreciate it, Mom, but I'm doing all right on my own." The lie tasted like a bitter pill, but Wylie refused to let her parents know that the balance in her bank account hovered near the hundred-dollar mark. "I think the weather down here is better for my asthma."

"But the air is so clean up here," her mother said. "The rain positively refreshes it!"

Wylie tried not to sigh. "I'm going to grab a few minutes on my own before I help out a friend with a food truck."

"Oh, I just love food trucks," her mother said. "So innovative."

Wylie smiled. *Just like those sandals with contoured cork and rubber footbeds. They've been around forever, but people try them out and think they've discovered a new trend.* "I think he's going for dependability before innovation. He's not the first person to power up a food truck."

"You should invite Dottie and the kids she nannies."

The smile fell from Wylie's face. "That's an idea, but we ended on bad terms."

"What happened? You always get along with everyone."

Wylie sighed. *Sometimes it's better to move on from mistakes instead of reliving them.* She scrunched her hair and resolved to take a shower before class. "She wanted her cousin to move in."

"Well, that's understandable."

Wylie stared at the phone.

"Either way," her mother said, "you're in a better place."

"I am."

"And that's all your father and I want for you—happiness and forward movement."

Am I happy? Wylie asked herself. *I'm no closer to healthcare and benefits.* "Thanks, Mom," she said. She tensed, waiting to see if the deflection worked.

"Of course." Then her mother chatted for a few minutes, sounding as happy as a lark surrounded by evergreen trees, gray-haired hippies and adorable homes.

* * * *

By the time Wylie got off the phone and had demolished a helping of noodles, she realized she was the only roommate in the house. She decided to swap her sweaty workout gear for a swimsuit, took off her top and considered going skinny dipping. Then the doorbell rang. *What the hell?* Beyond a set of double doors with frosted glass panels, two shadowy forms waited outside the home. She pulled her top back on. *Don't they have a sign that says 'no soliciting'?* She charged toward the door, intent on chastising away Jehovah's Witnesses, Mormons or a pair of Boy Scouts with popcorn to sell.

"Don't you know people" — she realized an elderly couple wearing track suits stood on the front steps — "love to have unexpected visitors?"

The man laughed and held out his hand. His clear eyes and clean-shaven cheeks looked sharp, but his shoulder stooped with age and the compression of a lifetime of worries. "We're Patricia and Jonathan Abramowitz, but please call us Patty and John. We live just up the street," he said.

Patty nodded. "The one with all the fountains in the front yard."

Wylie nodded, unwilling to admit that her new situation felt strange enough to occupy her curiosity and keep her from considering who else lived on the street. She smiled at the older woman, amused by the visible makeup line below her jaw. *Who bothers to wear foundation anymore?* Determined not to look out of place, she shook both their hands and recalled Antonia's explanation of her role in the commune. *'Neighborhood relations,'* the woman had said. *'We need someone to go to the community meetings and stay abreast of any council changes or code amendments.' Well, it looks like the council came to us.*

Mr. and Mrs. Abramowitz stared at her.

She took a deep breath and stepped back, gesturing for the couple to enter the home she barely knew. "It's a pleasure to meet you. Come right on in!"

The man gestured for his wife to precede him. She stepped into the living room and stopped in her tracks. "Oh, it's lovely. We haven't been inside since they finished construction."

"Just a minute," Wylie said. She retrieved her shirt and moved her dishes to the sink to buy time. *Where do I seat these people?* She eyed the couches in the living room, the stools at the kitchen island, the formality of the dining room chairs and the large sliding glass doors leading to the outdoor loungers. The number of options overwhelmed her before she recalled Nolan's comment about seamless indoor-outdoor entertaining. She eyed the doors to the pool and asked the older couple, "Would you like to sit outside?"

"That sounds nice," Patty said.

Wylie nodded, relieved to have a task to occupy her hands while she decided on the best way to handle her new role as the household director of neighborhood relations. "Would you like a glass of wine? When I get these doors open" — she shoved at the handle and almost lost her balance when the door slid along the smooth track — "the pool decking is like an extension of the room."

The husband and wife team looked at each other and shrugged. "Sure, why not?"

Ten minutes later, the older couple was occupying patio chairs and Wylie had located wine glasses, grapes and chardonnay. She had even remembered to put her shirt back on. "So what brings you over?" she asked the relaxed retirees.

"We have a meeting with Nolan at three o'clock."

Wylie checked her phone. The clock read three fifteen and she frowned. "I wouldn't expect Nolan to be this late."

John raised his eyebrows. "Have you known each other long?"

Is forty-eight hours long? Wylie tucked her hair behind her ears. "I just moved into the house."

The older couple exchanged glances. "Oh, are you a tech entrepreneur as well?"

A laugh bubbled out of Wylie's mouth and she clasped her hand over her lips to stifle the sound. "Not quite. I teach yoga." To fill the space in their conversation, she rambled about her freelance classes and the appeal of the beach locale. "Every other morning, we meet near the lifeguard tower in front of the rental stand. I have about ten regular clients, but extra people tend to drop in for occasional classes. It's decidedly low-tech."

"It must be hard to manage their different levels of expertise," Patty said.

Wylie popped a grape into her mouth and wondered what type of exercise had reigned during Patty's lifetime. She imagined the leg warmers of the 1980s and subtracted a few decades until she settled on home economics or group calisthenics. "Oh, I just modify the poses to give them the best workout possible. Even my regulars have different skillsets." She replayed the example of the man falling over at her last class and smiled. "I mean, take Price. He's one of my best customers, but I never know what state he'll be in."

"Is that Price Ross?" Patty asked.

Wylie nodded, relieved she had decided not to mention the time the man had shown up so high that he'd laughed through the entire session. "Do you know him?"

"He's our accountant," the older woman said. She looked at her husband and shook her head, a soft laugh suggesting the couple shared more than one memory of their wayward accountant's antics. "He told us the same story this morning."

"No way!" Wylie sipped her wine and wondered about the extent of Price's impromptu news service. "He must collect a lot of stories in his line of business."

John raised his bushy eyebrows. "He's not exempt from the stories." The man looked at his wife and buffered his obviously knowing statement with a kind smile. "But he does a decent job of keeping our accounts balanced and Patty likes him."

Wylie wondered how much John's demeanor had changed as he'd aged out of his professional obligations and assumed caregiving responsibilities. Then he told her about the time Price had bungled their property taxes and triggered an IRS audit. Her speculation dissolved into laughter. "Did you freak out?"

The older man frowned. "Freak out may not be the right description," he said as he explained how the couple had untangled the IRS auditor's administrative scrutiny. "I know Price owned up to his mistake, but the whole affair left me feeling frustrated. Too many people hear our last name and our address, make assumptions and double their scrutiny. They see Jews in Hollywood like a 1980s caricature of greed. I try not to draw attention to our wealth in the first place."

"Well, that's not fair," Wylie said. "I mean, that cultural moment was, like, forty years ago."

Patty laughed. "Forty years is a blip when you're staring down your ninetieth birthday and diagramming the family tree for nieces and nephews who know you'll soon be gone."

Wylie nodded, struggling not to touch on the woman's death. She thought about her family's approach to age and diversity across the generations. Both sets of grandparents had lived far enough away to reduce their relationship to holiday cards and awkward phone calls, but her parents had shrugged their shoulders when the school had prompted her to discuss issues of race, ethnicity and religion. *They were just liberal west-coast workers doing their best to have it all, but then again, it's not like 'Winidad' carries any cultural associations.* "Have you lived here your whole lives?" she asked, trying to steer the conversation back to common ground.

"I moved here when we got married," Patty said. "John's lived here his whole life."

"Where did you grow up?" she asked. *Look at me, making small talk.*

"Sonoma."

She laughed. "So, still California."

The woman's gaze softened. "Well, it felt like a big move to me at the time. I felt like an outlier when I landed down here and realized having children wasn't going to be as easy as I expected." She sipped her wine. "Are the politicians still threatening to separate California into two separate states? Some things never change."

"I'm not sure," Wylie said. "I generally stay out of politics."

"That's a mistake." John resettled his frame in the outdoor chair. "You can't sit on the sidelines and wait until it affects you. You might find yourself playing catch-up if you wait until you're passionate."

I heard 'Abramowitz' and just filed away their last name as a historical quirk. Does the stereotype of a 1980s Hollywood Jew still resonate in pop culture? Surely that's not why they got audited. Didn't most people my age disavow anti-Semitism and genocide at the same time that they got over religion? She swallowed, trying not to put her foot in her mouth and make assumptions about the couple's stances on Israel or the politics of tax cuts. Reform movements, immigration and human needs seemed equally fraught. "So you never had kids?"

Patty shook her head. "Tried and tried, but it never worked out like we planned. Nolan's parents lived on this lot before they separated and his mom built her new house on the other side of town. He used to wander up the hill to see me once or twice a week. It took some of the sting out of never having kids of our own."

I should have stayed with religion. I'm so glad my parents stuck with their marriage, but divorce can be hard. Is that why Nolan came back to this house after someone bought his childhood home? He had good memories of living up here? She thought of him as a little boy with laughing green eyes and round cheeks. "I can see him coming to visit you. He has a knack for making friends and I'm sure ten-year-old Nolan also had a sweet tooth."

"He was a good kid," Patty said, "and you're right. I always had cookies."

John shook his head. "Doesn't mean Nolan should be squandering his time the way he does." He turned to look at Wylie and tapped the table. "You're both chasing careers I would never have considered when I was a young man."

Patty reached for her husband's arm and stayed his rhythmic motion. "Dear, I grew up learning to cook, lighting Shabbat candles and preparing to run a beautiful Jewish home. If I'd let my youth define me, I'd still be worried about brisket and having the Rabbi to our home for Rosh Hashanah dinner. It's a whole new world for Nolan and Wylie. I'm glad they're trying to figure it out."

Wylie sipped her chardonnay, wondering if the other roommates had to tiptoe around significant cultural issues when they ordered groceries, settled accounts payable and coordinated maintenance. *Antonia's probably the only one who interacts with real people. The rest of their roommate duties probably happen online. That's a pity. You can't spend your life hiding behind a screen.* She considered thanking Patty for the vote of confidence but decided to focus on John's proud and cautious grumpiness. "There's not that much to figure out, but I have a lot of confidence in Nolan."

"I had a lot of confidence in Price, too," the older man said. "Look how that turned out."

"Oh, you're too hard on the man," Patty said.

John shook his head. "And you're too soft, my dear. There are a variety of reasons not to sell Nolan the kitchen. His venture could self-destruct and drag us into the news. His mother could sever her ties to our investment firm. It's better to leave the kitchen in the portfolio as a property holding. Let our executors deal with the fallout when we're gone."

I don't care where their families came from. She smiled like her conversations regularly touched on the pitfalls of personal wealth management. *Rich people are weird.*

"Chicken," Patty said.

Her husband shrugged.

Wylie cleared her throat. "I haven't known Nolan very long, but Price is one of my best customers. His yoga positions have gotten better in the last few months, so maybe he's hit his stride and you have one less person to worry about."

The older man looked at her. "I hope you're right."

Chapter Eight

The older couple took pity on her and transitioned their conversation to stories about the history of the hillside neighborhood. John took the lead on famous figures and the area's Methodist history.

"It's come a long way," Patricia said, "but you'd rather hear stories of Nolan."

"No, this is great. I love history," Wylie said.

"There used to be trees for miles. Where did you grow up?"

Not my history. I grew up in one of those tract houses that displaced your trees. She munched on her grapes and tried to ignore the differences between their life experiences. "The views from the top of the hill must be spectacular. Does the fog block often your view?"

"Sure," Patty said, who was polite enough to tout the weather and make it seem engaging. "The days are sunnier up here and less foggy than the coast, but we get it all when it comes to the weather." She looked toward the Pacific. "I'm grateful the summer temperatures are cooler than inland Los Angeles, but catching a breeze can be difficult, given the current housing density. So many modern houses do more than block the view."

Wylie smiled. *So much for my public relations skills.* "Like this one?"

John grunted.

"Still, I can't imagine there's much we can do about the weather." She grinned. "Aaron Spelling might have a bit of magic up his Hollywood sleeve."

"Patricia, he died in 2006," John said.

The woman blinked and stared at her hands, but she shook her head and smiled at her husband. "Of course, dear. It's not like I confused him with Jerry Lewis."

Wylie had no idea who the woman meant. *They could be my grandparents, but I have no idea what's normal at this age. Is Patty losing it? Was the town that small way back when?*

John took his wife's hand and comforted her confusion. "Of course not."

"Those old sitcoms were sweet," Wylie said to bridge the moment. "I think the core broadcasters have a good lineup, but I enjoy watching the mockumentary family sitcoms." *When I watch network TV, which is like, never.*

Patty laughed and they swapped opinions on the multi-generational sitcoms filling prime-time airwaves. Precious child actors brought their conversation back to common ground. "That show's such a caricature! Don't get me started on the number of inept realtors we've met over the years. Did you grow up nearby?"

"Mmm-hmm," Wylie said with a smile, prepared to deflect the conversation away from her life once again. "It's so interesting to meet new people" — her words trailed off as she heard the garage door open. Within minutes, Nolan appeared on the main level. He paused at the top of the stairs and she met his gaze, proud of her hosting ability and ready to introduce him to her newest best friends.

Instead of acknowledging her, he focused on the laughing couple and walked right up to them. "Patricia and Jonathan," he said, "I see you've met my friend."

Jonathan stood and shook Nolan's hand. "Delightful. I'm glad to see your taste in women has improved since your college years. Wylie is as refreshing as your food truck's business."

She choked on her wine and started to object.

Nolan released John's hand, turned and planted a kiss on her lips. "Please play along," he whispered in her ear.

She opened her mouth to object, but her senses stayed focused on his rich, exotic taste. It went straight to her core and mixed with the crisp chardonnay lingering on her tongue. Sinking back into her chair, she considered pulling him into her lap and claiming what she deserved for the last hour of chit-chat.

Nolan winked and stole a second kiss. "Thank you," he said.

"Hi, honey, welcome home," she said as she took a deep breath. Hints of citrus, mint and spice lingered on her tongue. She cleared her throat. *No more alcohol or you'll lose control and jump him in front of the old folks.*

Nolan grinned. "How's the chardonnay?"

"Delicious." She rose to get another glass and put space between them so she could process her thoughts.

John and Patty looked on and wore matching grins.

"Would you like some?" *The roleplaying feels like a high school drama, but doesn't every part of high school feel like a play?*

He winked at her. "That'd be great, dear."

If I keep swapping kisses with you, I'm going to have to skip the 1950s black-and-white sitcoms and head straight to the premium cable subscriptions.

Nolan engaged the older couple. He patted the small of her back and his hand brushed the top of her ass.

She shrugged it off and eyed their cozy trio, her cheeks coloring in embarrassment as she chided herself for first opening the door to Mr. and Mrs. Abramowitz. *Why did I assume I could bring something to the table by making friends with the neighbors? Of course they know each other. Why else would the two old people just pop in on a random weekday afternoon?*

"Are we out of wine?" Nolan asked with a wink.

His teasing gesture set her off. When thoughts of revenge and sabotage seemed more interesting than domestic harmony, she turned to fetch his wine. Then she pivoted and met his green eyes, prepared to put him in his place for assuming she would go along with his schemes. *Who gave you the right to kiss me like that? To touch me when I don't want to be touched?*

Nolan raised his eyebrows.

Or do I?

He glanced at the older couple with a pleading expression.

The sign of vulnerability softened her outrage and she realized something big underpinned his request to play along with the sitcom affection. Admitting she would seek him out under other circumstances, she shook her head and walked into the kitchen. Memories of sleeping in the SUV's front seat steadied her hands as she pulled supplies from the refrigerator. *It's my job to separate the pleasure of stealing kisses from my fierce insistence we remain friends. I started this mess, but what are the rules of this game and how long do I have to play along?* She grabbed a fresh bottle of wine, a hastily assembled cheese board and a glass for Nolan before she walked back to the pool.

John rose to take the board from her hands.

At least someone's a gentleman.

Patty smiled at Nolan. "I can't believe I got the date wrong for our appointment. Age must be catching up to me."

John looked at his wife, his expression settling into familiar worry lines.

"Not a problem," Nolan said, his arms wide along the back of the chair like he had all the time in the world to hang out by the pool and chat with his neighbors.

What happened to running your food truck? She set the second bottle of wine on the table. "Is that all, dear?"

He nodded, opened the bottle and refilled everyone's glasses. "Mr. and Mrs. Abramowitz, the date of our appointment doesn't matter. Too much time has passed since I've seen either of you. I'm glad you came by when you did and had a chance to meet Wylie. She's a gem."

Wylie thought about sticking out her tongue.

"You know us older people," John said. "We have our moments of spontaneity."

Nolan laughed. "We all have our moments."

Master of the house, Wylie mused, shaking her head. *It's almost fun to watch.*

"How's the food truck coming along?" John asked. "What's the profit margin on a three-dollar taco?"

Wylie lingered on the edge of the conversation, wondering if Nolan's 1950s alter ego would direct her back to the kitchen for hors d'oeuvres. She thought about the times her mom and dad had let her stay up late on Friday nights if she promised to let them sleep in on Saturday morning. Scenes of annoying neighbors, repeated catchphrases and serious episodes lingered in her memories like well-known friends. *Something about this situation just feels sweet, but the rhythm of a twenty-two-minute episode can feel too familiar and the protagonists hardly change from one episode to the next. Patty's right about times changing. I have little interest in playing the 1950s housewife, so I can either ride out this episode or make a quick exit.* Although her lips tingled with the memory of Nolan's kiss, the pleasure of sipping white wine beneath a hot spray of a shower won out. "It was so nice meeting you both," she said.

Nolan and John stood.

"You too, Wylie," Patty said, her head dipping in a small nod.

Wylie inhaled and looked at Nolan. "I'll catch you later…dear."

Instead of letting her escape to the white-tiled bathroom at the top of the stairs, he strode forward and caught her hand, pulling her close.

She wondered if he would kiss her goodbye. *Make it a good one.* Then she bit her lips, determined to keep them to herself. A second later, her body overruled her mind and she imagined the feel of his touch on her skin. *Damn feeling vulnerable. I want this attraction between us to be real.*

He glanced at her lips and took a deep breath, shaking his head like his thoughts had outpaced his capacity for words. "I'll explain later," he whispered in her ear, "but it means a lot to me that you're willing to play along."

The air between them simmered with unexplored needs. She nodded and straightened to break the connection between them. *If this is the second act, It's a script I've never read.*

Nolan failed to release her hand.

She looked at him and saw the sincerity in his jade-green eyes. Her shoulders softened and the urge to reprimand him fled. *I started this game of make-believe,* she admitted to herself, *but maybe that's because I never wanted it to end.*

Nolan winked and released her hand. "Go get a jumpstart on dinner."

"Jerk," she whispered.

The man laughed.

She shook her head and put some space between them. *Neighborly relations be damned. Whatever is going on, it had better be important.*

The white-tiled bathroom shared by the top-floor roommates felt like a refuge, but she half-expected Nolan to stride into the room and throw back the curtain. When the tiled room remained her domain, she left her mind drift, stroking her clit as she imagined what would have happened if she'd left the Social Club with Nolan. Exploring the tension of their first kiss gave her a reason to end her shower with an audible release. She smiled. *Maybe I should spend more time in the bath.*

The late-afternoon sun sparkled over the Pacific as she padded into her bedroom to trade her towel and wine glass for soft jeans and tennis shoes. *I have a feeling shifts at the food truck aren't high on sit-down breaks.*

When someone knocked on the door, she opened it and found Nolan standing in the hallway. She leaned against the frame, crossing her arms, and decided to focus on the limits they had defined on the small deck. "What was all that '*Hi, honey, I'm home*'?"

He raised his eyebrows and glanced at her lips.

She arched her eyebrows, wondering if a blush lingered from her shower.

"What? You're the only one who decides when we get to kiss?"

"I was saving your butt," she said, defending her actions at the club.

Nolan nodded. "Well, you might have just done it again. Patricia and Jonathan own a commercial kitchen that's sitting empty at the bottom of the hill. They've got everything I need to expand the food truck and reach a wider audience."

"So rent it."

"They won't budge," he said.

"Find another space."

"Why? Their space meets local health and safety code requirements for preparing food, but it's sitting empty while they strategize with their accountant."

"So?"

He ran his hand through his hair. "I've been trying to get a hold of their property for years, but I've been going about it the wrong way. None of the commercial factors matter if they decide they like you, and a steady girlfriend might be the sign of maturity they've needed from my end."

"But I'm not your girlfriend. We've known each other, like…three days."

He shrugged. "How hard can it be to pretend to like someone?"

How hard can it be to pretend not *to like someone?* She thought of Dottie and frowned. "I need to spend less time pretending and more time accomplishing something good in my life."

"So go on a real date with me."

"Not ready for that yet," she said.

"I know you like my kisses."

Grinning, she stepped back before he could prove his point. "You're confusing the traditional order of operations."

He ran his hand through his hair. "So we'll draw a line in the sand. Stick to the fake relationship when we have face time with the Abramowitzes. I'll be a devoted partner and you'll get chaste, guilt-free kisses. You'll know the winks mean nothing until you're ready to cross that line."

"You have more willpower than me. Don't you like my kisses too?" she asked.

"Oh, I like them very much."

She stepped away from the sudden intensity in his gaze. "That's why this is a bad idea, Nolan. This attraction between the two of us? It's too close to the surface for a fake relationship. We'll get confused."

"I'm very good at following rules. The minute John and Patty sign the purchase agreement, you're off the hook. We'll sort out the real attraction between us when you're ready."

And in the meantime, we pretend? She grinned, imagining the size of the reset button they would need to untangle their script. "We can do dinner, but no more lip-to-lip PDA in front of the cute old folks. I have my limits and I'd hate to embarrass them."

"So touching your ass is still in play?"

She rolled her eyes. "Keep your hands to yourself. I'll play along with your stories and tout your brilliance, but at the end of the day, we go to our separate beds."

"It's a big house. Lots of surfaces —"

"Nolan!"

He held up his hands. "Agreed. The Abramowitzes see me settling down and I'm eternally in your debt. Mini Mako gets free sweet potato fries for life. What could go wrong?"

I could fall for you and get my heart broken. She kept her mouth shut as misgivings rippled beneath the surface of her thoughts. She came up with additional reasons the Abramowitzes could hold out on him. Then she wondered if Price and a lifetime of John's suspicions stood between Nolan and his dreams of stainless-steel appliances. *This might have more to do with market conditions than he thought.* "I don't understand why you need that kitchen space. You already make food for Modesto. What's the difference between their kitchen and what you have now?"

"Scale," he said. "Right now, we use a commissary where food trucks and other food service providers prepare and store food. You can't imagine the chaos and logistics of that kind of shared space."

Sharing a space with you has already left my thoughts in chaos.

"The commissary also offers facilities for cleaning, servicing and parking food trucks."

"That sounds ideal."

He shook his head. "It sounds like one day I'm accidentally going to end up with a cooler full of taco fillings and no way to incorporate them into my menu."

She laughed but touched her lips to remember the stakes of the conversation. "I don't see what my presence has to do with convincing John and Patty. It's a property transaction."

Nolan reached for her but pulled his hand back at the last minute. "I've shown them my business plans and made them a competitive offer, but they won't budge and accept it. You managed to charm them. They liked you and they like the idea of young lovers."

"Everybody likes me after a free glass of white wine."

He smiled. "Maybe you should add cocktail hour to your yoga classes."

She raised her eyebrows. "Stick to running your own business."

He shook his head and ran a hand through his hair. "I'm sorry. That wasn't fair to you. I saw what you did on the beach during your class and you were great — calm and attentive to everyone who needed you. You see the subtleties of what people need to be comfortable."

I'm listening.

"I've been sucking up to Mr. and Mrs. Abramowitz for months. They've known me since I was a kid, but they've told me they won't budge on their property until they believe they're moving in the right direction. They might need to see me as a stable community member before they'll sign a contract. If that's it, then so be it. What's the difference between a friendship and a fake relationship?"

"Heat," she whispered.

"What?"

She cleared her throat. "So now I'm a gateway to respectability?"

He cocked his head and considered his response, the silence stretching between them. "You're fulfilling an older couple's fantasy for the next generation and giving them a reason to release their stubborn hold on their unused property."

I liked it better when I was the date you couldn't quite have. She shook her head. "That's just it. I don't want to time my moves to match a laugh track. I don't want the confusion and vulnerability of second-guessing every word you say and doubting my place in the world. I thought we had limits." Her voice cracked and she hiccupped.

He reached for her and pulled her to him.

She pressed her cheek against his chest and instead of tasting cardamom, she tasted the salt of her tears. Missing the passion and excitement of their stolen kisses, she struggled to stem her tears. "I don't usually cry this much."

Nolan rubbed her back, shifting his stance to absorb the weight of her feelings. "I didn't mean to put you in that situation, Wylie. I just saw the three of you laughing and I went along with it. For a minute, I thought you just wanted an apology for me touching your butt."

She hiccupped and wiped away her tears. "So you're saying you were desperate?"

"For your butt?"

She snorted and wiped her face of signs of her embarrassment. *When are the dynamics between us going to level out?* "Something like that."

He looked down at her and his posture stiffened as he held himself back. "I still want to take you out to dinner. I still want to see your eyes light up when I walk into the room. Nothing about my feelings for you has changed, but for a minute, I just forgot everything we said when we were alone. I saw the deal and I saw the effect you had on them without thinking of the ramifications. Chalk it up to poor impulse control."

She swallowed.

Nolan ran his hand through his hair, each stroke rekindling her warmth and attraction to the man.

"Give me a break, Wylie. I know I can do better."

But do I want you to?

"We can flirt and wink as much as you want, Nolan, but hands off."

He released her and stepped back. "That's what you want?"

She inhaled, holding on to the limits of a pretend relationship like the lifeline she needed to stay afloat. Hadn't she thrilled to his touch before reality had set in? *He's not the only one benefitting from a fake relationship. I can use the Abramowitzes as an excuse to keep my vulnerable emotions under control and still spend time with him. It'll buy me a while until I can trust my instincts.*

"It might not be what I want, but it's what I need."

"You're kind of amazing, Wylie, to do this for me."

She shook her head and ushered him from her room before she exposed her real desires and motives. "Thanks, dear."

* * * *

When they arrived at the commissary, Nolan turned up the music volume in the Bronco and jumped out of the truck. The facility buzzed with the chaos of a schoolyard, but he strode into the melee and dealt with the logistics of provisioning and preparing his food truck for the night. Workers in chef's whites greeted him before giving him updates on their completed work or changes to the menu. Drivers handed him clipboards to sign and asked about unloading freight.

Wylie tried to absorb the flow of information. *He was right about chaos and unimaginable logistics. How does he handle this level of activity every night?*

"Easy does it on the pepper in the tomato soup," said a honeyed voice.

Wylie recognized the familiar cadence and turned away from the orchestrated activity of the commissary's worker bees.

The speaker stilled the hand of a man holding a large shaker of red pepper. "Not everyone can hang with your masochistic Mexican taste buds."

The man moderating the tomato soup could have easily been the same one who had challenged Rusty's ego with claims of targeting and social profiling. His voice reminded her of old newscasts and classic movie heroes.

Searching for the actor, she squinted and scanned the women packaging baked goods. The woman raised her head and Wylie swore she saw neon green earrings hidden beneath the woman's pinned black curls and industrial hair net. *I'm surrounded by ringers. Did they all show up to the Social Club as a favor to Nolan?*

"We'll have a big crowd tonight." Nolan pulled a checklist from a basket waiting at the end of the prep table. "This event is part of a year-long celebration of movies, food and music underwritten by the *Los Angeles Times*." He jerked his head toward Wylie. "She's new, so I need someone else to come along and help us keep up."

Every person in the space dedicated to Modesto raised their hand.

"You won't be able to see the massive three-story inflatable movie screen, the local bands providing pre-show entertainment or visit any of the other food trucks until we're closed down." Half the hands went down and Nolan nodded. "On the bright side, tips will probably make up for your disappointment."

The man holding the red pepper shook his head and reached for the paprika.

"Come on, Esther," Nolan said to the probable samba dancer, "You're up."

"*Que sorte!*" the woman said. She unbuttoned her jacket and headed toward the exit.

Wylie smiled. *Well, they have more than one reason to like him.* She followed the woman to the parking lot and cleared her throat. "Hi, I'm Wylie."

"*Boa tarde.*"

Boa? Wylie a deep breath. *She's got to speak enough English to have responded to Nolan's offer.* "Tell. Me. What. To. Do?"

The woman laughed and Wylie inventoried everything she knew about Brazilians. Rio de Janeiro and the World Cup seemed like poor approximations for their culture, so she gave up on small talk, shook her head and walked toward the food truck. *She'll make friends when she's ready.*

A stack of painted bistro chairs chained through the legs and a box of multi-colored prayer flags told her she had found the right truck. Nolan exited the commissary building and entered the work yard as she wondered whether to load the items into the food truck or find the keys to his Bronco.

"Okay, Esther, let's bring the truck to the building so the guys can load the food and the bistro sets." He tossed his car keys to Wylie. "You load up the packaging and the utensils in the Bronco and follow me out of the yard."

She caught the keys and stared at them. "You want me to drive your truck?"

"Is that going to be a problem?"

No, just an unexpected perk. She gave thanks she had not offered to drive her vehicle. "Yes, chef."

Nolan grinned.

"*Então vamos meter o pé antes que o Rio de Janeiro alague.*"

"Do you have any idea what she's saying?" she asked Nolan.

He shook his head.

She sighed. "Maybe it's better if I don't know."

* * * *

The collection of food trucks at the event made Wylie blink in alarm. She had seen Nolan's truck perform well in front of the yoga studio, but the diversity of this scene overwhelmed her senses. The street food and catering options rivaled the population of the United Nations as she put the Bronco in park and surveyed the signs advertising Middle Eastern, Thai Fusion, Indian, Mexican, lobster, wings and fries. *We're just shilling healthy food at a decent price.* She frowned. *What's the competitive advantage?*

Nolan climbed down from the driver's seat and threw open the back doors of the truck. "Stack the paper goods by the door and Esther will put them where they go." He fired up the generator and plugged in a strand of patio lights. "After we finish the stock, jump over to the bathroom and give your hands a good scrub up to the elbows. The first customers will be here by the time we get everything set up."

She jumped into action and gave thanks for her tennis shoes against the cool traction of the grass. "Just tell me what to do, bossman."

They fired up the equipment, set up the bistro chairs and sanitized their hands as Nolan dished out gloves to her and Esther. "This event is too big for the inspectors to show up, but if anyone has questions on licenses or food handling, send them to me."

"Wait! Where will I be?" Wylie asked. The reality of the situation made her panic and second-guess her ability to be helpful. *Will the health department break down the door and cite me for some vague regulation I should have learned in a certification class?*

"Buttering sandwich bread and running the other room-temperature foods. Esther will man the heat and I'll take the orders. A twelve-year-old kid could do your job."

Thank you for small mercies. She closed her eyes and wondered how hard it could be to swill rice and beans with a sprinkling of cilantro. *I mean, if a twelve-year-old could do it…* She thought of herself at that age, one eye trained on adulthood. *I've come a long way since then.*

The truck next to them advertised Korean-Mexican fusion such as tacos and burritos filled with Korean-style barbecued meats and kimchi. A woman leaned on the windowsill, chewing gum while she waited for the gates to open and a customer to appear. The men loitering near the side doors wore tight white shirts that revealed large biceps and a heat-honed sheen that spoke of hours and hours spent working the food truck. She swallowed and dismissed her ambitions for a carefree, playful mood. *I think they've advanced beyond the cilantro.*

Chapter Nine

Wylie collapsed into a bistro chair. Her legs and back hurt, but she worried about the tightness in her chest. The constriction felt like weight and reduced her breath to a slow wheeze. *Now is not the time.* Pulling air into her lungs, she tried to fight the pressure of an asthma attack without using her inhaler.

Nolan, oblivious to her struggles, unplugged patio lights as the stewards of the neighboring trucks emerged to smoke, change their shirts and partake of their evening meals.

When the tightness persisted, she pulled a rescue inhaler from her purse and triggered the medication to open her airways. She watched the steady stream of cars leaving the venue as her lungs opened and she drew easier breaths. The neighboring workers watched her for a moment, still gauging her reaction and debating the need for intervention. "Damn allergies," she said to diffuse her embarrassment.

What about this night hasn't been embarrassing? She had updated her status and laughed when a few patrons mentioned the 'Mini Mako' promo code, but the rest of her evening had skirted disaster. Within the first hour, she had burned her arm, dropped two orders and developed a guilt-complex about the line of customers waiting outside Nolan's window. Free of the demand of hungry patrons, she pulled off her hairnet and crumbled it into a wad. *I doubt we got very many tips.*

"Not so bad, *Gatinha*."

Wylie winced and looked at Esther. The able-bodied woman had manned the hot plates and grill with an innate dexterity that must have predated her samba skills. "I'm sorry I messed up so many orders. I usually think I'm a quick study."

The woman laughed and adjusted her earrings. "When the popular trucks launched in 2009, people used to wander up to the truck like *dos mortos-vivos*. Zombies," she clarified. "I worked in my momma's clothing shop after school and I'd see the office workers staring at their mobile devices with puzzled expressions and fierce determination. They waited in line for hours to order fusion tacos and quesadillas drizzled with sweet chili sauce, but few of them knew what to expect until their first bite."

"That was a decade ago." Wylie hung her head and realized those hungry hordes had abandoned their physical keyboards and outdated operating systems. *How quickly will they abandon beachside yoga and the health emphasis that sustains my livelihood?*

"Don't matter in this town," Esther replied. "Social media trained them to be patient, especially at a venue like this one. Nobody comes out here expecting fast food and flawless service. They just want to have a good time."

"Well, I hope we met their expectations."

Esther laughed. "*Gatinha*, the night is just getting started."

"Well, it can't get much worse."

Esther looked at the group of employees hanging out by the next food truck. One man sprayed a mixture of water and bleach into a trash can while the other tied garbage bags and tossed them into a pile of refuse waiting behind the truck. The third employee, a woman with pale pink hair, looked at Wylie's coworker and smiled. Esther turned to Wylie. "So what's up with you and bossman?"

"Up?" She swallowed and looked for Nolan.

He stood shoulder-to-shoulder with another vendor in front of the electrical panel for a humming truck.

"Why does something have to be 'up' with us?"

"I've never seen two people work so hard to keep their distance in all my life. I'm friendlier with *o carteiro*."

Wylie smiled. "Maybe that's your cup of tea."

The woman stood and stretched, her millennial pink hair brilliant against her tanned skin. "Not exactly."

"Not exactly? Well, Nolan and I are not exactly seeing each other. It's complicated, but I'm here to work, just like you are."

"*Dá Deus nozes a quem não tem dentes.*"

Wylie sighed. "You're very selective with your English."

Esther looked at her and smiled. "I'm very selective with everything." She fixed her hair and responded to their neighbor's invitation with the sensuous walk of a woman who knew everyone within a fifty-foot radius was watching her move.

There's a difference between grace and flexibility. Right now, I'm not sure I have either one. What's the difference between friendship and a fake relationship? I thought the answer was heat and clear expectations, but what happens when the bleed of dishonesty stains other friendships? I can't play housewife with Nolan and ignore him five hours later.

She held up her arm and looked at the raised red welt of the burn. *Next time it won't be my arm that gets hurt.*

"Did you put some cream on that?"

She looked up and found Nolan standing at her side, illuminated by the vague glow of distant headlights. The slow bustle of decommissioning faded from her mind until the two of them remained in a cocoon of warm spring air. She scooted over and made room on the metal steps imprinted with a diamond pattern. "I'm pretty sure I slowed you down tonight."

He sat next to her and shook his head. "We made it work between the three of us."

"But you're paying me to carry my share of the load."

He exhaled. "Why are you so hung up about earning your place?"

She laughed, too nervous to ruin the easy comradery of the moment. "I don't want to calculate my contribution to your bottom line. It'd be low."

"Wylie," he said, looking at her, "it's not a matter of whether you earned your keep or not. I asked you to do a job and you did your best to accomplish the task. If anything, kudos for doing the work with little training and zero experience."

"I've been a waitress."

"I'd be more interested in your resume if you'd been a line chef."

She blinked to break the intimacy of his stare and focused on the splatter of food staining his jeans. The duck and weave of three people maneuvering in the shared space had thrilled and confounded her. *If his jeans are stained with beans and sour cream, mine probably look and smell a lot worse. But it doesn't matter. I still wanted him. I still noticed every time our skin brushed. Stick to your guns, Wylie. This gig is strictly look but don't touch.* She tucked her hair behind her ears. "Sorry, chef, no such luck."

"For what it's worth, I think you did fine. I don't want you to push yourself too hard." He picked up her arm and turned it to expose the red welt. "I don't want you to risk these kinds of burns." He lowered his head and kissed the exposed skin near the welt. "I don't want to see you get hurt."

She pulled back her arm and tucked it in her lap, ignoring the tingle from his lips and the soft scratch of his beard. Instead of meeting his gaze, she focused on the line of taillights leaving the festival. "Sometimes I can be too transactional about my place in the world. I guess it's a holdover from being an only child with too much access to my family's finances. I don't want to be a burden on anyone."

He stayed silent and adjusted his position.

She felt the wind slide between their bodies and wished she could lean into his warmth. "And the people who come to my yoga classes? You know, they're not like my friends. I know I'm providing a service and they're paying me to be nice to them."

"I'm paying you to be nice to me too," he said. "Does that mean I should be suspicious of every smile?"

Should I be suspicious of every kiss? She shook her head. "I think I'm getting the better end of the deal, assuming we can stick to our arrangement."

He sighed. "I know what you mean, though. It's hard to manage expectations and family is the worst. Patty and John were like grandparents to me, but they still think I'm a kid. My mom thinks this food truck is a hobby. I don't want her to be right about that assumption."

She wiped the grit from her forehead and glanced at her hand to confirm the grease she felt. "I can think of more relaxing hobbies."

He laughed, the sound deep and low, like the rumble of the first food trucks departing from the festival grounds. "I'm sure you can."

"Did you cook at a restaurant before you decided to open this food truck? Is it like your baby or something?" she asked.

He scratched his beard. "Something like that. I was standing on a street corner in Europe with a fifteen-dollar sandwich and a can of soda and it struck me I'd be just as full with peanut butter and jelly."

"But it wouldn't taste as good." She stretched out her legs and leaned against the next step.

"Taste is a matter of perspective. Have you ever eaten an apple when you feel like you're starving? That cold, crisp sweetness seems like manna from heaven. How could anything taste better? People in this city associate food trucks as being a source of gluttony and indulgence. We put calorie counts on the menus, but they don't do a cost-benefit analysis when they're deciding what to order."

"I've never thought of eating as an economic transaction."

Nolan smiled. "You were never truly down on your luck. Calories and nutrients-per-dollar count when you're counting pennies to cover the tax."

She thought about attributing her clumsiness to the restlessness of nights spent sleeping in the SUV, but the memory of sitting on the beach next to Penny Lane reminded her of the difference between forty-eight hours and a lifetime of upheaval. "So you think people come to the Modesto food truck for lowest cost nutrition?"

"Have you ever been to that town? Its slogan is 'Water. Wealth. Contentment. Health.' There's something so humble about laying out life's needs on an arch running through the center of town. People don't need luxuries to be happy. They need the building blocks of life. Fill a need and you're supporting the whole structure."

She wrinkled her nose. "I have been to Modesto."

He laughed. "At least I didn't name it 'Hollister'. Anyway, I think people will recognize a good deal when they see it, and we will work hard to reward them with good taste. Milk, eggs, potatoes, carrots, beans and peanuts aren't sexy, but they'll fill your stomach and give you nutrients."

"The yoga bunnies aren't worried about nutrient deficiencies."

Nolan laughed. "That segment of the population with unhealthy choices... We pitch our menu as a health-conscious alternative for the crowd in performance stretch fabrics. International fusion plays better to the Hollywood Night Market on Thursday evenings. A good marketer needs to be nimble and quick to respond to the needs of the crowd."

"But don't you lose your vision if you're always pivoting?" She thought of him standing in a steam-soaked bathroom each morning, trimming his beard. Did his bright green eyes register the small adjustments required by life or did he run a trimmer along his neck and trust a barber to take care of the rest?

"Do you want to hear my vision?"

I want to believe you have one, she thought, but took a deep breath, prepared not to laugh at his dreams to dominate a basin full of image-obsessed social media addicts.

"So picture a fast-casual restaurant without full table service."

She imaged him with a fork, a knife and a fifteen-dollar sandwich. Clever décor, but not so clever that it bordered on kitsch.

"The menu consists of high-quality seasonal food with few frozen or processed ingredients. It's the food people would cook for their families on a limited income."

"I can see how that homeliness would appeal to people." She left out the 'some' people.

"It'll meet their needs without making a mess in their kitchen. Low prices. No guilt, no empty stomachs."

She repeated, "No empty stomachs," and nodded, knowing people could subsist on cold sandwiches but they needed more to thrive. "It's a good concept."

"Except I don't want to create a concept that can support ten to twenty units. I'm thinking about the scale of McDonald's."

She looked at him. "Nolan, you're crazy. There have got to be thousands of McDonald's in this country."

"Try fourteen thousand," he said with a smile.

"But they're all franchises, aren't they?"

He nodded. "They started with a successful concept and proved it can work. I'm trying to do the same thing but without the deep fryer."

"The scale is mind-boggling."

He leaned back and shifted.

She felt the tingling warmth of skin just out of reach, but she kept her back straight. *I could relax into that warmth.*

"Well, at least you didn't laugh."

She waved at the dusty chaos of retreating food trucks. "So this is?"

"Proof of concept."

The scale of his ambitions took her breath away and she did collapse, wondering for a moment if his grandiose ambitions hid a stubborn refusal to accept reality. Then she thought of the way he had walked into the commissary and taken charge, as quickly as he had assessed her needs and taken charge of her life. *Wait! That's not right. He gave me an option. Isn't that what he's offering the rest of the world? A streamlined practical solution?*

She could see how the improvisation of running a business of wheels would transition to running a brick-and-mortar store. Nolan could pivot to changing conditions, navigating the weather and making do if he ran out of diesel or propane gas. The little hiccups of life on the road would help him beta-test Modesto with minimal overhead. "But you can't be everywhere when you open more than one store?"

"So you believe in me?"

"I believe you've got big plans."

He laughed and pulled her closer as the dust faded and the first stars appeared above the glowing skyline.

"I'll find leaders who take ownership. Just because someone is a great employee doesn't mean they'll be a great manager."

"Esther would be a good manager."

"Exactly. Everyone will start at entry-level so they can learn the ins and outs of the business. I'm not naïve enough to expect smooth sailing. At times, I know we'll need all hands on deck and I'll need a fleet of captains to get shit done."

She wondered if life in the valley would change with the introduction of Nolan's unpretentious food. "I'm probably not a good candidate for management."

"That's okay," he said. "I admire your tenacity and willingness to work for what you want, even if your goal is different from mine. There's a lot of pride in being the boss, even if the world requires you to get certification and insurance to do it."

Her thought jumped to her insurance needs. "Do you offer your employees decent health insurance?"

"Sure, but it's costing me a fortune. I'm hoping universal coverage will kick in before I have to review bids for a national network and consider the tradeoffs of large-scale benefit coverage."

She nodded, wondering how far her life would drift if practical considerations stopped weighing her down. She thought of her parents in Oregon, retired to a simpler life after spending decades grappling for a hold in the basin. There was something to be said for the people who stayed and fought, even if the odds remained stacked against them. "I know someone who would show up at the crack of dawn to get the job done."

"Good, keep that person in mind. I don't need them now, but one day soon, I should."

Will Penny Lane make it that long?

She turned to look at Nolan, but the intensity of his gaze took her breath away. She leaned forward, searching for an outlet to access the passion coursing through his blood. Before her brain could override her muscle memory, she cupped his stubble-tinged jaw and pressed her lips against his surprised mouth. He froze but remained beside her, clearly waiting to see what she would do next. She angled her lips and teased his, pulling against the reserve she had needed in a moment of vulnerability.

He caressed her back, urging her to deepen the kiss without taking control of it. She closed her eyes and let his taste surround her senses. *How many first kisses will we have? Does it matter if this is the one? The one that finally means something exists between us with enough necessity and desperation to flavor our attraction?*

When she began to pull back, to give him space to object, his hold tightened and he kissed her back, gently at first, until the need in her core swelled and she demanded more.

He smiled against her lips. "You know, I have a pretty good bed back home."

Instead of slapping him, she laughed. "What's wrong with mine?"

His eyes darkened and he reached for her. "Nothing if you'll let me join you there."

She listened to the alarm bells ringing in her subconscious. "We've got rules, Nolan. No lip-to-lip PDA."

"Show me the Abramowitzes," he said. "Those rules are for them."

She bit her lip.

"That kiss happened because we both wanted it to happen. Use a different label for our offstage actions. To me, it's organic attraction."

Rising, she brushed the dust from her clothes. Kissing Nolan felt like a luxury, one that seemed out of reach until she felt like she needed him the most. "Not in my budget."

Esther coughed. "I'm generally not into threesomes, but that kiss looked hot."

Nolan cleared his throat. "Good. We weren't offering you one."

"Did you forget about the food truck?"

Wylie rubbed the diamond imprints from her ass and wondered if the stain of lipstick on Esther's neck was an oversight or a purposeful addition. "Nope. Break's over."

Esther smiled. "All right, Mr. and Mrs. There's-Nothing-Going-On-Between-Us. Let's get this truck back to the commissary so we can all get down to business."

They retraced their steps to the abandoned playground, Nolan and Esther in the food truck while Wylie drove the Bronco.

Instead of minimizing her desire, the distance from Nolan gave her an excuse to inhale the scent of him and open little compartments in the truck, searching for clues to the treasure she would find when she got brave enough to strip him naked.

The preparers had clocked out, so Nolan parked the truck while Esther climbed into her car and waved goodbye.

Wylie lingered near the Bronco, not shy but not sure if she wanted the full scrutiny of the security cameras.

She shoved her hands into her pockets and rocked back on her heels.

"Who says we need to wait for a bed?" he asked.

She tossed him the keys. "I've spent enough nights trying to get comfortable in a bucket seat. I'm not interested in repeating that experience."

"What does interest you?"

She thought of the sun glistening on his sweat-soaked muscles and the allure of a hot shower, drenched in sin. "Clean sheets. Stress-free mornings. A year without evictions."

He laughed and climbed behind the wheel. As soon as she followed and secured her seatbelt, he leaned across the center console and turned her chin. "Wylie, we can play these games for a very long time, but make no mistake, I want to spend time with you. You've got a twenty-minute ride to decide if you're ready to do this or go back to being friends. I don't want to stumble into that house and have to ask again."

The night air warmed her skin as she faced the wind and let the pulsing beat of the radio waves lift her mood. *Twenty-six-year-olds are not only figuring out their lives. They're also getting laid. It's called having friends with benefits.* She glanced at Nolan, who wore the same self-confident smile that had graced his cheeks since the moment they had pulled out of the commissary. *This man knows what he wants. Can't I admit that I want it too?*

The truck climbed the hills of Pacific Palisades and she let her senses drift, wondering if Monument Street would feel foreign or carry the enticing appeal of a well-lit home. The silhouette of the eucalyptus tree loomed above the streetlights and well-lit houses, and she recalled the view from the rooftop deck. *When I stand up there, I feel like I'm on top of the world.*

Economically diverse neighborhood, my ass. Three cheers for the commune and being twenty-six.

She laughed when she caught sight of her homely SUV sitting on the street across from the late-model Mercedes. Someone had moved it to its rightful place on the street but, instead of being insulted, she found the passive-aggressive gesture charming and relatable. *That will teach me to leave my keys on the kitchen table.* "No parking permits required for the weekend?"

Nolan shook his head, triggering the garage and claiming the empty spot next to the Corvette. "Not on Sundays."

"I wonder if the tow company takes the day off."

He put the truck in park. "I doubt it."

The light of her bravado dimmed beneath the fluorescence of the garage lights. Why shouldn't they be together? She was an independent yoga instructor finding her footing, and Nolan was a food truck vendor serving the masses. Strip away the gleaming mansion and no-one would blink if two adults succumbed to a night of passion and ignored the possibility of lingering regrets.

"Do we need to sneak past Antonia's bedroom?" Wylie asked. "She doesn't strike me as the possessive type, but it'd be nice to know if you two have shared history so I don't have to worry when she prepares dinner."

"That is not what I want to think about right now."

"What do you want to think about?"

"You. Making good on every stolen kiss I've had to pretend I didn't want to chase to its rightful conclusion."

Wylie smiled and opened the passenger door. "You did offer me a hotel room outside Rusty's club."

Nolan inhaled. "You should have taken me up on the offer. We both would have slept better that night."

Her dancing retreat faltered as she realized that Nolan's appreciation of her life spanned two days. Her lean muscles and blonde hair existed somewhere between cocktail waitress and homeless beach entrepreneur. *What do I expect him to see?* She took a deep breath, remembering his resolve on the deck and his praise on the steps of the food truck. Her plans for security might not involve thousands of franchise locations, but they meant something to her and Nolan had acknowledged them.

"I'm trusting you'll remedy the situation once we get to the second level." She opened the door to exit the garage and blinked against the blue light of the media and game room. An action hero glared from the drop-down projection screen and the semicircle of eclectic seating held every one of her new roommates. They turned toward her entrance and she caught the glint of cinema light reflecting off their curious expressions. "Pull up a seat," Antonia said from the comfort of a boxy, overstuffed chair. She picked up the remote and paused the action. "We're just getting started."

Wylie lingered in the doorway as Nolan left the garage and closed the distance between them. On the far side of the impromptu theater arrangement, snacks graced the ping-pong table and a stack of red plastic cups waited on the bar. Wylie saw her bedraggled, food-stained reflection in the mirror behind the shelves of liquor bottles. *We're not the only two people living in this house.*

She turned to Nolan. "It's going to be obvious if we skip movie night and host our entertainment on the second floor."

"I didn't know you were such an exhibitionist."

"Seriously?"

He eyed the stairs leading to the next floor and adjusted the fit of his pants. "I think they'd understand."

"Do you always get what you want?"

"No," he said, glancing toward the collection of recliners, "but I'm willing to give you what you want."

"Why?" she whispered.

He smiled and claimed a quick kiss while every person in the house watched them. "Because I'm starting to see the value of the reward." He slid past her and settled on the autumnal-colored loveseat with velour fabric and scrolling dark wood trim.

Well, at least a few extra food stains won't destroy it. Taking a deep breath, she sat next to him, thought better of it and nestled beneath the weight of his arm.

Neil tapped away on his phone, but Jack stood and stretched. "Do you want some popcorn? A gin and tonic?"

Wylie thought of Dottie's towel-clad dismissal and the four months they had spent sharing a Montana neighborhood apartment. More bonding over Netflix and takeout might have given Dottie second thoughts, but Wylie knew she would have never found her way to the hills of Pacific Palisades without a lavender-scented kick in the butt. She smiled at Jack. "Yeah, popcorn and a drink would be great."

Antonia resumed the movie and the action on the screen reclaimed the group's attention. Wylie dropped her head against Nolan's shoulder. "You didn't mention movie night."

He toyed with the end of her ponytail. "I had other things on my mind."

"Like what?"

He glanced at the stairs and shifted on the floral fabric. Wylie smiled, knowing that a decade ago she might have pulled a throw blanket over their laps and done her best to test his patience with an illicit hand job. Now she just smiled and closed her eyes, knowing the movie probably would not last more than two hours. *Some things are worth the wait.*

Chapter Ten

Sunlight seeped beneath the door. Wylie blinked and found her bearings. Despite the size of her room, the bed felt as cozy as a new slipper. She longed to burrow into the blankets and spend the day oblivious to the window-filled hallway, but she threw back the covers and shook her head. *I have a studio interview today and I'm not running down the hill to get there like Nolan did.*

Sleepy confusion twisted her features and she reached for the curtains to let sunlight clear her mind. *I'm not supposed to be waking up alone. There's supposed to be a snoring, hot-blooded man next to me.* Sunlight highlighted the imperfections of the particle board furniture as she braced her hands on the edge of the bed. *Okay, maybe we wouldn't have both fit, but what the hell happened?*

Nothing about the aches and pains of her body spoke of midnight pleasures. She felt stiff muscles and a tight back earned from manning the food truck. An ache behind her eyes hinted at too many cocktails. To top off her frustration, she a sneaking suspicion she had missed the lauded return of the cinema hero. *Damn it, I hate it when I miss the climax.*

A morning stretch and strengthening sequence helped Wylie clear her mind, but as she came out of Downward Dog, she wondered whether sheepish regrets or banked desires waited beyond the bedroom door. *Only one way to find out.* She searched for clean clothes, wrapped herself in a bath towel and left the enclave carrying her toiletries.

Beyond the glass-paneled door, Nolan sat on the small outdoor couch with views of the surrounding hills and the glittering Pacific. Instead of lounging against the all-weather fabric, he was leaning forward and toying with a glass of orange juice sitting on the table.

She considered ducking into the bathroom for a shower, but she needed to know whether she owed the man an apology for passing out cold. "Did I finish all the gin?"

He smiled but left his sunglasses in place. "I doubt you could have finished all the gin. Neil just made a grocery run to the warehouse club."

Exhaling, she remained by the door and shaded her eyes against the sunlight. "I mean, I'm pretty sure the movie was supposed to be the aperitif and we were supposed to be the main course."

"Does that make me the side of meat?"

"Not exactly," she said, "but I definitely had thoughts of licking you clean when we left the food truck."

His hands stilled. "You fell asleep."

"You should have woken me up." She took a step toward him.

He grinned. "I tried."

Two steps and a smile. "Next time, try harder," she said.

"That type of encouragement would be off-putting to most men." He turned to face her and ran a hand through his hair.

She stopped and eyed his orange juice, wishing the man had carried two glasses up the stairs so she could be sure he was waiting for her. *Maybe he changed his mind about what he wants.* She recalled Rikard's advice. *Maybe this is just his private space.* The newness of their arrangement felt like a thin veneer of history separating her particle-board enclave from her nights on the street. She cleared her throat. "Well, thanks for being so chivalrous."

He took off his glasses and the intensity of his gaze stole her breath. *That's the man I should have seen when reality pulled me from my sleep.* She wondered if his rigid posture had less to do with the comfort of the couch and more to do with the possibility of self-restraint. "In fact, let the record state that I'm all in."

"All in?" He rose and closed the distance between them, reaching for her and pulling her close, his hand anchoring their connection at the small of her back.

Wylie looked up and forgot about the practicalities of bathing and maintaining appearances. She felt the steady assurance of his drive as he'd strode into the commissary, issuing orders and calling for updates like he owned the place. She trusted the type of man who noticed a burn wound and asked her if she had found time to address it after her flubbing her way through a night inside the food truck. "Yeah. Quite frankly, Nolan, I'm ravenous."

His gaze softened as he focused on her lips. "Last night you told me I tasted like a turmeric-laced mojito."

She wrinkled her nose. "That sounds disgusting."

"I know. I half-carried you up the stairs and put you to bed."

"How many drinks did I have?"

He kissed the side of her neck and she closed her eyes. "Just two, unless you and Antonia were taking shots while I took orders."

Wylie tilted her head, hoping he would take more than the simple liberty of a warm kiss. "We weren't. I meant to say that you taste like citrus, mint and spice, all at the same time. Like something fresh and cool I never expected to find."

"Hmm." The sound reverberated in his chest as he pulled back. "I never expected to find you either."

She cocked her head. "Give me fifteen minutes in the shower and your tongue can play hide and seek on every last inch of me."

"Tempting offer," he said before he released her, "but I have an appointment with John and Patty."

Frowning at the growing distance between them, she adjusted the towel separating her pride and her desire to feel the heat of his skin. *I'm laying myself out on a platter. Everything's been so easy until this week. Life has just fallen into place.* She smoothed the front of her towel. "And I have a job interview."

"So we'll reconvene?"

"Sure." She turned to leave and smiled. "Nothing says 'young love' like the pink stain of a hickey."

"And you're offering to give me one?"

"No, I'm pointing out that not everything you see is as simple as it seems." She winked. "Give my regards to Jonathan and Patricia."

* * * *

The strip mall studio building catered to Warm Seas' local yoga clients, but it also served as the hub for a network of studios scattered throughout the basin. The red-tile roof and cream stucco could have occupied any west coast street corner, but Wylie saw potential behind the tinted windows and steady stream of customers walking through the door. She reread the company's job description and repeated the words that could connect her skillset with the benefits of full-time employment.

Warm Seas LLC seeks a beautiful, experienced, spiritually grounded and lovely Yoga Instructor for our network of Los Angeles studios. Our Warm Seas Yoga Instructors are responsible for providing yoga instruction through a variety of transformative, impactful, entertaining and educational classes. Instructors will lead group classes in a safe, enjoyable and positive environment that promotes member wellness, engagement and transformative bliss.

"I can be lovely and transformative." She adjusted the vents as the idling SUV struggled to keep up with the demands of the sunbaked asphalt. "We'll just gloss over 'spiritually grounded'. Who the hell can claim that with a straight face?"

The clock ticked closer to the time of her interview, but she stayed in the car, working up the courage and self-confidence to win over a hiring manager with anecdotes of entrepreneurship and examples of how she liked trouble-shooting poses.

Her phone pinged with an incoming email and she clicked the app to soothe her nerves.

Dear Students and Aspiring Instructors,
We are canceling our classes for the next forty-eight hours. Please stay posted for further details. Thank you.
Cynthia

Wylie blinked to force the words to rearrange themselves into more meaningful sentences. *What is this 'we' business?* Her phone pinged again.

Join us at our temporary location, The Setting Sun Spiritual Center. Existing membership or class passes can be used at this location. New to our studio? Drop in for only $20 per class!

She exhaled and flipped to a messaging app to contact Cynthia and get information about the certification program. Before she could compose her text, she realized she had five minutes before the start of her interview and scrambled to get out of the SUV and arrange her wrap dress. *It's just a hiccup,* she told herself.

The hiring manager looked like he'd skipped every yoga offering for the past decade. His belly protruded past his belt and his shoulders slumped with the added weight left by decades of computer work and no desire to stretch. He gestured toward the office chair reserved for guests and settled back behind his desk. "Take a seat. I reviewed your website and client reviews. Very impressive."

She beamed, pleased to find her footing and get the interview off to a good start. "I'm very proud of what I've accomplished and have a lot of ideas to enhance the class offerings at Warm Seas."

He nodded and picked up her resume before she could list her ideas. "It says you're pursuing accreditation with Cynthia in Playa Vista?"

Swallowing, she glanced around the room and wondered who had picked out the motivational posters. *I hope there's no bad blood between them.* She took a deep breath to center her thoughts on the interview at hand. "Cynthia and her staff host a well-received accreditation class equal to two hundred hours of instruction. I've already completed forty online hours and the bulk of my classes. I have about forty hours left in the classroom to meet the national certification requirement."

The man set down her resume. "But Cynthia's studio is closing."

She shook her head, confident there had been a misunderstanding. "Oh, no. I think they're just relocating or consolidating or something."

He raised his eyebrows and her phone pinged again.

Dear Yoga Family,

Our hearts feel heavy as we announce we will not be reopening The Setting Sun Spiritual Center. Please know this was not an easy decision and we would like to take a moment to address the many rumors flying around town.

For a myriad of reasons, we fell behind on our Playa Vista rent. The owners of the building terminated our lease amid negotiations. They gave us a few days to vacate, but at no time did they serve a legal eviction.

It has been our most sincere pleasure to serve and share the benefits of yoga with the Los Angeles community for the past decade. The friendships we made mean as much to me as the life-changing moments etched in our memories. We want to thank every soul who walked through our doors to experience the benefits of a daily yoga practice.

The light in me bows and honors the light in you.

Namaste

Wylie buried the rage she felt and took a deep breath. She bit her lips to compose her thoughts before she met the hiring manager's curious expression. "How many people knew this was coming?"

The man shrugged. "It's not the first time she's fallen behind on her rent. We've hired a few of her past instructors and people talk."

"But it's a national accreditation program," Wylie said, "I'm sure the credit will transfer to another studio."

He handed her back her resume. "And I'm sure we'll have more job openings when you get it all straightened out. Until then, we can't hire you as an unlicensed professional."

She stood and scanned the file cabinets stacked with paperwork. "Would you have hired me before this debacle?"

"Probably," the man said. "Most of your students said you were quite lovely."

* * * *

Monument Street looked desolate when Wylie parked her SUV in front of the commune. Without the street-side Mercedes and the clutter of neighborhood vehicles, she could almost believe the house belonged to her. She eyed the spacious rooftop deck crowning the three levels. *I don't care how many neighbors are pissed off about that feature. It's built. Right now, I just want somewhere quiet and safe to be alone with views of the Pacific. I want to pretend my mess of a day was nothing but a bad dream.*

She hung her new parking tag from the rearview mirror and sighed, grateful she had accomplished one thing, despite the rest of her plans crumbling around her. The house code let her onto the ground floor and she climbed the stairs to the main floor, listening for signs of occupation. *The last thing I need is small talk with Neil and Jack, but I would settle for a cocktail with Antonia.* Then she remembered the frustrating loneliness and rejection of waking up alone. *Maybe I should lay off the cocktails.*

A cluster of apples sat on the table near the European kitchen. She picked one up and admired the main level. *Whoever designed this house has style.* She followed the open floor plan as it flowed from prep space to dining and living rooms. *Who am I kidding? This kind of place will never be mine.*

Then a breeze caught her attention and she glanced toward the large sliding glass doors. They stood open, creating the seamless indoor-outdoor living space Nolan had advertised. He sat in a patio chair, shirtless and facing the infinity pool. A chilled wine bucket and an open bottle of wine sat beside him. Steam rose from the heated pool water and hovered beneath the fog-tinged blanket of the spring air. *Who gets the other glass?*

She imagined the indulgence of slipping into that warm pool, naked as the sun set over the Pacific. Nolan would walk down the steps and join her, wordlessly pulling her close as he claimed her lips.

'*Hard day, honey?*' he would ask as he reached for her.

'*Shh,*' she would reply, '*let's not talk about it.*'

Instead, she strolled outside and took a bite of her apple, the loud crunch announcing her presence. "Well, the weather's nice enough."

Nolan laughed and nodded. "I wondered when you would get home."

She remained standing, wary of getting too close. "What did you do with the other roommates?"

He shrugged. "Various commitments."

Wylie's gaze narrowed. "Real or manufactured?"

He rose and faced her. "Does it matter?"

She took a deep breath. "I've had a shitty day. I'm not sure you want to deal with the fallout."

The memory of sitting on the diamond plated steps of the food truck felt more realistic than the pleasure of coming home to sun-heated pool decking. She scanned the mansions dotting the hillside as Santa Monica faded into the glow of the ocean. *This is just a game of pretending. What happened to the other man who could strip me naked with a glance?*

He poured another glass of wine and handed it to her. "I'm fresh out of gin-and-tonics."

She sipped the crisp white wine. "After a day like today, I might need tequila."

"Well, I'm sure we find some downstairs. At least sit down and tell me what's got you all riled up."

She sank into a chair, grateful for his intent and his ability to regroup. "Do you know what 'namaste' means?"

He sipped his wine. "Session's up? Pay on your way out?"

She smiled and sipped her wine, letting the cool tingle of the alcohol relax her senses. "When I was in high school, I assumed it had some deep religious connotation. Like, it sounded authentic and holy when the wizened man who taught my high school yoga elective said the word. Then I started going to studio classes and made friends with a girl named Natalia. She told me it means 'goodbye'."

"That's it?"

"Goodbye, person I respect."

He laughed. "Fair enough."

She looked at the hillside and frowned. "But people don't use it as a simple signoff. You see it everywhere now. T-shirts. Coffee cups. Nama-stay in bed. Namaslay. Namaste, Bitches. Who would buy a T-shirt that said 'Goodbye, bitches'?"

"I can think of several people," he said.

She looked at him and laughed, the moment releasing some of the steam and frustration that made her feel restless. "But they don't know what they're saying when they indulge in their little moment of cultural appropriation. It's like assuming that everyone from South Asia speaks the same language. Namaste literally means 'I bend to you', like you'd bend to a god. Hindi speakers use it as a respectful greeting, but the rest of the world slaps it on coffee cups like the bus map."

"Did someone say it at the wrong time?"

"No, worse," she said. "Cindy"—she waited for a reaction, but his expression remained relaxed. He toyed with his beard, content to let her to finish her story—"namaste'd me and the rest of her studio clients with a poetic, meaningless email. Instead of apologizing for bad business decisions, she sugarcoated her studio closing with a bunch of yoga-ese crap about good intentions."

"She closed down her studio with zero notice?"

Wylie swallowed another mouthful of wine. "The divine light in me bows to the divine light within you, but not enough to respect your time or your assets."

He offered to refill her glass.

She shook her head. "I'd like to take that divine spark and light a fire under Cynthia's ass. Without her, I don't have accreditation, I don't have a chance at job interviews, and I'll probably have to throw in the towel and retreat to my parents' house." She looked up from her glass. "That's not what I was planning to do with my life."

"Are you still thinking tequila?"

She stared at him. "How can you absorb all that crap I said and just let it roll off your back?"

"I learned to separate the things I can and cannot change."

Wylie rolled her eyes. "Please don't tell me you have a magnet with the serenity prayer."

"What?"

She thought of her mom's coping mechanisms and the way they had bonded over a 2003 animated film. Her mom had nodded in the darkness when a little blue tang fish reminded them to 'just keep swimming'. "Can't you take a moment to be bad when things don't work out?" she asked Nolan.

He reached for her hand, waiting until she set aside her empty glass to pull her into his lap. "I'm not big into yoga or prayers, but I know how to define a problem and look for solutions. It sucks that Cynthia closed her studio, but Modesto will still have a line of customers on Monday morning."

He traced the line of her collarbone and she shivered, wondering how the soft sweep of skin could capture her attention.

"But I've still got a lot of options and so do you. So, we can spend the rest of the night researching yoga stuff."

She laughed.

His hand dipped and skimmed the edge of her breast. "Or we can accept that Cynthia's an idiot and move on."

She held his gaze, feeling the warmth of his arousal beneath her leg. "I can see the appeal of what's on tap."

He nodded and reached for his wine, taking a sip. "And what is that?"

"Satisfaction," she said, meeting his gaze and looping her hands around his neck. "I've had a shitty day and I'm perfectly willing to swap relaxation for satisfaction."

"What about the rules?" he asked.

She inhaled, forced to choose between being right and being happy. Could she suspend the frustration of the day for the pleasure in his touch? His polished edge and cool authority had grabbed her attention from the start, but the moment their lips had touched amid the chaos of the Social Club, she'd known she wanted him. *Who else could shill sweet potatoes, rebuff my advances and still have the audacity to tease me with 'Mini Mako'? It doesn't matter how long it takes me to complete my certification and get my life back on track. Boundaries seem irrelevant when life keeps threatening to collapse around me.*

"We'll let them slip. This is just" — she waved her hands and glanced at the pool — "a release. No need for pretenses and cinematic diversions."

He laughed and set down his wine glass. "Is that what we call it when we suspend the rules?"

She shifted, watching his eyes widen as she licked her lips. "Organic attraction? Just call a spade a spade. I'm down for calling it pleasure."

He cradled her hips and dipped his head to press a kiss against her neck. "You're still thinking too much."

Wylie laughed. "It's called self-preservation. I'm too smart to jump in head-first and trust I'll never run out of air."

He slid his hand up to cup her ass and press her more firmly against him.

She closed her eyes, feeling the heat of his touch and wondering what it would mean to go all in. Last night's bravado and excitement paled against the intensity of Nolan's attention.

His hand stilled and his thumb rested in the small dip of her hipbone. "You're just getting started."

"I've still got plenty to lose."

He raised his eyebrows as she stepped away, crossed her hands in front of her chest and removed her athletic top. Freed from the shirt's built-in restraints, her nipples hardened in the evening air, and Nolan took a visibly deep breath. She smiled as she shimmed out of her pants and stood before him, proud of the naked desire reflected in his eyes.

Then he took a deep breath. "Why do I get the feeling I'm the one putting everything on the line?"

Wylie traced the ripple of his abs. "Why should either of us feel like we've got something to lose?" Before he could answer, she turned toward the pool and dove into the water. Breaking the surface, she blinked to clear her eyes and found him standing on the decking, backlit by the gorgeous house.

He picked up her wine glass and walked to the edge of the water, handing the glass to her. "Tell me about your day."

She stood in the water and took a sip. "Stalling?"

He shook his head and sat on the edge of the decking, a defined erection proclaiming his interest despite his continued absence from the pool. "No, just admiring the view."

The promise in Nolan's gaze allowed her to relax in the heated water and trust him to do just as he had promised. "I had a job interview, but I had to admit to the hiring manager that the instructor running my accreditation class had just closed her studio."

"Cynthia."

She nodded and saved her string of expletives for another time. "I don't know what happened. Her announcement email bordered on terse and defensive."

"What do you want out of life?"

Health insurance? A warm bed? None of the answers seemed worthy of the question. She looked toward the edge of the pool and imagined life running ahead of her like a well-rehearsed soap opera. "I don't know," she admitted. "I feel like I've never gotten started. I know the ending point—a house, some kids—but I have no idea how to get there."

He sipped his wine. "That's it?"

She nodded, letting the water absorb the weight of the question until her hair floated around her like a darkened halo. "It never occurred to me to dream of franchises and doing something that big."

"Sometimes 'big' is a penance."

She laughed and leaned back. "Tell me all your sins."

He abandoned his seat and walked toward her. "I spent too much time living in the moment."

She stood and smoothed back her hair, determined to meet him head on. "Living in the moment can be very rewarding." She swam closer to Nolan and rose from the shallow end. "The ending point seems inconsequential when we're both naked in the water."

He laughed and reached for her. "So you noticed that fact?"

She stepped forward until the heat of his arousal pushed against her stomach, as undeniable and present as the heavy air between them. "And what do *you* want?"

"Resolution." He grabbed her wrist and turned to kiss it. "The satisfaction of knowing I'm doing something good with the resources I have."

She shifted her hips and wondered what would happen if she abandoned the tension of the moment and climbed into his arms. "And what do you have?"

"Right now?" She nodded. "A beautiful and willing woman."

"You think I'm beautiful?"

He rolled his eyes and exhaled. "You're impetuous and fragile, loyal and determined."

"I'm not sure those were compliments." Doubt crept in and she pulled away.

He shook his head and drew her close once again. "You're living in the moment and it's beautiful, even if it gets you into trouble now and again."

"You don't feel like trouble," she whispered.

He lowered his head and captured her lips, his heat and spice covering the memory of apple-scented wine. He tore his lips from hers. "Tell me you'd be here with me in another place and time," he whispered. "Tell me your eyes would still fill with desire if we were standing in the middle of Oklahoma in an above-ground pool."

She laughed and pulled his head down until she could return his kiss. "That's not fair. I'd tell you anything right now."

"This commune has its perks?"

She unwound her arms and pulled him toward the edge of the infinity pool. When he resisted, she slipped behind him, winding her arms around his waist and pressing a kiss against the defined muscles of his back.

"Look at the city, Nolan. You can spend your days lost in the details or wake up every morning and be thankful for the sun."

He inhaled when she slipped her hand beneath the waterline and stroked his thigh, teasingly close to where she wanted to land. He turned and looked at her. "You are an unusual woman."

"Me?" she laughed. "I'm a beachfront yoga instructor. I'm a dime a dozen in this town."

"Wylie…" he began.

She replaced his view with her body, wrapped her hand around his cock and stroked his length until he took a deep breath, his eyes darkening as his pupils expanded and told him she had found her mark. "You're loyal."

She shifted her hips and tilted her head, softly biting him below the line of his collar and using her teeth to tug his skin as she worked his length. "I believe in better things when I'm with you."

He stiffened. "Like what?"

"Like more than a glimpse of satisfaction."

"If you keep stroking me like that, I'm going to need more than a minute to recover before you get your satisfaction." He cupped her face and claimed a kiss.

Her hand stilled and her attention faltered.

Pulling back, he grinned. "Right now you seem like the best thing I have going."

She smiled and looked at their reflections in the rippling water of the pool. "Better than pouring wine down my chest and tasting my nipples? Carry me to that lounge chair and let's do more than toast my shitty day."

He picked her up and she wrapped her legs around his waist. "I'm sorry your day went to hell."

"Don't worry about it."

He walked back to the decking, hitching her legs higher when she started to slip.

She tightened her muscles and gave thanks for every second of yoga that had toned her muscles and taught her how to hold a pose. "Worry about how I'm going to make you yell loud enough to wake the Abramowitzes."

His laughter kept the mood light between them. "I'm sure they won't mind."

She rubbed her chest against his and smiled when he groaned. "And do you mind?"

"Mind what?" He sank onto a chaise and settled her on his lap.

"Blurring the line between convenience and attraction."

He reached for the bottle of white wine and raised his eyebrows. When she arched her back, he filled the dip of her collarbone with cold white wine and they both watched the honeyed liquid overflow and trace the proud lines of her curves. She gasped at the contrast of his heat and the crisp liquid until he leaned forward and licked the trail, lingering to kiss her breast and draw her nipple between his lips. "The sweetest thing I've ever tasted," he whispered when their eyes met. "Don't doubt for a second that the attraction is real."

She leaned forward, desperate to push that attraction to its limits, but reality refused to release its final hold. "Nolan, do you have any protection?" He reached for his shorts and removed a condom, handing it to her like a final challenge. "Just one?"

He laughed. "I have plenty in my bedroom, but I don't want to risk putting on a show when the roommates get home."

The reminder of shared space pushed her to action. "I don't care whose bottom line gets the benefit of our rent. Right now, I'm happy to play along, and the only thing I want to feel is you inside me, my clit pressed against your fingers until I come."

"Wylie," he said, but she rolled the condom over his length and raised her eyebrows. "You want this?"

She raked her gaze over his naked, wet form. "Right now, I want everything on the menu." She straddled him and watched his eyes close in pleasure as she lowered her heat over his length. "Touch me, Nolan. Hold my hips while I rock against you and push us both over the edge."

He reached for her and she flexed her hips, feeling the pleasure of his presence deep inside her core. She shifted, picking up the pace until he met her thrust for thrust, their bodies rising together and falling until she began to moan and he pulled her close, slipping a hand between them to find her sensitive spot, his thrusts matching hers as she gripped his shoulders and set the pace until her world came undone in waves of rippling pleasure.

"Fuck me," he yelled, finding his release and tightening his hold on her hips as he rocked into her core.

Their breaths slowed and she dropped her forehead to his skin. "I'm trying."

"Trying what?" he asked.

She laughed, loving the way her thoughts scattered while their bodies remained connected. When she felt the wind against her skin, she disengaged so he could deal with the condom and the mess of their coupling. "You're the best roommate I've ever had."

"That's not saying much."

She smiled as memories of Dottie crept into her consciousness. *Keep it easy. I slept in my SUV because I thought I needed to control the lease. He's not asking for anything but a little trust.* She searched for solid footing beneath the chaise, then rose and stretched, ignoring the doubt creeping through her consciousness. *What if I folded too soon?*

His gaze remained fixed on her body.

Shaking her head, she inhaled, determined to hold on to the afterglow of her desire. "Well, given the alternatives, I can't imagine living alone ever again."

Nolan looked up and blinked. "I don't make a habit of getting naked with the people staying in this house."

The words hung between them. *Staying, not living. Not permanent.* She reached for her shirt. "Good. I'm feeling very territorial about our fake relationship. I didn't read the lease line for line, but I'm pleased with the fringe benefits."

He exhaled and looked toward the soft glow of the ocean shimmering beyond the hills. "I wasn't waiting for a fuck buddy. I was waiting for you, Wylie."

Stop looking at him like any of this is real, she told herself. *I haven't earned comfort and independence. This life is just make-believe until I go back to being myself.* She scanned the contemporary home and thought of the small room filled with the clothes and duffel bags that had transported her life from one pit stop to the next. She looked down and tried not to let the long lines of his body mean more than the quiet implications of his statement. "What did you expect when you opened that bottle of wine?"

"I don't know," he admitted. "It's hard to separate goals and desire when there's a beautiful naked woman in the pool."

She laughed, doing her best to center their confessions on common ground and preserve the possibility of a repeat performance. "What about when you find one in your bed?"

"Is it you?"

I want it to be me. She smiled as the sound of the garage door opening broke their moment of isolation. "Rikard's home."

He stood up. "I'm not sharing."

Laughing, she picked up a wine glass and finished the contents, hoping it would give her the courage to test the limits of what she had started and already feared to lose. "My place or yours?"

He eyed the third-floor windows. "Mine."

Chapter Eleven

The next morning, Wylie opened her eyes and watched Nolan sleep, looking at his eyelashes for much longer than necessary. His short brown hair and neat fade matched the hip street aesthetic of his food truck, but those eyelashes teased his skin like feathery crescent moons. She wanted to trace the line of his cheekbone and find the hidden strength behind his beard.

He opened his eyes and blinked, focusing on her. "Good morning, gorgeous."

She kept her head on the soft white pillow, content to let him wake up before she assaulted him with her demands for morning sex. When he smiled, she propped her head on her hand and passed the threshold between sated comfort and stated intent. He opened his lips to hers and wrapped an arm around her, pulling her onto the heat of his blanket-wrapped chest. "Good morning to you, too." She glanced toward the connected bathroom, wondering if they could multi-task.

He tightened his hold. "Where are you going?"

"To teach a beachside yoga class—every other day, rain or shine."

He frowned. "You can't teach yoga in the rain."

"No, but I usually huddle up with my customers at the nearby café and sip coffee while they indulge in the benefits of maintaining a community."

"They don't include you?"

She shrugged and sat up, savoring the soreness in her limbs but content to discuss the reality of her coming day. "I mean, they pay me, but I wouldn't consider them friends. We share coffee, but no one has ever suggested eating at the farmer's market or grabbing a cocktail. Why would they? We come from different worlds. You must see some of that at the food truck. There's always a line between the customer and the vendor."

He shook his head and reached for her. "I'm interested in blurring that line."

She scrambled from the bed and laughed. "Mini Mako already has plans. Got to make the money to pay the rent."

He threw back the covers. "But that sounds lonely. Shouldn't you enjoy what you do?"

They stood on opposite sides of the bed, each naked and ready for each other. Wylie shrugged. "I enjoy the people. Most people respond to that warmth and treat me well."

"Except Dottie."

"Maybe that says more about her than it says about me."

"Maybe there wasn't much there."

She wondered if Dottie had revealed her candy stash to her cousin or kept it ferreted away. *I found more satisfaction from savoring Nolan than treating him like something I couldn't have.* "Her loss. It is what it is."

* * * *

Fifteen people showed up at the class time and unfurled their beach towels beneath a cloudless blue sky. Wylie walked between them, greeting the regulars and taking time to connect with the new faces in the crowd. *Will they stay and make this a regular habit or fade into the anonymity of one-hit wonders?* The regulars greeted each other like old friends and Wylie cleared her throat as she began to lead the class. "Namaste."

For the next hour and a half, the group followed her instructions and Price Ross remained upright, grinning through the most complicated poses. At the end of the session, she smiled and headed straight toward him. "I met some of your clients. Patty and John Abramowitz. They spoke very highly of you."

"Oh, yeah?" he asked. "How did you put two and two together?"

Wylie smiled. "They were guests in the house where I live."

Price raised his eyebrows.

She searched for a way to clarify her statement. "I mean," she said, debating how far the relationship lie had to travel to give Nolan a chance of getting the kitchen, "my boyfriend's house. He already knew them. They're neighbors." She added the last-ditch comment to come off as genuine, but now it sounded lame.

"I've known the Abramowitzes for a long time. They were some of my first clients."

She smiled. "It can be a small town."

"So who's your boyfriend?"

The man who showed up shirtless and watched you fall on your ass? She swallowed, struggling to remember Nolan's last name. The commune's lease had listed everyone's identity, but she had focused on the clauses most likely to give her regrets. *I remember the 'W'. Wylie Winidad and* — she smiled — "Nolan Wilson."

Piece's eyebrows rose. "Their families go way back."

"Well, it's new construction, so I guess they tipped him off when it came up for rent." She blinked in the sunlight and ignored the ups and downs of the forty-eight hours she had logged in the contemporary house. "It must be nice to come back to that kind of continuity when you've been gone for years."

Price looked at her, his mouth opening then closing. He finally shook the sand from his beach towel, reached for his personal belongings and pulled a business card from his leather wallet. "Like you said, it can be a small town. Give me a call if you ever need my services."

She thought about Price bungling the Abramowitzes' property taxes and smiled. "I normally skate by with online software. I imagine they're making decisions on a whole other scale."

"Things can change," he said. "If you're lucky, that software won't be enough."

"What?"

The man saluted her. "Have a good day."

Wylie remained in the middle of the sand while the crowd encroached on the space formerly occupied by her class. *Things can change. Nolan can expand his truck into franchises. I can find a way to finish my accreditation, and* — she stopped and stared at the ocean — *it can all disappear in a moment.*

The house in the hills felt so far removed from the beginning of the week that she wondered how long the pleasures would last. She looked north toward tower eight and thought of Penny Lane. *Nobody wants to feel obligated to the needy, but don't we all need someone?* Life streamed through the lush oceanside park, but she walked to clear her head. Her calves ached and she stopped to stare at the scrubby hills on the other side of the Pacific Coast Highway. *People live there, and I don't want to live among them. I need health insurance. I need to finish my accreditation.* Narrowing her gaze, she followed the hint of a trail winding through the distant bushes. *I need to call Cynthia and give her a piece of my mind for dumping us on our asses. Nobody should treat other people like she did.*

Tower eight looked empty in the mid-morning light, but children played on the rope playground and Penny Lane stood at the edge of the water, singing off-key while the other beach-goers gave her a wide berth. Wylie walked up to the woman and considered what she could do to support her harmony. "Don't you know any other songs?"

The woman smiled and turned until Wylie no longer saw her tanned skin and age spots but saw the sunlight reflected from her blue eyes and the laugh lines that lined them instead. "It's such a pretty day. Why are you doing walking along the beach by yourself?"

"Looking for you," Wylie said.

Penny Lane laughed. "I told you I have too many people."

Wylie recalled the woman's backstory and realized there was nothing she could do to balance out Penny Lane's dearth of family resources and account balances, but Wylie knew she had more than pride and ambition — she had the ability to serve as the woman's friend. "I found a pretty sweet rental deal up in the hills."

"The hills can be dangerous," Penny said as a gull flew overhead.

"I don't think a bunch of tech-focused hippies are going to do me any harm. It's a bit of a commune, where everyone chips in and gets ahead on economies of scale." The older woman wrinkled her nose and Wylie continued to talk. "I don't think they want anything from me but rent and some household chores. It's a safe place. You could come sit by the pool with me. Take a hot shower and leave well-fed."

"You're always trying to feed me."

Wylie shrugged. "It's all I've got."

Penny Lane continued to stare at the ocean, humming to herself.

She strained her ear, trying to catch the point where lyrics gave way to spoken words, but the words never came. "You could tell me about your best friend, Larry, the one with Parkinson's disease."

"You remembered his name."

It was a memorable day. She shifted. "I'm sure you still miss him."

"He died."

She nodded but acknowledged there were some things about Penny Lane's life she could never understand.

"But I took care of him and stuck with him until the end," Penny Lane said.

"So let me take care of you for a day."

"You'll have to take me back to the bus stop."

She nodded. "I can do that."

"And find a new hobby after you're done clearing your conscience."

"Hobby?"

Penny Lane smiled. "I'm not above spending the day with you, but I told you, you've got to offer the whole package to make a difference in someone's life. One day of playing savior to the homeless isn't going to help either of us figure out what to do next."

"What about one day of eating ice cream and forgetting about our worries?"

The woman smiled. "I've always had a soft spot for ice cream. Did I tell you I grew up in New Jersey?"

Wylie nodded and turned to retrace her steps. "You told me about your mom."

"She was lovely," Penny Lane said.

* * * *

An hour later, they sat by the pool sunning their legs with an oldies station filling the gaps in their conversation. Penny Lane adjusted a borrowed baseball cap and dropped her metal spoon into the melted remnants of her ice cream bowl. "Are you sure this isn't a scam?" she asked. "I feel like the music's going to change and your roommates are going to emerge from the house in their cult robes. Am I the first victim?"

Wylie laughed and considered the strawberry ice cream she had found in the freezer. "Each roommate has a sphere of influence to help the household run seamlessly. Their method of governance cuts down on duplicate expenses and builds a sense of community dependence. The chatter I've seen on the messaging app reads like the newsfeed for a boring club—local events, house details and zero gossip."

Penny Lake opened one eye. "Cult."

"I swear, so far, so good. They were friendly the other night when Nolan and I came home to find them watching a movie."

"Who's Nolan?"

She cocked her head. "Good question. He's"—she hesitated, wondering how to describe a man she still wanted to get to know—"one of the original roommates and he owns a food truck that serves basic food for fair prices. I think he envisions expanding the truck into a kind of nonprofit restaurant chain."

"Nobody's going to invest in that," Penny Lane said.

"I know," Wylie admitted, "but it's nice to have a dream."

She thought about the intimacy of the previous night and the pleasure of knowing Nolan had been waiting for her, his arms wide with an open invitation. Well, at least an open bottle of wine. *Although, theoretically, I paid for a fifth of that wine.* She smiled. *Aren't we modern?*

Penny Lane slouched on the chair and closed her eyes. "Maybe you need your own dream."

"I have one," Wylie said, unwilling to challenge the older woman's statement and turn it back on her. "Baby steps toward self-sufficiency. Isn't that the badge of honor in this town? You've found a way to make it."

"Make it and thrive," Penny Lane said. "I wish I could have taken Larry somewhere other than the beach. He would have enjoyed sitting by the water without worrying about the sand."

Wylie laughed. "Why didn't he like the sand?"

"Parkinson's disease is a movement disorder that affects the nervous system. The symptoms become worse over time."

"I hear getting old sucks."

Penny Lane laughed. "Tell me about it. But Larry's personality changed as well between the time I met him and the time he died. He lost his motivation and became more inverted and withdrawn. The beach used to cheer him up. *'People pay millions for this view,'* he would say, *'and we're getting it all for free.'* But during the last few months, he hardly saw anything good or bad in the world around him. It was like he began to process the world more slowly and just couldn't take it all in."

"The brain's part of our nervous system," Wylie said. "Maybe his disease just advanced."

"I think he knew what was coming," Penny Lane said. "Whatever spark of personality remained in him didn't want to die in a hospital bed, but I have a hard time understanding why he killed himself and extinguished the possibility of experiencing anything else but that final white light. That's not something the man I first met would do."

"But you were there for him," Wylie said. "That counts."

"Yeah. I hated his choice, but he still got to make the final decisions."

"You could help a lot of families navigate their experiences. You called yourself a caregiver without the right credentials, but what if you called yourself a counselor?"

"Same problem," Penny Lane replied. "Wealth of experience, but zero credentials. I'm too old to go back to school, even if I could afford it."

Wylie protested the woman's defense. "You're not old, but in a decade, you'll be older. Why put off what you can accomplish today?"

"How's that accreditation going? They offer credits for lounging by the pool with a bum?"

"Point for Penny Lane," Wylie said. "I'm working on that." Her phone pinged with a notification and she ignored the device, choosing to respect the sun-drenched afternoon she had devoted to her guest. The device pinged again. "I need to change my notification settings to a daily review. Maybe I can just mute the channel for a while." Picking up her phone, she cupped her hand over the edge to read it in the bright sunlight.

Who the fuck ate my ice cream?

Wylie swallowed and struggled to remember whether she had checked the carton for a name.

And who left their dirty dishes in the sink?

"Um, I'm just going to slip inside and check on something," she said.

Penny Lane waved her off, the rest of her body unmoving as she soaked up the sun beneath the blue suburban skies.

She entered the house, blinking to adjust to the dim interior.

Jack stood at the kitchen counter and stared at the empty carton of ice cream she and Penny Lane had abandoned. Their lunch dishes rested in the stainless-steel sink, just as they'd left them. He looked up, anger stiffening his shoulders as his bloodshot eyes peered at her through smudged glasses.

"Hey, I just saw your messages on the messaging app," she said.

"Did you fucking do this?"

Wylie swallowed. "I didn't realize you'd bought the ice cream for yourself." He turned the package and she shook her head at the stenciled black marker that spelled 'Jack' next to a list of ingredients. "I mean, to be fair"—she swallowed—"at first glance, that just looks like part of the packaging."

"You have to notice the details, Wylie. It's not part of the list of ingredients. It's my name and the only thing that separates what's mine from what belongs to the house."

"What happened to spheres of influence and helping the household run seamlessly? I made a mistake and I'm sorry. I'll buy you some more ice cream."

"I don't want ice cream when you get around to it. I want it now. I want fifteen minutes of peace and quiet so I can check out of my high-stakes world and just relax."

She glanced at Penny Lane, who sat at the edge of her chair, aware of her isolation in a place where Wylie had intended to treat her like an invited guest. "Come out by the pool and sit with us."

Jack threw up his hands. "You don't understand. My world requires more than peace, love and harmony. I told you it'd be hard to empathize with a bunch of stressed-out entrepreneurs." He looked at her and shook his head. "You're just a stupid yoga instructor with a good ass."

She bit her lips and discarded a stream of defensive responses.

He scanned her body and raised his eyebrows. "What are you doing to add to the community? Screwing Nolan doesn't count unless we're all invited to take advantage of this community benefit?" He walked toward her. "Is that how you're planning to make amends?"

"That's enough," Rikard said.

Wylie turned to him, embarassment flooding her cheeks, though she'd never been to happy to see another person in her entire life.

"Fuck off, Rikard," Jack said. "This conversation doesn't concern you."

"Everything in this house concerns me. I live here and I'm not interested in exploring other options." The blond came to stand beside Wylie. "You're about to cross a line we'll all regret."

"Could you stop thinking about yourself for ten minutes? My whole damn business is about to explode and take me down with it."

"Then go cool off in your room and find a way to save it."

The men stared at each other until Jack swore and stormed from the room. Rikard turned to look at her. "Did he touch you?"

She shook her head and rubbed the fear from her skin. "It was just a carton of ice cream."

Penny Lane walked to the threshold and stopped before she entered the house. "Wylie?" she called into the tense silence permeating the room. "I think I'd like to go home now."

"Where is home?" Wylie whispered as her gaze swung back and forth between the hovering presence of Rikard and the wavering uncertainty of Penny Lane.

The woman turned toward the hills. "Wherever I belong."

Wylie drove the SUV down the hill, using a maps application to guide her through the city streets. Penny Lane stayed quiet in the passenger seat and stared out of the window. "Is this better than the seven-twenty?"

The older woman smiled. "I appreciate the concessions, but I hope I didn't get you into too much trouble."

Wylie kept her foot on the brake at a red light. "You and Larry lived together for a long time. Is it possible you had a common-law marriage?"

Penny Lane shook her head. "It wasn't like that between us. Is that even a thing?"

"I've heard of it. Maybe in, like…Montana," Wylie said. Penny Lane laughed as the light turned green and Wylie accelerated with the traffic. "Hear me out. Widows are eligible for survivor's benefits. The time you spent caring for Larry could keep you from sleeping on the streets."

"I'm not going to claim something I'm not entitled to receive."

"But what if you were entitled to receive it?"

Penny Lane shook her head. "Sometimes friends take care of each other and it just works out." She pointed to the cluster of tents behind a commerce center on Whittier Boulevard. Fifty colorful shrouds and a bike chop shop filled the space between the commercial loading dock and a stand of trees.

They passed the entrance to a parking lot serving the big box store and Penny Lane reached for the door handle. "You can let me out here," she said.

"I'll take you all the way." She stared at a line of red bollards designed to block cars from crashing through the store's plate glass windows. *What will block cars from crashing through the tent city Penny Lane calls home?* A pile of trash marked the edge of the encampment and Wylie wondered what happened when the pile grew too big and began to slump.

She knew rental rates had outpaced wages for people living near the margins of minimum wage, but she prided herself on her professional skills. What about the people like Penny Lane who had lost that source of pride? Could she walk into the chain store and 'present her credentials' with an address 'just around the back'? Thick brush might hide the rows of tents from passing drivers, but the hiring manager would see the traces of indignity from a lifestyle that depended on public toilets, sinks and donated supplies. She shook her head and looked at her friend. "You live here."

The woman nodded. "Home sweet home."

"I can take you back with me. We can figure something else out."

Penny Lane reached for the door handle. "You are like a scrappy little coyote, aren't you? I told you a day wouldn't matter. This isn't your problem to solve. The city wastes tens of millions of dollars each year cleaning up these messes. They sweep in to scare away the rats, remove used needles and piles of garbage. Hell, they'll even powerwash the sidewalks if we have one. You know what happens? The camps come back when the cleaning ends."

Rats? Wylie closed her eyes for a moment. Cholera, typhoid and hepatitis A could run through this camp like wildfire, but rats conjured images of typhus and old-school plagues. Sleeping in the SUV felt like a joke when the reality of a homeless camp sat before her. She slammed the steering wheel to vent her frustration. "But this is America! You shouldn't have to live like this!"

The woman smiled. "I remember what it felt like to be twenty-one."

"I'm twenty-six," Wylie whispered. Her job searches and petty complaints felt like childish exercise when she compared them to the burdens Penny Lane had to overcome to get on her feet. *I thought I could take credit for the beachside yoga sessions and the income I earned, but mom and dad sat with me at the kitchen table. They gave me family resources I never knew I had.*

She looked at the camp and thought of Nolan's food truck and the momentum he would have if he managed to get it off the ground—low prices, no guilt and no empty stomachs. The scale of his ambitions had taken her breath away, but Penny Lane's reality brought it all rushing back. *He can't be everywhere when he opens more than one store.* She focused on Penny Lane. "I'm going to get you a job and a place to live."

The older woman laughed. "Get yourself one first."

Chapter Twelve

Wylie drove back to the hillside mansion and climbed the stairs, her thoughts a kaleidoscope of vague ideas and the frustration of navigating rush hour. She found Rikard sitting at the kitchen table with a bottle of clear liquid and two empty cordial glasses. The silence of the house loomed in her consciousness. "Thank you for coming to my defense."

"Jack and Antonia went to dinner to help him cool off."

"And Neil?" she asked.

"In his room."

She stepped into the common space. "Did you orchestrate that?"

Rikard pushed a glass across the table. "I orchestrate a lot of things. Care for a drink?"

Scanning the open space, she eyed the next flight of stairs, intent on finding a quiet place to research local outreach organizations. "Not really."

Rikard raised his eyebrows. "It's an herbal *rakija* known as *travarica*. My family likes to drink it at the start of a meal with some dried figs."

"Did you label it?"

"No." He smiled as he filled her glass. "Who else could stand it?"

She swallowed.

"As my family says, the more the merrier. I gave up smoking, but I didn't give up this crutch."

Pulling out a chair, she faced the man and raised the glass to her lips. The fruit-flavored brandy packed a punch and she coughed. "It's like forty percent."

He smiled and looked at her.

She cleared her throat. "Like I said, thank you for defending me."

"Yeah, let's talk about that little incident."

"It was a mistake," she said. "I didn't know that ice cream belonged to Jack."

"Do you know the house belongs to Nolan?"

She put down her glass and looked at the man. "Say that again."

"You're not among peers, Wylie. Neither us should trust these people. Nolan rents out rooms in his million-dollar mansion to fulfill a high-minded quest for community."

"So you're not loyal to him."

He raised his glass. "*Živjeli*. I know a good deal when I see it."

She took a deep breath and considered the implications of his claim. Nolan's custom-built Bronco should have been her first clue. The easy relationship with Patty and John Abramowitz? The accountant's respect when she dropped his name? *He hasn't just lived in this house for a few years.* She swallowed, fighting the realization that threatened to steal her breath. *He built this house on the site of his childhood home. Shit. Does he enjoy my company or see me as a quirky diversion?* Shaking her head, she replayed their interactions but couldn't ignore the reality of Rikard sitting across the table, cataloging her reactions. "I asked Nolan if his daddy had money."

Rikard smiled. "Did you ask about his mom?" She shook her head and he finished his drink. "What kind of word do you live in, little girl? The first thing I do when I consider a new relationship is to find out everything I can about the woman. Why wouldn't you do the same for a man?"

"That's mercenary."

He shrugged. "That's the real world. Nolan's mother turned a ten-thousand-dollar bank loan into a multi-billion-dollar empire. Her privately held real estate investment company, Isla Investments, is one of the largest commercial landowners in California. Just think of what that means. Millions of square feet of office buildings, apartments, marinas and hotels line her balance sheets. And Nolan's set to inherit it all."

She shrank in her chair as she felt the weight of the implications, realizing Nolan's food truck schemes meant as little to him as any other man's hobby. "No wonder he's not worried about attracting capital investment for Modesto."

"There you go, finally putting the pieces together."

She had told Nolan she wanted to avoid the confusion and vulnerability of second-guessing their interactions, but he had kept quiet about his place in the world. *Will his mother group me with Penny Lane before we ever have a chance to interact? Do I care?* She faced Rikard as the memory of Nolan's cardamom-laced kisses faded like a treat she would never be able to savor. "Thank you for telling me."

He smiled. "My pleasure."

She rose from the chair and moved toward the stairway. "Why didn't you let Jack scare me away if you wanted me out?"

He shrugged. "You didn't deserve his anger."

"Just like I don't deserve Nolan?"

He refilled his glass and looked at her.

Realizing his critical assessments extended far beyond the daily weather report, she shook her head and climbed the stairs.

"Maybe you do deserve him or maybe you don't. The last roommate to occupy your space didn't deserve to hook up with Beth the cougar, but he did. If it all works out, they might pop out a few cubs and live the American dream."

She stopped and looked over her shoulder. "I've lived here for, like…three days."

"Three days." He leaned back and spread his arms wide. "Three days and you're already sneaking out of Nolan's room and camped out by the pool like it's somewhere you own." Leaning forward, he dropped his voice to a whisper. "What happens when three days turns into three months? Co-living isn't a practical solution for entrepreneurs once they acquire spouses and children. I'll be out of a home before you two little lovebirds make it to three years."

"I don't think Nolan would do that," she said, trying not to think of happily ever after like a balance sheet asset.

He shrugged. "Why not? I've done plenty of stupid things for a woman. I told you about Lisa." He straightened and refilled his drink. "I followed her here, but she formed a new strategy the minute she met Nolan. He wasn't interested and I was no longer her favorite. It's a brutal transition to watch your love life go from *Romeo and Juliet* to friend-sidekick."

"Romeo and Juliet never worked out."

He leaned back and raised his hands to encompass the co-living commune. "Who says? I realized how much I had been missing person-to-person communication and community interaction, but I had also been missing wealth."

She took the first step toward packing her bags. "You're going to lose it all one way or another."

"That's a bet I'm willing to take."

She considered the resignation behind his words and wondered if he recognized the coldness in his heart. Nolan's generosity and capability pulsed just beneath his skin, but she wondered if the blond man's touch would chill her to the core. He would do everything necessary to see life's drag race finish with a win. "But how do you come out on top?"

He shook his head. "I'm still trying to figure that out, but I highly doubt you'll be there to see the outcome. Run away, little girl."

* * * *

Wylie considered the piles of clothes on the floor and wondered whether to bother putting them away. She put her phone on 'Do Not Disturb' and sat on the floor, folding her body until she found the comfort of Child's Pose. *Why couldn't he have just shown up like a knight in shining armor and waved his magic wand? At least then I would have known where I stand.* She closed her eyes and listened to her heartbeat. *Because I wouldn't have let him.*

No wonder he's not in a hurry to recoup the tow fees or cash my check. She shifted her hips and sank deeper into the pose. *Rikard's in charge of Accounts Payable. I bet he'll cash it.*

A solid knock on the door let her narrow the field. Assuming Antonia had not returned from dinner, she took a deep breath and rose to face a man. "Nolan."

He smiled and leaned against the doorjamb. "Care for a swim?"

"I spent the day with my friend, Penny Lane," she said. "She's homeless. Her best friend died and she lost her apartment."

"That sounds fun," he said, his voice as even as the expression on his face.

"I didn't make any progress on a new source of certification. I didn't make any progress on sorting out my life or hers."

He straightened and folded his arms. "You can't fix people's lives for them. The best thing you can do is to give them the option to make a good choice and help them understand the consequences, but it matters that you care. It matters that you're trying."

She exhaled, knowing the insecurity of sleeping rough had triggered her emotions, but the reality of seeing the camp where Penny Lane lived had brought it all home. *I see how much I have left, but what does self-sufficiency get me? Smug independence and no one to share it with?* "You're so good at putting other people first. How did that even happen?"

"Sometimes you have to accept what you have to move on with your life."

She closed her eyes and sighed. "I have my health, mostly. A roof over my head. A family that will welcome me home. Why isn't that enough?"

"When is it ever enough?"

"When you're dead and you've got nothing left to prove."

Nolan laughed. "There's always tomorrow. In the meantime, I'd rather focus on using what we've got. How did your class go?"

She shook her head and scooped up a sweatshirt, sliding past him and aiming for the anonymity of the rooftop deck. She needed somewhere she could breathe and establish the equilibrium between her and Nolan. Her attraction to the man had felt like an indulgence when she'd thought they were two adults journeying to claim their status as full-blown Santa Monica residents. Now she realized that Nolan had the property and pedigree to claim an unfair advantage. *Rikard told me nobody ever goes out on the deck but Nolan. Was he trying to warn me and save me the embarrassment of this heart-to-heart conversation? How far would he have let the relationship progress before he brought it crashing to the ground?*

Nolan followed her but kept his distance and his back to the views of the Pacific. "The Abramowitzes invited us to dinner tomorrow night."

"Did they keep an eye on the lot for your mother?"

His gaze narrowed. "What does that mean?"

She wanted to hear surprise in his voice. She wanted denial and the humble bravado of a food truck vendor whose motives went beyond profit margins and sweet potato fries. *I can fall for a home-fry hottie with a heart of gold, but what right do I have to fall for a millionaire? Is everything between us a competition? Rich boy only wants what he can't have?*

Rikard's comments had given her a reason to retreat before Nolan or his family rejected her humble origins, but they failed to give her a place to hide. She wiped away a tear and recalled telling Nolan her tears were an anomaly. Now she wondered if her subconscious recognized the gap between their worlds and gave her the pretense she needed to slip into her shell of self-sufficiency. "Just give me a minute to get my act together."

Nolan nodded and followed her to the deck.

Pressing her body to the railing, she breathed deeply, filling her lungs with the cold humidity of the ocean air. She needed space to build a wall that would preserve her pride and rebuff Nolan's rejection. She needed to remember the vulnerability and determination of choosing her SUV over a one-way ticket to Oregon. The pleasure of her prior evening with Nolan felt like a dream sequence, but she needed Nolan's response to keep her from feeling like a convenient perk of the household. "Rikard told me your mom's loaded."

He rolled his eyes and sat on the outdoor couch. He looked at her, as ready and confident as a boardroom executive. How had she attributed that confidence and generosity to a heart of gold?

"Rikard's an ass, but he's loyal."

She frowned, remembering the way he had left his friend sitting in the back seat of the truck like a faithful hound. *The hound doesn't bite the hand that feeds it, but he knows how to scare off the competition with a well-placed growl.*

Nolan remained seated and gave her time to process her thoughts.

What happened to the Mooney Mansion? It burned down. Chesterfield Square? A legacy of violence. Isn't it better to keep your head down? She shook her head and decided to leverage Rikard's cutthroat intervention to regain her standing on shaky ground. "Not a little bit loaded, Nolan. Rich like Midas. I'm not comfortable with that lifestyle."

Nolan smiled. "She would prefer Cybele."

Wylie wiped away another tear and wondered why her body chose to release the waterworks when her frustration had nowhere else to go. "What does that mean?"

He looked at her for a long time, his thoughtful gaze making her feel a hundred times more vulnerable than when she had been naked in his arms. When he stood and reached for her, she widened her stance, prepared to hold the moral high ground, but instead of tugging, he trailed his fingers along her arm and she closed her eyes at the gentle touch. His sweetness overcame her reluctance and she softened as he pulled her into his arms. "It means my mom's a force of nature, but only because she'd rather have me on the board of Isla than shilling potatoes from a food truck."

"But you're not just shilling potatoes," she said against his chest. "You're trying to interrupt the market and give people a new alternative."

"My mother doesn't care about projects unless they'll turn a profit."

She opened her eyes and looked up. "But you do?"

"I spent a lot of time trying to prove myself when I was younger. People always wanted something from me—a party, a favor, a referral. I got tired of people asking for things and tuned the world out. Then something opened my eyes. Ask not what your wealth can do for you... Ask what you can do with your wealth."

"What happened?" she asked.

He smoothed her hair.

The heat of the connection encouraged her to dry her tears.

"I saw a man I could have helped, but I did nothing. Millions of people die every year." He exhaled. "I can't improve the world unless I start by helping one person."

"You're helping a lot of people," she said. "What you're doing counts."

He nodded and tipped her chin up until she caught the reflection of the light in his deep green eyes. "Where we come from doesn't matter, Wylie. It doesn't matter to me and it shouldn't matter to you. What matters is what is happening between us."

"You're not just taking advantage of me like I'm another household perk?"

He frowned and glanced toward the house. "Who would do that?"

She thought of Jack but kept her mouth shut before she hiccupped. "I was okay just being hot, but not okay being hot and convenient. The balance of power is off between us. I felt more comfortable when you told me you just liked my butt."

His hand dropped and rested at the small of her back. "I do."

"I'm not a convenience store."

"Wylie, where is this all coming from? I'm baring my soul but it's falling on deaf ears. Rikard pointed out a difference in our upbringings and you're falling apart on me?"

"I'm not falling apart," she whispered. "I'm just trying to figure out where I stand. I don't want to be the next charity case you're working to forget."

He stroked her cheek. "The contract downstairs says you have as much right to be in this house as any other member of the commune."

"But you own it."

"Yeah. So, go file your lease with the courthouse and call the authorities if I don't honor the terms of our agreement. In some ways, you have more power over me now."

The thought of holding Nolan to a list of rights and responsibilities made her smile, but she doubted the contract extended to interpersonal relations. She looked at him and saw a man who had gone out of his way to be kind to her and give her the space she needed. He had helped her to bed and given her the lead when she wanted more. "But you lied to me."

He took a deep breath. "Is there a difference between lying and omission?"

"There is when we're talking about a lie this big!" She pulled back and looked at him. "We're not peers. We're never going to be peers."

"Is Rusty your peer?"

She shook her head and thought of her ex-boyfriend's beat-fueled club. She had called him for a job, not for a personal reference, but she still felt ownership over his fate. *What would I have done if Nolan and his friends had come to the club for more than social intervention? I would have done my best to get Rusty through the tight spots and help the two men find common ground. By doing more than kiss Nolan?* She shook off her visceral attraction to the man and faced her reality. "No, but at least I can relate to what he does and the place he calls home."

Nolan widened his stance. "Well, let's see. In the last few days, we've sold low-cost street food to a hungry crowd, cleaned up a food truck and had mind-blowing sex. Which part of my life can't you relate to?"

"The part where you also stormed a racist club like a hipster Robin Hood, bailed out my SUV from the tow yard and gave a homeless woman a place to live for below-market rent. I don't want to feel indebted to you. I thought I was standing on my own."

He dropped his hands and she felt the cool wind against her back. "What's wrong with leaning on someone when you're down?"

She thought of Penny Lane and the crowd of community members lined up to explore the Social Club. Wouldn't it mean more if they did it on their own? She stepped away from the heat of his chest and traced the soft contours of his beard. She knew strength existed behind the soft veneer, but she had yet to find her bearing. "What happens when the support steps back? You have to trust your accomplishments and know you can do it again."

He captured her hand and brought it to his lips. "Exactly. Modesto is *my* accomplishment. It doesn't matter if I feed thirty people or thirty thousand. I'm still making a difference."

"I'm just trying to feed one."

"One?"

She added Penny Lane to her roster. "Or two."

He raised his eyebrows.

She counted the people who had shown her kindness over the preceding days—Rusty, his girlfriend and their flock of ambitious waitresses, the patrons who had come to her classes, even the librarians who had ignored her lingering presence and given her a place to rest.

"The point is" — he flexed his fingers — "I don't want fake relationships in my life."

"Great, we're getting divorced."

He frowned. "We were never married."

"Conscious uncoupling," she said.

He cleared his throat. "It doesn't matter what you call it. John and Patty still want us to join them for dinner. So much hinges on their property. I don't want to disappoint them."

"Nolan, I can't pretend to be your girlfriend. Nobody believes the two of us are together. Price Ross gave me a funny look. John and Patty seemed like they were just humoring my presence."

"That's not true. They believed our relationship when they spent the afternoon sitting by the pool."

"At your house!"

He smiled. "Not a problem. You don't want to play house? I'll introduce you as my mistress."

She rolled her eyes. "I don't like it when you keep things from me. Rikard tried to scare me away from you, but he had a point."

"Rikard's a control freak who hates the unexpected. That's why he makes such a good accountant. Straight and narrow. Unlike you, he doesn't see the depths within people." He picked her up and tossed her over his shoulder. "But I hear you loud and clear, roommate. You want to treat this thing between us like fringe benefits? I like your ass."

He slapped it and she winced, realizing she deserved the quid pro quo for smacking his chest.

"I like your quiet determination to get back on your feet, even if it means sleeping in your ridiculous SUV."

"It wasn't that bad." He paused on the stairs and she sighed. "Okay, I was terrified."

"Good. You're too young to end up as a statistic on the evening news." He turned to close the door and strode toward his bedroom. "So before you go accusing me of being a spoiled brat, remember I tried to do the right thing. I tried to be a gentleman. I asked you out to dinner and you declined."

"Well, it wasn't like I could get ready for a date."

"Now you've got several to choose from. I still want to take you out to dinner. I still want to order cocktails and tease out your thoughts. My interest in you hasn't changed — has yours?"

"Slightly."

He paused. "Slightly?"

"I have some questions."

He laughed and kept walking. "Fine, but right now I want to see you naked and remind you what it means when a man and a woman are interested in each other."

She landed on the bed and braced herself on her elbows. "Do you always get what you want?"

He shook his head. "Sometimes I have to earn it." He looked at her until she shifted, aware of the way she ached for him. "How do you feel when we're together?"

How do I feel? Like you've got all the power. Like you're the prince in the castle I dreamed about but discarded when life asked me to grow up. He braced his arms on either side of her and the distance between their worlds shrank to the span of an inch. His erection pressed into her thigh, answering his stated question with a physical response. "I feel good," she whispered. "I feel like I want more, and that scares me. What if I can't hold on to what I have?"

"What if you can?" He cupped her cheek, cradling her face with a heat that matched the intensity of his eyes.

She nodded.

He closed the gap between them and kissed her.

After one taste, she indulged her craving. *Have I ever wanted another man like this? Would I still want him without knowing the world classified him as rich?* The truth of her attraction and trust fired her response. The days of uncertainty and tear-streaked frustration sent her desire crashing to meet his. She succumbed and reached for his shirt, unwilling to entertain the excuses that could keep them apart. She slid her hands up his back, savoring the play of muscles as his tongue caressed her, diving and plundering in search of the satisfaction that came from letting go. "Lose the shirt," she whispered when he took a breath.

Nolan released her and rose to his knees, pulling his shirt over his head until her mind flickered like an old television set. *Chest. Lips. Erection. Repeat.* She grinned and reached for him. "Rikard's an ass."

He tugged her shirt free. "Let's talk about something else."

"Like?"

"Like making you shout my name instead of his." He reached for her head and lifted her from the bed, pulling her toward his body until she arched her back, straining to reach him as he stood on his knees.

She felt the tension in his hold and smiled. *I'm claiming what I've got.* She cupped his length, stroking him beneath the fabric of his jeans until he inhaled and shook his head.

"We're too old to play that game," he said.

Wylie smiled and pressed her mouth against the fabric.

He made a fist in her hair and exhaled. "You're a tease."

"No," she said. She smiled and scrambled to her knees, shucking her shirt until she met him skin-to-skin, heaving breasts to muscled chest. "I'm just reminding you that we both have power."

He shook his head and tucked a strand of hair behind her ear. "I submit."

Wylie raised her eyebrow. "What if I don't want you to submit?"

His green eyes widened as she gripped the back of his head and held him close, sucking and biting the tender skin of his neck until anyone with a clear view would know she had marked him. *You'll be wearing collars for a week, rich boy, and they'll know you liked it.*

He pulled away and sucked her bottom lip into his mouth, teasing her with the scrape of teeth. "So you like that?" he murmured as the urgency of their first coupling gave way to detailed exploration. She nodded and he pulled away to meet her eyes, chasing and exploring her responses as he caressed her skin.

"I do like it," she whispered. "I like it when you look at me and touch me, when you give me enough room to make choices without tying me down."

The words hung between them before he smiled. "Is tying you down an option?"

She watched his chest rise and fall, his breathing deep and relaxed. *What would it feel like to surrender to the very thing that sapped my control? Can I trust him to care for me when I have no other option?* She took a deep breath. "Does that turn you on?" He grinned and reached for the bedside table. "Wait! You've never done that?"

His laughter chased away the last of her concerns. He pushed her hands above her head and secured them with a necktie. She tested the silken restraint and smiled at the security of the knot. "You *have* done this before."

"Taking charge of the situation?" he asked.

She nodded, a gnawing desire beginning to coil in her stomach.

Nolan slid her pants over her hips. "Yes, I'm very good at that. My prep school had a class on douche-baggery and authority."

"No," she said, laughing.

He ran his hand along her stomach and spread his fingers wide, holding her still as her laughter died and her hips arched to his touch.

"Figuring out what you need and giving it to you?" His thumb dipped lower, rubbing small circles against her clit as he watched her respond to the tightening need building in her system. "I was born knowing how to do that."

Her hips bucked and he shook his head, pressing a trail of kisses against her skin until he found the tight peak of her nipple and drew it into his mouth, replacing teeth with tongue.

She arched from the bed and felt the wetness pooling between her legs. He moved lower, skimming her hips until his tongue teased her clit.

She squirmed, desperate to feel more.

"You're already so wet. I think you like this."

She opened her eyes and focused on his lazy grin. "I do."

Nodding, he held her hips, his tongue pushing her closer and closer to her limit.

She bucked against the restraints, cursing as they held fast. "Nolan, I need more."

He raised his head. "More?"

"More of you," she whispered.

He stood and shed his jeans. She stared at him as he rolled a condom over his length and raised his eyebrows. "More of this?" Her hips bucked and his smile widened. "I think you want it all."

He climbed on the bed and told her to lift her hips. She raised them from the bed, but he shook his head. "Higher, like you're doing a bridge."

Wylie complied and spread her legs, shifting her weight until she felt like a bound offering for his lascivious tongue. "Angling for easier access?"

He grabbed her butt, lifting her higher and easing the weight from her back. She looked at him, curiosity and anticipation quickening her heart, and he held her in tension, her arms anchored to the bed as tightly as he held her hips, and eased between them, seeking entrance with his dick to where his tongue had been.

"Nolan..." He raised his eyebrows and she stopped, giving herself up to the sensation of losing control. He held her fast and eased into her, slowing as she shifted and wrapped her legs around his waist to pull him in.

"You like this?" he asked, easing back and sliding into her once again.

She nodded and opened her eyes, surprised to find his gaze focused on hers when she had been so absorbed by her pleasure. Sweat beaded on his forehead as he fought to maintain control. *I don't want you to maintain control.* Arching her hips, she tightened her legs to pull him closer.

"Wylie," he moaned, closing his eyes as he thrust again. "Tell me this is okay."

She chose a more concise response. "Fuck me, Nolan."

His control snapped and he held her fast, thrusting into her depths.

She felt the slap of skin meeting skin. Her body ached to meet his, tethered and wanting more. Then he shifted his hands, lifting her higher and changing the angle until he found the spot that made her vision dim. "Nolan," she cried.

He answered her with a thrust. "Say it louder."

"Nolan!" The tension in her core spilled into the freefall of a mindless orgasm.

He squeezed her ass tight enough to leave bruises, rocked against her heat and submitted to his pleasure. Then he held her close, exhaling and lowering her to the bed while he remained on all fours and hung his head.

She looked at the tie binding her wrists. "Are you going to release me?"

He laughed and looked up. "Are you going to run?"

A slow smile replaced the blush of satisfaction heating her lips. "Not yet."

Chapter Thirteen

Nolan stroked her shoulder, pulling her toward consciousness. "Don't give me that line about every other day, rain or shine. You taught class yesterday, so today you're all mine."

She blinked as the sunlight cleared her mind of lazy, lust-filled dreams and replaced them with possibilities. *What happened to letting a body wake up before temping it?* She stretched and felt Nolan trace the line of her sternum. When his hand moved south and dipped beneath the covers, she laughed and turned to look at him, leaving his hand to rest on her thigh. "So now you've memorized my schedule?"

"It's not a difficult one."

The simple truth of his statement pushed her into full consciousness. She sat up and pulled the sheet to her chest. "I need to get my accreditation back on track."

"That sounds like a mobile, bed-bound activity if I've ever heard one."

"What type of accreditation are you talking about?"

He laughed and flopped on his back. "Your mind is somewhere else."

"Where it should be," she said, reaching for her shirt. He had confessed to his wealth, but it had taken her longer than an evening of pleasure to understand the consequences. She froze in mid-air and shimmied toward him on the wide bed. "Nolan, you're not going to do anything to help me, are you?"

"By 'help', you mean call in favors and leverage family connections?"

She pulled the shirt over my head and stared at him. "That's exactly what I mean."

He closed his eyes for a minute and sighed. "Let's define some terms."

"What happened to 'fuck buddies'?"

He opened one eye. "I thought we'd just ruled that out?"

She swatted his chest and he sighed.

"Wylie, I don't have any interest in being idle rich. Most nonprofits run a deficit and exist for the certainty of tax write-offs and the possibility of doing good. I could spend my days keeping a seat warm with Isla's board of directors, but I don't want to oversee the work. I want to do it."

She considered shucking her shirt and reclaiming her favorite position. Then she thought about the previous night and smiled. *Make that my second favorite position. It never occurred to me that I'd have a thing for altruistic entrepreneurs.* She frowned. *It also never occurred to me I'd even meet one.*

"Plus, my resources won't be enough to scale Modesto to compete with the size of a fast food giant. I still have to build value if I want it to succeed."

"Or turn a profit."

"Profit doesn't interest me. People do."

He rubbed her thigh and her muscles responded to the pressure of his touch.

"It's easy for rich people to give away their money and let someone else do the work. Look at The Giving Pledge. Billions of dollars and brilliant minds serving on advisory boards... What if those signatories got in the trenches and did it?"

"Maybe it's not their specialty."

"Well, it's certainly not mine. Do you know I had to teach myself to cook before I could even begin to think about Modesto?"

"Did you go to cooking school?"

He smiled. "I didn't want to learn how to make formal food. I wanted to learn how to make things people post on the Internet." He winced. "I recommend reading the reviews before giving a recipe a chance."

She grinned and hugged her knees. "Were they bad?"

"Terrible." He ran a hand through his hair and scratched his beard. "At the other end of the spectrum, you've got people with no assets but a heart of gold. Their loved one passes away from a drug overdose while living on the street and it stirs them to action. Thousands of meals and thousands of pounds of winter clothes, but what happens when they're gone?"

"Someone else takes their place?"

"If we're lucky. But I want to create the value chain. Maybe the tip jar goes toward offsetting the meals for people who can't pay. Maybe it's a benefactor's program. I'm not sure what I'm going to do to serve everyone who needs help."

"You need to start in the trenches."

He nodded. "So I was being sincere when I said I admire your tenacity and willingness to work for what you want. It might be narcissistic, but those are the same traits I try to cultivate in myself."

"Even if my goals are different from yours."

He reached for her. "Some of them align."

She shook her head and sat on her heels. "Let's make a deal."

"A deal?" He sat and his honed stomach muscles shifted beneath the edge of the sheet.

Confronted with the slipping fabric, she momentarily forgot to what she had wanted to say. Nolan's hair stuck out at odd angles and the shadow of a beard crept down his neck. She spied the red marks she had left and smiled. "Yes, a deal. The Abramowitzes own a commercial kitchen at the bottom of the hill, but they won't sell it to you."

"Correct."

"You think they'll rent it to you if they believe they're supporting young love."

He shook his head. "Not rent it, *sell* it."

Geeze. She inhaled, but she knew her assumption had served his needs from the moment she'd made it. *Why rent when you can own? Fine, we're playing a game with different stakes.* She waved off the distinction. "I'll go to dinner with the cute old couple. I'll play the fawning girlfriend of a stable community member" — he raised his eyebrows and she clarified her statement — "without overdoing it, but I want you to take your food truck to Whittier Boulevard."

He rubbed his beard. "Why there?"

"I spent yesterday afternoon by the pool after my yoga class. My friend, Penny Lane, came with me, but Jack started acting like an ass."

Nolan dropped his hands and narrowed his gaze. "What did he do?"

"It doesn't matter. Rikard ran him off before anything could happen, but afterward, I took her back to the homeless encampment she shares with about twenty or thirty other people. She means well, but she needs the kind of help you're trying to provide." She swallowed. "She lives in a tent, Nolan—a tent surrounded by garbage and rats. I don't want that life for her or anyone else."

He rubbed his eyebrows. "You're not above using me to get help for someone who needs it, but you won't accept help for yourself. Did I get that right? You don't want to doubt your place in the world, but remaking Penny Lane's life? You're all over that?"

"This isn't about me and it's not just about getting her help, Nolan. It's about opening your eyes to what you can accomplish with your resources. What if you aim higher than good food? Look at the lowest rung on the social ladder. If you want to make a difference, you need to spend time in the trenches instead of selling food outside a business park."

"I can't plant an outpost next to every homeless encampment in the city. There must be thousands of them, and even my resources will run out."

"Then go where the people congregate. Go to an intersection off Santa Monica Boulevard, where international charitable organizations partner with local food trucks to make a difference. I'm sure the regular volunteers would appreciate a night off."

"I'm not running a charity. I'm lowering the barrier to good food. A day of redeeming glass bottles should be enough to buy a decent meal."

"You're also not thinking about the people who've run out of choices. Do the people who need your food the most like the taste of it? Can you figure out a way to make the economics work to serve the entire community?"

"Wylie, there has to be a bottom line."

She thought about the restless nights she'd spent in her SUV and the anxiety triggered by aimless days. "Trust me. Once you get close to that bottom line, you realize how much farther you have left to fall. I'm not asking you to siphon out your bank account, Nolan. I'm asking you to push your limits and take a risk."

He closed his eyes. "You want me to give the food away."

"Just this once. The most discerning critics in the world are the ones with the fewest dollars to spend."

He nodded and opened one eye. "This act of charity will buy me dinner?"

"And a new perspective. Esther can run a franchise with her eyes closed, but can you find a way to employ the men and women who are fighting their circumstances?"

"Anyone who wants to work should be able to do so."

"Good." She thought about calling the accreditation institute and planning the rest of her day.

"I'm holding you to a dinner without rules." He reached for her and pressed a soft kiss against her forehead. "And also without obligations."

"What did I do to deserve that?" she asked.

He smiled and pulled her shirt from her shoulder. "You spent the afternoon by the pool with someone named Penny Lane."

"She's my friend."

He brushed his hand along the edge of her breast. "Speaking of friends and benefits."

"What happened to no obligations?"

"Just tell me to stop."

She leaned into his touch. The warmth of his hand built against her skin and she blinked, struggling to focus on his words.

He cupped the full weight of her breast and sighed, dropping his hand. "We all need friends to look out for us, but most of the people I know only see those people who mirror themselves."

"And?"

"You see everybody, Wylie. You see the people on the streets who might disappear into a crowd. That kind of empathy is rare and precious. After dinner tonight, I'm going to do my best to look after you, whether you need it or not."

She raised an eyebrow, smiling at the thought of someone considering her rare and precious. She spent so much time looking toward the future that Nolan's statement felt like a luxury. Still, she doubted the feeling would last. "Is that so?"

He nodded and reached for her. "I can see your thoughts as easily as I see your beautiful blonde hair. Don't run away from me yet. Don't plot your escape. We'll fight those battles another day, but right now the only thing I can think about is savoring the first course."

* * * *

The national organization's pre-recorded telephone message gave Wylie a lot of options, but none of them addressed her needs—'What to do when your instructor closes a certified studio with zero notice.' She pressed the zero key until the system hung up on her, then she called back and tried again. When the list of options expired, a customer service representative took her call and greeted her with the pleasantries of a scripted response.

This isn't her fault. She cleared the negative energy from her mind, laid out the entire chain of events and fought to keep her frustration from clouding her word choice. "So" — she injected a note of optimism to buffer the desperation of her question — "what do I do now?"

"This is a very unfortunate situation," said the receptionist.

"Tell me about it." Wylie tried to visualize the seamless transition that would alleviate her worries about achieving certification. She imagined the sound of the receptionist's keystrokes as she found a receptive teacher and arranged Wylie's life along the well-trodden path of a collegiate transfer. *That's not how this industry works.*

She had heard rumors of yoga instructors who got burnt out trying to live above the poverty line while depending on the success of someone else's studio. Most of the rumors ended in depression and anxiety. To make matters worse, she knew studio owners often asked new yogis to teach 'community' or donation classes after attaining certification. Instead of twenty-five dollars a student, the new instructors pulled in twenty-five dollars a class while everyone in the back office hoped these aspiring yogis and curious community members would stick around or make a commitment to the studio.

The representative sighed. "The organization carefully assesses each studio's training program and takes a holistic approach to certification. When we certify or approve a training program, we are certifying the program as a whole and not its parts," the representative said.

Wylie took a deep breath. "I'd like to transfer my course credits to another certified studio."

"The current pathway to certification is to complete a full training at a registered school."

The pressure of unshed tears made Wylie blink and she struggled to contain her frustration. *I am not going to cry about this policy. I am not going to cry about this policy. I am not...* She sniffled. *What the fuck am I supposed to do now?*

"Due to program constraints, it is not possible to complete parts of your training at different schools or to transfer completed work between programs."

Wylie got to her feet and paced. "But don't you lay out the coursework? Don't you strive for consistency? I mean, what's the whole point of this certification if you can't guarantee that students are receiving homogenous instruction?"

"It's a certification program, not the SAT."

"If it was the SAT, it wouldn't have cost me two thousand dollars!"

The representative cleared her throat. "Of course. Can you send us a copy of the records? I'll elevate the issue and see if management can offer you a path forward."

Wylie frowned. "I assumed the studio owner submitted them electronically or something." The receptionist's silence made her squirm. "Maybe I can get them from her."

"That would be the easiest solution. In the meantime, why don't you visit neighboring studios and find one with an instructor you'd like to use in the future? Attending a few classes might give you a better perspective on this adventure."

"Would you be able to transfer my course fees to the new studio? I paid Cynthia nearly two thousand dollars." More silence. "Or at least a portion of them?"

"It's a very giving community," the representative said.

Wylie heard the subtext beneath her words. *You have to be independently wealthy or have another job to work at someone else's studio. I need organized healthcare, but I also need my beachside practice. How long can I get along without the twin support?* She cleared her throat. "So I'm on my own?"

"Our mission is to promote the integrity and diversity of yoga instruction."

Wylie closed her eyes and acknowledged a truth she had long suspected about her chosen profession. *Teaching yoga instructors is like a multilevel marketing scheme and I'm right in the middle of it.* "Thank you for your help."

She got out a pen and a piece of paper as she scanned job listings and looked for benefit buzz words that might get her out of this mess. *Maybe I should go for an overall fitness certification, like working as a group exercise instructor, or I could get financial aid and study kinesiology and physiology at the local community college.* She thought of her past asthma attacks and shook her head. *At least at a gym, I'd be an employee, know what I'm getting paid and have workers' comp. If they didn't have enough participants for yoga, I could teach something else.*

She thought about the looks her parents had exchanged when she'd laid out her plans for the beachside class. *'But I'm good at this,'* she had said. *'You* taught me that everyone should find a way to live their passions.'

Her parents had locked gazes, giving her just enough freedom to flounder.

She closed her eyes and flopped onto the floor. *But I'm good at this!*

Leaving her bedroom, she grabbed her mat, determined to clear her mind before dinner. She messaged her roommates.

Leading a yoga session on the deck in an hour. Join me if you can.

Jack opened the door to his bedroom and raised his eyebrows. "Most people expect more than an hour's notice."

"I'm spontaneous," she said, walking past him.

The distance between them grew.

"Oh, I hear you. We all heard you last night."

She flinched but kept walking, determined to ignore Jack's contempt for the choices she made. *I signed up for roommates, but if I controlled the lease, I would have never let him move in.*

* * * *

Antonia came to the roof deck session. Afterward, she stayed to chit-chat and share community gossip. "You can use my shower whenever the upstairs one gets busy."

Wylie smiled, figuring she could slip into Nolan's suite if she needed immediate hot water. "What I need is a pretty dress that doesn't scream 'yoga gear'."

The other woman laughed. "Like a cocktail dress or something more fluid?"

Wylie imagined the wind-swept effect of riding in the Bronco. "Fluid. Definitely fluid."

Two hours later, Wylie stood in front of a mirror and examined the results of her efforts and Antonia's loan. Her hair fell in soft waves and her skin glowed from the abrasion of a citrus-scented exfoliator. *I'd rather let Nolan's stubble do the hard work. Will he care that this is a borrowed dress? Has he seen Antonia wear it?*

Her self-doubts vanished when he knocked on the door. "Hey, are you ready?"

As ready as I'll ever be. She took a deep breath and opened the bathroom door.

"You look amazing," Nolan said.

"More amazing than naked?"

He pulled her close and kissed the soft spot beneath her ear that would leave her light makeup intact. "Different, but just as good."

"So, dinner with pseudo-grandparents is equivalent to sex?"

He straightened. "Is that what you heard?"

She shook her head and linked her hand with his. "No, I heard you making promises about what happens next." He raised his eyebrows and she glanced toward his room. "At some point, this dress has to come off. Do you plan to be there?"

"I do."

"Then let's go make polite conversation and small talk."

He laughed and led her to the garage. "You drive a hard bargain."

She smiled and followed him to the main level, pretending to ignore the way Rikard and Jack locked eyes as they walked through the room. The drive to the restaurant seemed as easy as the classic rock songs coming from the radio station. At the coast, a breeze blew in from the water and tourists took pictures of the oceanside village.

A waiter brought them to a table where Patricia and Jonathan waited, cocktails in hand. The older couple rose and greeted them with handshakes and cheek kisses, one smelling of white wine and the other of rose. Wylie smiled through the encounter, wondering if their pleasantries would persist when Nolan got to business. *Am I taking advantage of them by pretending to be more than Nolan's friend with benefits? Or is this dinner a scheme and we're all here just here to see and be seen?*

"I think you'll like this restaurant." Jonathan looked up from the thick paper menu he held. His aged hands and suntanned skin stood out against the heavy white cardstock. "They serve classic American comfort food from breakfast to dinner. I particularly enjoy the wild mushroom burger."

My dad makes a mean burger, but it doesn't come with mushrooms. She scanned the menu and raised her eyebrows as ribeye transitioned to organic juices and soups made with bone broth. She glanced at Patricia and the confused frown marring the woman's pale skin. Her lipstick matched the outline of her lips, but she wondered how many times the older woman had blotted it with a tissue and an unsteady hand. "They've certainly got something for everyone. Matzo ball soup?"

Patricia smiled. "Oh, I just love that soup, but Mort's Deli makes it better."

"Mort's Deli closed." Her husband took her hand. "What about some fried chicken?"

She rearranged her iced tea. "I'll just have a salad."

"Have you tried Nolan's food truck?" Wylie asked to break the silence. "He's doing amazing things with basic ingredients."

"You used to make sand soup on the beach when you were a kid," Patricia said. "I remember watching you during school breaks when your mom and dad had meetings they couldn't miss."

Nolan scratched his beard. "Those were good times."

The older woman smiled. "I got the best of both worlds. A sweet, cheeky little boy that I could send home after dinner." Her husband laughed and took her hand. "What?" she asked. "It's true."

Wylie smiled and imagined running into a chubby-faced adolescent on a public beach. *We would have viewed each other as just another kid. I mean, unless we're talking twelve again. I would definitely have noticed his abs.*

The waiter came to take their orders.

Wylie fidgeted, wondering when the business conversation would begin. She looked at Patricia's hazed expression and ever-present smile. *Well, she might be as lost as I am.*

Jonathan wiped the condensation from his water glass and looked at her. "So you teach yoga?"

She raised her napkin and blotted her lips. "Freelance beachside yoga classes."

Patricia blinked. "That's nice."

"Price Ross comes to my classes," she reminded them.

Jonathan's brow wrinkled. "Is he better at yoga than accounting?"

"I mean, there's no 'good' in yoga. We're all trying to get better and find balance." She blinked and remembered to play the role of the poolside hostess. "I guess he hasn't fallen lately, if that counts."

The older couple laughed and Nolan squeezed her hand beneath the table. She wanted to ignore the flush of awareness that came when his thigh brushed hers, but her body betrayed her and warmed to his heat. *This is just business to him.* Shifting her legs beneath the white tablecloth, she suspended her resistance and tried to relax. *Why can't I enjoy the perks of playing along?*

"Wylie's being modest. She's a yoga instructor, but she's also got a heart of gold. She's been petitioning me to bring the food truck into the communities that might need it the most. I did a little research this afternoon and realized the homeless population is growing much faster than I thought. There must be three thousand people seeking shelter near Skid Row."

"Hot food isn't going to cure their ailments," Jonathan said as the waiter delivered their salads. He picked up his fork then set it down and adjusted his position in the chair. "Bunch of misfits just looking for handouts. Didn't we approve a bunch of new taxes to shelter them until they get their acts together?"

"That's what I thought too," Nolan said. "Residents have approved hundreds of millions of dollars for new housing and services, but the tax money's going to longer-term projects. Proposition HHH was a huge housing ballot measure, but those projects are taking years to get off the ground."

"Your mother wouldn't let red tape stall her projects. If she can do it, the city should be able to do it faster."

Wylie shifted in her chair.

"I'm trying to tackle our city's problems from another perspective," Nolan said, conceding the man's point. "The economy is booming and people like my mother make money off progress, but most people live on wages that aren't keeping up."

"Now you want to solve income inequality and the wage gap? That's ironic."

Nolan held his ground. "I want to leverage my resources and give people a way to do more with what they've got."

"You're chasing a fool's dream, Nolan. The men and women sleeping in parking garages aren't looking for steady work and balanced nutrition. At some point, I guarantee they had that option and decided on something else."

Wylie opened her mouth to defend Penny Lane, her one point of contact.

Patty set down her fork and blotted her mouth with the soft linen of her napkin. "Jonathan, you know better than to stereotype an entire population," she said, beating Wylie to the punch.

The older man winced, looking chagrined.

"Jewish law demands that everyone has access to adequate and permanent housing. We take the poor into our homes and feed them. It's a hallmark of our religion. Why can't we help Nolan do the same?"

John spread his hands wide to encompass the restaurant. "Not the time or place, Patty. If you want to get into the subtleties of Jewish law, we'll table the issue and discuss it with the scholars and the academics."

Patty rolled her eyes. "You know as well as I do that the point of Jewish law is to be good citizens and help repair the world. That's why I filled my days volunteering with grassroots organizations when I realized we wouldn't have children."

Her husband stared at her.

Patty stared right back.

"What a rich faith," Wylie said, trying to fill the void in the conversation.

The older woman laughed. "You grow up with ideas, but you don't understand them until you have the perspective of an adult. Girls these days have a bat mitzvah and the religious education to go with it. My mother taught me the subtleties of her social and cultural experience, but she was right about one thing. If my husband wants to argue about law and tradition, we'll do it at home."

"Patty—"

"Suffice it to say that taking in the poor and feeding the poor... We do them both, and I don't see a single reason we can't throw weight behind Nolan's outreach as well."

"Why can't the city manage the crisis?" John asked. "It's not just food. It's the liability. The threat."

"Food is a good starting point," Nolan said.

The older man shook his head. "Homeless shelters and transitional housing can meet their needs. I have no problem donating money."

Patty snorted. "The county doesn't have enough resources to shelter everyone. The cost of living in this city has grown so high that wages can't keep up with rent. People want to work, but they still need somewhere to live and something nutritious to eat."

John smiled. "You've always had a big heart."

The older woman took a deep breath, unwilling to give up ground to a loving compliment. "Let the city fight the housing crisis and let Nolan make good food."

"What are the chances his venture will implode while we're alive to see it?"

Patty sighed. "We should all enjoy the breeze while we can."

And we've lost her.

"Jonathan, you've been through a million excuses to hold on to the commercial kitchen. Let it go already. Nolan's a good kid. He's not going to turn it into a strip mall. He wants to make food. I spent my whole life making food."

Nope. She's still there. Wylie smiled at the woman, imagining the stained apron strings and dog-eared recipes that filled her afternoon hours. "And he wants to hire people to work," she said, adding what little clout she carried. "He wants to give them the means to solve their problems on their own."

Jonathan looked back and forth between her and his wife.

Yep, you were young and idealistic too. Wylie wondered when it would be safe to eat her salad.

"The U.S. Supreme Court already weighed in on this matter. Authorities can't stop people from sleeping on public property if no other shelter is available. The city's got to build more permanent supportive housing and temporary shelters to get people off the streets. Until that happens, isn't cheap food just enabling the camping we're trying to eradicate?" He turned to Nolan and crossed his arms. "That same little boy who built sandcastles also wanted to be an astronaut. What happens to my property when you're over this altruistic whim?"

"Sir, it's not a whim and it's not just about the homeless population." He took a deep breath. "A few years ago, I went carousing through Europe with my roommate from school. My mom told me to do it. '*Sow your oats then come back to Isla Investments and sit on the board.'"*

"It was solid advice."

"Except she didn't count on the reality check that came with sending me into the real world. My friends and I spent an evening at a nice restaurant next to our hotel. I gave my leftovers to a man sitting on a street corner who had nothing but a sleeping bag to ward off the night's chill. He had to sit on a pile of cardboard boxes and I chose to give him a swan made of aluminum foil."

"I'm sure he appreciated it," Wylie said. "The food, I mean."

Nolan shook his head. "The next morning, I went out for coffee and paramedics were zipping that man into a body bag. Anything could have caused his death, but I started asking myself if I should have done more to help him."

"He needed more than food," Jonathan said.

"But what about the single mothers trying to hold down a job and manage their kids? What about the blue-collar employee who signed over his paycheck to cover unexpected medical bills? What about the seminary student who's studying on a scholarship to pull himself up? They're all humans and they all need food."

John and Patty looked at each other. "You can't separate the two," Patty said. "You can't offer sustenance with one hand and dangle shelter with the other. Either you're committed to being a good citizen of the world or you're not."

Nolan nodded. "I might not be able to fix local housing markets, but I can do more with what I have — and you can too. By combining our assets, we can transform cash and goodwill into tangible benefits. I brainstormed what I could do to help people in need, but nothing clicked until I attended an event for the food community. The organizers had styled the event after TED Talks, but none of the attendees felt content to sit in a dimly lit auditorium. They milled in small groups, clustered around high-top tables and circulating tapas."

"You'd be amazed at what good food can do to improve the mood," Patty said.

Nolan smiled at the woman. "I think it was a setup. One of the speakers challenged chefs to feed the people in their restaurants but to also feed the people who lack access to healthy foods or need a helping hand. There's a McDonald's in Marseilles that's known for giving people their first jobs along with a side of fries. The residents don't throw their wrappers on the sidewalk. They stay loyal to that community for years."

Jonathan sighed. "The LA riots didn't touch McDonald's."

"Exactly!" Nolan said. "Communities safeguard organizations that earn their respect. Your commercial kitchen could be the next step toward turning Modesto into a concept that meets the needs of the twenty-first century. It could be the anchor for the local community."

"Or your mother could flip it when you get bored with your pet project," Jonathan said.

Nolan shook his head. "I give you my word."

"Well." Patty smoothed the napkin in her lap. "What more could you ask for than that?"

Jonathan kept his gaze focused on Nolan and raised his eyebrows. "Fair market value."

Wylie swallowed.

Nolan laughed. "You know as well as I do that my offer is competitive. I told Wylie I don't want to oversee the work. I want to *do* it. I'll tell you the same thing. This project means something to me, and Wylie's passion for the city's most vulnerable citizens has brought clarity to my mission."

Beaming with pride, Wylie started when she felt Nolan squeeze her hand under the table. The gesture surprised her and she squeezed it back, realizing that she'd forgotten how long he had been holding it. She met his gaze and smiled, feeling that the passion behind his speech eclipsed the work of a dozen script writers. *Oh, I'm going to do all the work tonight.*

"There are benefits to being rich," he said. "We're not helping blue-collar workers. We're opening our doors to help every man, woman and child who needs food, because we're the richest nation in the world."

Wylie kept her mouth closed and picked up her salad fork. *Nolan, you have no idea what kind of benefits I have in store for you.*

Chapter Fourteen

"See? You didn't need me to close the deal," she said the next morning. "The only thing you needed to secure John and Patty's support was to open up to them and share how you got to this amazing place in your life."

He skimmed a hand along her side. "I'm pretty sure this amazing place started with arrogance and a kiss."

The invitation hung between them, but drowning his insecurities with a burst of pleasure felt like a disservice. "Patty and John don't think you're a kid, Nolan. I've never met your mom, but I'm sure she wants to support you, whatever you choose. Tell her what you're doing. Let her see that Modesto isn't just a hobby."

His hand stilled. "Your influence is messing with my business plan. It's not the right time to get her involved in my projections."

Get involved in this or get involved in us? Sighing, she let his hand wander along her skin, giving in to the pleasure of his touch before she made a stand. *I could get used to waking up like this, but where will it end?* She rolled onto her back and stared at the ceiling. "So let's keep going on the business plan. Today's the day you get to test drive some of the menu offerings?"

His hand stilled and he sighed. "Yeah, I emailed the coalition yesterday. They're getting the word out. Wraps tonight, and if we're successful, we'll schedule another week for soups and stews over grains." He took a deep breath. "What if they don't like it?"

She turned and propped herself on one elbow, smiling at the hint of uncertainty keeping a smile from his clear green eyes. "What if they do?"

* * * *

Jack, Antonia, Neil and Rikard stared at the bustle of the commissary yard. "Dude, I just thought you guys made, like, quesadillas on a stove. What is all this stuff?"

Nolan stopped loading supplies and stared at the line of employees preparing the food truck. Esther and the man with the honeyed voice checked their inventory while a third worker confirmed fuel levels. "We're going to have a big crowd. Wylie, get this crew to load the Bronco up with serving utensils and paper products. We won't have any extra room in the food truck."

She swallowed and faced the four roommates who had turned to stare at her. "Okay, so everything goes in the back, then we ride together."

Rikard raised his eyebrows. "You're driving?"

"Are you volunteering?"

He scanned the row of coolers stacked to form a narrow aisle inside the main truck. "No. I just volunteered to be on crowd control."

"Thanks." She smiled. "We're going to need it."

On the way to the urban site, Wylie explained how the food coalition previously served meals out of a food truck near Sycamore Avenue and Romaine Street. When local demand exceeded the capacity of their vehicle, they partnered with an international charitable organization to bring their food-service operation indoors.

Jack stared out of the window. "So this idea brings nothing new to the table."

She glanced at him. *You're assuming these men and women have a table.* She cleared her throat and thought about the outing from Jack's perspective. "There have always been people in the community who wanted to help—churches, charities, civil services."

"Exactly."

"But the problem hasn't gone away," she added. "Decades of nightly meals testify to a persistent need, but Nolan's thinking bigger than a food line. He might have started with the blue-collar people who want better options, but what if people have zero options? I love that he wants to create sustainable infrastructure. I love that he's willing to serve anyone who walks in the door."

She cleared her throat and kept her eyes on the road before she lost control of the tears stinging her eyes. *I love that he would have helped me when I needed it the most.* "Modesto can model community support and upward mobility, but Nolan needs to learn what our community's marginalized populations will accept.

Man cannot live on peanut butter and jelly sandwiches alone."

"We're going to get mobbed," Rikard said as the Hollywood Freeway carried them past a series of tents.

Antonia met his eyes in the rearview mirror. "Or worse."

Wylie ignored their fears and glanced at Neil. "What do you think?"

"I think this is ridiculous. I'm an entrepreneur. Let me focus on that and I'll do more good writing donation checks than handing out plastic-wrapped utensils."

"You'd like to think that, but you're missing small opportunities while you bury your head in code. Sometimes it's the little things that matter the most."

"Says who?"

"Says the people who have nothing to lose."

Nolan turned the food truck in to the charitable organization's parking lot and she parked the Bronco behind the vehicle to ease the task of unloading their excess supplies. A uniformed officer from LAPD waved in acknowledgment and a group of security guards and volunteers moved toward the far side of the campus to begin patrolling the street for loiterers or emerging encampments.

"It's too quiet," Antonia said, peering at the empty lot.

"The customers start lining up at six p.m. in the building's gated hallway. They try to keep people from waiting in line on Hollywood Boulevard."

"Customers," Jack said.

Wylie turned to face him. "I don't care what you think of me, but you volunteered to be helpful. If you can't treat these men and women with respect, you get on the bus and ride it back to the Pacific Ocean. I hear it's great for worrying about what you're going to do next with your life."

"My lease didn't come with a volunteer requirement."

Rikard opened the door. "Consider it amended."

They lined up outside the wood-paneled food truck and discussed how to manage crowd control and the needs of their future guests. "We've got two wraps today," Nolan said. "They're both high-protein, but one's bean-based and the other's got tuna, walnuts and raisins."

Esther nodded. "Quinoa and corn for a side dish. Water comes from the cooler." She scanned the group and focused on Jack. "You can be on trash duty."

The trash piled up as the roommates came face-to-face with members of the local homeless community.

"I got shot in Desert Storm, came back and it's like the people running the government forgot I had ever existed." The man took off his stained fedora and scratched his short black hair. "They forgot what I'd done for my country."

"Don't we have Veteran's Affairs?" Neil asked.

"It's the PTSD, man. I can't always control it, and people in the mainstream work forget we're people too. We've just fallen on hard times."

Wylie walked down the line, doing her best to direct people into the building or give them a chance to try Modesto's wraps.

"How long you been on the streets?

"Since I was sixteen years old. I'll be fifty in March and you don't have to bother doing the math. I've never owned an apartment or a house. Sometimes I'm not even sure I own my tent."

Jack frowned. "How can ownership be confusing?"

The woman laughed. "People get used to having zero rights when they live on this side of town. There are thousands of people sleeping on the streets in the shadow of the financial district. We're in the homeless capital of the world."

Wylie looked at Nolan, leaning out of the food truck's window with a tuna wrap and a welcoming smile. *At least we're trying to do something about it.*

"So where are you from?" Jack asked.

The woman shook her head and her processed blonde hair obscured her face for a moment. "Columbus, Ohio. My best friend died twenty feet from me during a winter storm. I found her frozen to death, curled up in the fetal position. So, yeah, I'd rather not die like that."

Jack swallowed. "What keeps you going?

The woman scanned his bold glasses and all-American warm brown eyes. "I sell a little speed and I sell a little of myself. Used to be a lot harder, but now they all have cell phones and things like that. You got a cell phone?"

"Yeah, but I'm not interested in that business."

The woman laughed. "No problem. You change your mind, you can find me on Facebook under Clover Anne."

"I'm going to pretend I didn't hear that."

The people listening to their conversation laughed.

Antonia came from the back of the line and pulled Wylie to the side. "We've got a problem."

"What kind of problem?"

"We're going to run out of food soon."

Wylie inhaled, knowing Nolan's facilities limited the truck's ability to ramp up and meet demand. "What's the margin?"

"Maybe three of four people more," Antonia said. "I can't pin everyone down. They shift away from strangers and skip the line to be closer to the people considered friends."

"Okay. Go tell the site coordinator. I'm going to stand at the end of the line and be the bookend." She walked past the snaking line and focused on the last man who had joined them. "Why'd you pick the truck over the food coalition?"

"Is it any good?"

She nodded.

"Novelty's hard to come by in my life."

A woman walked up with a worried expression. "Is there going to be enough?"

Wylie closed her eyes for a minute. "I think we're about to run out, but the coalition is still serving hot meals. We'll come back another day," she added, hoping Nolan wouldn't mind her promise.

The woman's shoulders fell and she turned toward the permanent building.

"Wait," Wylie said. "I'm sure they set aside some food for the employees. You can have my wrap."

The woman frowned. "No, you eat it."

She shook her head. "I didn't come here for food. I came here to help. What's the nicest thing someone's done for you this week?"

"I saw my son."

"What?"

"I was in a living program with my son, but it turned out to be a bad situation. The woman running it stole my identity and used my name to launder money she made at a crack house. When I found out, she threatened my life and I had to put my son in DCFS."

"How old are you?" Wylie asked.

The woman smiled. "I'm twenty-six."

An hour later, the uniformed officer from LAPD shut the gates and the roommates stood in silence as they replayed their evening conversations. "I had no idea," Antonia said.

Rikard looked at her and nodded, but Jack and Neil stood firm, arms crossed as they debated the merits of what they'd heard.

Nolan opened the back door of the food truck and stepped out, sweat staining his shirt and exhaustion straining his smile. "Most of these people are employable," he said. "Maybe not forty hours a week, but something close to it—something that allows them to contribute while getting the services from the city they need."

"But that's no way to run a business," Rikard said.

Nolan put his hands on his hips. "What's the alternative? Close your eyes and pretend you don't see this side of town?"

Wylie walked up to him and put a hand on his back. "You did great today. Nothing but compliments on the food."

Antonia smiled. "I heard one lady ask if the wraps came with French fries."

The group laughed and Nolan shook his head. "There's not enough space in the truck to accommodate a fryer. Next time, we can deploy the baked sweet potato fries if they want something besides quinoa."

Esther yawned. "I need a nap before the evening rush begins."

The group stared at her and she shrugged. "What? I'm Brazilian. Only old people eat dinner before ten."

They thanked the site coordinators and retraced their steps to the commissary and the house on the hill. Instead of movie night, they convened by the pool with leftovers from the refrigerator and their opinions about what Nolan should do next.

"If you can feed these people, you can feed the world," Wylie said with a mixture of challenge and pride.

Nolan raised a beer and saluted her vote of encouragement. "I pictured a fast-casual restaurant with the food people would cook for their families on a limited income—low prices, no guilt and no empty stomachs."

Antonia raised her head. "But what if you've got nothing to give?"

Neil stared into the distance. "My father threatened to leave me as a dishwasher if I reached for the restaurant bill and refused to pay it."

"Why would he do that?"

"It's hard to be a curious kid," Neil said, his gaze softening with the memory. "Why can't people contribute to the community tab? Let them write checks or work. There's no reason for food insecurity in a twenty-trillion-dollar economy."

Jack stood. "I appreciate the endorphin-laced group sentiments, but I'm not in this for the win. I have no interest in feeding drug dealers and prostitutes who can't get their shit together from one day to the next. Fuck the Tragedy of the Commons. I'm a capitalist."

"You're an ass," Antonia said.

The man raised his hand, but Rikard moved faster and intervened. "How many times do I have to tell you to stop threatening the people in this house?"

"Let the Games begin," Antonia said.

Nolan looked up. "What are you talking about, Rikard?"

The Croat shook his head and considered his choices. "When I moved into this house, you offered me kinship and told me to extend that offer to everyone else who moved in. Sometimes kinship hurts."

"Spit it out," Nolan said.

"I found Jack stalking Wylie in the kitchen. I'm pretty sure he asked her if he could fuck her before he called her the newest community benefit."

Jack stepped back from the group.

Nolan rose to his feet and faced the man. "You have a thing for threatening people? Or is it just women?"

"Fuck off, Nolan. It was just a joke."

"Look at Antonia and Wylie. They're afraid to meet your eyes. Do they think it's a joke? Do they think it's okay that you're disrespectful and selfish?"

Wylie swallowed, unsure if she deserved Nolan's heated defense. *I could have handled it, right?* She looked at Antonia, hoping to see relief in the woman's expression. But instead of relief, she saw anger. She saw Antonia's short brown hair, narrowed eyes and hard resistance. *This isn't the first time Jack's threatened her. Did she tell anyone? Did I?*

"It's not a joke," Antonia said.

Jack sneered. "Bitch. Go back to West Hollywood to hang out with your new friends."

Nolan took a step toward the man and inhaled, crossing his arms likely trying to avoid a physical resolution. "Your lease is up. Consider this your first and last notice of eviction."

"I have rights."

"Leave," Nolan said, his voice no longer full of the good humor that indulged hungry customers and Wylie's waffling advances.

Jack stared at him then swore and turned, upending the poolside table holding their drinks and phones. Glass shattered as the metal rim of the table bounced against the concrete, but nobody moved.

Wylie swallowed. The strength of character behind Nolan's hip street aesthetic had never been more obvious to her. Rusty's bravado and Jack's menace paled against Nolan's disciplined control. Even as her cracked phone swam in a pool of sugar-laced liquor, she smiled and acknowledged the power lurking beneath her lover's sweat-stained shirt. *Doesn't Jack realize Nolan's trimmed beard and meticulous sideburns require the kind of dedication that goes above and beyond writing a business plan?* She shook her head and dismissed the ousted roommate's protests, knowing Nolan had the situation under control and the other roommates stood ready to continue the offense.

Nolan raised his eyebrow when Jack remained on the balcony. "I don't think the police would be interested in defending your rights. We've got a room full of witnesses and I hear they've got more pressing problems to solve."

"You're an entitled asshole."

Nolan laughed. "Yeah, what of it?"

Wylie smiled as Jack departed. *He might be entitled, but at least he's doing something good.*

* * * *

"Egg and black bean burritos. Ham, white beans and cornbread. Chili with pinto beans."

Nolan laughed. "What is it with you and beans?"

She looked up from her new phone. "Beans?"

Nolan had insisted on replacing the device, but she had insisted on a like-for-like model without considering the tradeoffs. Outdated smartphones should have been a dime a dozen, but so many of them ended up recycled, underground or sold on gray markets that legitimate vendors had no interest in carrying outdated stock. The phone in her hand worked, but the off-brand replacement screen flickered and she worried about battery life.

"Beans are great," she said. "They're cheap protein sources. They're rich in iron and fiber. What's not to love? They're like glorified nuts and seeds."

He pulled her close and rested his chin on top of her head. "That's cute. Have you considered the effect of upset stomachs and flatulence in a camp environment?"

Wylie winced and dropped the phone on the bed. "Okay, so people might want to temper their consumption, but this article says the longer beans soak, the fewer lectins and phytates remain to cause problems. Don't put them on your menu every single day and people won't eat them every single day. God, just imagine the institutional outrage if students had a healthy, cheap alternative to the cafeteria plan."

"Um, they'd still choose fried chicken. Hangovers demand comfort food."

"Well, I mean, Modesto could be the bridge between a cafeteria and a soup kitchen. Somewhere people want and accept in their neighborhood."

"You're getting it," he whispered.

"Besides, we're meeting the needs of half the population, but just the ones who are down on their luck. Beans are full of fiber and protein, Nolan. Everyone needs them."

He smiled. "That's the thing I like about you, Wylie. You see problems and find solutions. You're all in."

She tried not to stiffen at his soft tone. Had she gone too far and co-opted his ideas before he felt ready to share them? She reminded herself that fake relationships came with real limits. "What does that mean?"

"It means you tackled your crap eviction by finding a new job and sleeping in your car. You're googling cheap protein sources for a menu you have no stake in selling. Most people would temper their response with a little moderation, but you? It's pure enthusiasm."

"I have a stake it in," she whispered, thinking of Penny Lane and the nameless man who had sparked Nolan's quest. "Shouldn't we all have a stake in this?"

He shook his head. "I just wanted to revolutionize diners and give people an easy way to eat and earn a living. You've brought the personal perspective back to it. You've reminded me why I started this fight."

"You would have remembered," she said, looking up at his profile. *Just like you'll remember me one day when I move out.* She closed her eyes and focused on the Modesto menu ideas occupying her imagination and distracting her from memories of Jack's eviction. *Was Nolan reacting to Jack or to the threat he posed to me and Antonia? Did he measure his roommate's worth by the man's actions or the value of his victims?* "You see problems and try to fix them too," she said.

Nolan nodded and shifted on the outdoor couch. "So why don't you make this partnership a full-time gig? Keep your beachside classes but work for Modesto full-time? You'd get all the benefits of your pro bono work."

But would I get you? She thought of Esther and the measured banter between Nolan and his employee. Dottie's lease position had given her a similar measure of authority and the power to enforce her whims. She struggled to envision a scenario where her work at Modesto ended but her relations with Nolan continued. "I'd rather not mix business and pleasure. I'm going to get my accreditation hours transferred or maybe switch to a general fitness certification if I have to save my money and start all over again. Either way, Nolan, I like helping you out, but I don't want to clock in to do it."

"I get it,' he said, but his gaze remained focused on the distance. "The commercial kitchen's a big step, but it will bring my vision for Modesto one step closer to fruition." He turned and lifted a strand of blonde hair. "I just thought you might want to chip in."

Because all I have to offer is my time and my body. She stood. *And in your world, neither of those currencies will get me very far.* Rikard's intervention loomed in her mind. *'You're not among peers, Wylie.'* The memory tempered her enthusiasm for Nolan's heroics, but she trusted him. "I do want to chip in. I want to help you do something for the community that will have a lasting impact."

He inhaled and turned to face the city. "That's all?"

She stretched her hands above her head and yawned, trying not to notice the way his eyes followed her every move. "That's all for tonight. Honestly, I'm beat and thinking of turning in."

"You can stay with me," he offered, but the city had reclaimed his concentration.

"That's all right. It'll do me good to get some sleep."
He smiled. "We sleep."

Wylie nodded. *But tomorrow, we've got to do more.* "Let's talk in the morning. You can come to my beach session."

"Do I get a discount?"

She smiled and searched for the easy banter they shared before she had realized his net worth. "Only if you carry my gear and earn it."

"Deal." He stood and pulled her close for a kiss that warmed her lips but terrified her heart. "Goodnight, Wylie."

"Goodnight, Nolan."

She punched in the code to open the house and blinked as Antonia slipped into Rikard's room. *Good for them.* Shaking her head, she faced the white particleboard furniture filling her rented bedroom. *It's a few steps above the SUV, but I pay the rent for this room.*

Chapter Fifteen

Wylie stared at Nolan, standing shirtless near the refrigerator and looking as tempting as the cold glass of orange juice he held in his hand. *I could have spent the night squeezing him.* She smiled and walked toward him. "Well, good morning to you too."

He grinned. "I thought I'd get a head start and meet you down there."

"What happened to working off your discount?" He bent and brushed his lips across hers, the taste of fresh orange juice a sweet reminder of where she should have spent the night. "I'm confident you can handle it."

"I can."

Antonia strolled through the kitchen wearing a long T-shirt.

She made eye contact and Wylie grinned. "Walk of shame?"

The woman winked en route to the lower level. "It's only shameful if you can't handle the consequences."

Wylie exhaled and looked at the infinity pool, remembering the pleasure of having Nolan to herself and the bitter reminder of her place in the household when he'd evicted Jack with a single word. "I can handle it."

She grabbed a protein bag and filled her water bottle before inventorying the foam blocks and extra beach towels in the back of her SUV. They needed to be washed, but the roster for this morning's class had stayed at seven participants. *Last time I had twelve. I'm sure the other regulars will make it to my class.*

The regular short-term parking lot on Barnard Way felt like an indulgence and Wylie wondered what had happened to the musician in the park. Penny Lane's empathy had secured her identity amid the crowd, but Wylie wondered what would happen as Nolan and his employees began to recognize the faces and stories of the needy. *Will they be able to stick to their mission statement and let other agencies and nonprofits take care of housing and treatment? He's got to recognize the danger of stretching himself too thin.*

The sand beneath her toes felt refreshingly cool as she set down her supplies and waited for her regulars to report to the beach. Nolan's presence might distract her, but she assured herself that she had the patience and experience to handle it. The first pair of women arrived and waved their phones in the air to acknowledge that they'd transferred funds. Wylie greeted Isabella and her friend by name, but she left them to their chatter and scanned the beach for familiar faces.

Price smiled as he walked up, but he glanced north. "Have you heard about your competition?"

Wylie shrugged, noting how he chose his words. As an approved commercial fitness trainer, she had the right to conduct classes on the sand near Palisades Park, but she valued the loyalty of her customers as much as she valued her permit. "I trust the city of Santa Monica to enforce their permit system. A few rogue classes won't hurt my long-term revenue."

The man scanned her meager assembly. "Are you sure about that?"

She nodded and checked the time. With a minute to spare, an older couple joined their group and brought the total to five paying participants. Wylie pulled up the sign-up sheet and shrugged. Her missing regulars had paid their fees, but nothing could compel them to come. She took up her position near the front of the group and smiled. "We've got a small group today, but I'm glad you could join us."

Nolan jogged toward them and swiped a beach towel from her stack. He dried the sweat from his bare chest and winked as he took up the flank, bringing them to six.

"Allow your eyes to softly close," Wylie said. "If it's comfortable, breathe in and out through your nose or breathe with your mouth when needed." Price snorted and she struggled not to smile. "Listen to the rhythm of the waves, then begin to bring your awareness inward, to the muscles controlling your breath. Notice how your breath feels and begin to open your senses."

She watched one of the women sneak a peek at Nolan's shirtless form and contained a grin. *Good luck, Isabella. That one's all mine...for now.*

For the next hour and a half, the group of six participants worked up a sweat as they followed Wylie through a series of poses. At the end of the class, she folded her hands. "Namaste."

The older couple waved and departed before Wylie approached Price, Nolan and the two women.

Nolan's forehead wrinkled and he toyed with his beard as she surveyed the empty sand. "Small class today," he said.

Isabella grinned and rubbed her lips together, her immaculate lip gloss capturing grains of windblown sand. "They don't know what they're missing!"

Price cleared his throat. "I got a direct message this morning about a competing class farther up the beach. The instructor said she wanted to revolutionize my beachside practice and offered the class based on a donation."

"Oh, I have plenty of ideas about how to revolutionize my practice," Isabella said. She stepped toward Nolan. "I haven't seen you here before. Are you new in town?"

He stepped toward Wylie.

She tried not to smile, but the show of allegiance warmed her heart.

"I watched Wylie's last practice. It seemed like a good way to start my morning."

"I'm Isabella," the woman said, refusing to take a hint.

Price leaned close to Wylie and dropped his voice to a whisper. "She's trying to poach your breakfast date. Does Nolan Wilson know about him?"

Wylie narrowed her eyes. *Five breath cycles aren't going to be enough to return my heart rate to a normal and comfortable pace.* Nolan's shirtless, glistening torso and black running shorts had tested the limits of her professionalism for the entire class. She shook her head, knowing there would be time to replay her fantasies back at the house. She looked at Price and smiled. "That is Nolan Wilson."

The man's eyebrows shot up as he reevaluated Nolan's presence. "Rich and good looking. Honey, you do your best to hold onto that."

Or what? Wylie asked herself. *You'll never find anyone better?*

Nolan continued to fight off Isabella's advances, evading her questions and redirecting her interest in yoga to Wylie's skillset.

Undeterred, the woman showed no signs of backing down.

He dropped his subtle pretense and wrapped his arm around Wylie's shoulders. "Oh, I agree. She's the best. We're dating, so I'm enjoying the private practice."

We're dating?

Isabella and her friend exchanged glances.

Wylie smiled around the lump in her throat.

"Well, I hope we see you around." The guest saluted Wylie and winked at Nolan. "I always my enjoy yoga with a view."

"I'll see you next week?" Wylie asked.

Isabella and her sidekick looked at each other and nodded. "Of course! This class has helped me drop two pants sizes," Isabella said. "There are only so many things in life I'm willing to give up."

Like pride? Wylie asked herself. She kept smiling while the women departed, then took a deep breath and introduced the two men left standing beside her. "Nolan, this is Price. Price, Nolan. You guys, uh, both know the Abramowitzes."

Price congratulated Nolan on the news of the commercial kitchen. "I think it's going to be a positive change for Jonathan and Patricia. She's losing her short-term memory and he wants to focus his energy on making her comfortable without managing a portfolio of properties. I guess they could hire a property manager" — he grinned — "but I guess you know all about that side of the business?"

"More or less," Nolan said. "Wylie, you ready to go?"

"Yep, just a minute," she answered him as she lifted the stack of beach towels. Then she looked at Price. "Just out of curiosity, what was the name of the account that messaged you this morning?"

Price brushed the sand from his arm. "Um-hm. The woman we call 'Silicon Cindy'? Her account mostly consists of sunlit selfies and over-filtered facial expressions. I almost deleted the message because I thought she got hacked or tried to send me porn." He winked. "Not that I don't have my favorites."

Wylie stared at the man. *What are the chances?*

"I think she must have messaged everyone that had liked your previous posts. I passed Rex on the way down here and he said he was headed north to test drive the park's newest offerings."

"That bitch," Wylie said.

Nolan laughed.

She turned on him, disappointment erasing the familiarity between them. "It's not funny."

"I told you Mini Mako was memorable. C'mon, Wylie. They're going to see right through Cynthia and come back to you. Fight fire with fire and offer a discount for established practitioners. Maybe they'll bring a friend when they come back."

Wylie shook her head. "Not if she pulls in the regulars from her studio. Nobody likes participating in a six-person yoga class. They feel too exposed."

"Well, they don't like sixty either," Price said. "Who's going to help them adjust their poses and help them when they face plant in the sand? You're the best instructor I've ever had."

She let the praise wash over her sensitive feelings and took his hand. "Thanks, Price. I appreciate hearing that compliment."

Nolan rubbed a hand through his hair. "I guess that should have been my line."

Wylie heard him, but she stared at the silhouette of the distant lifeguard tower. "I'm going to report Cynthia." A gull landed at her feet, startling her to draw a sharp breath. "Better yet, I'm going to confront her."

Nolan and Price exchanged looks. "Are you sure that's a good idea?"

She nodded. "About as good as poaching your student's prospects when you know she's down. Cynthia's not the mother hen. She's the wolf." She marched toward the next tower and left the men to guard her stuff, but her steps slowed as the distance grew. *What if she's not there? What if it's someone else and I've made a complete fool of myself?*

As sure as the tides, Cynthia stood amid a crowd of people, the sun bouncing off her dyed bob like an impervious helmet. She held court amid her practitioners like someone who shirked social responsibilities and had long ago decided to get ahead, taxes be damned.

Wylie shook her head and marched forward until they locked eyes. "Can I have a word with you, please?"

Cynthia's eyes widened, but she smiled and turned to the crowd. "An old friend of mine! I hope you don't mind if I step away and say hello!"

"So now I'm an old friend?"

"Well, it sounded better than a disgruntled student."

Wylie widened her stance in the sand. "I feel like you owe me a few things. Cash, for one thing. You took my money without completing my certification. I doubt you have the funds, so I'll settle for an apology and a vow to stop poaching my students."

Cynthia brushed her bangs from her eyes. "Unfortunately, I'm avoiding commitments at the moment."

"It's one thing to close the studio on a whim, but targeting my students? What happened to professional courtesy?"

"Human feelings and behaviors are extremely complex," Cynthia said. "You should spend time meditating on your anger."

"Seems pretty cut and dried to me."

The woman cleared her throat. "You're young," she said, trying another angle. "So young that you have unrealistic expectations regarding other people's behavior. You've got to let go of those expectations and learn to roll with the punches. If you hold on to every little slight in your life, you'll accumulate so much disappointment, frustration, resentment and anger. Those burdens will weigh you down."

Wylie bit her lip, giving the woman a chance to finish her statement when she wanted to slap her face.

"I've found it's much easier to stop expecting so much from people. I didn't plan to close the studio with zero notice, but the landlord refused to give me more time to pay back rent. You understand, don't you? It's life and economics. You'll be so much happier and healthier if you rethink your expectations and learn to go with the flow."

"Go with the flow?"

"Yes! Exactly!" Cynthia nodded, exhaling like Wylie saw her as the voice of reason. "It's a tough break, but you'll get over it." She lowered her voice. "Do you think I want to be out here glad-handing the masses and scrambling to cover my ass?"

"No, but here you are, and I can see why our lessons stopped before you got to philosophy, ethics and lifestyle. Did you know the credits I completed are a total wash? That I'll have to start over again? That you stole from me and my peers? That instead of getting a side gig to cover the gaps in your business, you took the easy way out and screwed the rest of us?"

Cynthia rolled her eyes. "Whine, whine, whine. Please, just listen to yourself. At least I still have my pride."

"But not your reputation!"

Cynthia laughed. "That's the beauty of social media. You can rebrand your business in thirty seconds. Nobody reads the comments."

Wylie exhaled, hoping the lingering customers had heard their exchange and spread the word about Cynthia's business practices.

Nolan stood behind her, prepared to offer backup or something like it.

She looked over her shoulder and saw Price holding up his phone. *I don't need backup.* She exhaled and faced her former mentor. "Whatever, Cynthia. You'll get what's coming to you. If it doesn't come from me, it'll be the next person who you fuck over. I believe in community—and you're not part of it."

The woman laughed. "It's so cute how you've mixed up expectations and dependence. Take it from me. You're on your own in this life, kid."

"I'm a grown-ass adult!" Wylie muttered, holding on to the last of her restraint. Her fingers curled into a fist as she turned to walk away. She wanted to swing like a boxer gone wild in the ring. Her dad's self-defense lessons at the gym had included throwing punches and he had been her first and only victim. She knew that if she landed a punch, her first two knuckles would skim Cynthia's chin, the woman's eyes would go wide and she would recoil from the impact, stumbling backward until she lost her balance and landed in the sand. *It would be so much more satisfying.* She envisioned the jolt of contact but shook her head. *Violence never solves your problems.*

Cynthia's laughter rode the spring breeze. "Poor little girl's just starting in the world. She should have read her contract."

She turned, losing control. "Oh, Cynthia?"

"What is it now, kid?"

"Here's some customer feedback. Do you know people call you 'Silicon Cindy' and take lewd selfies when your back's turned? They do it because you're a joke, because you feed off being the center of attention and it's so annoying and desperate that they don't even bother respecting you."

"Girl fight!" a spectator yelled.

Wylie shook her head. "Before you start offering me life lessons, follow that hashtag and read the comments. I promise nine out of ten of them are mocking you. You want to get ahead in this town? Try being fucking authentic!"

Cynthia's chin shook like she had absorbed a physical blow. "Is that true?"

Wylie shook her head as the adrenaline wore off. "I don't believe in violence, but I do believe in fighting back."

The instructor bit her lip. "Did that make you feel better?"

She breathed deep and looked at Price to keep her body from succumbing to the exhaustion of the week. "No, but I'd much rather open your eyes and go viral than let you feel superior about what you did to me." She locked eyes with Nolan. "You're better off not hiring me. I'm a vulnerability. I could go off at any minute."

He walked up to her and swung an arm over her shoulder. "She had it coming."

"Yeah."

"But she'll think twice before she lets it happen again."

Wylie closed her eyes. "I won't give her the chance."

He kissed the top of her head. "Do we need to sign you up for anger management classes?"

"Seriously?" she asked, looking up. "I thought I deserved a medal for not decking her."

He kissed her lips. "No, not seriously, but your words were sharp enough to wound. I'm going to think twice before I leave you hanging in bed. I'm not sure my fragile ego could stand it."

She laughed and leaned into his weight. "A stronger woman would have walked away."

"I doubt it," he said, looking over his shoulder. "Nobody wants to spend their life as a punching bag."

* * * *

Nolan poured her a glass of juice and stood in the kitchen while she sipped the sweet and familiar nectar. How often had her mother done the same thing and given her space and room to voice her thoughts? *This man is not my mother, but he knows how to take care of people. Maybe I should thank his mother for those lessons — or his nannies. Whatever. Scratch that. I never want to meet the woman.*

During the ride home, she had replayed her conversation with Cynthia and struggled to identify the point where she'd lost control of her emotions and chosen to lash out rather than have a calmer resolution. *I'm twenty-six, but I still act out like I'm the kid.*

Nolan pulled breakfast from the refrigerator and walked toward the stairs.

"Hey," she said, reaching for his arm, "I wanted to say thank you."

"For what?"

"For letting me handle it, even if I did a terrible job."

He leaned down and brushed his lips over hers. "Plenty of people would have started with the punch."

"That doesn't mean it was the right call."

He caught her chin in his hand and tilted her face up like she had taken the blow. His eyes scanned her face and he nodded. "Would you do it again?"

Maybe? It hadn't solved anything. *What would my family say if they found out how I behaved?* She shook her head. "It didn't solve my problems."

He leaned forward and kissed her again, his lips tasting of comfort, cardamom and coffee. Then he changed the angle of the kiss and stole her breath, holding her fast as he pushed her to accept the intrusion of his tongue and the honed strength of his body pinning her to the chair. She groaned as her lips parted under his, then blinked in confusion when he released her. "What was *that*?"

He stared at her and drew a deep breath. "I think I understand what set you off, but she wasn't worth your time. You want to burn off some aggression? Come tangle with someone who can handle it."

Wylie rose, closing the space between them. "And you can?"

"Yes." He lifted her to the countertop and caged her with his arms. When she cocked her head, considering his response, he cupped her breasts and lowered his head to suck her nipples through the fabric of her tank. "I'm beginning to figure out what makes you tick and how far you're willing to go."

She wanted to rip off her shirt and throw it to the floor, but she grabbed the back of his head and pulled until his eyes met hers. "What if I don't know the answer to that question?"

"Then we'll figure it out together. Right now I need a shower."

She nodded, prepared to give him the space he needed.

He pulled her from the counter. "Don't get me wrong, Wylie. This thing between us? It might not be clean and it might not be easy, but it's worth it."

"I can handle those conditions."

"I had no doubt."

They climbed the stairs, as solemn as a procession, and she looked at the bed. *I trusted him to tie me up and take care of me. I trusted him enough to know when to hang back. This thing between us… How far will it go?*

He turned on the shower and stripped off his running shorts, as proud and naked as any statue of Adonis.

Amy Craig

Wylie smiled, pulling off her tank and black pants until she and Nolan stood in the steam-filled room, primed and ready to go. "Let me wash you," she said, attempting to prolong the pleasure she knew would come.

"That can wait."

He reached for her and pulled her close, turning her in his arms until she felt his lips against the nape of her neck. His hands spanned her waist and dipped lower, caging her hips until he shifted her position and brought her flush against his erection.

"I don't think I have that kind of patience," he said.

The heat and promise of his arousal pressed into her backside and she shifted, eager to turn and accept the challenge. "You have a thing for women behaving badly?"

She felt the laughter rumbling through his chest and he pressed kisses along her shoulder. "I have a thing for you."

"Nolan"—his name escaped with a sigh as she closed her eyes and arched against his chest, thrusting her breasts into his hands as he cupped them, his thumbs circling the tender peaks while his lips cruised her shoulder—"I thought you were an ass man."

"I'm broadening my horizons."

She closed her eyes, savoring the strength that kept her upright and the pleasure that kept her pinned to him. His kisses teased the limits of her control as he used his teeth to graze her skin.

"I missed you last night," he said. "I missed having you in my bed."

She smiled. "There's still time for that."

"Not right now."

The muscles in her core tightened as he released one breast and grazed the soft skin of her stomach, pausing briefly to tangle in the hair between her thighs before he found her clit and began to stroke, pinning her solidly against him.

She knew she could break away, spin and reclaim the momentum, but the allure of letting go felt as compelling as the steam and perspiration that held them together. Her body trembled as she succumbed to the pleasure, letting her head fall against his shoulder as he proved just how many ways there were to win.

Her breath escaped in soft pants as she began to move her hips and match the rhythm of his fingers. Then she hooked an arm around his neck and held on, rocking against his touch as his fingers penetrated and teased her, as rough and possessive as her body could stand. The tension in her built until she fell over the edge, hanging on to him for dear life as she cried out in the steam-soaked room and went limp in his arms.

"More?"

The hard length of his cock pressed against the heated flush of her skin. She turned in his arms, reaching up to nip his ear before she whispered her response. "Yes."

He picked her up and carried her into the shower, the spray like a soft caress on her sensitized skin. "I want to be inside you."

"I want you there. I want to feel you inside me, hips pumping, muscles straining as I try to hang on."

"Shit, Wylie," he swore, pushing her against the tiled wall.

The longing in his voice felt like honey against her sensitive nerves, more empowering and tasting as sweet as sin. She locked eyes with him, finding his gaze steadier than she felt. "I'm clean, Nolan, and I want you inside me. I want you now."

He dropped to his knees and parted her folds, licking her until she squirmed against him. "Wylie, I'm as clean as you are, but are you sure? There are other ways to get this done."

She laughed, stroking his hair beneath the spray. "I don't want to get this done. I want to feel you inside me, Nolan. I want to give every roommate in this house something to talk about. Stop stalling."

"Little voyeur." He laughed and turned her to face the tile, parting her legs as he ran his hand along her spine. "So soft and strong at the same time."

Panting, she braced her hands and shifted her hips up, feeling his gaze and wanting more. She looked over her shoulder and waited until he looked up from the sight of her inner folds on display. "You make me feel strong."

"You can still change your mind," he said, gripping his cock and stroking it until her nostrils flared with jealousy. When she shook her head, he closed his eyes for a moment, then grabbed her hip with one hand and slipped inside her, hotter and stronger than anything she could imagine. The first thrust left her breathless and she shuddered as he pulled back and slid deeper, urging her to take and accept him. He found her clit with his free hand and set the pace, pressing her where she needed it the most.

Each stoke left her wanting more. She felt her release coming and urged him on, thrusting her hips as they found their rhythm. The pressure burst and she cried out his name. He pulled out and hot semen spurted between them. As their bodies came down from the high, he dropped his head to hers and pulled her from the wall. "You okay?"

She smiled and turned in his arms, pressing her hand against the rapid heartbeat within his chest. "Now we definitely need the soap."

Chapter Sixteen

Wylie pointed to the cluster of tents behind the commerce center. Fifty wind-blown domes of polyurethane-coated fabric sat in the shade. Scattered tools and a cluster of bikes destined for a chop shop littered the common ground. "Penny Lane lives somewhere in that community. I don't have a way to contact her, but I'm guessing close to a hundred people live in those tents and would appreciate hot food."

"I've seen this encampment through the trees bordering Whittier Boulevard," Nolan said. "I never imagined it would be this big."

Wylie nodded. "Well, now you get to serve the people who inhabit it."

He smiled. "I have a feeling you'd bankrupt Modesto within six months if I let you pick the destinations."

She grinned from the passenger seat. "Well, at least we'd go down swinging."

He parked the food truck near the edge of the loading dock and scanned the curious faces who turned to greet their arrival. A separate squad of men and women in red matching shirts held clipboards and tablets. They stood among the tent residents like looming attendants. "I don't think we're the only ones paying a service call to this encampment."

Wylie matched the T-shirts with the magnetic plaque stuck to a nearby truck. "It looks like an outreach organization. They're probably trying to help in any way they can. Good for them."

"Do you see the best in everyone?"

She raised her eyebrows. "Don't you?"

He leaned across the center console and kissed her. "I do where you're involved."

She blushed and considered the lack of privacy afforded by the expanse of glass fronting the food truck. *There's a quickie, then there's an exhibition.* She cleared her throat. "Are we going to feed them too?"

Nolan nodded. "Why not? We're collecting data and customer feedback, aren't we? But I want you to stay close to the truck when we take breaks. Penny Lane will come find you if she's here. Esther's on her way to help, but we're going to be conspicuous."

"Are you scared?"

He banged on the thick metal of the truck paneling. "No, but I'd feel better if we had reinforcements."

She laughed. *Where's the threat?* "I think you ought to be more concerned about the people inside the truck. It's chili and rice. I'm pretty sure I can serve it without burning myself or sending your truck up in smoke, but what if I'm wrong?"

He rolled his eyes and checked the side mirror. "I'd feel better if you stuck to grating the cheese." She punched him in the arm and he raised his eyebrows. "Ready to go again?"

Wylie blushed and shook her head as she reached for the door handle. "Let's get this crowd served and satisfied before you get any more ideas."

"Oh, I have plenty of ideas," he said.

The food truck's first patrons strolled toward the truck with the suspicion and hesitancy of feral cats. They milled in small groups, eyeing the truck's wood paneling until Nolan raised the flap, leaned on the sill and raised his voice to be heard above the roar of nearby traffic. "Menu's limited, but the price is right. Come on down for free chili, rice and cornbread."

"You with the aid group?" the first man asked. He held the line and wore a black sweatshirt. His skin looked like it had weathered more than one type of combat zone.

"Nope. My crew and I are just here to give out food and see how you like it."

The man scratched his head. "What's not to like about it?"

Nolan lowered his voice to a conspirator's whisper. "I dumped a bowl of carrots and zucchini into the chili and let them cook down. I hate to admit this, but it's good for you. Now, be a good sport and come eat your vegetables."

The man wrestled with Nolan's playful tone then laughed and gestured to his friends to join them. "Man thinks he's a comedian."

Wylie exhaled. Nolan seemed capable of being everything to everyone. *Will he be there when I need it?* She watched him hand over the first bowls of steaming chili. *So far, he's never let me down.*

Esther parked next to the truck and climbed out, the wind teasing her soft pink hair. "Sorry, I'm late. I had an, ugh, pressing engagement." She checked her phone and smiled. "Well, in Brazil, we'd consider this on time."

Wylie smiled as she opened the back door of the truck to admit the employee. "Did your pressing engagement have pink hair?"

The Brazilian laughed and reached for hand sanitizer and work gear. "Now it's purple."

Wylie handed over the ladle and set to work organizing the cheese and chopped onions that would pepper the food. She slid past Nolan and set a bottle of hot sauce next to the stack of napkins on the sill. "What? Some people like it hot." When he laughed, she scanned the growing crowd and spotted her friend's tanned skin and sun-streaked brown hair among the crowd. "Penny Lane!"

Several heads turned in her direction and Wylie swallowed, hoping the woman would roll with being singled out. She climbed down from the truck and came around the front to greet her friend amid the stagnant air and asphalt fumes of the parking lot. "Hey! I hope you don't mind we brought dinner."

The woman smiled, but she glanced over her shoulder, rocking on her feet with nervous energy. "We're not used to getting this much attention. That aid group showed up with a load of donations, but they're unwilling to hand out the gear until they identify the addicts and find out who's been stealing supplies." She shuddered. "They're not like the EMS, social workers and housing counselors who come to visit. They've got an agenda."

"Well, we brought unconditional food."

Penny Lane smiled. "People will be glad to get it." She waved to a friend and nodded at the woman's unspoken questions. "Do you want to meet some of the people you'll be helping?"

Nolan's request hovered in Wylie's subconscious. "I should probably stay by the truck since I came to help them out."

"Who's paying for the food?"

"The owner wants to get feedback on his menu before he opens a healthy, low-cost chain."

Penny Lane laughed. "Is that why the man hasn't taken his eyes off you?"

"Possibly," Wylie said with a smile.

A woman with coarse braids approached Penny Lane and jutted her chin toward Wylie. "Who's your friend?"

Wylie met the woman's inquisitive greeting with a warm smile. "Hi! I'm Wylie. Modesto is a new concept for food service. Low prices, no guilt, no empty stomachs." The catchphrase seemed to solidify each time she said it. She attempted to channel Antonia's enthusiasm. "Right now, we're adjusting the menu and looking for feedback on the food. It's like a popup."

The woman eyed the truck's wood siding and scratched her head. "It's free food?"

Wylie laughed. "Yep, and you don't even have to smile, pretend you like it or pretend to listen to a sermon. Just give us your honest thoughts."

"Bunch of rich white folks come to do their penance," the woman said. "You going to sleep better at night knowing you gave away some free food?"

Wylie's smile faltered. *No. I'm going to sleep better at night knowing I did something to make the world a better place. Seven or eight billion people live on this planet, but at least I'll go to sleep knowing I tried to do something good.* "Do you like cornbread and chili?"

The woman's gaze narrowed. "Are you profiling me?"

"No." Wylie swallowed. "I'm just trying to support people who want to help you and others like you."

The woman rolled her eyes. "Others like me. You think you can just parachute into this camp and make a difference with a bowl full of beans and rice? You workin' with those dicks in the red shirts?" She scanned the parking lot. "I swear, if this a publicity stunt with a hidden camera, I'm not signing no release."

"I had no idea they would be here."

"Shit. If I wanted this kind of crap, I'd have gone to the shelter."

"She's good, Lori. I vouch for her," Penny Lane said.

"Who said your vote counts? You come and go as you please. Where were you when times were tough? Holed up on the beach or playing house in your la-de-dah apartment." She spat. "Someone call me when Social Services turns up with real help!"

Penny Lane linked arms with the woman and started singing *If I Fell*.

Lori seemingly tried to resist the soothing lyrics, but the familiarity of Penny Lane's voice won her over. She glared at Nolan and Wylie. "You gonna be brave enough to bring us the chili?"

"You want cheese with that?" Wylie asked, trying to smother a grin.

Lori wrinkled her nose and returned to the perimeter of the encampment in the company of Penny Lane.

"I'll take them some bowls," Nolan said. "Why don't we make up a whole tray and I'll bring it out into the camp?"

"I'll take it."

"No, you won't."

She frowned. "Why not?"

"Because I'm nervous and the chances of something going wrong escalates with proximity. I'd rather be in the middle of it than worry about what's happening to you."

Wylie put her hands on her hip. "Who would hurt me? Who would hit a girl?"

"You expect the best from everyone. Everyone makes mistakes."

She swallowed and changed tactics, determined to take ownership of the tense situation. "Nolan, I appreciate your intention, but you're not the only one who wants to feel good about what they're doing. You have everything. Let me have this moment."

Nolan tipped her chin and kissed her, stealing her breath. "I don't have everything. You did a good thing, Wylie. You pushed me to test the boundaries of my business plan. I don't know whether my original designs will work out or if I need to spend time reconfiguring them. Either way, you've done your part to encourage my dream. You're still doing it."

"So you're going to keep me on lockdown, far away from danger?"

He scanned the crowd, shifting with tension as he pitted his wants and needs against the agenda of the red-shirted workers. "Not lockdown, but not exposed to every threat."

She cupped her hand, feeling the connection between them. "But I want to do more, Nolan."

"Rikard was wrong about you," he whispered. "You do belong in this world and so do I."

"So you'll let me bring the food?"

He shook his head, laughter sparkling in the green of his eyes. "No way. I paid for it and I own it."

"You're a bully," she said.

"And you like it."

She dropped her hand. *What if I love it?*

Penny Lane returned, humming a tune Wylie failed to recognize. She turned to smile at her friend, determined to shelve her feelings for Nolan and use Penny Lane's presence like an armed accompaniment.

A man on a light blue bicycle fitted with a string of lights began to circle the aid workers' truck. His wheelies and tricks might have delighted a teenage crowd, but a worker in a red shirt broke from the pack and shooed him off, yelling as he waved his hands in the air. "Hey! Get away from the truck."

"That's just Dougie," Penny Lane said with a smile. "He's harmless."

Wylie's skin prickled as the aid worker and the bicyclist exchanged words. "It's not him I'm worried about."

Penny Lane shook her head. "Sometimes we squabble over donated items, but the arguments don't swell into serious violence."

"I think Dougie needs to back off from the truck."

Penny Lane frowned. "We're a community. He's just trying to break the tension."

Two more aid workers abandoned the group and strode toward the aid truck. Their peer had started yelling at Dougie and the whole encampment went silent when he ripped the string of lights off Dougie's bike. "Is this how you treat your benefactors? Parading around like a circus freak with what little you've got."

Dougie held up his hands. "Whoa, man. I was just horsing around. Give me back my stuff. I don't want any trouble."

"Then get away from the truck!"

"Wylie," Nolan said from the window, "bring Penny Lane around back and show her the kitchen."

Wylie shook her head, mesmerized by the violence simmering below the surface of the confrontation. She knew what it felt like to hold back her anger then finally let it rip. The arrogance and acknowledgment she had seen in Cynthia's eyes told her that the woman had known it too. *Will these men take the high ground or sink to her level?*

Dougie lunged for the lights, but the aid worker's peers mistook his intent and the echoing blast of a gunshot ricocheted through the community. The world seemed to stand still as Wylie braced for a second shot. Newsreels of active shooter coverage flipped through her consciousness like the wheels of a faceless slot machine. Had her time come? When silence reigned over the parking lot, she scanned the camp and the workers. Dougie lay on the ground, clutching his leg. Blood soaked his jeans. The steady drum of traffic obscured his moans, but she saw his face contort, wrinkling his weathered skin. His eyes clenched in pain.

Penny Lane screamed, ran toward Dougie and collapsed on the black asphalt ground "No! I can't lose another friend."

Bile rose in Wylie's throat. She shook her head and covered her mouth as the severity of the moment punctured her disbelief. She scanned the assemble, but both groups had closed ranks. *Who fired?*

In the moment of crisis, she remained rooted to the spot, unable to choose a side. She felt the pressure of an asthma attack starting to build, but she ignored it, chastising her cowardice as she scanned the crowd for the gun owner and weighed her safety against her desire to run toward Penny Lane and her blood-soaked friend. Nolan gripped her arm, his hold an anchor that refused to release her. "Esther's calling nine-one-one," he said. "Stay out of it."

"He's a nice guy!" Penny Lane's wail released the residents of the encampment. Half of them ran to her aid and half turned on the aid workers. "He doesn't deserve to die like this! Nobody does!"

Esther climbed down from the food truck and Nolan shook his head. "This is a line we don't cross. I'm telling you that as your boss and as your friend."

Wylie pulled against his grip as her vision blurred. The sense of disbelief and breathlessness that had underpinned the situation suddenly got worse. She gasped, struggling to draw in a breath of air laden with fear and mobile fumes. "Inhaler." The shortness of breath constrained her words to terse phrases. "It's in my purse."

"Call nine-one-one again," Nolan yelled. He helped her to the ground, cradling her head like she might lose consciousness at any moment.

Wylie wheezed and reached for him, her hand braced against his chest. "No! Take me to the ER. Prednisone. Nebulizer treatment or both. We've got plenty of time."

"Your fingertips are turning blue," he said.

Wylie closed her eyes, waiting for the sweet release of the rescue inhaler.

"I can't find it!" Esther stumbled from the truck and loosened a stream of Portuguese profanities before she turned on the operator who had taken her second call. "Send another ambulance." She described Wylie's condition and listened, turning to Nolan. "The regional nine-one-one operator has to route the call to the local police to send help. She's a screener. She can't do it herself."

"Can't afford it." Wylie gasped. The thought of financial ruin sent her panic into overdrive, accelerating her asthma attack as the muscles in her airway tightened and restricted her airflow. "Take the car."

Nolan shook his head and rubbed her back. "I can afford it. People die from asthma attacks. You're not going to be one of them."

You're not responsible for me. She tried to form the words, but her vision blurred and she blacked out.

* * * *

The upright gurney bounced and shook as the ambulance driver pushed the vehicle through the rough streets of Los Angeles. In the back of the cab, the lead paramedic administered a nebulized bronchodilator to open Wylie's airways. She blinked and focused on the man, trusting his uniform above all else. He nodded as the mask over her mouth clouded and she strained to pull in the life-saving medication that would open her airways.

This is ridiculous. She felt the tension in her chest begin to ease. Her body ached, but each breath gave her relief as the beeps and alarms of the emergency equipment gave proof of her condition. *They wouldn't have taken me if I hadn't needed it.*

"Your boyfriend looked worried sick," the paramedic said as the medication stabilized her system. "We had to listen to your lung sounds, measure oxygen levels and take a peak flow reading before we could load you." He glanced at the small window separating them from the driver. "Most of the time we just have to worry about overprotective pets."

He's not my boyfriend.

"Gave you an adrenaline injection to open the airways first. If your heart had stopped beating, the attack could have starved your brain of oxygen." The paramedic shook his head. "That was a severe attack, but your man almost passed out too. I don't think he's a big fan of needles."

Wylie closed her eyes as the narrative eclipsed her financial reserves. Living in her SUV had seemed like a low point, but selling the vehicle to cover her medical expenses would feel so much worse. She registered the ambulance sirens and drew in the life-saving medication. *Life is a series of emergencies when you don't have any money. How long before I can teach again?*

"You're lucky someone was with you. The GPS coordinates provided by your friend's cellphone carrier gave us an approximate location, but fifty to three-hundred meters is a big area to search."

She struggled to open her eyes and respond.

He shook his head and placed a comforting hand on her arm. "Relax and trust the nebulizer."

This is worse than the dental hygienist. She wanted to thank the man for his professional intervention, but the mask constrained her response. *When was the last time I even visited a dentist?*

The paramedic sighed. "Emergency infrastructure hasn't adapted fast enough to deal with our wireless world. What would have happened if you'd been out in the desert?" He shook his head. "You're lucky we're all familiar with that homeless encampment."

She straightened, desperate to know what had happened to Dougie.

"The older man's going to be okay," the paramedic said.

"I can't say the same for that aid worker. Who brings a gun to a charity mission?" The driver asked from the front seat.

Someone who's afraid.

"Imagine…shooting Dougie. His sister tried to find him a place to live and get him off the streets, but he said living outdoors felt like home and he never wanted to leave." The ambulance came to a stop and the paramedic released the restraints. "An attack like that's going to hurt for a while, but you'll be on your feet again soon enough."

Wylie squeezed his grip on the side of the bed rail, hoping her gesture conveyed her gratitude. When the hospital staff opened the back of the ambulance, she blinked against the intrusion of bright sunlight and struggled to get her bearings. Amid the onslaught of practiced procedures, she took comfort in the worried expression on Nolan's face. He'd ridden to the hospital with her and stayed by her side through thick and thin. *If that isn't love, what is?*

She closed her eyes and remembered Penny Lane's scream as she ran toward her injured friend. *How many times has Penny seen blood during her time on the streets? How many times has she worried for her safety?* She had lived with Larry for a few years and called him her best friend, but then claimed they had never had a relationship. *'I'm more of a caregiver without the right credentials.' Is she too afraid to admit she loved and lost him or too afraid it might happen again?*

Chapter Seventeen

"Even though your symptoms responded to the medications, we want to keep you in the ER for a few hours to make sure your symptoms stay under control," the doctor on call told Wylie.

She shifted on the emergency room bed, anticipating the cost of an extended stay. *At least they're not going to admit me.*

"I'm mainly worried about your oxygen levels. Your lung test results are still a little low and you had so much trouble breathing that I'm worried it exhausted you. We'll have the nurses monitor your progress and ensure you won't go into lung failure when you get home."

She swallowed. "I'll take my medications like a champ. What are you sending me home with? Corticosteroids?" The doctor raised his eyebrows. "It's amazing what kind of medical knowledge you pick up when you're managing a chronic condition." Nolan peeked into the room and she nodded to admit him.

"My roommate will help me stay on top of the medication."

The two men exchanged glances and Nolan smiled. "She's downplaying our relationship. I won't let her leave my bed."

"That's inappropriate," Wylie said.

"You want to come home with me or stay in the hospital for a few more days?"

She considered a range of outraged responses, but the creeping exhaustion of the attack stole her will to fight back against his display of possessiveness. "I appreciate your help."

He smiled. "We'll see how long that lasts."

The doctor cleared his throat. "The best way to prevent another severe attack is to follow your asthma action plan and avoid the things that trigger your attacks. Do you know what set you off? For many people, it's dust, smoke, cold weather, exercise or viruses."

She thought about the preceding week. Dottie's eviction, the tow truck and her shift at the food truck had tightened her airways, but her body's response had paled in comparison to this attack. "What about stress?"

The doctor glanced up from his chart. "Stress can do it too. Add a dose of irritants and you can understand why it's so important to carry your rescue inhaler."

She exhaled and shook her head. "I must have ten of them stashed in purses and pockets. It was a careless error." *And it's going to cost me.* She sat up straight and projected the last of her strength into a smile. "I'll rest better in his bed than in the hospital."

When the doctor left, Wylie and Nolan stared at each other amid the sterile odors and quiet beeps of the emergency room. She wanted him to sit next to her, sharing the heat and spice of his presence without making demands and discussing what to do next. Instead, he pulled his phone and wallet from his jeans and settled into the rigid chair at the side of the bed, waiting for her to talk.

She sighed. "Thank you for calling nine-one-one."

"You needed it."

She bit her lip, afraid to admit what she needed. Her fingers had started turning blue from lack of oxygen, but what about her heart?

"Do you want to call your mom and dad in Oregon?"

"No!" The word flew from her lips so fast she choked. Coughing, she wrung her fingers to keep warm and give herself time to process her thoughts. "They told me to try living in this town, but they said I wouldn't make it a year as a freelance instructor."

"They don't have a lot of confidence in your abilities?"

She shook her head. "It's not that. It's just that my mom thinks our family is stronger when we're together. She told me to tag along with them, but what would that get me? I've always been their third-wheel, tagalong kid. I wanted to stay in LA and do something by myself."

Nolan stared at the speckled linoleum. "I'm an only child too." He looked up. "Did you know that?"

She shook her head.

He smiled and looked toward the bustle of the emergency room, seeing things no one else could see. "I understand wanting to do something by yourself, but I also think you can set a course without doing everything yourself."

"All my friends left. They made compromises or moved to the suburbs. I don't want to depend on the wrong person and find myself leaving town. That would be my grave and there'd be nothing left of what I wanted here but memories and ghosts."

"And if you have your next asthma attack while you're hell-bent on proving your independence?"

She coughed. "Don't use my diagnosis against me! Would you be this brave if you didn't have mommy's millions warming your back pocket?"

"I don't know," he said, running his hand through his hair. "They've always been there, like a weight I couldn't shake off." His hand stilled and he dropped it. "But ever since I developed feelings for you, the weight has meaning. I told my mom about you, Wylie. Before you got sick, I called her and told her about what's been driving me and what you've helped me see in this world. She accused me of lust and puppy love."

Wylie opened her mouth to defend his actions.

"Then I explained how you've been helping me and encouraging me to take risks. I explained your friendship with Penny Lane. It boggles her mind that you'd be friends with a person whose pockets are literally empty."

"Anyone would love Penny Lane," she said, dodging the compliment. "She's got this vibe."

"You've got a vibe too, Wylie. You see the best in people."

She blushed.

"I called my mom again."

"Seriously?"

"I explained what we've been doing" — he blushed — "well, not all of it, but enough about Modesto to challenge her to see what I have planned. I pushed her to make more commitments to the communities where she does business."

"How'd that go down?"

"She waffled, but I used Patty's challenge as leverage. What are the optics of one family member offering sustenance while the other dangles shelter out of reach?"

"Were you disappointed she didn't immediately want to help?"

He laughed. "No. If you knew my mom, you'd know she has strong opinions. It meant a lot to me that she accepted my plans for Modesto without trying to talk me out of them. Sometimes silence is the best compliment."

"But she's your mom," Wylie said, thinking of her parents and the intimacy of her childhood. Beneath the financial awareness, she knew they always loved her.

"My mother's also a businesswoman. I know Modesto can't compete on economics, but the appeal of a public image boost gets her involved until she sees the impact firsthand."

"That was clever," she said, "but don't you want more from your mom?"

"I want her to take me seriously."

"Is she?"

He smoothed her hair. "Seriously enough. One day, I hope she'll be proud."

Wylie swallowed, thinking of the days and weeks that waited at the end of the calendar. *I worry this thing between us will fall apart when the novelty wears off.* "She has a lot of reasons to be proud of you. You showed up at the Social Club to protest a discriminatory dress code that didn't affect you. You're planning an empire of franchises to help people with whom you have nothing in common. I don't want to worry that you're propping up my emotions as your next cause."

"Damn it, Wylie!" he said. "You've never been a cause! You've never asked me for a single thing for yourself."

"Mini Mako?"

"Did I give in to your beautiful blue eyes?"

"No," she said, swallowing.

"My house created the extended family I craved as a child. Our roommates don't pay rent for shelter. They pay rent for kinship, community and the relationships we all know we need, even if we can't define the need."

"You kicked Jack out."

"Yeah, and sometimes families fall apart. That doesn't mean we should avoid them at all costs. It means we should recognize the time and commitment required to build our extended families."

"Only a week passed," she said.

"I want more time with you if you'll let me have it."

She bit her lip. "It's just so much to take in at one time."

"Take all the time you need, but let me know you're willing to give this thing between us a real shot of succeeding."

She nodded. "I want to be with you, Nolan, but I don't know if I can do it while we're under the same roof, while the balance of power between us feels so off."

"Is this still about the money?"

"I don't want your money, Nolan." She swallowed. *I want your heart.*

He stood and walked toward the bed, closing the distance that loomed between them. "Aren't there perks to letting me take care of you? You wouldn't dismiss my assistance if we'd met standing on a street corner."

She closed her eyes and relished the memory of their first encounter. "We did meet standing on a street corner. At least I was standing… You already had the height advantage." She opened her eyes and patted the space beside her.

He took a deep breath and claimed the offering, lifted her hand and traced the lines on her palm that determined her fate or formed as a result of it. "You're a good person, Wylie, probably a better one than I am. And I'm happier when we're together. I'm happier when your spontaneous kisses and generous nature brighten my day. You compel me to be a better man." He looked up. "Can't you let me take care of you when you need it the most? I promise the rest of the time, I'll let you stand on your own."

She thought of her dreams of independence and the thrill of accomplishment she felt when she deposited her yoga fees into her bank account. *How long will that feeling last as I move farther and farther into Nolan's world? How much longer will I exist in my own right before I live in Nolan's shadow?* She closed her eyes and inhaled. "What were you doing while the doctor and I met?

"Changing your hospital records to reflect my financial responsibility. I got you into this mess. I'll pay the bills when they come in."

Her eyes flew open. "I didn't ask you to do that!" *I didn't ask you to be kind, caring and exactly the opposite of the rich playboy I expected. You want to do the work, but you don't have to. How can I trust that motivation when I'm still fighting to cover my ass?*

He dropped her hand. "What if a charity paid them off? Erasing medical bills is quite the fad. Would you accept their assistance?"

I wouldn't owe them anything. I wouldn't constantly doubt where I stood. "It's not the same," she admitted. "I don't know why it's so hard for you to accept me as I am. What's wrong with me? I'm too damn independent to hold on to friends by myself?"

"I don't want to be your friend, Wylie. I've been falling in love with you since the moment you sassed Cynthia and asked me for a discount at the food truck."

"That's impossible. You said you've met a million social media influencers and turned me down."

"A million faces I easily forgot—but not yours."

She opened her mouth to unleash a self-deprecating comment, but he shook his head and reached for her, sliding his callused thumb along her cheekbone. She closed her eyes and savored the rough caress and the mark of effort from a man who could have chosen to sit back and just have fun.

"And not a single one of those influencers fought back when I let them down gently." He tucked her hair behind her ear. "You're so fierce and generous, so genuine. I'd do anything to have you by my side."

And hold you. And keep you in the back of the truck. She shivered and opened her eyes. "Nolan, you've got a big heart, but I need my independence. We didn't meet on the street corner as equals. I trust you here, but the minute we get out of bed, I want to reclaim my control. The pleasure comes from letting go and knowing you can claim it all back. I can't do that if you govern every facet of my life."

He shook his head and sighed. "I'm still going to take care of you when we get back to the house. I'm still going to remind you to take care of yourself."

"Because I can't do it by myself?"

"No." He reached for his wallet and phone. "Because I see more in you than you see in yourself."

His soft, sad smile tugged at her heartstrings, but she refused to melt into his arms.

"Pierce posted the video of you taking down Cynthia. He tagged Modesto and #Authentic. I don't know whether the quality of the food truck's food even matters right now. People are curious and our follower count is through the roof."

"You need to capitalize on that and share your message."

He reached for the door. "Thanks, Mini Mako. Give me a call when they discharge you so I can bring you back to the house."

You mean, give me a call so we can admit we're all done.

Penny Lane smiled at Nolan and stopped him in the hallway with a full body hug.

Wylie tried to read their lips and the easy smiles passing between them. *Life's easier when you understand the terms of the transactions.* She flopped back on the white, chlorine-scented pillows. *At least Penny Lane knows where she stands.*

When the woman came into the room, Wylie summoned a smile and raised her head. "Thanks for coming to visit."

"Dougie's going to be fine."

Dougie. I've been feeling sorry for myself while surgeons have been laboring to repair the damage to his leg. "I'm so glad to hear it."

"Nolan's going to take care of whatever medical bills Medicare doesn't cover. Plus, he's going to pay for a rehab facility to get Dougie on his feet again."

Of course, he's footing those bills. The man would take responsibility for the sun if he thought it needed help. I just don't want to be another one of his projects. She smiled to hide the dejection stemming from her thoughts. "That's great to hear."

Penny Lane's forehead wrinkled as she frowned. "You know, one of the first things you learn in the homeless community is to share what you've got. Propane heaters. Extra bags. Repair patches for the tents. It doesn't matter. You never know when you'll need something or someone else will have something to spare."

"Seems like people would spend more time guarding what little they have."

"No, that's no way to live. People who go rogue? It's miserable. Every night, they're trying to sleep with one eye open. How can you rest?"

Wylie faced the white wall and thought of the days she had spent drifting from building to building, wondering what to do next. "You can't."

Nolan had offered her an easy solution. Exchange part of her freedom for the pleasure of his bed and the achievement of supporting his dreams. Exchange part of her pride for the trust of finding someone beside you on those nights when tossing and turning precludes sleep. Why was this step such a no-brainer for everyone else? Why couldn't she let go of every decision?

He ran Modesto for personal satisfaction, knowing his family and peers probably saw it as a way to relieve his boredom. Hadn't the Abramowitzes accused him of just that? She could no more see Nolan as an astronaut than she could see him in the boardroom. He thrived on connecting to people, and for some unknowable reason, he wanted to form a more permanent connection with her. *He doesn't need to prove himself, but I still can.*

She turned to Penny Lane. "I don't want you to worry about sleeping on your own. I don't have a lot to share, but I'm going to get an apartment and give you first dibs if you want to be my roommate. We'll find you a job or find a way to leverage your existing benefits. Even if you say no, I want you to understand you're always welcome on my couch."

Penny Lane smiled and sat on the edge of the bed. "I always wanted a kid, but you're a lot more fun than a decade of puberty and stinky underpants."

Wylie laughed and coughed as her aching throat muscles protested the sudden movements. "I'm a grown-ass adult."

A pair of reporters with press badges and high-tech cameras knocked on the door. "Ms. Lane? Are you still willing to do a segment?"

Wylie raised her eyebrows. "What's this?"

"They heard about Dougie's shooting and they're doing a piece on the problems with Los Angeles' growing homeless problem. They asked if they could tape an interview with me, but I wanted to come see if you were all right first."

"Yep, you can totally lay claim to my couch, when I get one."

Penny Lane smiled and looked at the reporters. "Wylie was there too. She had an asthma attack, but she saw the whole thing happen."

The reporters exchanged looks and the younger one pulled out a pen and piece of paper. "Can you spell your name?"

* * * *

Wylie moved into the Sun Salutation and turned her face toward the bedroom window.

In the last forty-eight hours, social media comments had prompted Cynthia to reevaluate the way she'd shut down her studio. Multiple clients and trainees had peppered her posts with frustrated comments about the spirit of the discipline. After the hundredth comment, she'd called Wylie, apologized for her behavior and offered to cover Wylie's beachside classes. "Nobody's ever held me accountable before you did," she said.

Wylie's phone had some interference. "Sorry. I can't hear you too well."

Cynthia continued to chatter and add caveats to her admission.

Hell hath no fury like Internet backlash. She took a deep breath and grinned, knowing enough about wolves in sheep's clothing to be wary of exposing her regular customers to Cynthia's false contrition. Then she paused. *What if Cynthia wants to turn around her approach to running a practice?* "I appreciate the offer. I have the class covered, but it'd be great if you can attend."

"I'll be there."

Two minutes later, Cynthia updated her posts with plans for reconciliation.

Wylie shook her head and put down her phone, knowing the comment trolls criticized her actions as well. She closed her eyes, remembering how the pleasure of taking down Cynthia had receded faster than the pain of finding a new path to certification. Between Pierce's viral video and the publicity from her interview with Penny Lane, she knew she possessed enough time and momentum to let her body heal, but she worried about her heart. *I can't solve all my problems with a social media post.*

Nolan had escorted her home from the emergency room and turned her over to the care of the other housemates, but she felt his presence in the house. She could not creep down the stairs without one of her roommates hearing her footsteps and running to her side to offer to help. The support should have buoyed her mood, but she chafed against the public barrier.

Her formal and informal press coverage had caused a surge in her follower count. Sore knuckles and embarrassment might keep her from choosing violence for a very long time, but she recognized the benefits of the notoriety and the opportunity to support someone else. If only it had allowed her to understand what had happened between her and Nolan.

This time, she checked the messaging for activity before venturing from her room. Seeing no chatter, she tiptoed down the steps and locked eyes with Nolan. He sat on the other side of the living area, laptop and papers spread across the dining table that had once housed a jury more opinionated than the board of a New York co-op. *At least the commune environment encouraged them to act in the community's best interests instead of for their benefit.* She smiled at Nolan, knowing he had enabled that environment.

"Hi!" Antonia said, bobbing up from the couch like a curious sea otter.

"Hey," Wylie said, gripping her arms and aware of the other woman's scrutiny.

"Are you cold? Let me get you some coffee."

"I'm good," Wylie said.

Antonia ignored the claim, took her hand and settled her on the couch like a small child. Before Wylie could object, Antonia had ignored the reading on the thermostat and plied her with enough blankets to spike a fever. Wylie smiled and offered her thanks, but Antonia wrinkled her nose as she judged her efforts for completeness. She offered Wylie hot chocolate and brewed tea, but Wylie refused them both. Antonia scratched her head. "Straight whiskey?"

"Antonia, I just want to relax." She patted the couch cushion beside her, wondering if the coordinated furniture had ever housed more than one occupant. Most of the bonding action occurred around food, the pool or the mismatched furniture on the first level. "Come sit with me. It was an asthma attack, not a round of chemotherapy."

The woman sank to the couch and cradled her cheeks. "Oh my God. Do you have cancer?"

Wylie winced and met Nolan's gaze. He smiled and focused on his work, leaving her to fend for herself. "Nope. Just asthma."

Neil and Rikard climbed the stairs from the ground floor and paused to take in the scene. Neil mumbled a few words about chores and the men disappeared to the top floor without further comment or concern for her well-being. *Well, at least they're getting back to normal.*

When they returned, they carried Jack's belongings back to the ground floor. The creaking garage door and the sound of steady footsteps told Wylie the techie's brooding threats would soon be gone for good, but she could not ignore the pang of empathy she felt for him. *Where will he go? I can't let Nolan solve one problem and leave two in its wake.* She considered Antonia's hovering presence. "Antonia, would you mind giving Nolan and me a few minutes to talk alone?"

"I could draw you a bath."

"Just some quiet time would be good."

Her face fell.

Wylie reached for her hand. "Thanks so much for looking after me these last few days."

"Any time! You deserve it. The way you spoke about Penny Lane and the things she's been through? It was just so humanizing. I mean, I'm never going to look at a homeless person the same way again."

But do I deserve it? Wylie wondered, hoping she had found a way to do good. Reservations for her next yoga session had gone through the roof. She knew people would come to satisfy their curiosity but wondered if they would stay to develop their practice. "Penny Lane deserves the credit," she said. "Dougie is her friend. The only thing I did was legitimize her story, and that worries me more than anything else. Why does my testimony mean more than hers?"

"Because you're putting yourself out there. You've got something to lose."

She nodded, remembering Penny Lane's admonishment on the windswept beach. *'You're so young. Don't you see how many options you have left?'*

When Antonia left to give them a reprieve, Wylie dropped her pretenses and looked at Nolan with blatant curiosity, wondering what effects the last two days of distance had wrought on the bones of their relationship. When the contrivances were stripped away, was there anything left but lust?

Every time she had descended from her room, she had found him hovering at the perimeter of the common space, laptop and cell phone in hand while he kept her in sight. His constant presence had allowed him to plan Modesto's expansion and given her the reassurance she needed that he would be there when she felt ready to discuss their next steps. "I'm fine," she said to break the tension when he remained quiet and returned to his work.

"I know you're fine," he said without looking up.

"How do you know that?"

Their gazes met. "Your color's back."

Wylie touched her cheek. *He's seen so much of my color. Am I willing to throw away that type of intimacy to maintain my independence?* She stood and wrapped Antonia's blanket around her body like a shield. "Metro Movement asked Penny Lane and me to be ambassadors for its program, Steps to End Homelessness."

He raised his eyebrows. "What does that entail?"

She thought of the ubiquitous social organization guiding community charities throughout her childhood. Every holiday seemed to come with a tie-in to the city's humble defender. Metro Movement collected funds for local charities, coordinated relief services, counseled and referred clients to cooperating agencies, and stepped up to the plate with emergency assistance grants when they ran out of partner resources. "Pro bono work."

"You're going to teach yoga?"

She thought of the homeless camp and wondered how many residents would humor her efforts to refine their mind, body and spirit. "Not quite. I'm leaning on my new notoriety to keep spreading the word about their efforts. Their 5k is coming up soon."

"Mini Mako strikes again."

She pulled out a chair and tried not to look at the contract language and columns of numbers spread before him. His camaraderie with Cynthia had seemed so approachable, even from the vaulted height of the food truck. She wondered if she would have bantered with him if she'd understood the scope of his ambitions.

"They've partnered with businesses, philanthropists and government services to end homelessness by providing long-term housing and supportive care to those who need it."

He nodded and kept typing, answering messages she had no right to see. She sighed and propped her head on her hand, wondering if his question had been rhetorical or an easy way to keep the conversation flowing between them.

"They've already got a bunch of social media ambassadors, but Penny Lane made it clear she wants to do more and I feel like I'm in a position to help her with the transition. She reached out to me when I needed a friend. I want to do the same for her and help her navigate this."

Nolan's hands stilled. "Her life has changed a lot in forty-eight hours."

Wylie bit her lip, knowing he spoke the truth. Her friend no longer needed Wylie's offer of a couch or a place to rest her head. If the woman maintained her current momentum, she would be the person offering roofs and warm beds to those who needed them.

After the interview, an organization focused on limited equity cooperatives had tapped Penny Lane to be their social services liaison. The organization created and preserved affordable housing for very low-income individuals and families, but needed someone who understood the needs of the residents they served. Penny Lane's televised testimony about the needs of their community members had struck a chord with their leadership. While they assembled sites and funding to expand the supply of affordable housing, she would collect a paycheck by earning the trust of the people who needed their help the most.

"You were right about something, Nolan. So many people are trying to solve the homeless problem with grassroots campaigns. They're attempting to make an impact through events tailored to their specific communities. But what if they're only tackling the things they see? The things they feel they can bite off?"

His hands stilled and she kept talking, seizing his attention. "The week before Thanksgiving is National Hunger and Homelessness Awareness Week. It started at Villanova in 1975. That's, like, forty-five years ago."

He smiled. "I'm pretty good at math."

"Well, I'm not." She adjusted the blanket cradling her chest. "I would have just rounded it and said two decades."

"Two decades ago was the year 2000."

She bit her lip and enjoyed the glimpse of humor that had first drawn her to him. *This man needs to do more than sit behind a boardroom table.* "The Greater Los Angeles Steps to End Homelessness 5K run-walk has mobilized close to a hundred thousand participants and raised close to nine million dollars. It's happening in May and I want Modesto to be there."

"Wylie, I'm glad you read your talking points, but" — he held up his hand when she tried to cut him off — "Modesto's not ready for that kind of launch. *I'm* not ready for that kind of launch."

She loosened her grip on the blanket and let it pool around her. "How long are you going to fine-tune your menu?"

He turned the laptop screen and revealed rows of menu items and neat columns describing cost, preparation time and caloric content. "The menu's done."

"So bring the food truck to the event. Sponsor one of the stages and tell people how they can help you accomplish your goals—low prices, no guilt, no empty stomachs."

"Why does it have to be me sponsoring their event? Why can't they help us deliver our message? You can just slip it into your speech if you get a chance."

His quiet resistance stirred the embers of her heart. She had listened to him move through the house and recognized the stillness when he paused at the top of the stairs. He had so many resources, but years of second-guessing motives had taught him to hold on to his dreams until they were perfect and defendable. *Is that why he opened his heart and his home to me? Because I asked nothing in return?*

She had lain in bed, weak from the asthma attack, wishing she could roll over and take comfort in his arms. For a while, she had simply wanted to open her door and tell him they could go back to being friends with benefits, no questions asked. She imagined them spending their days sitting on the beach like anonymous tourists, on vacation from pursuing their dreams. Experience told her that wouldn't be possible. She had learned enough about Nolan's fierce loyalty to refrain from distracting Nolan with that path. She had done nothing to deserve his interest or jeopardize what he could accomplish. The best thing she could do would be to move out of the house.

"It won't pack the same punch," she said. "I've already got my marching orders. Beachside yoga and social ambassador. You're the one with the dream to transform a community. You're the one who needs to articulate it."

Nolan closed his laptop screen. "I'll think about it."

"You'll think about it?" She cocked her head. "Are you afraid to launch?"

"No, but I'm as stubborn as you are, Wylie. I'll do it on my terms. That's the thing about finally putting your heart on the line. You have to be willing to accept the consequences if you fail."

"You're not going to fail," she whispered.

"Then join me. Think about what you're going to do when Penny Lane picks up the tab for your next coffee. Think about how many people you could help by building something big. I'm not asking you to give up your yoga practice, I'm asking you to give me the time you would have spent at a corporate gig. Drop the accreditation schemes and come to work for Modesto."

"I need health insurance," she said.

"Great, you'll have it. What else do you need to feel secure?"

She noticed the dark shadows beneath his eyes and wondered if she had been the only one wide awake in the middle of the night. "We just met, Nolan. How can you ask me to jeopardize my independence to support your dream?"

He came around the table and leaned toward her until she closed her eyes, memorizing the hint of citrus, mint and spice that lingered in her dreams, knowing she could soon lose it.

"Wylie, I'd ask you to marry me if I thought you'd say 'yes'."

"What?" she asked, eyes wide open now.

He pulled back and met the surprise in her gaze. "Do you understand how serious I am? I'm asking you for the chance to build something greater than the two of us. Our fake relationship is the best thing that has happened to me in a long time, but I don't have the luxury of looking over my shoulder and wondering if you're all in. I need to know you're there, by my side, happy with the decisions we're making together."

"I just needed a place to stay," she said.

"Well, you've got a hell of a lot more, if you want it." Her mouth opened, but he left her feeble protest lingering between them as he climbed the stairs to the third floor.

Wylie closed her mouth. Twenty-six felt a long way from the romance of sixteen and the practicality of thirty-six. *Who mentions marriage in Los Angeles unless they mean it?* Her lease said she had as much right to be in the house as Nolan did, but the man had changed the stakes. She stayed seated at the table, staring at her reflection in the picture window.

Now which one of us is afraid to launch?

Chapter Eighteen

A night spent tossing and turning had left Wylie feeling restless. *I live in a mansion, but money can't buy peace of mind.* She swung her legs over the side of the single bed and stretched. Her phone buzzed with an incoming call. "Hi, Mom."

"How're you feeling, sweetheart?"

"Good. I feel a little bit stronger every time I eat something. My strength is coming back too. The attack was just so hard on my body."

"I put some muffins in the mail. It's a new recipe. I want you to eat some and share some with your roommate, Nolan."

Wylie closed her eyes. "He's a little bit more than a roommate."

Silence dominated the line. "Well, I assumed that must be the case. Nobody pauses their life to take charge of a stranger's care."

Some people do.

"I could still come down there," her mother said. "Play nurse. Make sure you have what you need."

"No, I'm okay." She cleared her throat and thought about Patty's education and the social and cultural experiences conveyed by her Jewish mother. "You already gave me what I need to keep going. You got up every day and finished your list of tasks because you wanted to have it all, nineties style. I'm not sure that combination will work out for me, but I appreciate what you and Dad did to have it all. Your work ethic is good and I'm starting to think it's the most valuable asset I have."

"Your dad and I are proud of you, sweetheart, but you don't have to do this all on your own. We could help."

"That's not necessary."

"I couldn't have raised you on my own. Your dad loves you dearly, but he's also a lifesaver when it comes to getting things done."

"Yeah, he's pretty great."

"So, it's okay to lean on someone. Sometimes having a partner is the greatest risk and the greatest reward."

"My yoga practice is kind of a one-woman show," Wylie said, unwilling to elevate Nolan's presence in her life when she had no idea how she wanted the script to play out. "I guess I could find another instructor and offer more classes. I like what I do, but I need a path toward benefits."

"A studio job might also give you a pension."

"I doubt it."

Her mom sighed. "We should have brought you along when we refinanced our mortgage and reviewed our annual retirement contributions. It might have helped you choose another route."

Wylie could imagine the angst of shifting in a pleather chair while a suit droned on about tax brackets and refunds. "Please, no." *Give me the people.*

Her mom sighed. "I mean, we did the best with what we had. You know that?"

"You did well," Wylie said, sensing her mom's uncertainties and hurrying to alleviate them. "Your lessons on money management didn't turn me into a corporate lawyer, but you taught me to keep fighting and planning. I appreciate those traits and they've made me a better person. There's no way I would let down my clients like Cynthia did."

Her mom *tsk-tsked*. "What was that woman thinking?"

Wylie decided to save that conversation for another day. "The point is, being a pampered princess might have been fun, but understanding the ins and outs of life was, like, good, you know — good in the long run. So, thanks."

"Sweetheart, what kind of drugs did they give you at the hospital?"

Wylie laughed. "You know, I'm glad the sellers accepted your offer for the contemporary home you showed me. You and Dad deserve it after decades of working hard, and one day I'll have room to come visit."

Her mother laughed. "We could have worked a lot less, but we wanted you to have the best. Maybe we should have tried harder to hide the daily stress, but you always wanted to help. You always wanted to understand the tradeoffs behind the benefits."

"I wanted to be the blasé princess," she admitted, "but I think it helped me understand your moods when life got hard. It wasn't me stressing you out."

"No. It wasn't you. It was everything we wanted versus everything we had—month after month of trying to make it all work out. Looking back, the work paid off."

"You're not disappointed in me?" She closed her eyes, expecting her mother to soften her response. "You're not disappointed I bailed on college and decided to do this whole yoga thing?"

"We could never be disappointed in you, Wylie. You were worth every moment of stress."

She walked toward the window, giving herself time to digest the comment. *Well, there was that time in high school I stole a pack of cigarettes from the corner store.*

Her mother cleared her throat. "You've always been very observant and sensitive to other people's needs. Instead of nursing or psychotherapy, you found a way to guide people toward inner peace that makes you happy. It's very new age, but we're proud of you for making it work."

"But?" Wylie asked, hearing the note of hesitation in her mother's response.

"Just make sure it's still the right decision. There's nothing wrong with spending a few years on one venture before trying another one. You're only twenty-six."

Twenty-six feels like an eternity when you're in high school and a blink of the eye when you're looking back. She smiled. "It's hard to keep track of what that means. Sometimes I feel like I'm clueless and sometimes I feel like I've made decisions that will impact the rest of my life."

Her mother laughed. "Well, you just get out of bed each morning and keep going as long as you can. Your father and I never saw it coming, but we're enjoying our new life in Oregon. You never know what's waiting just down the river."

I'm not even going to think of Nolan, asleep in that big bed just down the hall. "Thanks, Mom," she said. "I have to go. It's my first class back on the beach."

"It's so soon. Couldn't you take a longer break?"

"Maybe, but I'm already out of bed. I might as well keep going."

"Eat the muffins," her mother said. "They're full of protein."

"Maybe you could send me the recipe?"

"You've started cooking?"

"Not exactly," she said, "but I think Nolan's always on the lookout for new items."

"Interesting."

Wylie shook her head. "Just the recipe, Mom."

"I'll email it tonight."

That's so cute and old school. She pressed the home button on her phone and navigated to the app she used to monitor class reservations. It had been two in the morning the last time she'd checked her class count. Now she had twenty-three registered participants. *That's a good class, but a fraction of what I need to chart a new course. I'll just keep going until I get it done.*

Instead of emitting a cool beacon of light, her phone flashed and left her with a faceless black screen. "Shit." She threw back the covers and judged the sky to tell the time. Twenty-three participants expected her to be prompt and perky. Without those guarantees, she knew they would find somewhere else to stretch, strengthen their muscles and breathe in the fresh salt air.

Nolan stood at the kitchen island with his orange juice. Wylie lamented the shirt he wore, but she scanned the room for electronic devices. "What time is it?"

"Seven-forty-five."

She collapsed in a chair and pressed a hand to her racing heart. "I worried I overslept."

"Bad night?"

She looked up. "It could have been better."

He met her gaze and put down the glass. "Have dinner with me tonight?"

"We've eaten together almost every night this week."

"Just the two of us," he said. "I've wanted to take you out since the moment I recognized you outside that ridiculous club."

She thought about the first time she had seen him at the food truck and stifled her jealousy as he bantered with Cynthia. "Not before?"

He grinned. "Well, it seemed inappropriate to blur the lines when we were discussing business."

"Mini Mako," she whispered. "How much did I make? Three dollars?"

"I think you can claim a free meal."

She snorted. "You've been giving away free food all week. I would have done better to stand in line with everyone else."

"It's a sliding scale." He shrugged. "But I'm not talking about dinner on the steps of the truck. I'm talking about you and me and candlelight. I'm talking about taking this thing between us back to square one."

"What happened to marrying me?"

He raised his eyebrows. "Would you say 'yes'?"

She shook her head.

"Then it's not a question I'm willing to ask." He spread his hands on the countertop, as unyielding as a master of the boardroom. "I've learned there are some questions you should only ask once."

Should I help this man? Should I marry this man? Can I go all in before I even know myself?

"And maybe it's my fault I feel as strongly as I do," he said before she could voice her thoughts.

"You've tried to take care of me from the start," she whispered. "I couldn't be any more of a distraction."

"Take your clothes off and meet me by the pool if you want to test that statement."

She smiled. "I'm not sure I'm back to full form."

He nodded and took a step toward her before he stopped himself. "We skipped a few steps. I want to start over again. Just two people who make plans to share a meal."

She glanced at the pool. "You've seen me naked." When he failed to respond, she turned and looked at him, remembering how much she had loved waking up in the cocoon of his arms, laced with musk and citrus.

He raised his eyebrows. "Naked barely counts. I've seen your eyes roll back while your world shattered."

But can I walk away and put it back together again? She rose and met his gaze over the expanse of polished countertops. "I'll agree to dinner for two if you'll agree to two ground rules. Neither one of us brings up Modesto or my yoga practice. We're strangers."

"Strangers who like to fuck."

She smiled. "I know people tend to mix up the steps, but life as a freelance yoga instructor has taught me a few things. Lightning's bad for business and I'm good at fixing awkwardness and getting people back to form."

"Does it always work out?"

She focused on their shadows, blended into a perfect hourglass against the smooth countertop. *How long do he and I have to get this right before his house no longer feels like a haven? Until he wonders if my presence justifies the distraction?* She raised her eyes and met his gaze. "I don't know how often it works out, Nolan. I'm only twenty-six."

"But you know your mind."

She smiled. *That doesn't mean I know my heart.*

* * * *

They rode down the hill together in Nolan's Bronco and she gave thanks that he had control of the wheel. Twenty-three participants would stretch her leadership when she normally managed ten to twelve. *If this is the outcome of notoriety, I'll take it.*

"Nervous?" Nolan asked her.

She glanced at the crowd. "I'll be happy if half of them stay. My phone spazzed out, so I'll just have to honor everyone's presence and consider it a community class if people choose not to pay." She eyed the crowd assembled past the café and frowned. "That's way more than twenty-three participants."

"I, um, retweeted your class announcement," he offered as he put the truck in park. "But most of this probably came from the news coverage and idle curiosity."

She counted fifty people and swallowed. "How many people liked your post?"

"Hmm-m."

"Nolan?"

"Two hundred and fifty-six."

She swore and reached for the handle. *I'm the guppy, not the shark.* She wanted to face him and give him a piece of her mind for putting her in this awkward situation, but she recognized his good intentions and wanted to preserve the pleasure of meeting him across a white tablecloth. "I guess I should say thank you."

"It'll be better for all of us if you just went out there and kicked butt."

Wylie's regulars greeted her from the front row as she walked around the milling crowd. Their unfurled beach towels and coordinated yoga mats felt like an island of familiarity designed to calm her mind. She made a point of greeting each of them by name, bowing her head as the wind lulled. "Namaste," she said, and her respectful comment lingered above the crowd.

Then someone coughed and the first person stood up. Within seconds, the peace of the communal session dissolved into factions.

She looked past the front row and saw Rusty with Candy, who was wearing an outfit cut so low she wondered if Candy's cleavage might spill out of her top. The man's pathetic first attempts at beachside yoga had left him fumbling for purchase, but she applauded his willingness to try it again. She turned away from the sight of Rusty's chest hair and smiled to see Dede and Jeanie amid the crowd.

The women stood side by side as the morning sunlight reflected from the remnants of body glitter that suggested they had come straight from the Social Club. Despite their practiced customer service skills, they eyed the crowd, shifting to find their place amid the newbies and neighbors. Wylie waved at the pair and smiled when Dede gave her a thumbs up. *They're here, and that's what counts the most.*

"I want to thank everyone for coming to the beach this morning to refine your practice. It doesn't matter if this is your fiftieth class or your first, I want you to get something out of it. My name's Wylie and I'm going to do my best to lead you through this morning's poses. I don't know whether you found this class through social media or Modesto's post, but I'm glad you're here." She swallowed and counted the haphazard rows of participants. Fifty sets of eyes remained focused on her. "Let's form an aisle down the middle so I can move around while you hold your poses."

A woman with the toned arms of a lifelong practitioner strolled toward the group and Wylie inhaled, wondering when common sense would allow her to acknowledge too much of a good thing. Then she blinked and recognized the woman's white teeth and dyed black bob. "Cynthia," she said, hoping the woman heard her name above the chatter of the growing crowd.

"Figured you could use some help this morning." Her former instructor dropped her mat near the front of the group and scanned the assembly. "Word to the wise, you should cap classes at ten to twenty participants. People feel more engaged when you maintain a small group setting and a small student-to-teacher ratio."

Wylie surveyed the crowd of fifty. *The beach can expand. Why can't I?* She recognized the intent behind Cynthia's peace offering and shook her head. "Did they also tell you to bring a small army of assistants when things don't work out like you planned?"

"Nope, kid, just me...if you'll accept the help."

"I insulted you," Wylie said.

"Yeah. Life's a bitch. Don't do it again."

Wylie nodded and realized sweat and hard work were only two of the things separating her from Cynthia's studio success. The woman knew when to cut her losses and when to stand on her two feet and try again. "I appreciate the help."

"I'll appreciate a hundred bucks if you have it."

"That's fair," she said, hoping her regulars were not the only paying participants.

Cynthia stood at her side and appeared to be considering the skill range of the crowd. "You know, the only way to protect yourself from personal injury liability is to make use of effective releases. You have insurance, right?"

"I mean, I have an umbrella policy," Wylie said.

"Make sure your insurance covers all your activities and, for God's sake, never ask about preexisting injuries. All these newbies? They need to sign waivers."

Wylie faced the woman. "What?"

"You know asking about student injuries before class may increase your liability? Once you're aware of a student's medical concerns, you have a higher duty of care to make sure the class doesn't cause further injury."

"That's ruthless."

Cynthia shrugged. "Sometimes you have to draw a line between compassion and legal precedent."

Or decide to take the money and run. She recognized that Cynthia's business experience could be just as valuable as her credentials, but wondered if she could trust the instructor's loyalty beyond pitching in at an impromptu session. *I just have to recognize the differences between partnership, deference and respect.*

She faced the crowd of eager faces, knowing that those who had registered online had signed an electronic waiver and she would just have to risk the implications of teaching the rest of them.

Nolan stood in the back row, shirtless and surrounded by a crowd of mismatched yoga enthusiasts.

Their faded and eclectic athletic gear stood out against the uniformity of the regular crew, but she recognized their presence and the potential impact on her bottom line. She had plenty of respect for Palisades Park, streamlined sets and glossy magazine advertisements, but a few nights of vulnerability had given her a desire to serve the rest of the world.

She cleared her throat and addressed the crowd. "I'm excited to see so many new faces, but technology has both lifted me and failed me." Several participants laughed and nodded at her honesty. "I didn't prepare for a group this size, but Cynthia's going to help me run the class and adjust poses. Given today's constraints, we'll keep our practice gentle and give our new friends their best opportunity to participate if they're beginning their practice. Those of you who want more instruction can stick around for an extra thirty minutes and focus on flexibility. We'll staff up if interest continues at this level. Everyone can find their yoga home with us."

Esther and Penny Lane crossed the sand to join their group fifteen minutes later. The pair laughed throughout the entire session, drawing looks of ire from Isabella and the few participants clinging to discomfort amid the unfamiliar crowd. When the session ended, Wylie kept her back to the ocean and planted her feet, prepared to answer questions and honor her offer for thirty minutes focused on flexibility.

Rusty leaned on Candy and led the waitresses to the front of group. "I can't believe you do that shit every other day. No wonder you always jumped out of bed on the mornings you had to work."

"Well, maybe you should come to a few more sessions," Wylie said. She avoided meeting Candy's curious gaze but responded to Dede and Jeanie's laughter. "What's so funny?"

"Rusty said he's going to build something new with the Social Club, but he's out of his mind if he thinks the neighborhood wants to spend their leisure time learning to touch their toes. We told him that yoga's for upper-class women who want skinny white friends." Dede rolled her eyes.

Wylie thought of the journals she'd seen while waiting for her studio during her job interview. Every single cover had featured a white woman, and she had nothing to rebuff the waitress' impressions. "It's a big space. He could host classes where people borrow mats and drop donations for a community fund."

"We don't need this kind of mind-body preaching," Dede said. "It would take some pretty heavy lifting to get the community to buy into this shit."

"So do it at the church," Wylie said. "Do it where you feel most comfortable and with someone from the studios who defies your expectation of a skinny, white friend."

Rusty shook his head. "Wylie, we're trying to build a reputation for the Social Club. You want to increase the size of your practice or what?"

"Not at the expense of forcing it down their throats," she said. "An average one-hour yoga class in Los Angeles costs twenty bucks, and most require students to bring equipment. Mats cost around twenty dollars, so people're already down forty dollars to satisfy their curiosity. You want to do something good? Host the classes at the church. The Social Club can sponsor the mats."

Candy clapped. "Like logo merchandise."

Dede and Jeanie looked at each other. "I do feel better," Dede admitted. "Imagine the church basement full of all our neighbors. There'd be something cool and unifying about seeing the neighborhood's beautiful women working together. You saw this crowd. Nobody cared about different ages and sizes."

The other woman rolled her eyes. "You're not seventeen anymore. You're going to crash as soon as you get home."

Dede put her hands on her hips. "Yeah, but my doctor said I have to spend more time focused on wellness and preventative health."

Jeanie slapped her thigh. "Your doctor's your best customer at the club!"

"We'll think about it," Candy said. She took Rusty's arm and pulled him close. "It's an interesting idea, Wylie. Thank you for the input."

She smiled. *'Thank you for the input?' Is there an MBA hiding behind those layers of foundation and silicone?* "It's all yours. Take it and run with it."

Esther and Penny Lane moved through the crowd and watched the club owners depart. "You need more spice for a group this size," Esther said.

And you're about to fall out of your sports bra. She grinned and embraced the samba dancer and her friend. "I'm learning to go with the flow. What did you think, Penny Lane?"

The older woman shook her head. "My last group exercise class required legwarmers. My body's not used to this kind of stimulation. I'm glad I ate breakfast this morning, but I'll be honest with you, I could do with a nap."

"What is that American expression? Sleep when you're dead?" Esther asked. "I bet half these people would enjoy shaking things up. Mixing up Brazilian samba and yoga poses could be the next big thing."

"I think most of them were just curious and wanted to gawk," Wylie said. "Penny Lane and I are ten-second celebrities."

"No, you're not giving yourself enough credit. Girls in my *bairro* grow up dancing samba, letting their bodies flow with the music and learning how to gather strength from their mothers and sisters. Movement and celebration can heal the body, but if we add in the rigor of yoga's steady poses, we might be able to transform the heart."

Whose heart are you trying to transform? Natalia and Dottie might have been absent from today's crowd, but their existence neither proved nor disproved Wylie's ability to make friends. She thought of her parents in Oregon and wondered whether anyone in the commune besides Nolan had considered calling them after her asthma attack. *Who would have known how to reach them?*

Esther's enthusiasm for bringing samba into the practice continued as Nolan walked up. She waved her thanks to the last of the departing customers and smiled at him. *We could do this,* she told herself. *Together, we could break the mold and make so much happen in this community. Fusion classes. No empty stomachs. No empty hearts.*

"I think I owe you an apology."

He pulled his shirt over his head. "For what?"

She tried not to show her disappointment as his sun-warmed abs disappeared under the thin layer of fabric. "Mini Mako couldn't mobilize this kind of turnout."

He shrugged and looked at Esther and Penny Lane. "Who knows what motivated people to break out of their shells and come give your class a try? Sometimes life gives us the little nudges we need."

Penny Lane snorted. "Or sometimes a kick in the head."

The group laughed and Wylie replayed the previous few days. Even though Metro Movement had asked Penny Lane to be an ambassador, that unpaid effort would not put a roof over her head or give her a way to jump the wait for subsided housing. The organization focused on limited equity cooperatives would probably hit Penny Lane with weeks of pre-employment screening before she could cash her first paycheck. "Did you go back to the camp after the shooting?" She narrowed her gaze and considered Esther and Nolan. "I'm so sorry. I was so focused on my recovery that I didn't think of what I could do to help. Did one of you put her up?"

"She spent the first night at the hospital with Dougie."

"I told you... I'm a caregiver without the right credentials," Penny Lane said. "Dougie couldn't have asked for a better patient advocate. Who else is going to berate the nurse at two in the morning when she's late with the pain medication?"

The group laughed and the woman smiled with pride. "Dougie'll be okay and you don't have to worry about me right now. Nolan's mother caught wind of the coverage and spent some time networking with the city department focused on housing and community investment. I don't know what motivated her, but she dedicated a substantial number of affordable housing units in exchange for a bevy of tax credits."

Wylie bit her lip. *I know what motivated her.* She looked at Nolan. "You didn't have to do that."

Penny Lane pulled off her hat and swatted Wylie's arm. "And you don't have to move out just to prove you're willing to share your new apartment with me."

"You're going to move out?" Nolan asked.

The lighthearted moment collapsed until the world contained just enough space for the two of them. "I've always wanted to prove that I can take care of myself," she said, hoping Penny Lane and Esther would recognize the moment.

He ran a hand through his hair. "Nobody doubts that fact."

She closed her eyes. *But are there more important things to prove? Do I need to prove it to myself?* She took a deep breath and offered him a tentative smile. "Maybe we can talk about it over dinner?"

Esther whistled. "Oh! It's date night. Wear something sexy."

What do I wear to camouflage my heart?

Chapter Nineteen

Surveying her closet, Wylie came up with two dress options for dinner — the wrap dress she had worn to her job interview and the cocktail dress she had borrowed to dazzle the Abramowitzes. The wind-swept effects of riding in the Bronco called for fluidity, but she had no idea what to expect from an evening alone with Nolan. Fearing neither dress would leave her comfortable enough to suss out her feelings for the man, she abandoned formalwear and choose skinny jeans, a pair of black heels and a black top with puffed sleeves that bared her abdomen. *Work with what you have.* She tossed her blonde hair over her shoulder and left the tiny room with a twenty-dollar bill, a credit card and her new, financed smartphone jammed into her back pocket.

Nolan stood at the base of the stairs in jeans and a button-down shirt. The setting sun came through the wide windows and picked out the red highlights in his dark brown hair. When he smiled, she gravitated toward the invitation on his face. "I didn't know what to wear," she said.

"You look perfect."

"Where are we going?"

He raised his eyebrows. "Does it matter?"

"Maybe," she admitted. "I'm starving."

"Well, I promise there will be food." He turned toward the kitchen and plucked a bowl of hulled strawberries from the communal refrigerator. "Will this tide you over?"

She eyed the ripe red fruit and hoped she could keep the tiny seeds from worrying her teeth. She knew he would delay the rest of her plans if she decided to pull food from the fridge and eat. "I might end up with red-stained lips."

"I can think of worse outcomes." He reached for her and offered her a strawberry.

She opened her mouth and took it, sucking the juice from his fingers. "Is this how you treat all your first dates?"

The color of his eyes darkened until they beckoned her to drown in them. "I'm considering an emergency cancellation. You look good enough to eat."

She danced from his arms and retained the bowl of food. "Not a chance, Nolan. You promised me real food." Her expectations of the evening turned her stomach, making her realize she craved more than physical sustenance. "Stand and deliver."

He pulled out his phone. "Our car's here."

"What about the Bronco?"

"I told you... They steer like tanks and the death wobble is enough to make you second-guess the quality of American engineering."

She shook her head. "Not yours. It's got a smooth ride."

"But I still have to drive it. I'd rather focus on you." He held up his hand. "Ride-sharing apps are very normal."

She walked to the front door and peered at the waiting car. "That is not a late-model Ford."

"And you're not an average woman, Wylie Winidad. Let me indulge you."

He took her hand and pulled her toward the front door. She held firm to the bowl of strawberries and teetered on her heels, wondering whether to lay down the rules that would keep her on solid ground. "You'll scare me away," she whispered.

"Let go for a night," he said with a smile. "I have you."

She nodded and followed him toward a chauffeur in a black suit who had no interest in making eye contact.

"Mr. Wilson," the man said, "Right this way." He held open the rear passenger door and averted his eyes.

Wylie clutched the bowl of strawberries to her chest as she climbed inside the car and her worn denim slid across the smooth leather seats. "This is ridiculous."

Nolan reached for a bottle of chilled champagne and grinned. "I'm so glad you brought snacks."

She noticed the gleam in his eye and grinned. "We're never going to make it through the night."

"I can manage to restrain myself if you can."

A ripe strawberry caught her eye and she plucked it from the bowl, teasing her lips until juice beaded on the surface and he stopped toying with the champagne cage. "Are you sure about that?"

He laughed and popped the cork. "I've never been more certain."

The driver brought them through the chaos of Los Angeles traffic while she told him about growing up with two loving parents who should have maintained a filter between their world and hers.

"It gave you an appreciation for life's challenges," he said. "I doubt you would have need extracurricular classes on adulting. Isn't that the new thing? A lot of kids have helicopter parents who protected them from reality, but they're fine with letting colleges fill the gaps."

"What else should they do?"

"Pop their precious bubbles and just go out and do it."

She glanced at the columned edifice on the corner of 7th and Olive Street. A uniformed valet waited in front of the neoclassical landmark, primed to open doors and whisk away vehicles without making eye contact. Twelve stories of repurposed splendor waited to receive them, but she shook her head and smiled. "It's a beautiful hotel, but we could have stayed home and saved you the trouble."

He laughed and took her champagne glass. "Home doesn't have the same 1920s elegance. The Bank of Italy might be responsible for the Doric columns, ornate golden ceiling and marble floors, but I thought you'd get a kick out of the green velvet lobby."

"How much green velvet?"

"Chairs. Curtains. Table fringe."

The promise of green velvet table fringe had her reaching for the door handle. "You've got to be kidding."

He laughed. "We grew up in the same hometown, but people don't move to Los Angeles for tract housing and residential grids. They move here for the glamour and possibilities of something more. Let me give you a taste of that something more."

So I can remember it when you've moved on. She kept her mouth closed. "Is this how you grew up?

"No, but I remember my excitement the first time my mother let me tag along."

The valet opened the door and a doorman smiled as Nolan led her into the hotel. Creative downtown denizens and aspiring visitors filled two stories of marble and art deco furnishings. She spied the promised green fringe and the mirrored reflection of a palm tree. "It's another world."

Nolan smiled. "It's la-la land. But they do have four bars."

"Four?"

He scratched his beard. "One on the rooftop. One in the restaurant. A coffee bar."

She shook her head and eyed the dark luxury of a bar waiting off the main lobby. "Let's do that one."

"Afraid to get in the elevator?"

"No," she said, "I'm afraid I'll never get out."

He led her through the sharp-dressed suits from the financial district, the New Age bohemians toting designer handbags, the aspiring models who coveted the handbags and the urbane out-of-town guests taking in the show. If their jean-clad presence stood out, the hip crowd gave them time to prove their worth. Nolan chose a quiet table for two and a waiter appeared within seconds. "Would you like to see a menu? We offer a selection of classic and proprietary cocktails crafted by our award-winning bar director."

Bar director? Wylie shook her head and tried not to finger the smooth leather beneath her hands. *Everyone wants to be a director in this town.* "Maybe we should stick to bubbles."

The waiter nodded and described a mixture of amaro, vermouth, ginger, lime and sparkling mineral water. Wylie eyed the green velvet lobby and decided to accept his suggestion. *Why not? I'm a fish out of water in this crowd.*

When the waiter left, she and Nolan admired the crowd, content to let the suspense of the evening supersede their silence. The waiter promptly returned with two cocktail glasses, their square bowls filled with bubbling cocktails and stylized flowers made from mint leaves. Wylie accepted her drink and stared at it. "It's too pretty to drink."

Nolan laughed and lifted his glass. "If I applied the same rule to you, I'd have never gotten you home." He toasted her and smiled. "To new beginnings."

Wylie held his gaze and sipped her drink. *And to memories that help to keep us warm.* She tested the boundaries of their conversation limits. "Tell me about your mom? What swayed her move into affordable housing?"

He put down his drink and wet his lips. "I'm suspicious she had it planned all along."

"The timing is convenient."

He spread his palms. "Convenience is the marriage of needs and resources."

She sipped her drink and looked at their opulent surroundings. *What happens when you can't afford the cost?*

"In the first part of 2020, the governor pushed a huge plan to tackle homelessness. My mom waited for an opportunity, knowing the legislature would have a deadline, the press would take up the problem and homelessness would become a national issue."

She snorted. "Too bad she didn't predict the coronavirus."

"Touché, but's a lot to ask, even in California."

She grinned. *The state always on the verge of secession. Forty million residents, pushing and pulling against the constraints of the nation, who can't figure out who they want to be but know they can do it better than anyone else.* She looked at Nolan, relaxed in an upscale bar, while she sat on the edge of her chair and the city's elite moved around him. *Maybe he should run for office.*

"Our residents have lots of compassion, but it doesn't hurt when the state has surplus tax revenue." He swirled the contents of his drink. "She knew there would be pie."

"We're not talking about Modesto."

"No, we're not."

"But she must have seen the news coverage. She must be proud of what you're trying to do."

He smiled. "I hope so, but that's not why I'm doing it. My mom and I have always been planets in the same solar system, never meeting but following the same orbit. She expected Isla properties to bring us together, but I found other ways to deploy my resources."

"But are you close? Do you call and celebrate when you've achieved something big?"

"What counts as something big?"

She thought of the Abramowitzes and their commercial kitchen. "Will she help you with the expansion?"

He laughed. "Well, I imagine my mom knew about John and Patty's decision before I did. They decided to sell the building to me based on my 'good deeds', but I felt compelled to confess that you and I weren't quite dating."

Wylie lifted her drink to her lips. *Because you were ashamed of me?*

"She told me to hurry up and make it official before I lost you."

You can't lose what you haven't found. She sighed, struggling to weigh the pleasure of his statement against her uncertainties. "I'm glad you owned up to the truth. It's hard to define what's going between us right now. Lust doesn't seem like enough."

"What happens between lust and love?"

She thought about her childhood fantasies and the outdated marriage proposals she had grown up watching. "Trust? Faith? I don't know the answer yet. My family's been small my entire life, but I want to make room in it."

"I don't know the answer either, Wylie, but I want you in my life."

She swallowed.

"And just so we're clear, my mother wants to meet you."

Wylie put down her glass. "That's scarier than the thought of you proposing marriage."

He tipped his glass. "Would you say 'yes'?"

"You haven't asked," she replied, hoping to put him off as she leaned forward and wondered if she would need the contents of the hotel pool to extinguish the heat between them.

"I'm afraid I know the answer," Nolan said. He took a deep breath and smiled. "Patricia told me every story has a beginning. We've muddled ours, but here's to starting on the right foot."

Here's to finding someone who can meet your passion. Here's to finding someone who's not afraid to go all in and give you what you need. She let her proposition hang between them as she finished her drink. "I'm not sure you can top this beginning."

Nolan stood and offered her his hand. "Care to find out?"

* * * *

Their driver glanced at Nolan and rose to open the rear passenger door.

"Has he been waiting the whole time?" Wylie asked.

"He's ours for the night."

She climbed into the car. "It's not good for him to sit still that long."

"Well, I'm sure we can stop for a stretch break if he's amenable. Is that what you'd rather do next?"

"No," she admitted, intrigued by his agenda. "But I feel a little conspicuous having a man in a suit drive me around."

Nolan shrugged and looked at the ride shares circling the block for the convenience of hotel guests. "Sometimes conspicuous pays the bills."

She rubbed her arms and hoped their next stop would replace the chilled air of the art deco lobby with something hotter.

"So, I confess I pulled a few strings to arrange our next step."

Her eyes widened. "How many strings?"

"It's not that bad," he admitted. "My university roommate works on a freelance basis as a curatorial assistant for one of the campus art museums. He offered to give us a VIP curator's tour before we stop for dinner."

"The strawberries were a good call," she said.

He leaned across the seat and kissed her lips, reminding her that they both tasted of mint and a week of heady memories. "You were a good call."

"Why the museum?" she asked to keep herself from climbing into his lap.

He cleared his throat and blinked. "The man who started it had two sides. He was the former chairman of an international corporation, but he used his wealth to collect old master paintings and drawings of a bygone era."

"That's not unusual. High-performing individuals often love the arts."

"High-performing individuals also have wills and strong opinions on what should happen next."

"Opinions aren't exclusive to the one percent."

Nolan smiled. "So the man died before many of the exhibit spaces were complete, but he left enough resources to the museum to ensure its success. The university assumed the management and operations of the institution, but they also leveraged their experience to do more than the man had ever envisioned."

"You're the institution, not the man," she said, aiming to keep things light.

"No, I'm building the institution from the ground up."

Wylie shook her head. "I respect what you're trying to do, but I thought we weren't going to talk about Modesto."

"I didn't say anything about the food truck." He reached for another bottle of champagne. "You won't make it to the end of the night if we start enforcing penalty shots."

She snorted and imagined the ineffectiveness of shooting champagne. "This isn't truth or dare, Nolan. It's a date."

"Then stop questioning my agenda. You can plan the next date."

The driver picked up speed.

There might not be a next one, and it definitely won't be this grand if I'm in charge of the budget.

He pulled her close and tucked her under his arm, kissing her hair then her lips when she turned her face toward his attention. "I'm not the university. I'm the art. *We're* the art. We can't help where we started, but we can hang in there, doing our best to shine against the white gallery walls and forcing other people to question what should happen next."

"Aren't they also on the gallery walls?"

He shook his head and looked away. "No. Most people are sitting in the storeroom, content to gather dust. I told you. I want to be among the people. I want to do the work."

So do I.

Their car arrived and Nolan's friend threw open the museum door. His rumpled shirt and expanded waistline made him look less like a chain-smoking artist and more like a man who treated sugar as a panacea. She smiled at the warmth of his smile as he and Nolan shook hands and embraced with the familiarity of long-time friends.

The man turned to Wylie and introduced himself as Nash. He scanned her frame and she stood firm, knowing his interest stemmed from his affection for

Nolan. *Nolan and Nash*, she repeated to herself. *I wonder how he would fare against Rikard?*

"So it took impressing a woman to finally bring you to the museum?"

Wylie laughed and asked Nolan, "You haven't been to your friend's museum?"

"The man's a freelance curatorial assistant," he said. "They just let him borrow the keys." Nash laughed and Nolan rocked back on his heels and grinned. "Plus, I've been busy since we got back from Europe."

"How's the food truck?"

Nolan shook his head. "Topic non grata tonight."

Nash shrugged and led them into the building. "We've got a few exhibitions, but Nolan said you might be interested in the permanent collection."

She eyed a kaleidoscope of colors spiraling up a white staircase and wondered how long she could get lost in their rhythm. The modern art called to her bubble-laced buzz, but she recalled Nolan's intent. "Show me what you've got."

"Most of the works of art stem from the sixteenth through the twentieth century, but our founder had broad interests. There might be a subtle emphasis on the nineteenth century, but who can resist the explosion of creativity brought on by that period? At the time of his death, the museum's collection boasted examples of realism, orientalism, impressionism, pointillism" — Wylie smiled when he gauged their interest—"and symbolism. Of course, generous patrons have given the museum the resources to expand that collection."

You forgot elitism. Wylie kept smiling.

Nash stopped at the edge of a side gallery. "These have always been some of Nolan's favorites."

Amy Craig

She peered around the corner and braced herself for heavy-handed oil paintings and horse-drawn carriages. Instead of a riot of colors, she found herself staring at portraits of a woman. In each painting, her square face and stoic expression confronted the audience without diminishing her appearance. She looked like a woman ready to face the world with thoughtfulness, whether in a ruffled cravat or a cocky hat.

"It's a series of self-portraits," Nash said. "The artist was a Russian diarist, painter and sculptor. Historians say she had musical talent, but illness destroyed her voice and she lost her chance to be a professional singer."

"So she painted," Wylie said, reaching for the canvas as she recognized the resemblance between herself and the female painter.

"I'm sure she kept singing as well," Nolan said. He walked up behind her and wrapped his arms around her chest. "The man who started the museum had two sides. This artist has two sides, but she wasn't afraid to look in the mirror and see herself."

Wylie relaxed against his chest and exhaled. "Most college boys have pinups on their walls."

His chest rumbled with laughter. "Nash didn't say this was the only poster we had, but he's right, I've always loved it. My mother has always loved it. This woman? She could accomplish things. She stared into the mirror and she worked the system."

"You don't need me to work the system, Nolan. You're more than capable of doing that by yourself. I don't want to be art on the walls. I don't want to be a reminder of someone else."

"What would you paint?" he asked her. "Would you paint yourself standing at the edge of the sand in

341

Triangle Pose? Would you paint yourself poolside with a cold cocktail?"

She shook her head and looked at the severe painting, seeing the highlights and the keen intelligence in the woman's eyes. "I'd paint myself on the beach next to Penny Lane, head raised to face the world."

"I could see that." He turned her in his arms and drew a deep breath. "I could see that defiance from the moment we first met. I could also see the vulnerability. You don't have to choose one persona, Wylie. You can be fiercely independent and still be willing to let go so the people you trust can take care of you."

She bit her lip to stem the tears gathering in her eyes. "Do you talk to all your first dates like this?"

"No, only the ones I love."

She remembered her fear as the echoes of the gunshot faded into Los Angeles traffic. *How can I take responsibility for the idea of more than myself if I froze when the moment called for action? The woman in the paintings didn't recede into history and the comfort of a dream. She left her mark on more than one canvas, like she had earned the right to be seen.* "I haven't earned this kind of chance, Nolan. I haven't earned this kind of confidence."

He glanced over her head and smiled. "That's the thing about art, Wylie. You're just looking at the masterpieces. You never see the mistakes and the moments of doubt. You never see the compositions that went in the trash."

Nash waltzed into the room, swinging his keys. "Are the lovebirds staying for dinner?"

Heat flooded her cheeks and she nodded, needing food to temper the rush of feelings brought on by Nolan's confidence. "Did you pack us a picnic?"

"Hell, no," he said. "At the end of the day, the last thing I want to do is cook."

She laughed and linked her arm with his, suppressing her fears and holding onto his words like the promise of morning sunlight. "So far, your favorite activities seem to be movie nights, winding down by the pool and rescuing women."

"Perfectly normal activities," he said, "but you didn't need rescuing."

"I was living in my car."

"You had options."

"Hmm-m," she said, thinking of the choices people made every day. Penny Lane had chosen to be with her friends over and over again. Instead of cowering in the parking lot, she had run toward Dougie without fearing the consequences. Wylie knew heroes went down in history for choosing love over life, but she wondered if she could be that brave. Her heart had grown large enough to make room for Nolan's success, but she wondered if her presence would distract him. She wondered if she would be strong enough to step back and take second place to the things he needed to achieve. *Aren't we all looking for that happily ever after?*

She scanned the white walls, wondering how long it would take her to digest the museum by daylight. The pieces reminded her of the people who came in and out of her life—Rusty's simmering aggression, Esther's bold swagger and Penny Lane's heart of gold. At the end of the day, she wanted the canvas of her life to be more than the gray flocking of a lifetime of dust.

Nash led them to an opaque glass door separating the gallery space from the museum restaurant. "It's not officially open for business yet," he said, "but we've hosted a few exclusive events. Nolan said you might have feedback on the menu." He opened the door and revealed an elegant mix of mint-green scalloped booths, laminate tabletops and brass mid-century pendants hanging from the ceiling. The room smelled like citrus polish and fresh herbs when it should have smelled like decades of dust and grease.

"Just the two of us?" she asked, turning to Nolan.

"Unless you want Nash to join us?"

She shook her head. "I don't think I'm hungry anymore."

He frowned. "You were starving when we left the house."

"That was before the strawberries and the cocktails." She looked over Nolan's shoulder and saw Nash reach for the dimmer switch. "Maybe we can take it to go?"

Nolan frowned like she had spent the evening on her phone instead of juggling her feelings for him. "Go where?"

"Griffith Park?" she asked, hoping to steer clear of the romanticism of the beach. It would be too easy to fall into the familiar, lulling pattern of the waves and believe fate wanted their relationship to work out. In contrast, the largest park in the city boasted fifty miles of trails that wound through woodlands and canyons. More than one homeless person had probably set up camp amid the native oak and walnut trees, but she knew police patrolled the trails. She always associated the park with hints of lilac and sagebrush. "I'm sure the observatory is open."

"We could just go home," Nolan said.

She stalled, unwilling to let the night end with the bittersweet agony of goodbye sex. "Why? You spent so much time setting up this night. Let's enjoy it."

Nash disappeared into the kitchen and left them standing amid the mid-century splendor. She laid her head against Nolan's chest and listened to his heartbeat. "I had fun pretending to be your girlfriend. It gave me a way to escape the unsteadiness in my life."

He rubbed her back.

She felt him hesitate as he neared the edge of her shirt and the stretch of exposed skin on her lower back. "I'm just not sure how long I can go on pretending," she said.

His old roommate returned with a canvas tote filled with white cardboard boxes. She heard the muffled clink of thick glass as he offered it to Nolan. "Good luck, man. The Fern Dell entrance closed at sunset. Send your driver up to Vermont. There's a drop-off area just past the horseshoe driveway. You could sit out on the lawn and have a picnic."

Nolan refused to accept the tote.

She reached for it. "Thanks, Nash."

"Are you sure?" Nolan asked.

She nodded, too afraid to meet his gaze. They rode in silence as the driver navigated Western Canyon Road and pushed the sedan to climb the hills. The food in the bag cooled as the hum of the car's vent fans filled the silence between them.

He reached for her hand. "What's on your mind?"

She let him toy with her open palm. "All the things you're going to do in the next few years."

"Why can't we do them together?"

"Rikard was right," she whispered. "Your life doesn't have room in it for me and the security I want."

"Let me make that decision," he said.

She shook her head. "I have to take care of myself — my wallet, my health, my heart. I could let myself fall in love with you, but what would you be giving up to return that love? You've got so much work do to, so much to build that's bigger than yourself."

He shook his head. "Wylie, we all need security, belonging and achievement. What happened to the girl who threw herself into causes? The one who went all in?"

She's scared and worried she'll drag you down. "I was never that girl."

Chapter Twenty

We're going out with a bang. Wylie watched the driver pass the observatory and head for a designated unloading zone. *If nothing else works out, I'll have the memories from tonight.* She looked at the world-famous Hollywood sign in the distance and wondered how many dreamers had come to the mountaintop to mark their first night in town. For her and Nolan, the visit might mark their end.

When they left the car, she ignored the sign's optimistic white letters and focused on the observatory. A crowd of visitors threaded their way across the lawn and a reel of headlights illuminated them as cars passed, circling for parking.

Nolan took her hand and she transferred the tote to her free hand, content to lose track of her thoughts amid the crowd of late-night stargazers. Like each of them, she wanted to suspend her earthly constraints, peer through a telescope and glimpse an echo of light. She wanted to confirm the presence of something bigger than her life, like Nolan and his ambitions. She knew that the minute she lost her nerve, the domed art deco structure and its durable concrete walls would remain to shelter her terrestrial form from the distant, blazing sun.

A car slowed as they weaved up the hill and the woman in front of them stopped and turned, shading her eyes against the car's headlights.

"Oh, my God," Wylie said. "That's Dottie, my old roommate." She craned her neck to look at the woman standing next to Dottie. She toted a full-sized backpack and a tourist's plastic bag, but the car's headlights moved on. Presumably, the woman was the wannabe actress who had upended her life. "I don't want to see her."

"Why not?"

"'Namaste' isn't the only phrase I would say to her."

He laughed and swung her hand. "You hit Cynthia's pride where it hurts. Most people would argue she deserved it."

"I should have walked away. What did my tantrum accomplish? Neither one of us feels good about what happened."

"Was it cathartic?"

She thought about the question.

"It's a double standard," Nolan said. "Society lets men and children beat up each other and indulge their impulses, but it's a novelty when a woman steps into the ring. You and my mom fight with words and you both get shit done. Say what you want to say. Society shouldn't expect women to rein in their emotions when they let everyone else take a fair swing."

"We still correct the kids when they act out."

"Yeah, but most of the time they get immunity." He raised her hand and kissed the back of it. "I don't think you should go around beating up people who give you a wrong look, but a physical release is a human response. Yoga's good, but the movements are too slow when you need to let off steam. You fought Cynthia with words and I don't think you should feel bad about that response. I'd like to see you get mad one day and take a swing at me. I'll know it's an honest blow and you'll know you don't have to hold back."

"So you want me to beat you up?"

He laughed. "No, I want you to know I'm still going to be there when you're done. I'm still going to help you depressurize, even if I deserved it."

"Like, in bed?"

"I want you to say what you mean and stand up for yourself — in bed, in business or in court. Have you ever gotten a traffic ticket?"

She shook her head. "I once stole a pack of cigarettes."

"Did your parents make you smoke every one of them?"

"Ew. That only happens in the movies. I tried to blame it on my friend Natalia."

"You threw her under the bus?"

Laughing, she remembered the easy pleasure of their date and resolved to savor it. "Exactly."

"Well, instead of decking your parents, we could go for a run. Take a Krav Maga class. Bed isn't the only option."

A man darted out of the park area and pointed a gun at Dottie and her cousin, his face shadowed by a baseball cap. Silhouetted trees and distant overhead lighting dramatized the snarl of his features. "Give me your bag," he said.

Wylie rushed forward. "Oh my God, we've got to help them."

Nolan pulled Wylie away from the threat, upsetting her balance. She stumbled and held fast to his hand, focusing on the cold metal in the hand of the criminal. *This place is too public for such a brazen crime. That man must be desperate.* "We've got to help them."

"It'll be over before you can blink," he said.

"Look what happened to Dougie."

He hesitated.

"Nolan, sometimes you've got to put yourself in danger to make a difference."

"The man's got a gun, Wylie."

She looked at his features and the way he swung the gun back and forth between the two women, waiting for one of them to react.

Dottie backed up, abandoning her cousin as she started screaming. "He's got a gun!"

"At least one of them has some sense," Nolan said.

The man with the gun focused on Dottie and grimaced. He advanced on her screams like a predator intent on silencing his prey.

Wylie wrenched her hand free from Nolan's grasp. "Call the police. I'm just going to get her out of the situation and distract him." Without waiting for his response, she waved the tote in her hand and walked past the screaming mess of her former roommate. "It's just food," she said when the man focused on the tote. She gauged the severity of his desperation beneath the shifting shadows.

His eyes remained fixed on the offering.

She thrust the tote toward him. "You can have it."

The man yanked the bag to his chest. "Where's your purse?"

Nolan put his hand on her back, a quiet reassurance while Dottie and her roommate clutched each other and wailed.

The man's gaze shifted to Nolan. "Your wallet!"

Nolan shifted and tossed the man his wallet. The offering buffered her vulnerability as he moved his frame in front of hers. "Get out of here," he said.

The man blinked, his gaze evaluating his intended targets.

Nolan jerked his head toward the cover of the tree line. "Security is bound to be here soon."

Wylie doubted their rescue would be that precise.

The man in the baseball hat's eyes darted toward the road. He sneered before he beckoned them to hurry up. "Give me what you've got."

She reached for the phone in her back pocket, ready to surrender what she had to convince him to retreat without inflicting real harm on her, Nolan or her screaming sidekicks.

'Relinquish your property and report the incident to authorities. Don't be a hero. Nothing's more valuable than a life,' her father had said during one of their school-age talks.

Nolan shook his head. "Get out of here."

She tossed the man her phone and watched her twenty-dollar bill and her credit card clatter to the sidewalk. She looked up and saw the hunger in his furtive glances. "That's all I've got."

Each of them stared at the items, unwilling to upset the tension.

The robber scanned the trees once more and swooped low, dropping his guard to reach for the cash and the card.

Wylie struck without thinking, bringing her knee up until it shattered the man's nose.

He screamed, dropping the gun and the other items in his hands. Nolan kicked the gun into the shadows of the trees and yelled for help. "Security!"

The man struggled to his feet and made for the parkland.

Nolan moved to chase him.

Wylie grabbed his arm and she felt the tension in his muscles as he considered further action. "Let him go. He won't get very far."

"How do you know?"

She looked at the splatter of blood marring the sidewalk like a line drawn in the sand. On one side, a population of strangers waited for empathy and a second chance at dignity. She stood on the other side, her pants stained with the man's blood, willing and able to help them. "He's desperate."

Her heartbeat echoing in her ears, she knew her self-defense move had nothing to do with releasing her emotions. The show of force had defused the situation before the man with the gun had made a decision that would cost him more than a clutch of pawnshop assets. She understood she could take meaningful risks and stand up for herself to help people get their second and third chances, but at some point, law enforcement should handle the action. "Tonight it was armed robbery. Next week, it will be worse."

"It won't end," Nolan said, "but you did good. Scared the hell out of me, but you did good." He looked at the blood and shook his head. "Where have you been hiding, Wylie the warrior princess?"

She shrugged, feeling the adrenaline flee her system. "You've never done that yoga move?" She laughed. "I guess my parents taught me more than I thought."

Dottie rushed toward them. "Oh my God! Oh my God! You saved us! We're not even friends."

Extracting herself from the woman's candy-scented embrace, Wylie stepped back and considered her former roommate's statement. "You've said that more than once."

"Why would you intervene?"

She shrugged, thinking of the times she'd held back or waited for authority and experience. "You needed help, and I thought I could make a difference. Honestly, Dottie, it had nothing to do with you."

Dottie gaped.

Wylie thought of Nolan's comment when they stood on the street corner at the beginning of the week. *'Maybe there's nothing there.'* She shook her head, acknowledging that some people in her life would treat her presence like a transaction and some would treat her presence like a gift. *People like Nolan and my parents.* She realized she felt more balanced and empowered with him by her side. "That man was desperate. I hope he gets the help he needs before someone gets hurt."

Dottie blathered her thanks.

Her companion cleared her throat. The woman's stout physique, mousy brown hair and circular glasses marked her for character roles as a studious friend.

"This is my cousin Billie," Dottie said. "I offered to show her around town while she gets settled in."

Wylie nodded, knowing she should introduce Nolan, but she craved a quick escape before the magic of their night dissolved into incident reports and polite conversation. She picked up the tote and looked at the security guards running toward them. "Good luck with your auditions."

"Wait! You're just leaving?"

She smiled. "Yep."

Nolan took her hand and they left Dottie and Billie standing on the sidewalk.

When the breeze picked up, she looked at the green grass on the hills swaying beneath the cloudless nighttime sky. The verdant grass would fade to brown when summer came, but she accepted that the shadows shifting in the breeze would never end. Somewhere in the brush, a desperate man was clutching his nose and feeling the empty pangs of hunger. She wanted to help that man find a solution without violence. She wanted to help Nolan fight back. "I hope he finds the help he needs, but in the meantime, Dottie and her cousin can explain what happened."

"You got mad."

"No. I just saw an opportunity to stand up for myself."

He kissed her palm. "You stood up for more than one person."

"Yeah. It might become a habit," she said. "Call the driver so we can get out of here before the whole thing ruins our night."

"It hasn't gone exactly how I planned."

She swung her arm, pulling his along for the ride. "I'm starting to understand a magnet my mom kept on the refrigerator."

"What did it say?"

"We plan. God laughs."

"I think that's a Woody Allen quote."

She laughed. "Well, maybe he was onto something."

She tucked herself under his shoulder and let the rhythm of traffic and the heat of Nolan's skin keep her thoughts at bay. She closed her eyes and let her mind drift until sleep claimed her attention.

The driver pulled up to the house on Monument Street.

"I don't want this to be the end," Nolan said, stroking her arm as he urged her awake.

She smiled, wanting to reassure him. "It's not the end, Nolan. I wanted to give that man my dinner. I wanted to give him a glimmer of hope and a night of security before he tackled the challenges he's facing." She pulled the heat and weight of his hand to her lips and kissed his knuckles. "Modesto is more than your dream. It's a way for the entire community to give back, including myself."

"You're not going to move out," he said, his eyes wide with hope. He gripped her hand like she would retract it and climb from the car at a moment's notice.

Tracing his knuckles with her lips, she shook her head and met his gaze. "I'm going to start over on my accreditation. I don't know whether that means working in a studio or expanding the kinds of classes I teach. I'll find a way to pay for high-deductible healthcare if it comes to that option. Either way, I'll cover my basic needs and spend the rest of my time helping you achieve your dreams."

"You don't have to be my helper," he said. "I want you to be by my side."

She pulled his thumb into the warm cavern of her mouth, unsure how to manage the prospect of standing by his side. *I'm much more comfortable with the other naked positions we've tried out.*

He stilled, seemingly fighting the pleasure and promise of her touch, his expression pained as he dragged his thumb along her lips and cupped her chin. "You can own this dream too. You care about the people you meet, offering little adjustments and glimmers of hope that brighten their days, just like you brighten mine."

She raised her eyebrows and stopped trying to postpone the conversation.

"You asked me to push my limits and take a risk. Why can't you do the same?" he asked.

"I'm so used to taking care of myself. What happens when you change your mind?"

His eyes narrowed. "I love you, Wylie. Do you understand that?"

She licked her lips and smiled. "Do you make a habit of going all in? Isn't this our first date?"

Pulling her close, he tilted up her chin. "If I have my way, there won't be any more first dates for you. Tell me you feel the same way or tell me you might get there one day."

"Or what?"

He shook his head and stared at her mouth. "Or you'll leave me in agony, but I won't bail on you while there's hope. I'll wait for you to figure it out."

Seeing the desperation and vulnerability in his eyes, she crawled across the seat and straddled him. *At the end of the day, we're just two people willing to expose our hearts, and that's the biggest risk of them all.* "I'm very close to figuring it out," she said, lowering to make contact.

His cock jumped in response to her heat.

She smiled and traced the line separating his haircut and his trimmed beard. *You're always in control unless you're with me. There're freedom and power in that piece of information, but I don't want your money, Nolan, I want your heart.* She raised her eyebrows, trying to play it cool. "There may be a few terms and conditions we need to iron out."

"I'll have my lawyer review the contract." He cupped her ass and held her like a priceless piece of art. "But your heart's beating as fast as mine."

She glanced at the million-dollar house that homed a community when she'd thought she only needed a place to live. And this man stood at the center of it all, anchoring the ties that brought them all strength. "We should go up," she said. "My heartbeat's betraying me and I don't want to control my impulses right now."

"Why? The driver will help us take a naked selfie if that's what you want."

Her eyes widened as she realized he was serious. Then she laughed and shook her head. "I don't want a naked selfie. I want *you*. I want your oversized dreams and your loyal heart. I want the man who can pop champagne corks and dish out hundreds of wrap sandwiches without breaking a sweat."

"You're not in it for the suits and fat cigars?"

She swatted his chest. "You shouldn't have kept your background from me."

"You would have bolted."

"How do you know that?"

"I came to your yoga class to ask you out and you were as skittish as a frightened colt."

"*'Power's only a bad thing if you don't trust the person who wields it,'*" she repeated.

"Exactly. I know how glimpses into another world can mess with your head. I almost bolted when I saw that body bag because I didn't understand it or understand my place in the world."

"Now you do?"

"It's a work in progress," he admitted. "The world is full of big challenges, and it's so easy to close your eyes to human need. Shame pushed me until I realized how much more I could have done for that man. But once I got started, I never stopped fighting. It takes a certain level of naivety to tackle dreams like ours."

"And a certain level of trust," she said.

"Do you trust me now? Do you trust yourself?"

She shifted on his lap. "I wouldn't call myself naïve, but I'm getting the hang of balancing my needs against what I want to accomplish in this world. Juggling the feelings I have for you might be the easiest part."

He put his hands on her hips and stilled her movement. "And the hardest?"

"Conflict resolution and anger management classes?"

He laughed. He smiled and pulled her flush, raising one hand from her hip to cradle the back of her neck. "I told you that I'm here to help you figure these things out."

"Why?" she asked.

"Because I love you."

Wylie sighed and leaned forward until their foreheads touched. "I wasn't looking for you," she said. "And you weren't even on the menu." He kissed her, his taste sweeter than any spice she could imagine.

"I'm glad you took a risk, Mini Mako. I'm glad we both learned to ask for what we want."

* * * *

A Year Later

Banners for Metro Movement's 5K filled Grand Park. The sea of people waiting to begin the five- and ten-kilometer races stared at the stage, eager to do their part to bring an end to homelessness.

Penny Lane stood behind the microphone and delivered her speech about the things the community had done to help her stabilize her living situation. She ended with a plea for the thousands of other people who were still waiting for help.

Afterward, Nolan stood on the stage amid the signage and paraphernalia of an event that would make the evening news. He announced his fast-casual restaurant chain and credited Wylie's influence for shaping his vision of success. "The people of this city want to give everyone the tools they need to achieve their dreams — a home to guard their bodies, food to nourish their souls and the community support they need. My girlfriend opened my eyes and personalized the needs in our community. She helped me structure Modesto to support everyone who walks through its doors."

She rolled her eyes from the wings. *He had to throw in that part about the girlfriend. Last night I was a member of the board of directors.* She smiled. *It doesn't matter what title I have. He knows I love him.*

When he walked off the stage, she smiled to encourage him. He had practiced the speech as he'd walked up and down the halls of the house, alienating his roommates until each of them could recite it in their sleep. She had been the only one to cradle him at night, flesh against flesh, as she told him how exciting it would be to see him take the stage at the main event.

"How'd I do?"

"You only went off script once or twice." She raised her eyebrows and toyed with the buttons on his shirt. "I expected more discipline from you."

He blushed and stilled her hands. "I saw more than one man lose his balance when you waltzed onto the stage in your yoga pants and kicked off the opening ceremonies."

"It's very important to stretch your muscles before you go for a run."

He leaned down and captured her lips. "I might need private lessons."

"You can visit the new wellness studio any time you wish. Cynthia holds classes on Tuesdays and Thursdays. We're big into this kinship vibe I heard about."

The man she loved pulled back and swatted her ass. "Should I sign up for a recurring membership?"

She draped her arms over his shoulders and smiled. "If you play your cards right, I'd be willing to offer you a lifetime commitment."

"As long as you're by my side, Mini Mako. Sign me up."

Want to see more like this?
Here's a taster for you to enjoy!

Love Repaired
Deana Birch

Excerpt

I parked the loaner SUV in line next to the other shiny overpriced automobiles, did a final check for personal belongings in the seat next to me — no need to learn the same lesson twice, my cell phone had spent the day in my car — and headed into the office. With the sun set, the cool evening air hit my cheeks and I perked up as I walked. My Cayenne sat in front of the large metal garage doors, a sparkle reflecting its recent wash. At least luxury came with attention to detail.

When I reached the glass door, I tugged it toward me only to find it locked. *Jesus.* I'd even failed at picking up my car. I stood on my tiptoes and rapped my knuckles against the glass. On the other side, the room was dark and the half-circular reception desk was abandoned, a black office chair pushed into its place. But from the hall behind it, a light peeked out — my ray of hope.

I knocked again and pressed my lips together while readjusting my shoulder bag. I shifted my body weight from side to side and banged louder.

Florescent beams flooded the showroom and I blinked. My skin flushed, and my mouth went dry. A legal aide at the firm had once said something about man candy, but I thought that was like a unicorn — not real, a legend in a forest I would never visit. But Man Candy had a warm smile, combed-back dirty blond hair and a build that screamed heaven through a tight, black, untucked work shirt. The last few buttons were open and matching pants hung low on his waist. He was also headed right toward me, tapping a wrench in his hand.

With dimples in his smile, he slipped the tool into his back pocket and unlocked the door. His sea-blue eyes must have been designed for skinny dipping.

"Mrs. Benton, I presume." The low, scratchy voice matched the light stubble on his cheeks. His dimples deepened, and the warm showroom air hit my already-heated body.

"Ms." I couldn't resist the urge to brush against him, and as I did, the perfect blend of motor oil and earthy spice came with me.

Testosterone, how I've missed thee.

I walked over to reception and placed the key fob on the desk.

He followed and squinted down at the neat paper piles next to the flat computer screen and keyboard. He picked up my keys from the tail of the stuffed squirrel that held them and dangled it like a time piece.

"Nice keychain." After a quick arch of his eyebrow, the damn dimples reappeared with his tight-lipped smile.

"Thanks" — I glanced at his chest — "Ben." I took the stuffed animal from his grease-stained hands and slid the other key toward him.

"Did you fill it up?" he asked.

"Uh…no." Add one more failure to my day.

Ben shook his head and grabbed the fob before popping it into a drawer. "No one ever fills it up. You know it costs double, right?" He peered up with one eye closed.

"Well, it was either fill it up or make you wait longer."

"Either way, it's my time. I'll have to do it Monday." He rubbed his face with both hands and a tattoo poked out from the tight sleeve around his bicep. His very full bicep.

I cringed and lifted a shoulder. "Sorry. Anyway, I only drove it to my office and back."

Ben walked out from behind the desk and over to the door. Holding it open for me again, he motioned for me to leave.

I'm too young to suffer hot flashes, right? And I was not dreaming of ways to sabotage my brakes or engine. That would be silly—and a further inconvenience that my schedule would not allow.

"You had a failed fuel pump. It's a pretty common problem. That was what was causing the stalling."

Note to self— Get another failed fuel pump.

When we stood in front of my car, he pulled up on the handle, swung the door open, and I froze. A big white pastry box sat on the passenger seat.

"Fuck me."

"Pardon?" he asked with an airy chuckle.

I brought my hands to my face and pulled them down slowly, probably ruining the effects of the anti-aging cream I'd put on that morning. "Fuck. Fuck. Fuck."

"Are you okay?" Ben leaned in closer.

"I forgot the fucking cupcakes. Fuck me. Fuck." I let my bag fall off my shoulder and dragged my feet over to the steel garage. My back met the cool wall and I slid down to the rough concrete. I stomped my sensible beige heel before slumping into a ball and whimpering into my hands. My entire day, week, month... They had all been colossal fails.

The motor oil and musk were back, now touching my wrist and seated on the ground next to me.

"Shitty day?" He draped his defined forearms over his knees with his fingers interlaced.

"I wish I could say it was the shittiest, but it just seems to be par for the course. *Fuck*." I stomped again.

"You have quite the potty mouth for a lady."

"Did you just call me a lady? Oh my God, now I'm really going to cry." Forgetting Shae's cupcakes was the cherry on top of my botched-Mom sundae. But being one step away from a 'ma'am' was the rainbow sprinkles. Asshole-expensive face cream... It obviously wasn't working. And I wasn't even forty.

"You wanna talk about it? I'm a pretty good listener."

If that were true, then Man Candy truly was a unicorn and I was in an enchanted forest. But the words flew out before I could stop them.

"My client lied to me and made me look like a fool in a deposition. I forgot my phone in the car this morning, which means my older daughter has probably called it three hundred times. And because I was behind closed doors with said lying client, I couldn't call her.

"It was my little one's last day at dance camp and I was supposed to bring the cupcakes. Which, as you can see, I did not do. Oh, and their father is in prison for vehicular manslaughter. Sorry you asked?"

He frowned and shook his head. "Where are they now? Your girls?"

"My sister takes care of them so I can keep working."
I wrapped the hem of my skirt around my legs.

"Who takes care of you?" The smile and dimples
were gone, but the warmth stayed in his eyes.

"Me, I guess." I shrugged and tried to recall any
moment my ex, Pete, had ever really taken care of me,
and I drew a blank.

He narrowed his blue eyes. "Is that enough?"

The beautiful stranger next to me had gotten as far
as my walls would let him. Although, I had to admit,
someone being concerned about me might have made
a tiny crack.

"That and the half-bottle of Chardonnay waiting in
the door of my fridge."

"That's depressing," he said, getting up. He offered
me his strong, rough hand and I clasped it. With a
gentle yank, I was on my feet. "You ready for me to add
insult to injury then?" He wet his lips and tilted his
head.

"Oh, God. I don't even care about the bill. Just tell
them to send it to me." I smoothed the front of my skirt
and dusted off my rear.

"It's not that." Ben cleared his throat.

I scanned my car for a scratch or dent.

He continued, "I'm really sorry, but I ate one of the
cupcakes."

I darted my eyes back to him and he hunched as if
waiting to be smacked.

"You eat cupcakes?" I leaned back a little. Whatever
moment sugar had spent on his lips, it was not
spending a lifetime on his hips. Bastard.

"It's my cheat day. And those damn things were
next to me in the car all day. Staring at me. Taunting
me. Like, *'Ben, you know you want me.'*" He wiggled his
fingers. "Then you were late, and, well…I made some

kind of weird justification that I could have one. I'm really sorry."

"You ate one of my daughter's pink frosted cupcakes?" I planted my hands on my hips.

Ben nodded with a clenched jaw.

"You're a fucking unicorn." I picked up my bag, tossed it in the back and climbed into the car.

With the seat belt fastened, I reached for the door, but he held on to it stopping me from closing.

He blinked hard. "Did you and your potty mouth just call me a unicorn?"

"We did." I smiled at the mythical man candy creature, shut the door and drove out of the enchanted forest.

Home of Erotic Romance

Sign up for our newsletter and find out about all our romance book releases, eBook sales and promotions, sneak peeks and FREE romance books!

About the Author

Amy Craig lives in Baton Rouge, Louisiana USA with her family and a small menagerie of pets. She writes women's fiction and contemporary romances with intelligent and empathetic heroines. She can't always vouch for the men. She has worked as an engineer, project manager, and incompetent waitress. In her spare time, she plays tennis and expands her husband's honey-do list.

Amy loves to hear from readers. You can find her contact information, website details and author profile page at https://www.totallybound.com